Thanks, N

Wow!! They
sure changed the
people for the movie.
Pat

many

Tulip

m of

l for a

ALSO BY DEBORAH MOGGACH

Marie Forster.

DEBORAH MOGGACH

The Best Exotic Marigold Hotel

VINTAGE BOOKS
London

Published by Vintage 2012

13

Copyright © Deborah Moggach 2004

Deborah Moggach has asserted her right under the Copyright, Designs
and Patents Act 1988 to be identified as the author of this work

First published in Great Britain in 2004 by
Chatto & Windus with the title *These Foolish Things*

First published by Vintage Books in 2005 with the title *These Foolish Things*

Vintage
Random House, 20 Vauxhall Bridge Road,
London SW1V 2SA

www.vintage-books.co.uk

Addresses for companies within The Random House Group Limited can be
found at: www.randomhouse.co.uk/offices.htm

The Random House Group Limited Reg. No. 954009

A CIP catalogue record for this book
is available from the British Library

ISBN 9780099572022

The Random House Group Limited supports The Forest Stewardship Council
(FSC®), the leading international forest certification organisation. Our books
carrying the FSC label are printed on FSC® certified paper. FSC is the only
forest certification scheme endorsed by the leading environmental organisations,
including Greenpeace. Our paper procurement policy can be found at
www.randomhouse.co.uk/environment

Typeset in Aldus Roman by Palimpsest Book Production Limited,
Falkirk, Stirlingshire
Printed and bound by CPI Group (UK) Ltd, Croydon CR0 4YY

This one is for Simon Booker.

Acknowledgements

My thanks to Sathnam Sanghera, Razia Hamid, Ian Robertson, Alan Hayling, Patricia Brent, Geraldine Willson-Fraser, Alexandra Hough and Tom and Lottie for their help. Those who know Bangalore may find the place somewhat shifted around, but then memory plays tricks on us all.

www.deborahmoggach.com

CREDITS

Anne Cushman & Jerry Jones: from *From Here to Nirvana* (Rider Books, 1999); Tim Dowling: from "And now for the Good News" in the *Guardian* (13/2/2003), © Tim Dowling, reprinted by permission of the publisher; Dorothy Forster (Words and Music): from 'Rose in the Bud', copyright 1907 Chappell Music Ltd, London W6 8BS, reproduced by permission of International Music Publications Ltd. All rights reserved; Peter Holt: from *In Clive's Footsteps* (Hutchinson, 1990), reprinted by permission of the author; Swami Purna: from *The Truth Will Set You Free* (Vega Books, 2002); Leo Robin & Ralph Rainger: from 'Thanks for the Memory' (Famous Music Publishing), administered by Music Sales Ltd; Jack Strachey & Eric Maschwitz: from 'These Foolish Things', copyright 1936 by Lafleur Music Ltd, reproduced by permission of Boosey & Hawkes Music Publishers Ltd; William Shakespeare: from 'Who is Sylvia?' in *The Two Gentleman of Verona* (1594–95).

Every effort has been made to trace or contact all copy-right holders. The publishers would be pleased to rectify any omissions or errors brought to their notice at the earliest opportunity.

Part One

1

Muriel Donnelly, an old girl in her seventies, was left in a hospital cubicle for forty-eight hours. She had taken a tumble in Peckham High Street and was admitted with cuts, bruises and suspected concussion. Two days she lay in A & E, untended, the blood stiffening on her clothes.

It made the headlines. TWO DAYS! screamed the tabloids. Two days on a trolley, old, neglected, alone. St Jude's was besieged by reporters, waylaying nurses and shouting into their mobiles, didn't they know the things were forbidden? Photos showed her lolling grey head and black eye. Plucky pensioner, she had survived the Blitz for this? Her image was beamed around the country: Muriel Donnelly, the latest victim of the collapsing NHS, the latest shocking statistic showing that the British health system, once the best in the world, was disintegrating in a welter of underfunding, staff shortages and collapsing morale.

A hand-wringing why-oh-why piece appeared in the *Daily Mail*, an internal investigation was ordered. Dr Ravi Kapoor was interviewed. He was weary but polite. He said Mrs Donnelly had received the appropriate care and that she was waiting for a bed. He didn't mention that he would kill for an hour's sleep. He didn't mention that since the closure of the Casualty department at the neighbouring hospital his own, St Jude's, had to cope with twice the number of drunks, drug overdoses and victims of pointless violence; that St Jude's would soon be closing because its site, in

3

the centre of Lewisham, was deemed too valuable for sick people; that the private consortium that had taken it over had sold the land to Safeways who were planning to build a superstore.

Exhausted, Ravi drove home to Dulwich. Walking up his path, he paused to breathe deeply. It was seven in the evening; somewhere a bird sang. Beside the path, daffodil blooms had shrivelled into tissue paper. Spring had come and gone without his noticing.

In the kitchen Pauline was reading the *Evening Standard*. The story had gathered momentum; other cases were printed, outraged relatives told their tales.

Ravi opened a carton of apple juice. 'Thing is, I didn't mention the real reason the old bat wasn't treated.'

Pauline fetched him a glass. 'Why?'

'She wouldn't let any darkies touch her.'

Pauline burst out laughing. At another time – another lifetime, it seemed – Ravi would have laughed too. Nowadays that place was unreachable, a golden land where, refreshed and rested, he could have the energy to find things funny.

Upstairs the lavatory flushed.

'Who's that?' Ravi's head reared up.

There was a silence.

'I was going to tell you,' said Pauline.

'Who is it?'

Footsteps creaked overhead.

'He won't be here for long, honestly, not this time,' she babbled. 'I've told him he's got to behave himself –'

'Who is it?'

He knew, of course.

Pauline looked at him. 'It's my father.'

Ravi was a man of compassion. He was a doctor; he tended the sick, he mended the broken. Those who were felled by accident, violence or even self-mutilation found in him a grave and reassuring presence. He bandaged up the wounds of those who lay at the wayside, unloved and unlovable; he staunched the bleeding. Nobody was

4

turned away, ever. To do the job, of course, required detachment. He had long ago learnt a sort of numbed empathy. Bodies were problems to be solved. To heal them he had to violate them by invading their privacy, delving into them with his skilled fingers. These people were frightened. They were utterly alone, for sickness is the loneliest place on earth.

Work sealed him from the world which delivered him its casualties, the doors sighing open and surrendering them up to him; he was suspended from the life to which he would return at the end of his shift. Once home, however, he showered off the hospital smell and became a normal person. Volatile, fastidious, a lover of choral music and computer games, sympathetic enough but somewhat drained. Of course he was compassionate, but no more or less than anybody else. After all, the Hippocratic Oath need not apply on home territory. And especially not to a disgusting old sod like Norman.

Barely a week had passed and already Ravi wanted to murder his father-in-law. Norman was a retired structural engineer, a monumental bore and a man of repulsive habits. He had been thrown out of his latest residential home for putting his hand up a nurse's skirt. 'Inappropriate sexual behaviour', they called it, though Ravi could not imagine what appropriate behaviour could possibly be, where Norman was concerned. His amorous anecdotes, like a loop of musak, reappeared with monotonous regularity. Already Ravi had heard, twice this week, the one about catching the clap in Bulawayo. Being a doctor, Ravi was treated to Norman's more *risqué* reminiscences in a hoarse whisper.

'Get me some Viagra, old pal,' he said, when Pauline was out of the room. 'Bet you've got some upstairs.'

The man cut his toenails in the lounge! Horrible yellowing shards of rock. Ravi had never liked him and age had deepened this into loathing of the old goat with his phoney regimental tie and stained trousers. Ruthlessly selfish, Norman had neglected his daughter all her life; ten years earlier, however, pancreatic cancer had put his long-suffering wife out of her misery and he had battened on to Pauline. Once, on safari in Kenya, Ravi had watched a warthog muscling its way to a water-hole, barging aside

5

any animal that got in its way. He retained, for some reason, a vivid image of its mud-caked arse.

'I can't stand much more of this,' he hissed. Nowadays he and Pauline had to whisper like children. Despite his general dilapidation, Norman's hearing was surprisingly sharp.

'I'm doing my best, Ravi, I'm seeing another place tomorrow, but it's difficult to find anywhere else to take him. Word gets around, you know.'

'Can't we just send him away somewhere?'

'Yes, but where?' she asked.

'Somewhere far, far away?'

'Ravi, that's not nice. He *is* my father.'

Ravi looked at his wife. She changed when her father was around. She became more docile, in fact goody-goody, the dutiful daughter anxious that the two men in her life would get along. She laughed shrilly at her father's terrible jokes, willing Ravi to join in. There was a glazed artificiality to her.

Worse still, with her father in the house he noticed the similarity between them. Pauline had her father's square, heavy jaw and small eyes. On him they looked porcine, but one could still see the resemblance.

Norman had stayed with them several times during the past year – whenever he was kicked out of a Home, in fact. The stays were lengthening as establishments that hadn't heard of him became harder to find. '*The man's a menace,*' said the manager of the last one, '*straight out of Benny Hill. We lost a lovely girl from Nova Scotia.*'

'Thing is, he's frightened of women,' said Ravi. 'That's why he has to jump them all the time.'

Pauline looked at him. 'At least *someone* does.'

There was a silence. They were preparing Sunday lunch. Ravi yanked open the oven door and pulled out the roasting tin.

'I'm so tired,' he said.

It was true. He was always exhausted. He needed time to revive himself, to restore himself. He needed a good night's sleep. He needed to lie on the sofa and listen to Mozart's *Requiem*. Only then could he become a husband again – a human being, even.

The house was so small, with her father in it. Ravi's body was in a permanent state of tension. Every room he went into, Norman was there. Just at the *Lacrimosa* he would blunder in, the transistor hanging on a string around his neck burbling the cricket commentary from Sri Lanka.

'He uses my computer.'

'Don't change the subject,' said Pauline.

The place stank of Norman's cigarettes. When they banished him outside, the patio became littered with butts like the Outpatients doorway at St Jude's.

'He downloads pornographic sites.' When Ravi entered his study the chair was skewed from the desk, the room felt violated. Fagends lay drowned in the saucer underneath his maidenhair fern.

Pauline slit open a packet of beans. They both knew what they were talking about.

'I'm sorry.' Ravi stroked her hair. 'I want to really. It's just, the walls are so thin.'

It was true. At night, when they lay in bed, Ravi could almost feel her father a few inches away, lying in the pigsty that had once been the spare bedroom.

'But he's asleep,' said Pauline.

'Yes, I can hear that, all too distinctly.'

'He is amazing,' she replied. 'I've never known anybody who can snore and fart at the same time.'

Ravi laughed. Suddenly they were conspirators. Pauline put the beans on the counter and turned to her husband. Ravi put his arms around her and kissed her – truly kissed her, the first time in weeks. Her mouth opened against his; her tongue, pressing against his own, gave him an electric jolt.

He pushed his wife against the kitchen unit. She was hot from cooking. He thrust his hand down her slippery cleavage, down beneath her blouse and her stiff butcher's apron. He felt her nipple; her legs buckled.

'Sweetheart,' he said. She moved her body against his. He slid his hand into the small of her back to cushion her from the cupboard knobs.

'Let's go upstairs,' she whispered.

7

There was a sound. They swung round. Norman came in, zipping up his trousers.

'Just had the most monumental dump. Must be those chick peas last night.' Norman rubbed his hands. 'Something smells good.'

Norman Purse was a vigorous man. Never any problem in *that* department. His work, building bridges, had taken him all over – Malaysia, Nigeria. He had sampled the fleshpots of Bangkok and Ibadan and was proud of his linguistic fluency; in six African languages he could say 'Show me your pussy'. Oh yes, he had plenty of lead in his pencil.

His wife Rosemary hadn't put up a fuss. She had been a pretty girl once, nicely turned ankles, a bloom to her. That was the trouble: she was too bloody nice. There were certain things a chap couldn't do with a well-bred English rose. Besides, she was his wife. After a few years, like all roses, she was past her best. She had grown into a mousy, middle-aged person who cooked his meals and scuttled around doing whatever women did, hardly a peep from her. To be perfectly honest, the woman wasn't a barrel of laughs. The only time he heard her giggle was behind closed doors with their daughter Pauline. 'What's so funny?' he would ask, opening the door. They would jump like rabbits. Then, when he went away, they would start all over again. Women were strange creatures.

And now Rosemary was long since dead and his own daughter had become a middle-aged matron herself. Pushing fifty, if he remembered it right. One of these career girls, travel agent, never seen her way to give him a grandchild. But a damn good cook, like her mother, better than that slop at The Beeches. Ravi could rustle up some decent grub too, he said it helped him relax. Norman liked teasing his son-in-law. 'Fancy a takeaway?' he would ask, wandering into the kitchen and rubbing his stomach. 'I could murder an Indian.'

Norman had been living with them for a month now and very comfortable it was too. He couldn't go back to the bungalow, of course, because it had burnt down. All the fault of that damned electrician, what a cowboy. They blamed Norman, said he must

8

have nodded off with a fag in his hand but that was a lie and a slander. What were they suggesting, that he was losing his marbles? He might have a dicky heart and an occasional problem with the waterworks but at least he had kept his wits unlike some people in the various penal institutions, a.k.a. Homes, in which he had been incarcerated. Stark raving bonkers, most of them, wandering around in their nighties muttering to themselves. His daughter had a heart of stone, sending him there. The Dettol-smelling corridors, the tap-tapping of Zimmers, the rows of chairs facing the rain-lashed sea, those ghastly prison warders who couldn't handle a red-blooded male, the miserable old hags. Lesbians, the lot of them.

And they called these places *Homes*. Somebody had a sense of humour. Home was with his daughter in Plender Street. It was her duty to look after her old Dad. And it wasn't as if it were a one-way thing. He made himself useful looking after the place when they were at work. Plenty of burglars around, even in Dulwich.

It was a gloriously sunny morning in May. Norman filled the saucepan, squirted in some Fairy Liquid and put his hankies on to boil. He was in a good mood. He'd had his morning wank, he had emptied his bowels and had thoroughly cleared his nasal passages. What with one thing and another, he got through a lot of handkerchiefs. He had eaten a hearty breakfast – Bran Fibre and three slices of toast with Cooper's Old English and that blithering low-cholesterol spread Pauline bought for him. The transistor around his neck – he hung it there to keep his hands free – burbled the morning news. *'The pensions time bomb'*, it said, *'is a disaster waiting to happen.'* The water came to the boil; grey scum rose to the surface. *'Over the next thirty years the elderly population will grow by two-thirds.'* Norman turned down the gas and let himself out of the house.

Plender Street was a pleasant street of Victorian villas – quiet; leafy; Neighbourhood Watch stickers in the windows. Ravi had done well for himself and Pauline must bring in a few shekels too. TWINKIES, they called them: Two Incomes and Something or Other.

A comely housewife pushed a buggy along the pavement; Norman doffed his hat to her as he walked past. She looked startled; good

9

manners were a rarity nowadays, of course. He gazed after her as she quickened her pace; nice arse. Probably wasn't getting much rumpy-pumpy, not with a little kid around. He whistled cheerfully; another thing you didn't hear nowadays, whistling. This place suited him, it was his home, for God's sake. Nice room, meals on tap. No, they weren't going to get rid of him this time. He knew Pauline was searching for another penitentiary, she was doing it on the internet, but no luck so far.

Norman was having too much fun. Ravi was such a fusspot; he had grown worse with the passing years. Everything had to be just so. Norman knew just how to tease him – flicking his fag-ends into the gas-log fire, removing his bottom teeth when he watched TV. He enjoyed his son-in-law's sharp intake of breath. Just that far, no further. Norman had a well-developed sense of survival.

And the man was such a prude. Funny, that, considering he was a doctor, plunging his hands God-knows-where. Norman had told him his joke about the gynaecologist's wife, '*Had a good day at the orifice?*' Not a titter. A while ago he had asked him to get him some Viagra. 'I'm afraid that's impossible,' Ravi had said. What a goody-goody! Once, on a train, Norman had seen his son-in-law reading the safety leaflet. On a *train*. The *safety leaflet*. He hadn't let Ravi forget that.

Norman pushed open the door of Casablanca Food and Wine. A dusky maiden stood behind the counter. He had never seen her before.

'Good morning, my dear.' He raised his hat. 'What's a lovely girl like you doing in a place like this?'

'My Dad owns it,' she said.

'Ah. And what's your name?'

'Sultana.'

Norman spluttered. 'Sultana! Fancy a date then?'

The girl gazed at him, coolly. Oh well, he thought, never mind. He bought his packet of fags and two cans of Tennants. Sultana was doing that text thing on her mobile, thumb skittering. Even so, she could see him. Norman gazed longingly at the rack of magazines. Just for a moment he felt that rare thing: embarrassment. He couldn't, not with this lovely creature here, so young and dewy.

10

There was nothing for it but to go down to the high street. It took him a good ten minutes, his back was playing up. Finally, however, he reached its welcome anonymity, cars thundering past, and went into a newsagent's.

'Morning,' he said to the man behind the counter. He scanned the top shelf of magazines. Lifting his walking-stick, he dislodged a copy of *Asian Babes*. It fell to the floor.

Norman bent to pick it up. A spasm shot up his spine. He froze. Bent double, he waited for the pain to pass.

'Here, Grandad.' The man came over and picked it up for him.

'It's for my son-in-law,' Norman muttered at the floor. 'He's Indian.'

'I'm sure he is.' The man grinned. 'I expect he'll be wanting it in a bag, too.'

Clutching the carrier, Norman hobbled back along the road. A siren screamed. He jumped. A fire engine rushed past. Suddenly he wanted to be home, safely ensconced on the sofa. Today the world seemed more than usually hostile – the traffic, the heedless passers-by, the newsagent with his insolence. Somebody unloaded a crate of bottles. Norman jumped again. He wanted his daughter to be home, instead of miles away in some office or other. She would bring him a cup of tea. She would rub Ibuleve into his back and tell him he wasn't that old, it was all right, he wasn't going to die. Everything was going to be all right.

Norman paused, leaning on his stick. Suddenly he saw himself as others must see him. Just for a moment, like the clouds parting. Then they closed again.

He thought: I miss my wife. Rosemary would understand.

This surprised him so much that he didn't notice what was happening at the end of the street. Something was up. What looked like a fire engine seemed to be parked outside his daughter's house. A crowd of people stood watching.

Norman hobbled closer. He stopped and stared. At 18 Plender Street, black smoke was billowing out of the side window.

2

Let us meditate on the Divine Light that is inherent in us,
May it dissolve all Ignorance and Darkness.

(Gayatri Mantra)

Ravi hadn't seen his cousin Sonny for years. The man lived in Bangalore, for one thing; they had grown up four thousand miles apart. Besides, they had nothing in common. When they met they regarded each other with mutual incomprehension. But Sonny was in London for a couple of days, *en route* to somewhere or other, and none of the other family members was around to pick up some stuff he had brought over.

They had arranged to meet in the lobby of the Royal Thistle Hotel, Bayswater. Ravi spotted his cousin straightaway – a portly man in shirt-sleeves, pacing up and down and shouting into a mobile. The fellow had put on weight. Hard to imagine that he was once a playboy, bopping the night away in the Lotus Room at the Oberoi Hotel, Bangalore, in the company of Bollywood starlets. Still talking, Sonny snapped his fingers at a waiter. 'Bacardi and coke, plenty of ice!'

Ravi's heart sank. Sonny was a wheeler-dealer, a businessman of boundless energy. Ravi had forgotten how sapping that could be for someone in a fragile state. He longed to go home.

Sonny turned. 'Ravi old chap!' He barked something into his phone and clicked it off. 'Come over here! You look terrible, you poor fellow. Overworking as usual?'

'No –'

'Don't know how you stand it, your hair's gone grey. You should

12

try the stuff I use, Tru-Tone, I'll get you a bottle, you'll feel a new man.' Sonny snapped his fingers again and ordered Ravi a drink.

'And *you* should lose some weight,' said Ravi. 'You're storing up trouble for later.'

'Aye aye, doc.' His cousin's face was shiny with perspiration, he had always been a sweaty man.

'Think of your heart.'

Sonny patted his chest. 'Sound as a drum.' He heaved over a carrier bag and dumped it at Ravi's feet. It said *Surinama Silk House*. 'Mangoes for you and your lady wife. Brought them from Lalit's farm – remember Lalit, your uncle's cousin? The best mangoes in Karnataka.'

Ravi watched two men cross the lobby. They fetched their keys from Reception. Suddenly, the thought of checking into a clean, empty hotel room was so seductive he nearly swooned.

'Flying to Frankfurt tomorrow,' said Sonny. 'You know Meyer Systems? They're relocating to Bangalore, to our very own Silicon Valley – these tekkies, they have their heads screwed on, they all want a piece of the action. You wouldn't recognise the place, *yaar*, you know how much software we're exporting? We have the satellite links, we have the know-how . . .' He counted on his fingers. 'Motorola, Texas Instruments . . . The world's shrunk, my friend . . .'

Ravi's temples throbbed. Outside an ambulance sped by, its siren wailing. Today he had failed to revive a cardiac arrest. Asthma attack, a young man with newborn twins.

The drinks arrived. Sonny was still blathering on. Ravi took a sip of orange juice and put down his glass.

'Sonny,' he said. 'I'm having a terrible time.'

That he confided in his cousin of all people, a man not overly interested in others, took him by surprise. Once he started, however, the words gushed forth.

'Pauline's father's come to live with us, we can't get rid of him and I'm going out of my mind. Last week he set fire to the kitchen. He was boiling up his revolting old hankies in my Le Creuset saucepan, nearly burned the house down. I can't tell you how

13

disgusting he is. The toilet stinks of pee, prostate problem, scatters it everywhere, he babbles on when I'm trying to concentrate, he makes horrible slurping noises on purpose, he tells the most offensive jokes, he farts, he belches . . .' Ravi's voice rose. 'He strains his tea through the fly-swat, he never lifts a finger to help, he drops biscuit crumbs everywhere, I can't stand him, I can't get any sleep, Pauline and I are quarrelling all the time, sooner or later I'm going to have to move out, I can't stand it any more, I think I'm cracking up.'

Ravi paused for breath. He thought: What a sign of my desperation, that I'm telling all this to a coarse, Bacardi-swigging little man I hardly know. Who I don't even like much.

'Jesus.' Sonny let out his breath.

Driving home, Ravi felt violated. He only had himself to blame. This, of course, only made it worse.

Ravi was a private man. *'Knock knock, anybody there?'* Pauline would ask. After the miscarriage he had never spoken of his grief. Twenty years ago, that was; their child would be an adult now. During the Flower Power years he had never let it all hang out, he was busy studying. Confidences made him uneasy; it was like handing over your luggage for somebody else to unpack, picking through your underwear.

Now he had blurted it out and soon it would be all around the family. His Aunty Preethi in Chowdri Road, Delhi would be phoning her sister, his mother, at present visiting his brother in Toronto (*The world's shrunk, my friend*). They would be discussing his problems, shaking their heads sorrowfully, hissing at their grandchildren to turn down the TV . . .

Ravi parked outside his house and sat there in the darkness. He had betrayed his wife and, much as he loathed him, he had betrayed the old boy. In the main, he considered himself a man of integrity. If Norman were lying on a hospital bed, he would be all compassion. But then, work was easy. It was appallingly, drainingly difficult, but it was easy.

Ravi looked up at the house. It was dismal, this reluctance to enter one's own home. The upstairs window was steamed up.

14

Pauline must be having a bath. Downstairs, needless to say, Norman had not closed the curtains. The room was exposed to the street. None of the lamps was lit, just the ceiling bulb which cast a pitiless glare like an operating theatre. Norman, the cuckoo in the nest, sat in a haze of cigarette smoke, watching TV.

Ravi let himself in. He had made up his mind: he would phone Sonny and tell him to keep mum about tonight's conversation. The living-room door was ajar; he glimpsed a pair of veined ankles in bedroom slippers. Tiptoeing past, he dumped the bag of mangoes in the kitchen. A burnt smell still lingered.

As furtive as a teenager, Ravi crept up the stairs. Even his study felt polluted now; he was certain that Norman masturbated in it. The bedroom was his only refuge.

Ravi sat down on the bed. Royal Thistle Hotel. He didn't know the number. The phone book was downstairs in the living-room.

I hate him, thought Ravi. Why can't he just go gentle into that good night? Why can't we just throw him into the care of the community like we do schizophrenics and psychopaths? Why can't we leave him to stagger round the streets of London, stealing ladies' knickers off washing-lines? He could get arrested for lewd behaviour. Why don't the old know when to give up the whole damn business and call it a day? *'Hope I die before I get old.'* Who sang that, the Kinks? Why didn't I have a misspent youth?

Ravi reached for the receiver, to dial directory enquiries. As he did so, the phone rang.

It was Sonny's voice, shaking with excitement. 'Listen, man,' he said. 'I've got a hell of an idea.'

Pauline's job as a travel agent had shaped her theory about love. Sexual attraction is triggered by the unknown. A foreign destination quickens the pulse. Even the anticipation of this made her customers fidgety, watching her with bright eyes as she downloaded hotel availabilities on her computer. She imagined them stepping into an unknown city, as alert as foxes sniffing the air.

Within a week, however, the senses became blunted and routines established (*Why isn't there any grapefruit? We had some yesterday*); what was thrilling became mundane (*Not another ruin*). She had experienced this herself, often enough. It was a speeded-up version of love's exhilaration, so soon dulled by domesticity.

In fact Ravi was the domesticated one. It was he who dug the garden and did most of the cooking, it was his way of unwinding from work. He liked things just so – soft lights, real napkins – a sense of style that had been sorely tested in recent weeks. Any taste, she had learnt from him. Left to herself, she would be as slovenly as her father.

The trouble was, Ravi had ceased to surprise her. No doubt this was mutual, though he was too well-mannered to say. The beach on to which she had once run, whooping for joy, had reverted to a strip of sand. She wasn't exactly bored; Ravi was an intelligent man and his beauty still had the power to startle her – fastidious profile, greying wings of hair. It was simply that, during a long marriage, a holiday mentality was hard to sustain.

Ravi wasn't an adventurous man. She put this down to his job. At work he coped with the victims of chance, its random brutality. Many years ago she had tried to get close to him by reading books about Hinduism. 'Surely it's all about predestination?' she said. 'If somebody's going to be knocked down by a lorry, that's their karma.' Ravi had looked at her, puzzled, as if she were talking a foreign language. He wasn't an Indian Indian at all. He was a doctor.

Hence her astonishment the next evening. She went straight from work to the restaurant. It made her uneasy, not to check in at home first; her father, like a dog, should not be left alone all day. But Ravi was insistent – seven-thirty prompt – and things were strained between them; she felt obliged to obey.

Sonny sat beside a bubbling aquarium. He was talking on his mobile phone. His shirt was strained across his chest. '*Every button doing its duty,*' her mother would have said. Black hairs sprouted from the gaps. 'Sit down, sit down!' he said to her, patting a chair.

Ravi was reading a fax. He looked up briefly and smiled at her as if she were a waitress. What was up? Both men had loosened their ties; there was a conspiratorial air to them. More papers, anchored by a salt pot, lay on the table. Their edges stirred in the breeze from the ceiling fan.

Sonny switched off his phone. 'That was my accountant,' he said. 'Tip-top man.'

'You remember Sonny, my cousin?' said Ravi. 'You met at Samina's wedding.'

Pauline nodded. 'Lovely mangoes. Thank you.'

Sonny waved this away. 'This evening, Pauline, is an evening to remember. Your husband and I are cooking up a plan.' He looked at Ravi. 'Who shall begin?'

Ravi opened his mouth but Sonny leaned across the table. 'I have a business proposition.' He gripped Pauline's hand. 'Big bucks all round, and a benefit to humanity. Sounds good so far, eh? Ravi's a good fellow, he and me, we're going to be business partners.'

Pauline looked at her husband. 'But you don't know anything about business.'

'Listen to Sonny, sweetheart. It's an ace idea.'

Ace? Ravi never said ace.

'I'm talking about the old people business,' said Sonny. 'In my country we care for our olders and betters – know what our pension scheme is called? It's called the family! Here in Britain what happens to them? There is nobody to look after the poor old buggers, their families are scattered hither and thither. People like yourself, what do you care for your old *apas* and *ammas*?'

'I care for mine,' said Pauline.

'Where's the money to pay for them?' asked Sonny. 'Your National Health Service is cracking up under the strain –'

'Don't I know it –' said Ravi.

'– this Muriel lady, I see her on BBC Worldwide out of her trolley, discarded like rubbish –'

'That's because she wouldn't let –' Pauline began.

'That's not the point,' said Ravi. 'I know she was a racist old bigot. The point is that we're facing a huge increase in the number of old people –'

'And what will be facing them?' Sonny interrupted. 'Poverty! People are living longer, my dear lady, and there isn't the money to care for them –'

17

'You and I will have to face that soon,' said Ravi.

'Not that soon!' snapped Pauline. She disliked being harangued. And she wasn't that old.

'The pensions time bomb!' Sonny spread out his hands. 'It's a disaster of epic proportions, my dear, already it's happening and it's going to get worse. First your Equitable Life, then the others, company after company is pulling the plug on final-salary schemes –'

'– low interest rates and the fall of the stock market –' said Ravi.

'– all that hard-earned money is vanishing into the air!' Sonny snapped his fingers. 'Year after year it's getting worse.'

Beside them, a waiter cleared his throat. 'Are you ready to order, sir?'

'No!' barked Sonny.

'Something has to be done!' Ravi's eyes were glazed; there was a hectic look to him that Pauline had never seen before. She felt a surprising throb of desire. Behind her husband the fishes darted to and fro, bright with their secrets.

'All day I have been on the telephone,' said Sonny. 'I should be in Frankfurt now but I have postponed my trip. This brainwave, it is a once-in-a-lifetime thing, the great eureka!'

'We're going to set up a retirement home,' said Ravi.

'A chain of retirement homes!'

'First things first,' said Ravi.

'OK, OK.' Sonny swung back to Pauline. 'Your good husband and I, we're going to set up a retirement home.'

'In India,' said Ravi.

She noticed, then, that one of the fish had died; it floated on the surface, buffeted by the bubbles from the pump.

Ravi was indeed a changed man. He surprised not just his wife, but also himself. The plan was so bold it felt like a shot of adrenalin. His normal caution had disappeared, for the scheme made sense, there was a large and beautiful logic to it. Only someone with vision could see this. Sonny had recognised this capacity in Ravi and had singled him out.

18

Ravi stepped out of the side door for a breath of air. Cigarette butts littered the concrete. Rubbish had collected in the gutters – a dusty baby's dummy, a crumpled examination glove. The maintenance contractors had gone bust and St Jude's had no funds to hire anyone else.

Third world conditions, thought Ravi. I'll give them third world conditions. As Sonny said: 'If we can't take Muhammad to the mountain, we'll bring the mountain to Muhammad.'

It all made sense, such staggeringly obvious sense he was amazed that nobody else had thought of it. Perhaps they had. Perhaps, at this very moment, retirement homes were being built in developing countries. Sunshine, cheap and plentiful labour, low costs. The elderly could be looked after at a fraction of the price, thus unburdening the social services. He and Sonny would form a company and set up a deal with local authorities. Sonny already had his eye on some premises, a run-down guest house near his office in Bangalore.

'It's not so far,' he said. 'Look at me, Stuttgart one day, Houston the next, fellows hop on a plane like they hop on a tonga, easy-peasy!' He clicked his fingers. 'We're all global travellers now, old boy, cheap packages to God knows where, Maldives, Seychelles, our own beauteous state of Kerala, cheaper than Connex bloody South-East to Worthing and probably faster too, went there myself on Monday and it took all bloody day. Who wants to be stuck there in some nasty little room smelling of cabbage? Why should they be mouldering away in rainy, dirty old Britain when they could be sitting under a palm tree, tanning their wrinkles and getting their false teeth stuck into a nice juicy mango? What would *you* do, eh?'

'Actually I'd stay here,' said Ravi, who hated India.

But *he* didn't have to go; he would be the London end of the operation, using his medical contacts, liaising with the residential sector. Sonny was right; even older people were sophisticated travellers nowadays, visiting children in Johannesburg, playing golf in Florida. This was where Pauline came in; Blenheim Travel Agency, where she worked, could fix a deal for low-cost fares to Bangalore. Sonny, who was now back in the subcontinent, was working on it that side. 'The head honcho at Air India, he's a pal of mine. Once we're up and running we'll put on special flights, discounts for relatives, sightseeing packages . . . mark my words, cousin, they'll be a lot keener to come to Bangalore than bloody Worthing on a wet Thursday afternoon.' Down the phone line, his voice crackled with excitement. 'This time next year, we're going to have some very satisfied customers.'

'They're not customers, Sonny, they're people.'

'Ah, Ravi man, you're such a prig.'

Back home, Pauline seemed doubtful about the whole business. 'It's a huge risk. Where will you get the money?'

'Sonny's raising the finance.'

'Do you trust him?'

'Of course,' said Ravi. 'He's a bigwig in Bangalore, got a finger in a lot of pies.'

'What sort of pies?' she asked.

His wife irritated him with her misgivings. It wasn't like Pauline, to be so unsupportive.

'You'll never get people to go,' she said. 'I mean, a nice warm country's one thing – but *India*. Think of the disease.'

'It's not all mud huts, you know.' Ravi felt a rare stirring of patriotism. 'If you'd been, you'd realise that.'

'You've only been back a couple of times yourself.'

'That's because I don't like it,' he said.

'Well, they might not either.'

'Then they can come home,' Ravi replied. 'It's not a life sentence. They can go out for the winter and see if it suits them.'

'Old people like the familiar.'

'What's familiar about the world they live in now? Britain's a foreign country to most of them these days, it's frightening, it's confusing –'

'And full of darkies,' said Pauline.

He looked at her sharply. Was she teasing him? 'Well, they'll feel at home in India then.'

Touché. They were lying in bed, whispering. Norman's snores were audible through the wall.

20

'I know the real reason you want to do this,' hissed Pauline.

'Why?'

'So you can get rid of my father.' She turned away, pulling the duvet with her. 'You want to send him there, don't you?'

3

Like Brahma, you do not become attached. You are not sorrowful at the passing of the past.

(Swami Purna)

The Best Exotic Marigold Hotel, Brigade Road, was a roomy bungalow built in 1865 by a box-wallah called Henry Fowler. He had done well for himself in the cotton trade, produced a large family and found in India a congenial home from home. The Marigold was indeed a pleasant place, verandas on three sides and a compound shaded by flame trees. One could imagine the tea parties and parasols. In those days Bangalore was a garrison town and favoured by the British for its mild climate, wide streets and parks. The old city, with its maze of bazaars, was seldom penetrated by them; they lived in the tree-lined thoroughfares of the Cantonment, of Cunningham Street and Defence Lines. They called it the Garden City; their heavy Victorian buildings gave it an air of permanence and authority though they themselves, being made of frailer stuff, passed away and were buried in the graveyard of St Patrick's Anglican church.

Fowler died, his successors died, the bungalow was occupied for a time by the Inspector of Waterways and then used as a primary school run by nuns. With Independence and the departure of the British it was converted into a guest house and had remained so ever since. In the 1960s an annexe was added; over the years air-conditioning was installed in some of the upper-rate rooms and bathrooms, with temperamental plumbing, added *en suite*. But it had remained largely unchanged: twenty rooms with flowered bedspreads and mismatched, cream-painted furniture. There was a lounge filled with chintz armchairs and a heavy teak bookcase filled with paperbacks left by former guests; there was a large dark dining-room. As in many such places, the furniture seemed either too heavy or too flimsy for the rooms, it looked as if the items had been shoved there on a temporary basis until somewhere better could be found. There was an air of somnolence about the place: ticking clocks, creaking ceiling fans and, from the kitchen, the distant clatter of pans. Outside in the garden budgerigars chirruped in the aviary and the flower-beds were planted with marigolds and roses, really you could be in Tunbridge Wells.

'A little corner of Britain,' wrote Sonny. 'An oasis of olde-worlde charm in the midst of the hustle and bustle of modern Bangalore.' He was drafting the script for the promo-video:

> The Best Exotic Marigold Hotel combines the tranquillity of yesteryear with exciting shopping and sightseeing opportunities. Enjoy the ambience of a bygone age with the advantages of modern living: all rooms, both de-luxe and standard, are equipped with direct-dial telephones and Star TV. First-class cuisine includes both English and South Indian specialities. Come and pamper yourself! You deserve it.

The Marigold was indeed an oasis. Around it a new city had grown up. Property prices had rocketed. One by one the neighbouring bungalows had been demolished and replaced with office blocks. Over the past twenty years, with the arrival of the high-tech revolution, business had boomed. The Garden City was transformed into the Corporate City and the Marigold lost its customers to the big new hotels springing up along Brigade Road: the Oberoi, the Taj Balmoral, the Ramanashree Comfort Inn. They offered convention centres and conference suites; they offered twenty-four-hour room service and health clubs where executives sweated out their curries. There was no way that the Marigold had been able to compete with that. Though it had a small clientele of budget travellers none of them stayed long, for despite Sonny's words Bangalore had little to offer the sightseer and was mostly visited as a stopover *en route* to somewhere else – Mysore or, for the adventurous, the ruined city of Hampi. Even then, most tourists were on some package deal tied in with one of the five-star hotels.

So the Marigold had gently declined. Its owner was an easy-going Parsee called Minoo. Through a combination of inertia and sentimentality he had resisted the offers of developers to buy him out, for he had inherited the hotel from his parents and was loath to see his childhood home demolished and made into an office block. Sonny Rahim's offer, however, was more attractive.

'Just think of it, my friend,' said Sonny. 'One hundred per cent occupancy guaranteed, no vacant rooms, no cancelled bookings, it's the hotel-wallah's dream!'

They were sitting in the deserted dining-room. Minoo knew Sonny because he owned the building opposite – Karishma Plaza, a concrete edifice hideous even by Bangalorian standards, with shops below and office space above. Sonny had get-up-and-go, that was for sure.

'A little updating is needed,' said Sonny, 'some minor alterations, but we're not talking old crocks here, these people won't be on their last legs, incontinent and senile –'

'What happens when they become so?' asked Minoo. 'It will happen to us all.'

'Then I will make arrangements for them to be transferred to the Victoria Hospital or to be sent home, these are the conditions that operate in British establishments of this kind. Of course we'll have a qualified doctor on call, I have already approached Dr Sajit Rama, he is a good chum of mine, he runs the Meerhar Clinic in Elphinstone Chambers, and of course on the premises we would have a trained nurse in residence – your good wife.'

This was true. Minoo's wife had been a nurse before their marriage. Well, a nurse of sorts. Everything slotted into place.

'My cousin, Dr Ravi Kapoor, lives in London,' said Sonny. 'He'll run the British side of the operation, we have set up a company together, Ravison Residential Homes. His own lady wife will be our co-partner as she'll be involved with the travel arrangements. We're talking big, my good fellow.' Sonny stretched out his arms, jolting a bottle of soda. 'Join us now, my friend, and you'll reap the rewards! I see an empire growing, retirement homes in sunny climes – South Africa! Cyprus! – away from the rain and the crime, where the living is cheap and the service excellent, I see a chain of homes so our customers will be able to travel freely between them if they wish, a time-share for the active elderly, this is the way the world is going. From little acorns, great oak trees grow, *acha?*'

The man was a human dynamo. Every few minutes they were interrupted by the squawk of Sonny's mobile. He paced up and down, shouting into it. A damp patch spread across the back of his shirt.

Minoo gazed across the dining-room. The curtains were closed. Shafts of sunlight blazed through the cracks, so bright they hurt his eyes. What happens when we die? he wondered. How can we truly know? Suddenly the room was filled with residents, their white heads nodding as they talked together. They were older than he, they had been shunted nearer that blaze of whiteness.

'What happens when they die?' he asked.

'The same as in England,' replied Sonny. 'Cremation, burial . . . I will make the arrangements, leave it to me.'

What happens to us all? Minoo wondered. Vultures will pluck out my eyes, for I will be dispatched in our Parsee manner, and then what?

The chair creaked as Sonny sat down again. The man was waiting for an answer but Minoo was lost in a kind of luxuriant dread. Surely there would be nothing to fear . . . just a sweet surrender.

'You wish to talk it over with your wife?' asked Sonny.

'She is at the beauty parlour.' The thought of Razia jolted Minoo to his senses. 'I must be frank with you, my friend. My wife's nursing experience is somewhat limited. She worked at a foot clinic.'

'A small matter.'

'She was an assistant chiropodist.'

Sonny shrugged and added vaguely: 'Once a nurse, always a nurse.'

Suddenly Minoo flushed with rebellion. For once, *he* would

25

make a decision. He pictured Razia arriving home, her nails blood-red and her mouth dropping open. He pictured his mother staring at him, the teacup half-way to her lips.

'Let's talk figures,' he said, surprising himself. He had never used the phrase in his life. From the kitchen came the crash of crockery. Fernandez, the cook, had been at the bottle again.

Sonny opened his case and pulled out a sheaf of papers. And so the deal was struck. It was June. Just a month had passed since Sonny's moment of revelation in the Royal Thistle Hotel, Bayswater.

Once he had secured the premises, marketing was the next step. Sonny planned to set up a website. Also to produce a full-colour brochure and promo-video, to be distributed to the appropriate agencies in England. With this in mind he arranged a meeting with his cousin's brother-in-law Vinod.

In his youth Vinod had dreamed of being a film director. He had pictured himself surrounded by Bollywood starlets like Sonny, whose playboy antics he read about in *Calling Bangalore* maga-zine. Fate, however, had written him a different script and after various financial disasters Vinod had found himself, in his middle age, running a photographic studio on the Airport Road. Weddings were his speciality, and it was while he was shooting a video of Sonny's nephew's nuptials that Sonny pulled him behind a clump of bougainvillaea and told him his plan.

The following week, Sonny clattered up the stairs to Vinod's studio and thrust a folder into his hand. He had already story-boarded the video.

'We open with the timeless beauty of our country.' Sonny pointed to a poster on the wall. 'A shot of the Taj Mahal at sunset.'

'Maybe sunset is not a good idea,' said Vinod.

'What? So we have to die?' Sonny shrugged. 'Okey dokey, sunrise. Some raga playing on the soundtrack –'

'Too foreign,' said Vinod.

'– and then a tour of the tourist sights of Bangalore.'

'What tourist sights?'

'Tipu's Palace, my friend! Cubbon Park and our splendid

Botanical Gardens! There is plenty to see here, for the discerning visitor. If you please, focus on the Raj aspect – the clocktower, the statue of Queen Victoria. My theme will be: there's a little corner that will for ever remain England.'

Outside, traffic thundered past on the way to the airport. Due to a power cut the air-conditioner wasn't working so Vinod had unwisely opened the window. The studio stank of exhaust fumes and they had to shout above the noise.

Vinod had to admit it: his life was a failure. The realisation had been creeping up on him but only now, in his fiftieth year, had he put it into words. His creativity had been destroyed by a thousand weddings and their numbing demands. Any attempt at artistic licence – cutaways to a stray cat, a montage sequence of dancing feet – was met with bewilderment and, on one occasion, a refusal to pay the fee. Vinod was also saddled with an irritable wife and heedless, disappointing sons. It was chastening to be a recorder of other people's triumphs when he himself had so little to celebrate. So his pulse quickened at the prospect of this job, despite Sonny's bossiness and his insistence that the section devoted to the bustle of downtown Bangalore should include shots of emporiums owned by his business associates.

'Kiddy Korner?' said Vinod. 'These people, surely they are past their childbearing years?'

'Don't they have grandchildren?'

'Drapes Galore?' asked Vinod. 'What will they be doing buying curtains? Surely their hotel rooms will be furnished?'

Sonny pooh-poohed this. Fired with entrepreneurial zeal, he saw that anything was possible. He himself owned a half-share in the Surinama Silk House. 'A sari imparts an air of timeless elegance, particularly to those of mature years.'

'But these are Englishwomen,' said Vinod. 'They're not going to start wearing saris.'

'Don't be bloody negative.' Sonny paused. 'Ah, that has given me an idea. Fashion shows! I shall lay on entertainments. Once they are living in our country our customers will have money to burn! The grey pound, it's called. Or the white pound.'

Suddenly, Vinod started to enjoy himself. Most jobs were a

simple matter of getting all the relatives in the picture and making sure the jewellery was in focus. It was a long time since he had had a creative argument.

Filming at the Marigold would include an establishing shot accompanied by Sonny's sales patter. 'And British music,' said Vinod. 'The Enigma Variations would be just the ticket. I have the CD at my residence.'

'A panning shot around the garden,' said Sonny. 'The trees, the flowers, the tranquillity. A humming bird sipping nectar.'

'Who's making this film?' said Vinod. 'Leave the shots to me.'

Sonny was unabashed. 'And a buffet in the dining-room, my friend. Birianis and cream cakes!'

Fighting, Fucking and Feeding, thought Vinod. In his youth he had wanted to make wildlife documentaries. You had to have the three Fs, otherwise viewers switched off. In this particular case two of the Fs were inappropriate, but the Food aspect was vital. After all, when you were old that was all you had to live for.

Sonny paced to and fro, across the backing sheet. Vinod willed him not to trip over the folds. Once, years ago, Vinod had sat his sons there, in their school uniforms, and taken their photographs. Perched on their chairs, they had radiated hope for the future. Twenty years later here he still was; nothing had changed except he was older, his sons had left him and the traffic had grown to a roar.

'And don't forget the doctor,' said Sonny. Vinod snapped to attention. 'He's first-rate, I've been there for treatment myself. Take a shot of him in his workplace.'

Dr Sajit Rama ran a clinic for sexually transmitted diseases. The next day Vinod loaded his equipment on to a rickshaw and directed the driver to Elphinstone Chambers.

The waiting-room was thick with *bidi* smoke. Rows of men sat there, gazing at their feet. *I'm not really here*, their bodies said. Vinod recognised the man who sold CDs in the street outside the Air India office. What brief pleasure has brought them here? wondered Vinod. Was it worth the price to be paid?

He was ushered into the doctor's surgery. Dr Rama stepped

28

out from behind his desk and shook Vinod's hand. 'Any friend of Sonny is a friend of mine.' He was a handsome man with a fine head of hair. 'To be perfectly frank, I'm not a geriatrician.'

'And I'm not Alfred Hitchcock,' said Vinod. 'But we all have to make a living, *acha*?'

He set up his camera. The idea was to film a consultation. As it was a clap clinic, the dialogue would be mute. Vinod planned to shoot sixty seconds of the doctor listening to a patient, and play music over it.

He positioned the doctor in front of the framed diploma on the wall. The man was unfairly handsome; film star looks, in fact. Vinod pictured the English ladies imagining all sorts of aches and pains just to get him to visit. This fellow would always be doted upon.

Who will look after me when I'm old? Vinod wondered. Not his sons, that was for sure. Their treatment of him was shameful; had they no sense of family responsibility? Of respect?

The nurse ushered in a patient. He was a thin, hunted-looking man. He sat down on the edge of his chair and ran his fingers through his hair.

'What seems to be the trouble?' asked Dr Rama.

'I have a discharge from my part,' said the man. He looked at the camera.

'I assure you, this is confidential,' said the doctor. 'My friend is filming for another purpose entirely.'

'It only happened the one time, Doctor-sahib,' said the patient. The doctor nodded in sympathy. They all said this. 'And now I'm punished for it.' The man lit a *bidi*. His hand shook. 'Please don't let my wife find out about this! She will kick me out of the house.'

'Step behind the screen, sir,' said Dr Rama, 'and lower your trousers.'

Once Vinod had enjoyed the pleasures of the flesh. For years he had visited Chula, a charming young lady who worked at an establishment near the Gandhi Market. Even his own wife had shown some enthusiasm in the early years before she started ganging up with their sons and dismissing him as a failure.

A yelp came from behind the screen. As Vinod packed up his

29

camera he thought: Already I feel past it and I'm fifty years old. What must it feel like to be seventy? Eighty? The only answer was to endure this existence, try to perform good deeds – look, he was helping his friend, and for a very small fee – and pray for better things in his next life. He would go to the temple that very afternoon and perform *puja*; it never failed to restore his spirits.

4

By the path of good lead us to final bliss, O fire divine, thou god who knowest all ways.

(Isa Upanishad)

By late August it was all set up. The Marigold had closed to passing trade and a new sign had been erected: THE BEST EXOTIC MARIGOLD HOTEL: RESIDENTS ONLY. Rates had been fixed – advantageously low compared to their British equivalent. With Sonny to crack the whip, a lethargic workforce had been galvanised into activity: the rooms were ready, the lobby had been repainted and a wheelchair ramp installed. Visa arrangements had been sorted out and cut-price flights had been negotiated through Blenheim Travel, where Pauline worked. As the brochure pointed out, India was a country of contrasts. Though baffling and frustrating, bogged down by bureau-cracy and corruption, it was also a place where, if you spoke in the right ear, things magically happened. Sonny saw to that. 'You soon get used to it, dear lady,' he told Pauline over the telephone. 'It's not called greasing palms. It's called *I wanna hold your hand.*'

And, as yet, the two cousins hadn't fallen out. Until this venture they had hardly known each other. Separated since childhood, the fastidious doctor and the brash entrepreneur had had little in common until now. There had been some snippiness over the company name: in Sonny's opinion *Ravison* gave his cousin too much weight – who, after all, was doing most of the donkey work? But *Sonnyrav* sounded clumsy and he had to admit that his real name, Sunil, didn't fit into any combination. This apart, they were united by their shared zeal.

31

At home in Dulwich, however, tensions were rising. Ravi had become a driven man. He shut himself away in his study – a room from which Norman was now barred – and spent the evenings hunched over his computer. He had grown even thinner, if that were possible, and there was a manic look in his eye. Unfamiliar words flew out of his mouth – *'prioritise'*, *'the bottom line'*. Pauline, however, suspected that the bottom line wasn't his newly discovered business flair, but hatred of her father.

Of course it was difficult, having the old man in the house. Indeed, after a long summer matters were at breaking point. Of course Pauline herself had complex feelings about her father. But she was allowed to.

'Why are you so nice to your patients?' she asked Ravi. 'And foul to him?'

'They're work.'

'Pretend he's a patient then.'

'He's not,' said Ravi. 'He's a disgusting, selfish old brute.'

'Don't say that!'

'You do.'

'I'm his daughter.' Pauline glared at him. 'It's easy for you to be a good son. Your parents live in India.'

'Exactly. That's why your father should go there.'

Norman refused to go.

'You're trying to get rid of me,' he bleated. 'Been travelling all my life. Doesn't a fellow deserve some rest?' His eyes grew moist. 'I'm seventy-six, dear boy. My one wish is to end my days near to my only child.'

'But she's at work all day,' said Ravi. 'Think of the sunshine and the company.'

'Don't worry, I won't be around long,' said Norman. 'Then I needn't trouble you any more.'

Nonsense, thought Ravi, you'll outlive both of us. At this rate, you will. Ravi felt breathless. Probably early-onset emphysema from the passive smoking.

'If India's so bloody marvellous,' said Norman, 'why did you leave?'

'Because the medical facilities are better here.'

'Ah!' Norman snorted with laughter. 'Bit of an own goal there!'

'I mean *were*,' said Ravi. 'It's improved out of all recognition.'

Pauline looked at her husband. Her father brought out the worst in Ravi; he became prissier, more self-righteous. She had a suspicion that Ravi found *her* less appealing nowadays. Sometimes he gazed at her oddly, inspecting her face, his eyes lingering on her chin.

Suddenly she realised: My marriage is at stake. She saw Ravi walking up to another front door, sinking into a strange armchair. She saw it with perfect clarity. Within a matter of months he would find another woman; he was needier than he looked. She laid the brochure on her father's knee.

'Have another look at it, Dad. I'll fly out with you and settle you in.' She smiled at him. 'You'll be our pioneer.'

'No fear,' said Norman. 'You mean I'll be all on my own.'

'Course you won't. We've only just started advertising. We've had a lot of phone calls already.' Two, in fact, but it was a start. 'And afterwards I'll come and visit you lots. Look.' She pointed. 'We've got this relatives' package. They can combine it with a week at the seaside, Bangalore's only two hundred kilometers from Kerala. Goa's not far. Toby and Eunice spend every winter in Goa – remember them? Your old neighbours?'

'Course I do. I'm not completely ga-ga, you know.'

'And no worries about the language,' said Ravi. 'Everybody speaks English there – after all, you used to rule the place. You'll find there's still a lot of respect for the British – good old-fashioned courtesy.'

Norman's eyes narrowed. 'Stop buttering me up. Send me somewhere in England and I'll go quietly –'

'None of them will take you –'

'But I'm not going to blasted India. It'll kill me. If this operation doesn't kill me first.'

On Monday Norman was due to be admitted to St Jude's for his prostate op. Ravi could no longer bear the smell in the bathroom, nor its urine-freckled carpet. He had made some phone-calls and

33

moved his father-in-law up the waiting-list. Besides, it would get the man out of the house for a couple of days.

Ravi drove him there on Monday morning. Sitting beside him, Norman was uncharacteristically silent. For a moment, Ravi was almost sorry for the old bastard.

'It's purely routine,' he said. 'Nothing to be scared of.'

'Now we're alone . . .' Norman lowered his voice. 'Man to man . . .'

'Everything will be fine in that department.'

'The old todger . . .' Norman took a breath. 'Between you and me, it's not what it was. Another nail in the coffin and all that.'

'Nothing'll change, except you'll ejaculate inwards rather than outwards.'

There was a stunned silence. Ravi felt gratified by the effect of his words. The traffic shunted forwards.

'Come again?' asked Norman.

'The semen travels back into the vascular sac. But you'll be able to get an erection, the same as usual.' Ravi said this with feeling, having just received his phone bill – proof that the old tosser had still been availing himself of his computer.

It was this conversation that gave Ravi an idea.

At lunchbreak he took the lift up to the Genito-Urinary Unit. He had a burning desire for Norman to sign up for the Marigold – not just for the obvious reason but as an augury for the future. If Norman went, others would follow. Beneath his rational exterior, Ravi had a deep and regressive streak of superstition. Back in India, in another life, he might have bargained with the gods – a trip to the temple on an auspicious day, a gift of sweetmeats.

Here he resorted to human intervention. He went into the office and sought out his consultant friend, Amir Hussain.

Norman had nothing against Indians *per se*. His daughter was married to one, for God's sake, though in that case his initial horror had been replaced by relief when he discovered that Ravi was more British than the British.

No, he was a broadminded fellow. On his travels he had bumped into a lot of them. In Africa they ran the place – shops, businesses

– working hard, working their way up. The same thing was true of England, of course: from Paki corner shops to the big companies they were over the place like a rash. Nobody could accuse him of bigotry.

Still, his heart sank when the consultant walked into the ward. Nothing personal, of course. It was just that in times of crisis, especially of such an intimate nature, it was reassuring to see a white face.

The chap sat down on his bed. He was accompanied by a comely nurse, probably Filipino.

'Any questions, Mr Purse?' asked the consultant. His name-tag said *Amir Hussain*.

'Nobody told me about the ejaculation business. Bit confusing, eh?' Norman grinned at the nurse. 'Won't know if I'm coming or going.'

'Ha! Glad to see you've got a sense of humour.' The consultant sent the nurse away and lowered his voice. 'In Bangalore, where I come from, they call this op the Great Rejuvenator.'

'Bangalore, you said?'

He nodded. 'In fact, many men request the operation before they actually need it. The effect on women is very powerful,' – Mr Hussain winked – 'know what I mean? Men, they have to fight them off, my God they're popular, bees round a honeypot. Removing the risk of pregnancy is a most liberating experience for a woman, and the women in Bangalore are the most voluptuous in India.'

'That true?'

'And famously inventive. In India, you know, sex is the very basis of our culture. I'm sure you've heard of our *Karma Sutra*.'

Norman nodded enthusiastically.

'The *lingam* is worshipped, of course – especially in South India, and especially in the area around Bangalore. In fact, we have some of the most erotic carvings in the world.' Mr Hussain leaned forward. 'My dear fellow, they'd bring your eyes out on stalks.'

Norman stared at him. The chap was a consultant, he must know what he was talking about.

'Trust me. If you were ever lucky enough to go there, I'd guarantee you wouldn't want to come home.' The fellow leaned even

35

closer; Norman could smell peppermint on his breath. Mr Hussain winked at him and whispered: 'So much pussy you'll be coughing up fur-balls.'

The day after the operation Ravi took the lift up to the G-U unit. Norman, in his pyjamas, sat in the TV room. Next to him sat an elderly Jamaican patient. They were watching *Gilda*. Beside them their catheter sacs, filled with urine, sat on the floor like hand-bags.

Norman pointed to Rita Hayworth. 'What a woman. Don't make 'em like that any more.'

The Jamaican man nodded. 'What a woman,' he said.

'How are you feeling today?' asked Ravi.

'Piece of piss.' Norman chuckled. 'Get it? Piss? Feel like a new man.' He nodded at his neighbour. 'Just telling my friend here about that Home you're setting up.'

The other man nodded. Ravi felt a sudden tenderness towards them, sitting side by side like aunties, their handbags on the floor. For he knew, when Norman spoke again, that his plan had worked.

'Can I have another dekko at that brochure, old chap?'

5

Speak or act with an impure mind
And trouble will follow you
As the wheel follows the ox that draws the cart . . .
Speak or act with a pure mind
And happiness will follow you
As your shadow, unshakeable.

(Sayings of the Buddha)

Evelyn Greenslade was a dear, one of the favourites at Leaside. She was a little vague, of course, and inclined to live in the past but that was hardly unusual. The past was palpable to the Leaside residents – memories of their youth so close they could feel the breath on their faces. Those far-off years remained inviolate; golden afternoons revisited as the elderly inhabitants sat in the lounge or watched TV in their rooms, their hands clasped around a cooling cup of tea. Evelyn drifted there, rudderless – why should she resist? The undertow pulled her back. They waited, her brothers and her schoolfriends; they waited like fairground figures, needing her only to throw the switch and set them in motion. Moments of her childhood returned to her, crystal-clear as if they had happened yesterday.

Evelyn had always been a docile, dreamy woman, no trouble to anyone. That was why the staff liked her. That was why she had come to live at Leaside, agreeing to her children's suggestion that she could no longer cope on her own. *'I don't want to be a burden,'* she said.

Her son and daughter had their own lives to lead. Besides, they

37

were far away. Christopher was installed with his wife in New York; he had an incomprehensible job and a young family. On his last visit he had bought Evelyn a computer so they could exhange emails but there had only been half an hour to learn how to use it. She had pretended to understand – she knew how fussed he became – but for the past six months it had sat there, reproaching her for her ineptitude. At first it sat on her dressing-table, taking up valuable space, but then she demoted it to the floor.

It was her son's idea that she should sell the house. Christopher was right, of course. Since Hugh's death she simply couldn't manage; everything seemed to break down at the same time, all the things her husband had normally fixed. How feeble she had become! It seemed to have happened overnight, that the stairs became too steep and bottle-tops too stiff; suddenly, for no reason, she would burst into tears. And the countryside felt threatening now she was alone in it. She would wake at night, her heart pounding. Had she bolted the door? Sometimes she woke, still groggy. For a moment everything was all right; Hugh was down in the kitchen, checking the corks on his disgusting home-made wine. A strange time to check, but still . . . And then she would realise.

When Christopher told her how much the house was worth Evelyn was staggered. In her part of Sussex, apparently, property prices had soared. To think what she and Hugh had paid for it! This, combined with breaking her hip, made the whole thing inevitable. She put herself in her son's hands. It was such a relief, to let a man take care of things again, and Christopher was a lot more efficient with money than his father. He suggested a place where she would be looked after but still retain, as he put it, a measure of independence – her own furniture around her, maybe a section of garden. Proceeds from the house sale should pay for this, he said, adding ominously, 'Until, as may be, more comprehensive care might be needed.'

Even after this transaction a substantial amount of money remained. This Evelyn insisted on giving to her children. They had, of course, protested but she reasoned that they had better enjoy it when they really needed it. Finally, they agreed. After all, better to use it now before the government clobbered them. Death duties were iniquitous. What right had the Treasury to seize forty per cent from those prudent enough to save and prosper? Christopher could get quite emotional on this subject. Hadn't it already been taxed? What message did this double whammy give the honest citizen?

So it was settled. 'Shrouds have no pockets,' said Evelyn.

'Oh Mum, don't be so morbid!' replied Theresa. Gratitude made her daughter snappy; Theresa had always been a turbulent woman.

Theresa lived up north, in Durham. Nowadays she seemed to be some sort of counsellor, though Evelyn couldn't quite imagine what sort of people would need her daughter's help. Theresa came down to visit, of course, usually on her way to some holistic weekend. Evelyn found these events curiously exhausting. Theresa did take things to heart. She cross-questioned the staff on her mother's behalf; when Evelyn made a mild complaint about the food, Theresa barged into the kitchen and demanded to see the cook.

Worse still were their tête-à-têtes. Theresa was processing the past, she said; she was working on her feelings of rejection. Had Evelyn felt ambivalent about her husband's hostility towards his daughter, when she was little? Did she, as both wife and mother, find her loyalties split? This sort of talk confused Evelyn. The past she remembered bore almost no resemblance to Theresa's version; the events might be the same but it was like seeing a foreign film – Serbo-Croat or something – that was vaguely based on it but all in black-and-white and somehow depressing. Then off Theresa would go to some Group Hug in Arundel. Why, thought Evelyn, does she hug strangers, and never me?

Evelyn missed being touched. She missed Hugh's arms around her. Without the casual contact of skin upon skin she felt brittle and unwanted; she felt like an old schoolbook, filled with irrelevant lessons, that somebody had shoved into a cupboard. The only hands upon her belonged to professionals – the visiting nurse taking her blood pressure or anointing the bruises that bloomed, after the slightest knock, on her papery skin. She had never considered herself a sensual woman, it wasn't a word in her vocabulary, and she hadn't expected this hunger. Nor the need to be needed. Nor the loneliness, in a building full of people. She was only seventy-three but, gradually, those familiar to her were deserting her by dying – her two brothers, several of her friends. People who understood what she meant. Now she had to start all over again with strangers – fellow residents whose wrinkled faces reflected her own mortality – she had to explain things to them. If, that is, they could be bothered to listen. Most of them didn't, of course; old age had deepened their self-absorption. Even after a year it felt like being at a new boarding-school, with no possibility of going home.

Evelyn hadn't predicted this. She had expected the aches and pains, the failing vision, the reliance on others. She knew she sometimes became confused. But she hadn't predicted the loneliness. She remembered Hugh, stuck with tubes, turning to her and smiling. 'Old age is not for sissies,' he said. And then he had gone, and left her to it.

That was why she loved Beverley. Once a week Beverley visited Leaside to do yoga and manicures. She was a chatty, affectionate girl and had taken a shine to Evelyn. She kissed her and called her darling, she brought in a blast of fresh air. Beverley's life was go-go-go; she whizzed around Sussex in her little car, running classes at a dizzying variety of venues: Pilates at the Chichester Meridian Hotel (Mondays), aerobics-'n'-line-dancing at the Summerleaze Health Club (Tuesdays), St Tropez tanning at the Copthorne (Wednesday evenings) and Table Decorations for Special Occasions once a month at the Billingshurst community centre. Then there was the acupuncture, which she was learning from a videotape, and her home hairdressing business. Amongst all this she found time for a packed and disastrous love life. It was no wonder that the arrival of Beverley's yellow Honda, radio blaring, lifted Evelyn's spirits.

After group yoga – only the less demanding postures, it was really an excuse for the old dears to have a snooze – Beverley would sit in Evelyn's room and do her nails, tenderly holding her hand while her cigarette smouldered in the ashtray and she told her about her latest love rat.

'How could he?' Evelyn would say when Beverley paused for breath. 'Fancy that!'

'And then Maureen saw him at the petrol station, filling up his car – three kids in the back and the bastard had never told me!'

'Which one is Maureen, dear?'

'The one with the allergies. Remember?' said Beverley. 'Her face blew up when she got that kitten.'

It pained Evelyn that she looked forward to Beverley's visits more than to those of her own daughter. They certainly saw more of each other.

It was Beverley who broke the news, one day in August.

'They're closing this place down!' she whispered. 'Heard the old bat in the office talking on the phone. Can't afford to keep it going, the grasping sods. They're going to knock it down and build houses on it.'

'Are you sure?'

'It's happening all over, sweet pea, it's in the papers. Like, there's new rules and regulations, nobody can afford them. Better just to flog the place and bugger off to Barbados.' She dipped her brush in the little pot.

'They can't just do that without telling us.'

'Keep still, sweetheart.' Evelyn's hand was trembling. Beverley held it steady and painted on the varnish. 'What's going to happen to you all, you poor things?'

It was true. Leaside, a large Edwardian building on a prime site three miles from Chichester, was to be sold. At this point Evelyn didn't panic. She would move elsewhere. All her life, somebody had taken care of her.

She phoned her son in New York. Christopher would know what to do.

'Slightly bad news, Ma,' Christopher said. She recognised that voice from his childhood, when he hid his school reports.

Christopher went on about the stock market and September 11, something about falling returns. It was all beyond her. In the background, somewhere in the Upper East Side, one of his children shouted, 'Dad, it's not working!'

41

The gist seemed to be that she had less money than she thought. She heard the TV, and a child crying.

'Sorry, Ma, Marcia's at the gym and I'm holding the fort. Got to go. We'll work something out.'

She phoned her daughter. Theresa was furious; she had never had an easy relationship with her brother and was even more hostile towards his wife. 'That bitch is bleeding him dry. You know she got a designer to do up their apartment? Know how much they cost? And private schools for the kids, skis and what not.'

Christopher sent Evelyn a sheet of incomprehensible figures. Oh Hugh, help me! Her pension, it seemed, had shrunk alarmingly. It was all due to the same thing, Christopher said: a slump in the world markets.

Theresa suggested that her mother come and live near her in Durham, an offer made with a palpable lack of enthusiasm. 'Trouble is, I'm away so often, courses and things. I'm off to Skyros next month.'

'What about your counselling?' asked Evelyn.

'Oh it's very flexible. Usually just a couple of days a week, I can rearrange it with my clients.'

How can you live on that? Evelyn opened her mouth, and closed it again. Of course she knew how.

'There's always the local council,' said Theresa. 'If you threw yourself on their mercy – I mean they'd have to help, wouldn't they? They must have homes, or sheltered housing. I can make enquiries.'

Evelyn didn't consider herself a snob, not really. However, she found this conversation depressing. Did her daughter understand nothing?

No doubt Theresa meant to be kind but the message was clear: her mother was redundant. No longer a human being, she was a problem to be solved by the local authority, like a drug addict or one of the homeless. She *was* homeless. She was to be shunted away out of sight. How quickly, after Hugh's death, had she become surplus to requirements!

'You can't go to one of those places,' said Beverley the next week. 'Not somebody like you.' Beverley understood.

'Anyway, I'm not old enough.' When reminded of it, Evelyn's age surprised her. Seventy-three wasn't *her*; it floated nearby, as irrelevant as a sum on a blackboard. She didn't connect it to herself. 'I'm not ill enough, either. You have to have something wrong with you, for one of those places.'

'I've been having a nose round.' Beverley produced a copy of *The Lady*. 'I nicked it from one of my clients – don't touch, your nails are wet.' She opened it and, squinting through the smoke, pointed to one of the advertisements. 'How about this place?'

Evelyn peered through her spectacles. 'The Best Exotic Marigold Hotel. My uncle Edward lived in a house called Marigolds. It was just outside Pontefract.'

'Well, this one's in India.'

The idea was preposterous, of course. *India*. It was a big enough kerfuffle just to get herself to Chichester. Evelyn had grown more fearful in her old age. The newspapers carried such alarming stories – biological attacks, rapes and muggings. That very week, according to the *Sussex Mercury*, somebody had set fire to a litter bin in the Cathedral precinct.

Beverley, however, thought the idea a hoot and sent off for the brochure. The next week she sat down in Evelyn's room and opened it.

'Look at that house – you could be in England. Except it's sunny.' Outside, rain lashed the window. It had been the wettest August on record – gales, thunderstorms. The management had had to switch on the central heating. 'What's the point of mouldering away in this bloody country? How long've you lived in Sussex?'

'All my life,' said Evelyn.

'That's *so* not adventurous. Isn't it time for a change? After all, what's to keep you here?'

How did Beverley guess? Evelyn hadn't talked much about her children and her grandchildren, it was too painful. Besides, she could never get a word in edgeways.

'It'd do you the world of good, petal,' said Beverley. 'It's never too late, and you're in terrific nick now your hip's better. If you don't like it you can always come home.'

All my life. Put like that, it did sound tame. But they had been fulfilled and happy years, Evelyn was sure of it, despite Theresa's bemusing version of events. With the passing of time, however, and the departure of its main characters, the mixture felt denuded and flavourless; she had thought about it too much, it was like meat with the goodness boiled out of it.

'I used to make an excellent stew,' she said.

'Pardon?'

'Though I say it myself. The secret was pouring Hugh's wine into it.' Evelyn paused. 'He never knew. I used his beer for killing slugs, too. You pour some into a dish and leave it in the garden, overnight. They climb into it and drown. Such a happy death. The best sort one could imagine, really.' She relapsed into silence.

'Here, stop babbling and try some of this.' Beverley squirted her with perfume. 'It's Arpège.' She always had some free samples with her. They tried them out together.

Evelyn roused herself from her reverie. No, the idea was mad. She gave back the brochure. 'I couldn't die in a foreign field.'

'Indians don't die.'

'Yes they do, dear. All over the place.'

'What I mean is, death's not important.' Beverley had learnt this from her friend Maureen, who knew more about yoga than she did. 'When you die you come back as something else. A woodpecker or something.'

'Why a woodpecker?' asked Evelyn.

'Search me.'

Until recently Evelyn had believed in heaven. Now she was drawing nearer to it she wasn't so sure; it was like someone shoving a page in front of her face – the closer it became, the more blurred the writing. There was so much senseless suffering in the world – what had Hugh done, to deserve those final months? To believe in heaven you had to believe in God, and during those last terrible months in hospital she had lost Him.

Beverley pointed to a photo. 'That's the doctor at the hotel. Dr Sajit Rama, he's called. Isn't he gorgeous?'

'He looks like Omar Sharif.'

'Isn't Omar Sharif about a hundred years old?'

'He wasn't always, dear,' said Evelyn.

'Actually, isn't he dead?'

Evelyn thought suddenly: This life, it's as if I'm dead already.

Beverley gazed at the photo. 'What do you think Omar Sharif should come back as?'

'Himself, but younger,' said Evelyn. 'And staying in the next room.'

They burst out laughing. 'Plenty of life left in *you*,' said Beverley, 'you naughty girl.'

Evelyn was surprised at herself. 'It's those big dark eyes. We used to have a spaniel with eyes like that.' What was the dog's name? Disappeared, along with so many others. Only that morning – was it that morning? – she had forgotten the name of Christopher's wife.

Oh Lord, what was it? If she tried to remember, it only became more frustrating. Sometimes it worked if she came at it casually, fooling herself that the name didn't matter. Sometimes it felt like grabbing at shoals of minnows; they darted away in the water, tiny slivers of silver, they would never be caught.

'Indian men are so fit compared to pasty English ones,' said Beverley dreamily. 'Honest, you'd feel ten years younger.'

Marcia. There, she wasn't completely senile.

This cheered Evelyn. She picked up the brochure and looked at a photograph. It showed the hotel garden. The place was bathed in a golden light, the light of long afternoons in her childhood garden, now tarmacked over to become the freight terminal at Gatwick. '*The timeless beauty of India*', it said. Time didn't really exist, not with the important things. Evelyn talked to Hugh in her head; his voice continued even though he himself had stopped. She could remember every inch of that garden – the brick path, worn in the middle; the moss beneath the water butt where she had found a newt.

'I remember now,' said Beverley. 'With Hindus you've got to do good deeds. Then you come back as something better.'

What had the newt done, to end up being a newt? Perhaps it had once been a cruel father who had beaten his children.

'What's so funny?' asked Beverley.

'Nothing, dear.' Evelyn found this conversation invigorating; nobody at Leaside talked about things like this. The very word *India* sharpened her senses, like squeezed lemon. Even if she never went there, which was likely, it was bracing to think about it. Hugh would have been amazed that she even entertained the idea.

She thought of her children and smiled. It was worth doing it, just to see their faces.

But of course she couldn't. What about the dirt and disease? 'What about those Muslim terrorists?' Evelyn asked. They bred out there, hatching their suicide missions. She feared for her grandchildren, living in New York. She feared for herself.

'Indians are Hindus, silly billy,' said Beverley. 'The Muslims are in Pakistan, that's why they made it. To put the Muslims there. Even I know that.'

'I know so little,' said Evelyn.

'Never too late to start.'

Christopher, who was inclined to lecture, had tried to interest his mother in wider matters. On his last visit, when he had given Evelyn the computer, he had said that it was all one world now. 'It's called globalisation, Ma. You see, I can download the kids on to your computer and you can talk to them.'

'I'd rather see them.'

'You *do* see them. It's as if they're in the room. Distance has become meaningless. I can work anywhere, all I need is my laptop. Time and space have been transformed – look, our lettuce comes from Kenya, our Raleigh bikes are made in Korea, our trainers in Taiwan –'

'I've never had any trainers –' said Evelyn.

'That's the new global economy –'

'Perhaps I should get some, they're supposed to be so comfortable –'

'I remember talking to a chap who was harvesting the next field – remember that huge field at the end of the garden? Stonking great combine harvester. Said he had a flat in Eilat, for the scuba-diving, harvested in Sussex and Israel and Saudi, travelled all over the world. Chap who drove the tractor came from Poland –'

'What are you talking about, dear?'

46

Christopher had stopped, with a little sigh. While she was pruning her forsythia, it seemed, the world had been transformed.

Beverley gazed at the doctor's photo. 'Honest, I'd go there myself if I was old.'

She left. Evelyn stood at the window and watched her manicurist scuttling through the rain. Beverley opened the car door. Faint sounds of yapping came from the interior; it was her West Highland terrier, Mischief. Beverley flung her case into the back seat. Then she drove away, the loose exhaust pipe rattling.

Evelyn stood there, watching the rain lash the rhododendrons. How strange, she thought; if I went to India, which I can't possibly imagine doing, it would be Beverley whom I would miss the most.

6

We are what we think, all that we are arises with our thoughts, with our thoughts we make the world.

(Sayings of the Buddha)

Dorothy Miller lived in a block of flats next to Madame Tussaud's. Outside, day and night, traffic roared down the Marylebone Road. Dorothy had always been a poor sleeper. Lying in bed, she listened to the cars passing in waves, rising then subsiding.

Through the wall, however, was silence. The waxworks stood, mute in their celebrity. Dorothy hadn't been in there for years but she sensed their presence, keeping watch with her through the night. Queens and murderers, mistresses and presidents, their selves had long since died but their replicas remained, for ever poised – a hand raised, eyes gazing nowhere. During the war they had been stored in an adjacent building. One night, in a bombing raid, the roof was blown off; when the rescue teams arrived they had stared, appalled, at the heap of limbs.

Dorothy lived alone. She thought: If these flats were bombed, people would rescue their photo albums before they rescued me. She was used to this sensation. Sometimes, in fact, she got a certain satisfaction from it. After all, she had had an interesting life, as interesting as that led by many of the effigies next door. Sometimes, half-asleep, she imagined them stirring themselves and stretching their limbs; she imagined them ageing.

Some of them, in fact, she had met during her career; some she had featured in programmes. Dorothy had worked at the BBC, in current affairs. She had travelled widely and been involved in some of the history on the other side of the wall. It was many years now, however, since she had retired. Arthritis confined her to the flat, sometimes for days at a time. It was on the ground floor. Each day, outside her kitchen, a queue formed for the waxworks – students, Japanese tourists. As she brewed her coffee the people gazed through the window. They peered closer, unnerving her, until one day she realised: Of course they're not looking at me. They're inspecting their own reflections in the glass.

Increasing years, of course, render us invisible as if in preparation for our eventual disappearance. Dorothy had never been a head-turner but she had always been smartly dressed – a sophisticated woman who had never married though there were rumours of an affair with an actor, himself married, now long since dead. Enquiries about her private life were not welcome; in fact, nobody would think of attempting to make them.

In recent years chronic pain had made her short-tempered. What was happening to the world? Had she missed something? People seemed to have pulled up the drawbridge and retreated into their own solipsistic little lives. Half of them didn't even bother to vote. In a way, Dorothy couldn't blame them. The rot had started with Mrs Thatcher, *there's no such thing as society*, but a worse betrayal was committed by her own party which had mutated into something so repellent that she was tempted to upsticks altogether and leave the country. Even the BBC, once so familiar, was now unrecognisable. The phrase 'market forces' had, like a cancer, eaten into the organisation she had most loved. That it was elderly to think this way only made her more irritable. Newspapers were full of interviews with people she had never heard of, famous for being famous, famous for being celebs; what had they done, what was the point of it all? No doubt Tussaud's was full of them now. At some defining moment a sea-change had occurred – around the time when train passengers were renamed customers, when ordinary dogs disappeared overnight, to be replaced by pit bull terriers. It was as if she were performing in a play and realised, quite suddenly, that the cast had been replaced by actors she had never seen before.

Dorothy started making breakfast. No oranges. Yesterday she had hobbled out to her local greengrocer's only to find it had turned into a SnappySnaps. Her own face, in the mirror, had been replaced by that of an old woman.

It was the rush hour. Outside, the traffic was at a standstill; even here in the kitchen she could smell the exhaust fumes. She knew that she was struggling against her own irrelevance. August had been miserable; the queue along the pavement was a hunched row of anoraks. On Radio 4 they were broadcasting an item about care home closures: '. . . *squeezed out of existence by regulatory overload and starved of funding by social services . . .*'

Dorothy tried to unscrew the percolator. What will happen to me, she wondered, when the time comes? Her BBC pension would hardly stretch to a private place, not for more than a few years, and her lease was soon to expire; a Hong Kong company had bought the block of flats and planned to refurbish the place and sell it off at a no doubt extortionate profit.

'*A spokesman said "Unless the government makes £1.5 billion available immediately, the sector will collapse and the NHS could be left with a bill for £15 billion."*'

Dorothy was seventeen when the NHS was created. Now it was cheaper to send people to France for new hips. They returned, glowing with praise and with a taste for red wine at lunch.

The phone rang. It was Adam Ainslie, one of her protégés at the BBC.

'Are you all right?' he asked.

'No. I need somebody to unscrew my percolator. I may be reduced to many things, but not to instant coffee.' Dorothy's joints ached. She thought: I need new hands. Maybe I could fly to France and get them fitted.

'Shall I come round?' he asked, over-brightly.

'Don't be silly. All the way from Fulham?'

She thought: I need a servant. After all, my parents had them. Sod socialism.

'Can I send you a video?' asked Adam. 'It's only a rough cut, but I'd love your opinion.'

'What is it?'

'It's a programme I've made about what happens to people after they've been on a chat show. You know, fifteen minutes of fame and all that.'

Dorothy's heart sank. Outside, the queue shuffled forward. 'Too Big to Wipe,' she said.

'What?'

She seemed to have spoken out loud. The last time in New York – years ago, when was it? – she had switched on Jerry Springer. Those were his guests: Too Big to Wipe.

'I'd really appreciate your input,' said Adam. 'I owe everything to you. A lot of us do.'

He was flattering her, of course. But she had given Adam his first job and he remained loyal. She would watch his awful video and try to be kind.

It took Dorothy half an hour to get the damn jiffy bag open. Adam had trussed it up with that sort of tape they used, in films, to gag prisoners. She scrabbled at it with her fingernails. On the *PM* programme there was an item about woodlands. Apparently they were too thick and dark. The government had decided that the countryside was now a leisure facility and that woods were too alarming for its citizens – sorry, customers – particularly ethnic minorities who weren't used to them, and after consultation with the community was putting in place a scheme to make them more user-friendly. Trees would be cleared to create more open, glade-type environments with seating, disabled access and leisure facilities.

'I'm seventy-four years old, Laszlo,' Dorothy said. 'I can no longer be surprised by anything. Maybe those who have suffered stress disorders caused by overpowering vegetation have been claiming for counselling. Maybe, once those messy trees have been cleared away, those too big to wipe will sue the relevant agency for making the seating too discriminatingly small for their enormous bottoms.'

She often spoke aloud to her dead sweetheart. It was one of the consolations of living alone. The relationship had been doomed but in her imagination Laszlo was for ever hers, leaping to help her in his polite Hungarian way.

51

'Help me to wrench off this blasted tape,' Dorothy said. 'Help me to survive.'

Life was full of incomprehensible instructions. The manual for her video recorder was twenty pages long, in tiny print that only an ant could read. It no doubt catered for possibilities undreamed of by those who, until then, had been content with their existence. The funny thing was that the more choice there was, the more powerless one felt.

'Am I just a batty old woman, Laszlo? Given the choice, would you have tired of me by now?'

Dorothy finally extracted the video from its jiffy bag. She slotted it into the machine, poured herself a whisky, and sat down in front of the TV. Adam, her surrogate son, was a charming young man. She owed him an honest opinion.

A picture bloomed on the screen. It was the Taj Mahal.

Dorothy gazed at the TV. She couldn't see the connection with chat shows, but then many connections escaped her nowadays. She could watch ads in the cinema and have no idea what they were going on about, not a clue.

The sun was sinking – no, it was rising. That dewy, pearly light . . . it was the dawn. The marble mausoleum glowed, radiant. The camera panned around to the Yamuna River; submerged in it, up to their necks, stood water buffalo. Sitar music played.

'*Welcome to India,*' said a voice. '*A land of timeless beauty.*'

'Was that a joke?' said Dorothy on the phone. 'If so, it was in very poor taste.'

'Sorry,' said Adam. 'I sent the wrong tape. It was meant for my parents.'

Dorothy seemed extraordinarily upset. He could see it could be construed as tactless, to send an old lady an ad for a retirement home, but where was her sense of humour? Dorothy had never been easy, but age was clearly worsening her temper.

Adam was standing at the window, poised for action. In his street there was severe parking congestion. His own car, like several others, was double-parked. At any moment one of his neighbours might emerge from a house and drive off, in which case Adam had to be ready to leap out and grab the space before anybody else got it. Some people, to avoid losing a space, never moved their cars at all and had resorted to public transport.

'Send the tape back,' he said, 'and I'll send you the other one.'

'Why don't you come round for supper?' asked Dorothy. 'Haven't seen you for a while. Then we can do it in person.'

'I'd love to sometime – oh, blast, must rush.' Outside, a car was pulling out. Adam slammed down the receiver and ran out of the house.

He meant to phone Dorothy back, he really did. But then Sergio came home with some squid he had bought for their dinner party and they had started hunting for the recipe they had torn out of the *Independent*.

Adam was fond of Dorothy; there was something intransigent about her strong plain face and gravel voice. During his days at the BBC she had been an inspiring boss and he owed her a great deal. In general, however, she had not been popular with her colleagues – too autocratic; too demanding, in others, of the standards she set for herself. She had been regarded with respect rather than love, and when he had told a fellow trainee 'I'm a friend of Dorothy' the chap had presumed he was gay and asked him out for a drink. Adam *was* gay, of course, but he hadn't meant it like that. Dorothy was good with gay men – maybe because, in common with many fag hags, her personal life seemed to have been a failure. She had subsumed it in her work.

Adam still valued Dorothy's opinion. That was why he had sent her the tape. But he also did it out of kindness, to make her feel needed. Over the years a subtle change had taken place in their relationship. Once she had been his mentor; he had been flattered to be asked to Dorothy's dinner parties in her book-lined flat with its Howard Hodgkin painting above the fireplace. Once he had met a Labour cabinet minister there. But now she had retired; the dinner parties had long since ceased and when he visited her it was out of a sense of duty. He was even starting to humour her, for her fine clear mind had become somewhat muddled – what had she blurted out? Something about being too big to wipe? She shouldn't live alone; with nobody to listen to them, her thoughts became confused. Age had shifted the balance between them. Dorothy was a proud woman; if she had suspected that he was patronising her, she would have been horrified.

His own dinner party consisted of Brazilian friends of Sergio – dull but good-looking, like most of Sergio's pals. Adam's attention wandered.

Suddenly he remembered the videotape. He had promised to phone Dorothy. *Shit!* He had also promised to send the tape to his parents, who were thinking about a possible retirement home. His father and mother lived in Devon. They were a game old couple, always off on some jaunt or other in their beige wind-cheaters, birdwatching in the Hebrides or driving to Portugal in their camper van. Recently, however, life had dealt them a series of blows. Their village shop had closed down which meant they had to drive to Okehampton to do their shopping – no bloody buses, of course – and recently his father had crashed the van. 'Eyesight on the blink,' he said. Neither of them, to be honest, was fit to drive any more and this had left them marooned in the middle of nowhere, suddenly shunted into dependency. Their neighbour, a farmer, had lost his stock in the foot-and-mouth crisis and had decided to sell up. People were sloughing off their responsibilities and decamping to warmer climes where the living was easy. No more leaky roofs! No more chores! Adam had heard about this retirement place in India, a country that had happy memories for his parents. He had written off for the details.

Adam was thinking about this as he chewed the squid (some-what rubbery). He was also wondering how long his relationship with Sergio was going to last. He thought: Those cheekbones are beginning to wear thin. Funny how a lover's friends suddenly made you see them clearly. Adam's sister, a frequent traveller along the bumpy road to love, said that relationships based on sex lasted exactly two years.

He also thought: This Indian place might make a good documentary. While ruminating on this, Adam drank a great deal of

54

Chilean Merlot. He forgot about the documentary and it was to be three more years before he plucked up the courage to leave his lover. But he remembered to get the video back and send it to his parents.

Who put their house on the market and prepared to uproot their lives, for that was the kind of people they were.

Dorothy had her dream again. She was submerged in the gully behind her house. This time she bumped against the bulk of a water buffalo; she grabbed on to it and heaved herself up. Now she seemed to be sitting astride its head. It reared up from the water, lifting her with it, the water falling off her in streams. And then it shrugged her off and she was drowning.

She woke, drenched with sweat. It was three o'clock. She waited for the images to dissolve and leave her safe. *'It'll all come out in the wash,'* her mother had said, though it didn't, did it? Her mother had lied. Dorothy willed herself to think of humdrum things: tea at Patisserie Valerie in Marylebone High Street; the *Today* programme with Jim Naughtie's soothing Scots voice. This slowed her fluttering heart.

Her throat was dry. She pushed back the duvet and carefully, achingly, got out of bed. Her bones felt like chalk, dry and squeaky as they rubbed together; one day they must break. Even walking to the kitchen made her breathless. She leaned against the fridge. Outside a taxi passed, its sign illuminated. She thought: I should tell Adam about India. He's closer to me than anyone.

This thought depressed her. Adam was a busy young man; weeks went by without his phoning her. Oh, he sometimes dropped in for a cup of tea when he was editing down in Soho but Dorothy knew, in her heart, that she came first with nobody.

The kitchen was dark. Dorothy hadn't switched on the lamp, it would be too much of a jolt. She stood there, drinking a glass of water. Across the Marylebone Road stood an office block. Its lobby was illuminated. At night a security guard sat there, a young Indian man. He talked for hours on the phone, swirling round on his swivel chair. When she wore her spectacles she could see him quite clearly. Every night he sat there, her unwitting companion during the small hours. But she, in the darkness, remained invisible.

Pauline had crippling period pains. She was going through the menopause, a journey that neither of the men in her life could share. It was a tumultuous voyage. She bled, heavily and erratically. The cramps were fierce, as if nature was kicking her in the stomach as a final punishment: *Even if you COULD have had children, now you can't.* She had hot flushes, her face turning brick-red like her father's. At work people looked at her curiously as she pulled at the neck of her blouse, fanning herself. Nights were the worst. She woke, drenched in sweat, her heart pounding with nameless dread. She feared her own mortality. *Fasten your seatbelts, it's going to be a bumpy ride.* For this flight was taking her to a destination that filled her with foreboding: old age, a foreign country from which nobody returned.

She couldn't confide in Ravi. Like many doctors he was breezily dismissive of the ailments, unless life-threatening, of those he loved. They were drifting apart – literally, in fact, when her night sweats forced him to abandon their bed and sleep in his study. Pauline suspected that he went back to work; sometimes, when she got up to get a drink of water, she saw a strip of light beneath the door. She was an outcast, she and her fluttering heart, she was alone amongst the insomniacs in this huge city.

It was early September. Ravi's study was being taken over by Ravison business – a new filing cabinet, piles of folders, post-it notes stuck to the framed photo of his class at St Ignatius Boys' School, Delhi. There had been a lot of enquiries, not just about the Marigold but about the possibilities of other Homes around the world – South Africa, Cyprus – prospects mentioned in the publicity material.

Ravi said: 'See – people want to get the hell out of this country.'

'Don't put it like that!' Britain was like her father; only *she* was allowed to slag either of them off. Underneath it all Ravi was still a foreigner.

Ravi was sorting through '*Fitness to Fly*' doctors' certificates. Eighteen clients, so far, had signed up for the Marigold. The rooms were nearly filled. Pauline knew their names because she was organizing their travel arrangements: Mrs Evelyn Greenslade, a lady from Chichester, who wrote in longhand; Mr and Mrs Ainslie from Beaworthy, Devon. They sounded genteel and, judging by the addresses, well-heeled. Plans for state assistance had long been abandoned as unworkable; this was a purely private enterprise. One of their customers had even enquired about shipping out her antique furniture; that was the sort of person they were attracting. Some of them would have already been installed by the time Pauline flew out with her father at the end of the month.

Why had her father changed his mind? Pauline never found out. Fully recovered from his operation, he seemed to be looking forward to his new life in Bangalore. 'Raring to go,' he said. He had had his jabs; he had even sorted out some lightweight clothes from his travels in the tropics and crowed over the fact that they still fitted him. Norman's imminent departure had changed Ravi's attitude towards his father-in-law; he had become more tolerant of the old boy, almost fond. The day before he had even managed a mild joke, about buying a new saucepan.

Pauline's own feelings were mixed. In her present state, the flight itself filled her with panic. What happened if one of her copious periods suddenly began? She pictured the charnel house it would create in the British Airways toilet. Would there be Tampax in India? She had always been curious about Ravi's home country but this voyage back to his roots was not the one she had envisaged. She was going to leave her father in a strange land, in the company of people he had never met. It was like taking a child to boarding-school – in this case, half-way across the earth – and leaving him there, the new boy in class. She would walk away, eyes swimming. She pictured him behind her, waving his stick in farewell . . . a small figure, growing smaller.

Pauline eased her way downstairs. She had wedged a Kotex between her legs; the plastic shifted. Her father sat in the lounge, reading the 'Deaths' column in the *Daily Telegraph*. He liked to sit there with his morning coffee, totting up the *suddenlies* and *peacefullies*.

She paused for a moment, looking at the blotches on the top of his head. 'Good day today?' She indicated the paper.

'Pretty good.' He pointed with his pencil. 'Eight of them older than me. Seventy-nine . . . eighty-two. Only a couple younger and they're *suddenlies*. Probably poofters with AIDS.'

'Dad!' Norman only totted up men. When it came to mortality, women didn't count. 'Could be car crashes,' she said. 'Could be anything.'

It was Saturday. Pauline should be going to the supermarket but she didn't feel like moving. There was a silence. She wanted to tell her father so much but she didn't know where to begin. And he wasn't going to start, not after fifty-one years.

'Got *punkawallah* in the crossword,' he said. 'Chaps who fan you, in India.'

'I wouldn't mind one of those.' She didn't say *for my hot flushes*. Though only too frank about sex, Norman was embarrassed by women's intimate arrangements. She said: 'Remember, you can always come home.'

'Not on your nelly.'

'The other people sound very nice,' Pauline said. 'There's a civil servant and somebody who worked in the BBC. A Dorothy Miller. Mostly women, of course.' She thought: They stay alive longer than men.

Suddenly her eyes filled with tears. These damn mood-swings. Now that her father was leaving, his possessions already had the power to move her – his slippers in particular. She would have to throw away the piece of paper she had pinned by the front door: CHECKLIST: TEETH. FLIES. BUS PASS. KEYS.

'Another old biddy left in Casualty,' Norman said, showing her the paper. 'Here, on the front page.' He started to chortle. 'Remember what's-her-face, the one who got your hubby into trouble?'

'Muriel Donnelly.'

'Wouldn't let darkies touch her.' He coughed his smoker's cough. 'Ha! Catch *her* going to India.'

Pauline laughed. 'I think we can safely say that she won't be joining you.'

Ravi came into the room. 'What's so funny?' he asked.

Pauline told him.

'Nothing funny about racism,' he said.

'Oh don't be such a prig,' she replied. 'You have to admit it would be funny if an old bat like her, who can't stand darkies, suddenly found herself surrounded by a thousand million of them.'

7

When Ignorance is shattered, Light overflows, Wisdom arises, the Mediator becomes fully delivered and freed from the bondages of cycles of Birth, Rebirth, Decay and Death . . . Herein lies the sole object and the very purpose of Meditation.

(Ven. Dr Rastrapal Mahathera)

When the Queen Mum died Muriel put up the flags – three of them, stuck in a vase in her window. She had removed them from her Diana shrine in her lounge. Diana was a story-book princess, of course – beautiful, doomed, a deer fleeing the hounds according to that Earl Spencer. The Queen Mum, however, was the real thing – royal to her bones rather than a beguiling traitor. She was special, the most special Mum in the world. Muriel's son Keith made her feel like that. He made her feel like royalty.

The last time Keith visited he had admired the Union Jacks. 'It's to set an example,' Muriel had said, indicating the flats opposite. 'To that lot.'

Muriel had lived in Peckham all her life, except for a short and traumatic period during the war. While she stayed put, however, the area had changed around her. The Blitz had been followed by equally savage destruction in the 1960s, when streets had been bulldozed to make way for high-rise blocks. As the years passed many of the families she knew had moved out, to be replaced by blacks. Nowadays crack dealers drove past in convertibles, music blaring, the thuds making her ornaments tremble. Huge girls barged into the *Only Two Schoolchildren at a Time* newsagent's. They shoved past her, shouting on their mobiles, while she tried to buy a tin of Whiskas. More recently illegal immigrants had moved in, grey-faced men from God knew where. They stood outside the tube station waiting to be picked up by cowboy builders. Crime statistics were soaring; her nights were punctuated by the sound of smashing glass.

Keith had urged her to move out. 'It's a dump, Mum. Come to Chigwell.' He lived there in some style, he had done well for himself. Muriel, however, was stubborn. She let him buy her a flat on the ground floor of a nice new block, round the corner from where she grew up. She let him fit it out, washing machine, satellite TV. She even took the money Keith pulled out from his wallet, so fat it didn't close properly, when he visited her. But she stayed where she was. She was an independent woman, she didn't want to be beholden. And she didn't want to live anywhere near that sarky wife of his.

The loathing was mutual. When Muriel had been stuck in Casualty, back in May, Sandra hadn't even been bothered to phone. It was only when Keith got back from Spain that all hell was let loose – newspapers, TV, Muriel did enjoy it. The neighbours made a fuss of her, the ones who could speak English, all of a sudden she was a celebrity.

Muriel loved her son. She had always been there for him. Wives and girlfriends came and went – '*Here we are, gathered together again*,' said the best man at Keith's last wedding – but they were like driftwood, washed back to sea while Muriel remained, the rock. That was mothers for you. Keith was all she had, Keith and her cat Leonard. In fact they had a certain amount in common. Both were sleek, handsome and predators of the opposite sex; both disappeared for days at a time on mysterious business of their own – in the case of her cat, returning with a torn ear.

Where did Keith's money come from? Muriel didn't ask. He said he was in property and that was good enough for her. It certainly financed a lavish life-style: the house in Chigwell, the house in Spain, the vast silver jeep-thing in which he arrived to whisk her out to Sunday lunch up west at places where they removed her coat with a flourish as if she had just arrived from Buckingham Palace. In Keith's presence Muriel was plugged into

61

a different world. His father would have been proud of him. After all, that was what sons were for: to do better than you ever did. Otherwise there would be no sense in it.

Life had to make sense. Muriel was a superstitious woman. She read tea-leaves – a lost art since the arrival of tea-bags. She scanned the skies of the urban jungle for supernatural omens and read her horoscope in the *Daily Express*. Her life had had its sorrows and though her husband, and the large tribe of Donnellys to which he belonged, had found solace in the Catholic Church she was suspicious of organised religion and pursued her own spiritual path. Cats understood this. Leonard sensed things, that was why they were close. He was an independent spirit, like herself in his own feline way.

She had named him after one of her dead husband's brothers. Leonard had died during a bombing raid; he was returning home from leave, carrying a bag of sausage rolls. She was a young girl at the time. The Donnellys lived next door and it was Leonard she had loved, more than all of his brothers. *When I grow up I shall marry Lenny*, Muriel had thought. His spirit lived on in her cat. She talked to him in a way she had never talked to her husband Patrick with whom she had shared a bed for forty-two years until he had smoked himself to death.

Muriel was talking to Leonard now, the day that she herself was to become a crime statistic. No tea-leaves had warned her. 'I fancy a spot of fish,' she said. 'It's Friday, see, though it's all the same to you.' She checked her handbag: purse, keys. 'Daft picture of Charles in the paper. Paddy called him Jug Ears, remember? We were on the same side, Paddy and me, we had that in common.'

Leonard lay draped over the back of the armchair. The fabric was worn, from where Patrick's head had rested when he watched the telly. It had remained her husband's chair; only the cat used it. She stroked Lenny's fur; he rose to meet her hand. That's what she liked about cats. They were so easily contented: a chair, a gas fire, a loving stroke. Humans needed so many things to make them happy.

Muriel let herself out of the flat. Pulling her shopping trolley she made her way past the school, the roar of the playground

62

behind the wall. Years ago there had been two fish shops in the high street. One was run by Ron Whiting. She had explained the joke to Keith, when he was little, his hand in hers. Now she had to go to the supermarket which was further away: across the main road, down an alleyway – her short cut – and past what had once been a row of cottages where her friend Maisie lived. They had fed sugar cubes to the milkman's horse. A man came into the stable once and showed them his willy. When she was sixteen Maisie had run off with a GI.

The sun came out. It glinted on the broken glass. Her neighbour Winnie went the long way round, by Cressy Road, but Muriel pooh-poohed that. Winnie was such a timid little thing, cowering behind her nets, never emerging after dusk.

Muriel walked past the Dixon's loading bay. There was nobody around. Why hadn't Keith phoned? It had been three days now, this was not like her son. He had given her a mobile phone. When she sat on the bus, her handbag throbbed in her lap. But she couldn't see the little numbers and she never remembered to plug it in. It was hard enough, working out the buttons on her remote.

Muriel didn't hear the footsteps behind her. She was thinking about her son when a hand grabbed her arm and wrenched it back.

She didn't feel the pain, not until later. It happened so fast – the wrench, the kick. 'Sod off!' she screamed, gripping her handbag. A hand clamped her mouth shut. She smelt the skin; she smelt sweat and fear. Something kicked her again, hard.

Muriel fell over. She hit the pavement heavily. She glimpsed a black face, hood pulled down. He wrenched at her bag and tripped over her shopping trolley. 'Fuck!'

Then they ran off. Lying on the pavement she saw them sprinting down the alley – two kids – and then they were gone.

They had punched the breath out of her body. Muriel lay spreadeagled, her knickers showing. For a moment, she was too shocked to move.

Maybe she fainted because now a man was bending over her, blocking out the sun. 'You all right, love?'

He tucked his hand under her arm and helped her to her feet. Muriel swayed, bumping against him. Her legs kept giving way.

Later, she didn't remember how she got there but she seemed to be standing in a shop, holding on to her trolley as if she were drowning.

'I been mugged,' she gasped, but the words seemed to come from somebody else. Her legs were trembling. And then she was in a back room, this Paki man helping her, and she sat down on a chair. A woman gazed at her. She had a red blotch on her forehead. Muriel's own face felt sticky; when she inspected her fingers it was blood.

'They took my bag,' said Muriel.

The newsagent gave her a glass of water but Muriel's hand was shaking; the water dribbled down her chin. She hadn't been in this shop before; the one she went to, it was nearer home.

'They were blacks,' she said. 'Not like you. Black blacks.'

'I'll phone the police,' said the man.

He spoke to his wife in a foreign language. She wore a sari, holding it against her mouth as if she had bad breath. Muriel remembered a girl at school called Annie Jones. Annie had a hare lip. When she talked, her hand strayed to her mouth. Nobody had wanted to be her friend.

Muriel's head swam. The newsagent must have called the police because now he was picking up the phone again. 'I shall call the ambulance,' he said.

'No! I'm not going to no hospital!'

'You've got a nasty cut.'

'Not Casualty!' Muriel's face throbbed. Her leg hurt and when she looked down she saw her stockings were torn. 'What about my cat?' she said. 'They got my keys, what about his food?'

'Fifteen times we've been robbed,' said the man. 'Fifteen times in two years. These kids have destroyed my business.'

'They got my handbag,' said Muriel. 'It only had twenty pound in it.'

'I've had enough,' said the man. 'I'm packing up and taking my family home.'

'Don't go!' she cried, grabbing his arm.

'Not now, love. When I've sold my shop. I'm going to take them home to India. It's safe there.'

'Safe?'

'India has a very low crime rate. You can walk the streets in Hyderabad, my home town, and feel no alarm. I wanted to make a life for my family in England but what sort of life is this?'

'I'm not going to no hospital,' said Muriel, but already she could hear the siren approaching.

Where's Keith? Muriel wailed silently. *Where's my boy?* In her distress she had forgotten his phone number. It was in her handbag, of course, but her handbag was gone. Without it her hands felt useless, like flippers.

The policeman looked like Keith when he was young. She had wanted to stroke his cheek. Now he was gone and she was lying on a trolley like last time, it could be the same trolley, with people hurrying past and somebody moaning on the other side of the curtain. The bin said *Contaminated Sharps Only*.

Muriel would have killed for a cup of tea but despite her asking twice nobody had brought her one. They had put her in Coventry, because of last time. The big black nurse who took her blood pressure looked like the same one, though you couldn't always tell. She had yanked the band so tight it hurt.

I've been mugged! Muriel wanted to shout. How dared they? Why had they singled her out – that brief blow that had sent her reeling, that could have cracked open her skull? What had she done to deserve it? And the indignity! Her damp knickers, because she had wee'd herself; the hole in her stockings that exposed her varicose veins and turned her into a bag lady, except she had no bloody bag.

She had felt threatened by them before, of course – the gangs of them jostling in the bus queue; the mad old lady in a poncho who spat at her in the high street. She had seen them smashing car windows and being chased by the police. And then in hospital it was all foreign people too, jabbing you with needles and shouting at each other over your head. It was like being mugged all over again. Did nobody realise that when you were frightened you wanted your own kind around you?

Muriel hated hospitals. It was this place, St Jude's, that had swallowed up her husband. Paddy had entered on a stretcher, never to come out again. She had returned home to an empty armchair and an oxygen cylinder.

She heard voices. 'It's that Mrs Donnelly again,' said a nurse.

'*The* Mrs Donnelly?' She recognised the doctor's voice. 'Oh well, we have to treat all sorts here.'

Muriel bristled. How dare he?

They pulled open the curtain and stepped in. It was the tall, grey-haired Indian doctor. 'Well well, Mrs Donnelly,' he said. 'So we meet again.'

They sent Muriel home in a community ambulance. It was dark.

Was it only that morning when she had set off for Safeways? Compared to last time, the doctor had seen her quickly. He probably wanted to get rid of her. Cuts and bruises, that was all it was, and a nasty black eye. No X-ray, no overnight stay. A new nurse had dressed her leg: a nice Australian girl.

'I'm not a racialist,' Muriel told her. 'Last time, the nurse was ever so rude. They got different manners from us. People pretend it's not true but they don't live with them. They don't know what it's like, them in their nice houses in Wembley or what not.'

There was only one passenger left on the ambulance, an old boy with a Zimmer frame. He was dropped off at the elderly folks' home down by Peckham Rye. Muriel gazed at them through the window. The old people sat there. A TV was on but they weren't watching. Some of them had fallen asleep, lolling in their chairs. The chairs were ranged around the walls, leaving the centre of the room empty, as if waiting for a significant event to happen.

Muriel leaned her cheek against the glass. It cooled her skin. Soon Keith will arrive, she thought. When he hears what's happened he'll drop everything and come over. He'll know I'm shaking like a jelly. He'll come over in his big silver jeep that all the neighbours stare at and he'll tuck me up in bed. He's a good boy.

The smell of urine rose from her clothes. Today she felt her age; those thugs had made an old woman of her. She thought: I need somebody to take care of me. The doctor had said that. She had flinched from his brown fingers, pressing her, prodding her, prising open her lids and shining a torch into her eyes. But he had been kind to her – surprisingly kind, considering. Maybe he had forgotten what had happened last time, so many people made a fuss about the conditions in that place.

The doctor had actually sat down beside her – him, a busy man. 'You shouldn't be living alone at your age,' he had said. His badge said *Dr Ravi Kapoor*. 'Have you considered some sort of residential accommodation?'

'My son'll look after me.'

'I know a very good place.' He had smiled at her, as if sharing a secret.

'Catch me being stuck in front of the telly with a lot of old bats.'

'I can see you're a woman of spirit, Mrs Donnelly.' When the doctor smiled his face was transformed. Like a lot of those Indians, he was a handsome man. 'Anyway, if you change your mind . . . I'll get your address from Admissions and send you a brochure.'

There had been something puzzling about this conversation but then the whole day had been disorientating. Muriel thought: I won't be beaten. Two kids aren't going to knock the stuffing out of me. *I can see you're a woman of spirit.* She hadn't lived through the war for this.

The war. One day she would tell her son what had happened – the whole story, not the parts she had told before. She had always put it off – tomorrow, the next week. It never seemed the right moment. All of a sudden it would be too late; the events of today had demonstrated that.

The bus jerked to a halt outside her flat. The windows were dark, of course. So were those of her neighbour Winnie; she was away, staying with her daughter in Bromley.

'Sure you'll be all right?' asked the driver.

Muriel nodded. 'I'll let myself in.' She didn't want him to see where she hid her spare set of keys.

She felt odd: light-headed, numb. Later she realised it was a portent. She crossed the forecourt to her front door. The keys were there, in their plastic bag behind the tub of geraniums. She thought of the real Leonard, the human one. Like the Indian doctor, he too had a smile that transformed his face. Say he had missed his train and taken a later one; say the bomb had fallen on somebody else. Then it would have been Lenny waiting in the flat with tea and buttered toast, ready to kiss her better.

But then, of course, her son would never have been born. The thought made her weightless.

The door swung open. She hadn't inserted the key. It just swung open.

Muriel stepped inside and switched on the light.

Something was wrong. Surely she had locked the door behind her when she went out shopping, a hundred years ago?

Muriel stood still. She felt a draught – a chill wind from the kitchen. In their vase, the peacock feathers trembled.

The back door was open, that was why. Somebody had been into her flat; maybe they were still there. Muriel stood in the hallway, her heart knocking against her ribs. *Keith, where are you?*

She knew she should get out of the flat but she stayed there, stuck. She thought: Those boys, they had my keys. They know where I live.

Then she seemed to be in the lounge. She switched on the light. The bookshelf had been knocked over. The ornaments lay on the floor – her Royal Family mugs, her glass animals. The settee was skewed sideways. Despite the disorder, there was an emptiness in the room. It took her a moment to realise that her TV was gone – the big wide-screen TV that Keith had given her.

Muriel whispered: 'Leonard?'

There was no sign of her cat. He must be terrified. Muriel went into the bedroom and opened her wardrobe. He wasn't there. She bent down, creakingly, and fished out the shoe box. The cash was still there – two hundred pounds, her money for emergencies.

Muriel felt a brief flush of triumph and then she burst into tears.

Ravi returned to an empty house. His wife and father-in-law had left that morning. At this moment they must be thirty thousand feet above Bahrain.

As he walked from room to room, he felt lighter. The invasion had been lifted; his house had been returned to him. There were no signs of Norman's habitation, except some sheets in the washing machine which Pauline had switched on before she left. There was a note to that effect in the kitchen. Ravi pulled out the damp sheets, stuffed them into the dryer and slammed the door shut. It was as if Norman had never existed. Ravi slotted *Così fan Tutte* into the CD player. How fleeting is our imprint upon this earth, he thought. Just a footprint in the sand, and soon the wind will blow it away. Ferrando's voice swelled out: '*Un' aura amorosa . . .*', a loving breeze brings balm to my soul.

Ravi drew the curtains. He sank back in the sofa and gazed at the armchair, the one occupied by Norman for the past four months. Soon it would revert to simply being an armchair again. How little we leave behind, he thought. He pictured the plastic bags of belongings in A & E: spectacles, a watch. He had lost a patient that day – a motor-cycle accident. There had been two muggings (including that Mrs Donnelly), a lacerated finger, a first-degree burn from a chip pan. So many near-collisions – knives slipping on chopping-boards, lorries skidding – it was a miracle that anybody survived into old age at all. '*What about karma?*' Pauline had asked. Like many English people, she was attracted by that subcontinental mumbo-jumbo. He resented her talking in those terms, it was a betrayal of what he had given up his life to do – to restore the casualties of chance, to mend the cracked vessels. Didn't she understand the most basic thing about him?

It felt odd, sending Pauline to his home country without being by her side. He would have been interested to see her reactions; in her present moody state she could swing in any direction. Besides, India had an unexpected effect on people; one could never predict who would surrender to its allure and who would be baffled and distressed. He himself had returned on a couple of occasions to visit his family but both times without his wife. The first occasion was when they were going through that rough patch and Pauline had moved out; the second time was when her mother was dying and Pauline had had to remain in England. For reasons Ravi was disinclined to investigate, he wasn't sorry.

On this occasion, of course, he was simply too busy to go. He couldn't take time off work, and then there was Ravison Ltd. It was thrilling, to discover in himself this aptitude for business. The very word *business* made his heart beat faster. All his life he had worked in a bureaucracy, ruled by its own caste system, stifled by budgets and management incompetence. Now he felt like a pit pony loosed into the sunshine. Anything was possible – large amounts of money, the power to change things by his own decision. Once the business was up and running he could even consider resigning from the hospital. He could get up when he liked, he could work the hours he liked. He could travel round the world, liaising with architects under coconut palms. Ravi's very body felt different, as if unknown muscles were strengthening. Really he should be grateful to that old sod Norman for giving him the idea in the first place.

Dorabella and Fiordiligi were singing of forgiveness. *'Fortunato c'uom che prende . . .'* Ravi wiped away a tear. He went into the kitchen. Pauline, bless her, had left the fridge well stocked. He pictured her tall, broad-shouldered body and felt a stir of desire. Now she was absent his wife had reverted, like the house, to her old self – brisk, amusing, undisturbed by the turbulence of the menopause and the presence of her father. Even Norman could be remembered more kindly now – a cheery old reprobate rather than his tormentor.

Ravi put a fisherman's pie into the microwave. He was a bachelor again, filled with vim and optimism. After supper he would go upstairs and catch up with work. Everything was going according to plan. The first residents had been installed with only minor problems. Sonny wouldn't lie to him; they were in this thing together, fifty-fifty.

Ravi tore open a bag of salad leaves and shook them into a bowl. In the old days he would be exhausted when he came home from the hospital. Nowadays, despite double the workload, he was filled with energy. How exhilarating it was, working for himself rather than for other people! He mixed a vinaigrette – walnut oil, lime juice. He even felt tenderly towards Mrs Donnelly. *'Here I am again,'* she had said, *'turned up like a bad penny.'* She was trying to be cheerful, even though she was shaken. Ravi no longer considered her a racist bigot, more a plucky old bird. After all, the world had changed so profoundly; it must be confusing for somebody of

70

her age. He would send her a brochure although, as Pauline had said, there was not a hope in hell that she would go. Muriel Donnelly, of all people!

For one thing, she wouldn't have the money. And then there was her other little problem.

Tossing the salad, Ravi smiled. The old girl was right, of course. They were all over the place nowadays, you couldn't get away from them. Especially, of course, in the health sector. In fact it was immaterial what country you happened to be in, when your time came. Whether you were in Watford or Wisconsin, in all likelihood the last face you would see, on this earth, would be a black one.

Muriel had been mugged. She had been burgled. Her cat had disappeared; Leonard must have fled when the robbers came and she didn't dare go out into the night to look for him. She was alone, and her son wasn't answering his phone. She just got the machine.

'Keith! Please come and get me. Wherever you are, Keith, come here quick. They're going to come back. They got my keys –'

A beep and she was cut off.

Her neighbour Winnie was away. The flat upstairs was empty. Muriel, still wearing her overcoat, sat trembling on her bed. She had lost all track of time. She felt woozy and disembodied, it must be the painkillers, she felt as if her body was sitting there but she herself was floating up by the ceiling fixture, gazing down at the old lady with the black eye and bandaged leg. Her soul had escaped, leaving her as light as a husk. She knew that her legs felt chilly – they had thrown away her stockings at the hospital – but the chilliness belonged to somebody who had no connection to her.

Muriel sat there, waiting for Keith to ring, waiting for the click of the cat flap. She knew that she should phone the police but then she would have to wait for them and they might take a long time. When her son came he would whisk her away from this flat that was no longer hers, that had been invaded by strangers who wanted to kill her. Evil was in the air like a gas leak.

Just then she heard a click. It was the cat flap.

'Lenny!'

Muriel heaved herself to her feet. Her Lenny had come home.

71

She would put him in his cat basket and take him to Chigwell. Keith would make a fuss of her and tuck her up in his spare room, it had its own bathroom, solid gold taps. Even his tart of a wife would be sorry for her now.

Muriel made her way along the corridor. 'Lenny, I'm here.' Maybe what happened today was a portent, a warning to her that she must leave Peckham for good. Maybe her son was right. She would let him pack up her flat and move her to Chigwell; she could end her days peacefully in the countryside with cows, not muggers, for company.

Muriel went into the kitchen. A ginger tom stood there, eating Lenny's food. Bold as bold, it didn't even turn.

'Get out!' Muriel kicked at it with her good leg. 'Sod off!'

It hissed at her. Its eyes were milky with cataracts. Then it sauntered off, tail up, anus in full view. With difficulty, it squeezed itself through the cat flap.

Muriel unbolted the back door. The cat had stopped at the end of her yard. It stared at her.

'Sod off!' she shouted, hobbling across the concrete.

She stood still, trying to catch her breath. Her lungs wheezed. The car park looked eerie, bathed in the sodium light. Somewhere a bird sang; they sang all times of the night nowadays, it wasn't right. The street lights made them think it was the day. Far off, beyond the next block of flats, a man bellowed.

Muriel steadied herself against the wall and waited for her heartbeat to return to normal. Then she turned to go indoors.

Next to her was a row of giant dustbins on wheels. Something caught her eye.

At first she thought it was a bit of fur coat – a muff or something – that somebody had thrown away. It was flung on to a pile of rubbish bags.

She stepped closer. No, it was a child's stuffed toy. Black fur, white paws.

She moved even closer. And then she stopped.

During the movie Pauline slept. She dreamed she was a little girl again, kneeling beside her mother on a grassy knoll. Her mother was already ill, though nobody was saying. Her face was grey and clammy. They were sitting in a place called India though Pauline knew it was the park in High Wycombe, where she grew up; she recognised the war memorial. Gravely, her mother passed Pauline a plate of food. When Pauline looked down, she saw it was monkeys' heads.

It seemed perfectly natural, those wizened faces sunk in gravy. They looked happy enough, smiling up at her like little old men. She wasn't going to eat them, no fear.

A shadow fell. It was her father. He sat down on the grass and lifted out a head. He put it into his mouth and started munching.

'Be a good girl and get me another one.'

Pauline woke up. Norman was holding up his empty whisky miniature.

'Be a good girl,' he said to the stewardess. 'Get me another one.'

The stewardess caught Pauline's eye and smiled. No doubt it was pity; Norman had been making a nuisance of himself throughout the flight. Then Pauline realised that her own face was drenched in sweat. Another hot flush.

'We'll be landing soon,' said the stewardess.

Pauline pulled up the blind. Outside dawn blazed, a rim of fire over the curved horizon. Five hours had been lost as they hurtled through time zones towards a new day. Her heart beat faster, or maybe it was just palpitations. This was what she did for others, sending them speeding through space, sending them to destinations on the far side of the earth. She too had travelled, of course. But tonight was no holiday; for her father, it was a new life. She pressed the dinner napkin to her face. The moon pulled at the earth's gravity; the tides pulled women's wombs – except for stewardesses, who criss-crossed the world and whose periods apparently stopped altogether, as her own would soon do.

What a strange dream. Maybe there would be monkeys in India. There would certainly be babies. It was painful, having her mother so briefly restored to her. Suddenly Pauline missed her so powerfully she felt nauseous. How could her mother desert her by dying? The old man in the next seat had sucked the life out of her, Pauline realised that now. There was no justice in the world. Her mother, a good woman, had died; her father, on the other hand, seemed indestructible. Selfishness was a powerful life-force, he would probably outlive them all, despite the abuse he had inflicted on his body by a lifetime of drinking and smoking – he had even lit up a fag in the toilet and been hauled out by the steward.

'In a few moments we will be commencing our descent into Indira Gandhi International Airport . . . please make sure that your seatbelts are fastened, your trays folded and your seats returned to an upright position . . .'

Norman seemed to have got his way. He unscrewed the cap and poured whisky into his glass. 'Going on to Bangalore,' he told his neighbour on the other side, a corpulent Indian who had slept most of the journey. 'My daughter's dumping me in an old folks' home there.'

'Bangalore is a charming city,' said the man. 'Very pleasant climate, very up-to-the-minute facilities.'

'See, Dad?' said Pauline.

'It's known as Pensioners' Paradise,' said the man. 'My countrymen live all over the world. Sometimes they have no family left in India, so they buy into new residential complexes for their old age.'

'See, Dad? It's not just you.'

'It's very similar to England, in many ways,' said the man. 'Wait for Christmas. They all go to Midnight Mass at St Patrick's Church, and then it's roast turkey and all the trimmings at Koshy's.' He tapped Norman's knee. 'And for a man who likes a drink, Bangalore is the place to be. The home to Kingfisher beer. A pub on every corner!'

Norman tapped the side of his nose. 'And a few more things besides.'

The plane hit turbulence. They jolted in their seats. The whisky slopped out of Norman's glass.

'You sure you shouldn't be in hospital?' said the cabbie.

'I've *been* in hospital,' said Muriel. 'Put your foot down and take me to Chigwell.'

'I live that way myself,' he said. 'Ongar. Couldn't live in London,

74

not nowadays, I mean look at you. How could they do that to a poor defenceless woman? Law and order, it's totally broken down, I mean where's the police, where's the bobby on the beat? Kids today, they're totally out of control. They come to this country – you know what I'm talking about – they come here, living on benefits, the dads fucking off, pardon my language, kids dealing in crack cocaine, they're off their heads half the time, little kids twelve years old. They know the system, see, they just laugh at the police, they just give 'em the number of their solicitor. Hardened criminals at twelve years of age! Lock 'em up, I say, lock 'em up and throw away the key.'

Muriel sat there, her eyes closed, as the cab drove through the streets. She had drunk half a tumbler of some liqueur Keith had brought back from Spain.

'I mean, did you read about that old lady, she was in the papers, left for two days in A & E. Call that a civilised society? Bring back hanging, that's what I say.'

Muriel's overnight bag sat beside her. She couldn't remember packing it. Normally a talkative woman, she seemed to have lost the power of speech. All she could do was will the cab to get her to Keith's house before she collapsed. When the flying bombs came that was what you did – count during the silence, waiting for the explosion . . . fifteen . . . sixteen . . . seventeen . . .

Leonard.

Muriel must have fallen asleep because now they had arrived at Keith's house and she was fumbling in her pocket for the money she had got from the shoe box.

'This the place?' The cabbie heaved out her bag.

The house was dark. Keith and Sandra must be out for the evening, enjoying themselves. Even his mobile had been switched off.

'My boy'll be back soon,' Muriel said. 'I got the keys.'

She had found them in her kitchen drawer. She had moved around like an automaton. It was like, when the systems were down, an emergency generator kicking in. Pacemakers did that, with your heart.

The cabbie escorted her up the drive. His hand cupped her elbow. 'Nice place. Must've cost a few bob.'

'There's a swimming-pool out the back.' Even now Muriel could summon up maternal pride; it was that deep-rooted.

Suddenly they were flooded with light. The house was thrown into relief – large, half-timbered, stickers scattered over Jordan's bedroom window. The kids were away at boarding-school.

'They're not my son's kids,' she said. 'They're Sandra's.'

The intruder lights made the house look flimsy, like a stage-set. They reached the porch. 'Blimey, this bag's heavy.' The cabbie lowered it to the ground.

'Don't leave me!' Muriel grabbed his arm.

'Course I won't, my love.'

The cabbie took the keys and opened the locks for her, one by one.

He had to push the door open; it was jammed by a heap of letters. They stepped in. The air was chill. Something went *beep-beep-beep*.

'Oh oh,' said the cabbie. 'Where's the alarm, ducks?'

Muriel switched on the light. She was too flustered to think. There was an unused smell in the place; the table was littered with dead lily petals.

'Must be somewhere,' said the cabbie, searching the passage.

Then the burglar alarm wailed.

Muriel was sitting in an unknown lounge. The cabbie had gone. Seated opposite her were a man and a woman who looked vaguely familiar. A Yorkie sniffed her leg.

'Stop that, Coco,' said the man. 'Sorry, sweetheart, it's your bandage.'

Muriel was clutching a mug of tea; some of it slopped on the carpet.

'Here, let me hold it for you.' The woman took the mug out of Muriel's hand.

How long had Muriel been sitting there? Slowly their faces assembled themselves into familiar people. They were Keith's next-door neighbours; Muriel had met them at a barbecue. The man was called Carl; he was a builder.

'Your poor eye,' said the wife, what's-her-name. 'You poor dear.'

She had bleached-blonde hair and wore a dressing-gown. There was a cabinet full of silver trophies against the wall. Muriel spotted a Diana mug.

'Where's Keith?' Muriel asked.

Carl looked at his wife. She said: 'I'll make you up a bed, Mrs Donnelly. We can talk in the morning.'

'Where's he gone?'

'He's gone abroad.'

'What, to Spain?'

Carl shook his head. He was a big, beefy man with a suntan. 'Not Spain, love. See, they'll be looking for him there, too.'

'Who will?' asked Muriel.

'The police.'

'The police?' Muriel stared.

'See, Keith's been in a spot of bother,' Carl said.

The wife turned to him. 'More than a spot, cherub.'

There was a silence. The dog started whimpering. It was sniffing Muriel's holdall.

'Coco!' Carl gripped its collar and pulled it away. Claws skittered across the parquet floor.

'What's been happening?' said Muriel. 'What's happened to my son?'

Rita! That was the name. Rita cleared her throat. 'What Carl's trying to say is that your son's in trouble. A business thing. We don't know nothing about it, but something's blown up and he's had to get out of the country. He told us not to say anything but seeing it's you. I don't know what's happened to Sandra, I mean there's the kids isn't there? I don't know if she's gone with him. But he's gone. I'm so sorry.'

The dog struggled out of Carl's arms and bounded over to the bag again.

'Coco!'

'The cat's in there, that's why,' said Muriel. She couldn't say the word *dead*, she would start blubbing. 'I couldn't leave him all alone.' There was a pause. They gazed at the bag. 'Keith wouldn't leave me all alone,' she said.

'He was in a bit of a hurry,' said Carl.

'I'm sure he would have told you,' said Rita. 'If he had time.'

Carl looked at the bag. 'Don't you want to let your cat out?'

'No,' said Muriel. 'He won't be coming out again.'

Somewhere, far away, a clock chimed. This house was even bigger than Keith's.

'Your son left on Tuesday,' said Rita. 'And that afternoon the police came round. They'd only just missed him.' She looked at the bag. 'Is there something wrong with it? Your cat?'

'My Keith's done nothing wrong,' said Muriel. 'Why're they wasting their time chasing my son when they should be catching criminals! They should be catching those boys.' Her head swam. Was it really that very morning that she had been mugged? 'He hasn't gone abroad. He's hiding, like he used to do when he was little. He's ever so clever at it. He's hiding and nobody's going to find him.'

Her words detached themselves from her and moved away. They were like a stream, babbling over stones . . . little hisses when she said an *s*. Muriel watched herself subsiding, like an empty hot-water-bottle. And then she was swallowed up in the darkness.

Part Two

1

Remove the Curtain of your Heart and see the Beloved sitting inside yourself. Close your Ears to the Outside and hear the Cosmic Sound going on within you.

(Mira, poet-saint of Rajastan)

'When they shake their heads, Evelyn, they don't mean *no*, they mean *yes*.'

'Well, not quite,' said her husband. 'They mean *yes if that's what you want it to be*.'

'Don't complicate things, Douggy. You're confusing her.' Jean turned back to Evelyn, leaning across the aisle. 'You see it of course in shops and things in England, but in India it's sort of symptomatic of the whole subcontinent, of their philosophy – of their very Indianness.' She sank back in her seat to let a passenger pass. Dinner was finished and people were making their way to the toilets. They stood in a queue, exposed in their need. Jean Ainslie leaned over again. 'It's an acceptance of karma.'

'Plus a strong sense of hospitality,' said Douglas. 'Pleasing the visitor to their country –'

'You can't ask a straight question, like how long is something going to take,' said Jean. 'It'll take as long as you want it to take –'

'And if you get rattled it only makes it worse,' Douglas shouted over his wife's head. He was sitting in the seat beyond hers. 'You just have to go with the flow –'

'We've learnt that, haven't we, darling?'

'Learnt it on our first trip –'

81

'Trekking in the Himalayas – a wonderful experience, wasn't it, Douggy?'

'Wonderful.'

'Extraordinary.'

The retirement company had put Evelyn together with the Ainslies; it was their policy, apparently, to arrange for people to travel on the same flight if it were at all possible. Evelyn felt relieved to have made friends so soon, and with such a pleasant couple. The Ainslies were obviously seasoned travellers; they seemed to have been everywhere. What an indomitable pair! Even in their sixties they had still been driving around Europe in their camper van. In comparison, Evelyn's life seemed timid and dwindled.

'Our other visit, we did the Golden Triangle,' said Douglas. 'Delhi, Agra, Jaipur –'

'We even went to Jessailmer,' said his wife. 'That was in the days before anybody went there –'

'Miles away in the Thar Desert –'

'Nowadays of course it's full of coach parties, but then it was quite extraordinary, wasn't it, Doug?'

'Fantastic.' He beamed across at Evelyn. 'Well, you only have the one life, haven't you?'

Evelyn was about to reply that in India it seemed you didn't, but she couldn't recall the details of the conversation with Beverley. It sounded so ludicrous now, she would only make a fool of herself.

'A couple of vagabonds, that's us,' said Jean.

Suddenly Evelyn missed Hugh so fiercely it took her breath away. Hugh's smiling face, that awful old jumper he refused to throw out, Hugh's skin flayed by the wind as they tacked out of Chichester Harbour. *'Ready, old girl?'* Evelyn ducked as the boom swung round. He called both Evelyn and his boat (the *Marie-Louise*) *'old girl'*, and with the same exasperated affection. She and Hugh had been vagabonds too, in their way, clinging together in this disorientating world with their children mutating into strangers.

'All you need is an open mind,' said Jean.

'And a cast-iron gut,' said Douglas.

This, of course, was one of Evelyn's greatest worries. What if she fell ill with dysentery or hepatitis? Typhoid, even? Some health tips had been included in the brochure – always eat peeled fruit, only drink boiled water – but the very mention of digestive disorders set her tummy fluttering. She already felt queasy, even though she had only consumed a British Airways dinner of chicken provençal and apple crumble.

When she tentatively voiced her fears Douglas said: 'Don't you worry, Evelyn. Everyone gets Delhi belly –'

'It's part of the Indian experience –' said his wife.

'You should see their loos! Talk about the Black Hole of Calcutta –'

'Doug, stop it! You're alarming her.' Jean turned back to Evelyn. 'Don't mind him. He's always had a wacky sense of humour.' On her fingers, Jean ticked off the items they had packed. 'Water purification tablets, mozzie nets, Sennacot . . .'

Evelyn drifted off. She thought of safe old Britain, left behind them as they hurtled through the night. Of course nothing was safe, she had realised that: your husband, your home, your money – all could be stripped away. But to fly across the world! The bravado with which she had signed the acceptance form, that startling burst of rebellion, had long since disappeared.

'The thing is, I haven't travelled much on my own,' she said. 'Since my husband died –'

'Ha! Count yourself lucky,' said Jean. 'Honestly, Doug can be more trouble than he's worth, always rushing up to people and talking to them in pidgin English, always dragging me off to see some old ruin or other. Sometimes one just wants to relax, don't you think?'

'Oh yes, I –'

'But I'm not really a beach person, am I, Doug? I mean, people said why don't we retire to Spain or Portugal, somewhere like that, but there's nothing to *do*, is there? I mean, imagine a lot of old biddies sitting around knitting, we'd die of boredom wouldn't we, darling?'

Evelyn was silent. Implicit in this, of course, was her own status as an old biddy. I'm not really! she wanted to cry. She thought of

83

Hugh's hands. Of course she missed his face, his voice, the whole Hughness of him – the smell of his skin, his barks of laughter – but it was his hands she missed just now . . . his forefinger rubbing a smudge of earth off her face when she straightened up from her weeding; his hand slipping into hers at night, when she turned over in bed. Sometimes they laced their fingers like teenagers. She longed for him to be beside her, the bigness of him, shifting in his seat. She longed for him so much that her ribs ached.

'How did you hear about this place?' asked Jean. 'Our son suggested it – he makes documentaries for the BBC.'

'How nice,' said Evelyn. She was going to say that her manicurist suggested it but hearing Beverley's voice in her head – *'What a hoot'* – made her miss her.

'Adam knows us so well –'

'That's our son –'

'He knew this was just our sort of place. We've always been adventurous, haven't we, Doug?'

Douglas nodded. 'Though we'd draw the line at bungee-jumping.'

'You're as young as you feel,' said Jean.

'Young people are drawn to India, aren't they?' said Evelyn. 'Theresa, my daughter – you may have seen her in the Departure Lounge – she goes to ashrams.' Of course, Theresa was no longer young. She was forty-nine. Theresa's own children, if she had had any, would be grown up now. This gave Evelyn a scooped-out feeling. 'Has your son had any children?'

Jean shook her head. 'Of course there've been plenty of girls who've been keen enough, but he hasn't found the right one yet.' There was a silence. Jean closed her eyes and sank back in her seat.

Later Evelyn tried to sleep but her old heart went pitter-patter. How could she cope with the terrors ahead when even the idea of catching a connecting flight filled her with dread? Beyond lay the unknown – a void.

> *Lead us, heavenly Father, lead us*
> *O'er the world's tempestuous sea;*
> *Guard us, guide us, keep us, feed us,*
> *For we have no help but Thee.*

All her life Evelyn had sat in a pew, boxed in by certainties, mouthing the words alongside first her parents and then her husband. One by one they had deserted her, leaving her amongst strangers.

On the third day He rose again . . .

Where were they now? The cabin lights were dimmed; for these hours of the night she and the other souls were in the care of the captain, whose disembodied voice warned them of turbulence ahead. Evelyn sat there, her seatbelt securely buckled. Under the blanket her hands sought each other. Her fingers laced together. Round and round she pushed her wedding ring; nowadays it moved easily on her finger.

Across the aisle Jean Ainslie was asleep. Her mouth hung open, slackly. Sleep aged her; only the blanket, rising and falling, showed that she wasn't already a corpse. Evelyn thought: These people will be my last new friends, this couple and whoever is there awaiting me at the hotel. She thought: I must make the strange into the familiar. Have I got the courage to do this, at my time of life?

She knew, of course, that she had no choice. Wherever she went, this was what she had to do now. Even if she came home again, which she might, this same situation would face her.

The Indian gentleman on her left side, to whom she hadn't talked, was snoring. His head lolled an inch from her shoulder. Evelyn shifted in her seat, trying to find a comfortable position. Her joints were stiffening.

'Try this.'

Douglas leaned across his sleeping wife. He passed an object to Evelyn.

'It's a neck cushion,' he said. 'I've blown it up for you.'

'But you can't –'

'Go on, take it. Makes all the difference.' He smiled at her, his face illuminated by the reading light. The beam shone down on to his thick white hair; it reminded her of the heavenly ray piercing through the clouds in her *Child's Book of Bible Stories*. 'Sweet dreams,' Douglas said. 'See you in India.'

2

Break the boundaries of limited mind and body. Experience bliss throughout yourself and around yourself. Find yourself in the Ultimate.

(Swami Purna)

Razia was still sulking. Her sulks could last for weeks; this one had. It was now the beginning of October and Minoo, usually an amiable man, was losing patience.

'Please, my dear love, my lotus blossom –' He tried to put his arms around her but she pulled away.

'What did I do wrong, to be married to a duffhead like you? You and that man, in cahoots together, wheeling and dealing behind my back, and I – silly me – I was thinking we could sell this place and enjoy a peaceful old age –'

'Please keep your voice down –'

'They're all deaf –'

'But isn't it going swimmingly?' asked Minoo.

'Swimmingly?' Razia hoisted her sari over her shoulder. 'Always they're complaining – the heat, the mosquitoes, the food –'

'No more complaints than is usual –'

'But those guests, they *left*! Now we're stuck with these ones, day in and day out, you have no consideration, I'm worn down to the bone, look at me, oh I should have listened to my family!'

Minoo nearly added: I should have listened to mine. He didn't care to voice this, however; it would only inflame things further. His stomach churned; arguments with his wife affected his digestive organs.

86

'A *prosperous* old age!' snapped Razia.

'Aren't we making a good profit now? Look at the figures. Sonny said that within three years –'

'Sonny! Your new good friend! Sonny this and Sonny that! You really think that man can be trusted?'

The bell tinkled. Minoo heaved himself to his feet and left the small, windowless office and his seething wife. Stepping into the lobby was like stepping on to a stage: he shed his private life and became a professional, faced with demands that were unmuddied by guilt and resentment. More and more, as the years passed, he felt this.

Mrs Evelyn Greenslade stood at the desk. 'I'm so sorry to trouble you,' she said. 'I don't want to be a nuisance.'

'Madam, I am at your service.'

Mrs Greenslade had only arrived two days earlier but Minoo had already taken to her. A small, fragile woman – the desk reached up to her chest – she had that unmistakable air of refinement he so admired in the British. She was a true lady; fine bone structure, wavy white hair and beautifully dressed, too, in a cream blouse and pearl necklace.

'You are settling in comfortably?' he asked.

'Oh yes, though of course it's all a little strange. The heat, of course, and all the people – I mean, so many of them everywhere and so poor, so terribly poor, it's very shocking. I come from Sussex, you see.'

'I've heard it's very pleasant,' said Minoo. 'Several of our past guests, they have their homes in Sussex.' He rummaged under the desk for his box. 'I have letters of appreciation here, one is from a Colonel and Mrs Penrose from Pulborough, Sussex, perhaps you are acquainted with them?'

'There's a legless beggar,' she said. 'Have you seen him? Just outside, at the crossroads. Somebody's made him a little trolley and he sits there all day, begging from the cars when they stop at the junction. Just a young man, and no legs at all.' She gave a little laugh. 'It certainly puts my hip into perspective.'

'This is India, madam, you soon grow used to it.' Mrs Evelyn must have been a dazzler in her youth. In fact she was still pretty, in a faded, self-deprecating way. Minoo, susceptible to beauty, felt himself becoming gallant. 'The situation of beggars I am powerless to solve, but if there is any way I can help to make the stay of such a charming lady more enjoyable, please feel free to ask me.'

'Well, to be perfectly honest, there is.'

There was a pause. From the lounge came a murmur of voices. The morning mah-jong session, organised by Mrs Rheinhart, was just getting down to business. Were there sufficient cold drinks in the cabinet? These old people certainly knocked it back – Fanta, Thums-Up. Until recently, of course, guests came and went. Nowadays, however, they were on the premises all day and he must remember to increase the order. It was usually Razia's job, to check on the stores, but Razia was sulking. At the moment she was on the phone to her sister. He could hear her aggrieved voice through the wall.

'It's Norman – you know, Mr Purse.' Mrs Greenslade cleared her throat.

'Ah.'

'It's just – well, you know his room is next to mine?' She fingered the pearls around her neck. 'Well, I was wondering – if it's not too much bother – if you had another room available which I could move into? A little further away?'

'What is the problem, madam?'

'It's just – you see, I'm a light sleeper and – well, he's so loud. Banging about, and his wireless and everything . . .' Her voice died away. 'And then, he and I, we have to share a bathroom . . .'

Her cheeks flushed pink. Outside, on the veranda, came the scrape of the sweeper's brush.

'We do have one vacant room,' said Minoo. 'But it's a little smaller. Your son, when he telephoned from New York, insisted that you occupy a room with a garden view.'

'I don't mind about that,' she said.

He fished for the key. 'If you would like to inspect the room first –'

'I'm sure it'll be lovely.'

He straightened up. 'Very well, Mrs Evelyn. I'll tell the bearer to move your things.'

She thanked him and left, crossing the lobby in her soft beige shoes. She made no sound. Such a self-effacing woman, it was as if she were already a ghost.

A mid-morning torpor had settled on the hotel. Outside the *mali* hawked and spat. Nirula was an elderly Tamil, naked but for the soiled *dhoti* tucked around his waist. He had worked at the Marigold since Minoo was a boy and would no doubt work until he dropped. Minoo was fond of him. Who would take care of this old gardener if the hotel was sold?

Beyond him, in the shade of the flame tree, Norman Purse sat with his pen poised over the newspaper. Every day he sat there doing the crossword; it kept him quiet for an hour or so. Sometimes he nodded off but even then he kept a tight grip on his *Daily Telegraph* in case somebody snatched it away. English newspapers, even last week's, were precious.

There had been several complaints about Mr Purse but Minoo felt a certain male solidarity with the gentleman. Exhausted by his own wife and somewhat stifled by the predominantly female atmosphere, Minoo found Norman-sahib refreshingly male, a cock in the hen-coop, with his coarse jokes and stop-me-if-you-dare smoking at meals. Besides, being the father of one of the company directors he was in a somewhat privileged position which he exploited to the hilt. His daughter had now returned to Britain but she frequently emailed to hear how he was getting on and would no doubt react badly to news of any problems. As both manager and owner, it was Minoo's responsibility to keep the place running smoothly and so far there had been no major disasters.

He put this down to the age and nationality of his new clientele. Minoo had a deep respect for the British – not the young backpackers who used to frequent his hotel but those of a different class and generation, one that was now dying out. He was only a year old when Independence was declared; over half a century had elapsed since the British had ruled his country but, to him, the elderly English would always possess an innate superiority and an elegiac air hung over their imminent extinction. What an honour it was, that they were to spend their last years under his roof, in the country to which their ancestors had given so much – even, sometimes their lives! You only had to look at the grave-stones at St Patrick's Church.

What piffle! Razia's voice was in his head. *You silly old snob!*

Minoo looked up. Mr and Mrs Ainslie were striding across the lobby. Mr Ainslie, dressed in shorts, clutched a water bottle. With his tanned face and thick white hair, he looked in prime condition.

'Just off to Tipu's Palace!' he called out.

'I shall order you a taxi, sir,' said Minoo.

'No no!' replied Mr Ainslie. 'We'll take Shank's pony.'

'Darling,' said his wife. 'He hasn't a clue what you're talking about.'

'We'll walk!' called out Mr Ainslie. 'Or take a rickshaw. Don't worry about us, we'll get to know our way around in no time!'

Hand in hand they strode out of the hotel. Minoo watched them walking down to the front gate. They stopped to greet the *mali*, their heads cocked cordially as he gestured at the flowers. Minoo felt a wave of misery. How contented they looked! The Ainslies were the only married couple amongst the guests, who were predominantly widows or spinsters; over dinner, Mrs Ainslie had told him that they had been married for forty-eight years. Their happiness drained those around them of energy. Next to them, the old ladies looked bloodless.

Minoo stood behind his desk, lost in dreams of what-might-have-been. Bapsi's face appeared before him. She was as he remem-bered her a quarter of a century earlier: smiling, placid, fixed for ever at twenty years old. How different his life would have been had he married her, as his parents had intended – a demure Parsee girl who would have been a comfort and support to him, who might have given him sons. Love would have blossomed between them, he was sure of that now – a love created by mutual respect. Minoo was aware of the irony: that this yearning was not for a lost romance but for an arranged partner, hardly the stuff of passion. But where had passion got him?

It was all the fault of those bloody shoes. Minoo had always been particular about his appearance. *Vanity, vanity, all is vanity* . . . If he had not bought those shoes – Bata, beautiful shiny brown

90

leather, antique finish, narrow fitting and just *just* a half-size too small – if he had not bought those shoes he would never have developed corns and gone to the chiropody clinic on Chundrigar Road where a luscious nurse had bewitched him, turned his life upside down and brought humiliation to his own family and that of his blameless bride-to-be.

Through the wall Razia's voice rose and fell. Minoo's stomach churned. She had snapped at the cook that morning; judging by the lack of smells emanating from the kitchen, Fernandez was also sulking. Minoo would have to investigate.

He sighed. How well-behaved the British were, compared to his turbulent wife! A new arrival was expected that evening: a Mrs Muriel Donnelly from London. She, no doubt, would also possess impeccable manners. *Manners maketh man* was a proverb he much admired. Look at that Mrs Greenslade, a vision in beige, so well-mannered she hardly existed any more. *Don't mind me*, said the British, *I'm not really here*.

Minoo opened the register and rubbed out Mrs Evelyn Greenslade's name. There! Gone, just like that. How fleeting is our stay in the Hotel of Life! (And how his wife would sneer if she heard him say that.)

He pencilled in Mrs Donnelly's name instead; he would put her in Room 15, next to Mr Purse.

'Any advice, I'm your man,' said Norman. 'Knocked around in the tropics, you see – Africa, Malaysia.'

'It's bloody hot,' said Muriel. 'And the taps don't work.'

'Water supply's a bit erratic, but you get used to it. In India you just go with the flow.' He chuckled. 'So to speak.'

Muriel Donnelly was unpacking a Coronation mug. She had only arrived that evening and was moving into the next-door room unexpectedly vacated by Evelyn Greenslade. The mugs were wrapped in an old newspaper but it was the *South London Echo*, so even Norman wasn't interested. She was a stout woman. Legs planted apart, she delved in her suitcase.

'I must say, you're the last person I expected to see here,' he said.

'Why's that?' She unwrapped a photograph of a cat and put it on the chest of drawers.

'My son-in-law, he was the doctor.' Norman explained the connection – the hospital, the fuss. Her being on the TV.

Muriel nodded. 'It was him who gave me the brochure.'

Norman stared at her. 'Why on earth would he do that?'

She turned round. 'You believe in fate?'

'These chaps here do. Indians.'

'Something happened, see.' She didn't explain further.

'Got some whisky in my room,' said Norman. 'Fancy a *chota peg*?'

Muriel shook her head. Norman felt rebuffed. Most of the old biddies here were eating out of his hand. Desperate for a man, of course – a healthy, red-blooded male like himself. Not that there was much competition. There were only a couple of other chaps here: Doug Ainslie, hale and hearty enough but out of bounds, being married, and Graham Turner, a decrepit old bachelor who was long past it, even if he had been up for it in the first place. The staff, though male, looked even more ancient than their customers, if that were possible. In general the Indians were a handsome race but somewhat effeminate; you only had to see them in the street, holding hands like nancy boys. No, Norman was having a fine old time, bees round a honeypot.

He wondered how this Muriel woman was going to fit in. How could she afford this place? It was cheap, of course, by comparison with England, but she came from a different class. A bit of a culture shock, in more ways than one.

'They're a friendly lot here, by and large,' he said. 'Nobody completely bonkers. You'll feel at home in no time. The grub's good too. Wait till you try Fernandez's treacle pud. Just like the old days. And lots going on – cards, quizzes, outings.' He looked at her scalp. The old boiler was thinning on top. 'And a hairdresser comes round, charming lass.'

'Always looked after myself,' she said.

'So have we all, my dear. But there comes a point when we have to put ourselves into the hands of strangers and this place is a sight better than some of the dumps I've been in. Stuck in the middle of nowhere looking at a bloody ploughed field. Wait until morning. Street outside absolutely teeming. Never a dull moment.'

It was true, of course. In these poor countries people lived their lives in full view of everybody else. No privacy at all. Some of them had no homes to go to and slept in the concrete passage-ways of the office block opposite.

Later, Norman lit a cigarette and strolled down to the gate. It was ten o'clock at night but the row of stalls beside the cross-roads were still busy. Smoke rose from a brazier where a man was roasting nuts. Spirit lamps lit a cigarette stall, a cold-drink stand and a place that sold plastic novelties, the sort of things Norman could never imagine anybody buying. This little bazaar was so familiar to him now that he felt he had been here for years. Behind it stood a crumbling concrete office block, three storeys high. It was named, somewhat pompously, Karishma Plaza. At street level was a row of shops the size of cells. Most were still open: Khan's Video Rental; Gulshan Crafts; a tailor's shop where an old man sat in the strip light, bent over a sewing machine. He seemed to be there day and night. When cars slowed down at the crossroads, beggars clustered around them, tapping at their windows.

Norman gazed at the scruffy little bazaar. He was used to this from his sojourns in the tropics – the destitute scraping a living amidst the traffic, the slums clustered around the five-star hotels. It made a chap pleased for his own good fortune. Besides, being British he was treated with a deference that had long since vanished in his own country. Here, he was still somebody and that was good for a fellow's ego. All his most intoxicating expe-riences had happened abroad, in places that smelt of dung and cheap perfume. It was the smell of adventure.

Norman nodded a cheerful good evening to the *chowkidar* who, perched on his stool, dozed at the gate. A pariah dog stood list-lessly, its dugs heavy with milk. *'The women in Bangalore are the most voluptuous in India.'* Not here they weren't. Where he stood they were either beggars, baby on hip, or else sweepers. Comely enough, of course, but sexual shenanigans were definitely out of the question. Maybe some of the shrouded bodies lying on the pavement were female but he could hardly prod them awake and ask them in for a tot of Johnnie Walker. They lay there, as still as the dead.

It was up Brigade Road, in the big hotels and shopping arcades, that he saw women with some flesh on their bones – flashing-eyed temptresses haggling over jewellery or sipping *lattes* in the coffee shops. He saw them on his trips to the Oberoi Hotel to buy yesterday's *Daily Telegraph*. Those wearing saris revealed, at their midriffs, seductive bulges of skin. These were sometimes bedewed with perspiration. Norman imagined grabbing the hem and spinning the women like tops until they unravelled. He imagined dark nipples, puckered like currants, and thighs *karma sutra*'d around his neck. He imagined nuzzling enormous breasts that smelt of gardenias. Norman closed his eyes and pictured pussies that tasted of mangoes and prawns, the surprisingly luxurious starter at last night's dinner. His carnal knowledge of Indian women was limited – to be frank, non-existent – but he knew they were tutored in sexual wiles from an early age and the prostate doctor's words had inflamed him. Surely here, in India, he could arouse his flagging libido?

There were, however, certain problems. To the younger, jeans-clad generation he was invisible. In recent years Norman had grown accustomed to this, of course, it was one of the penalties of growing older. The females of more mature appearance, however, presented another difficulty, for they were never alone. In India, as in Africa, there was no such thing as solitude. This made the lothario's task a challenging one; like a lion, one had to single out one's prey and separate her from the herd. So far he had not managed to accomplish this.

Norman flicked his cigarette into a bush. Behind him the aviary was silent; the budgies had settled down for the night. So had the old dears in their bedrooms. He too felt weary. His back ached; his varicose veins throbbed. He knew he was getting too old for this sort of caper but one had to show willing. He would make discreet enquiries. Sonny would be the fellow; no doubt he was acquainted with the hot spots of his home city. Or Norman could

94

have a man-to-man chat with Minoo Cowasjee, who ran the hotel. With a wife like that – what a harridan! – he was bound to have found solace in other arms.

Ah, the joys of coitus! After all, it was the only way a chap could tell that he was still alive.

The residents were eating breakfast.

'Listen to this, girls.' Madge Rheinhart adjusted her spectacles and read aloud from the *Daily Mail*: '*In a bid to control the London drugs epidemic, armed police are being recruited to patrol school playgrounds.*'

'I read that yesterday,' said somebody.

'It's yesterday's paper.'

'Actually it's three days old,' said another woman, whose name Evelyn hadn't caught.

'Aren't you glad we've got away from all that?'

'Good grief, Cooper's Marmalade!'

The bearer put it on the table: a pot of Cooper's Coarse Cut Marmalade, complete with saucer and teaspoon. There was a silence.

'Where did you buy it, dear?'

'A shop in Lady Curzon Street, it had Marmite too. Cost an arm and a leg.'

'Still, one's pension goes a long way here.'

'What did you say about the schools?'

'Oh do pay attention, Stella!'

Madge Rheinhart rolled her eyes. She was a bossy, good-humoured woman. Her husband, apparently, had owned half Kensington. Today she wore tracksuit bottoms and a T-shirt saying STARLIGHT EXPRESS. Her spectacles hung around her neck on a *diamanté* chain. Evelyn wished she had thought of this; her own glasses hung on a sort of bootlace. Evelyn wasn't a vain woman – her nails were her only weakness – but she admired pzazz in others.

Jean Ainslie leaned across from the next table. 'Doug and I've been reading the Indian papers, haven't we, darling?'

'Dull as ditchwater,' said Douglas. 'Full of cement tenders.'

95

Evelyn smiled. She liked Douglas because he had been kind to her on the plane.

'Anyway, they don't have the crossword,' he said.

This was a source of some grievance. Norman Purse was the only person who managed to buy the *Daily Telegraph* on a regular basis. This was because he knew where to go – a source he kept secret – and set off smartly after breakfast. Evelyn had seen him striding down Brigade Road, waving away the beggars with his walking-stick. Not only did he hog the papers all day – sometimes he managed to buy *The Times* too – but he always filled in the crossword, triumphantly scrawling in biro so nobody could rub it out. Worse still, it was often incomplete; this made it doubly annoying, especially when the clues he missed were easy ones. Even Evelyn could have solved '*Kentish town famous for its oysters (10)*'.

He was out now, buying the paper. Breakfast was being served by Jimmy the bearer, an elderly man in turban and stained white jacket. He was very slow, and only brought out one item at a time. Evelyn watched him cross the room carrying a bottle of ketchup on a tray; he carried it with care, as if it might explode. Still, they were in no hurry. Cereal was available, plus omelettes or hard-boiled eggs. Evelyn had once tried the sausages, but it was not an experience she cared to repeat. The dining-room was gloomy, Indian buildings being constructed to keep out the sun, and some rebellious souls took their tea out on to the veranda.

Fifteen residents were already installed, and some more were expected in the next few weeks. Evelyn couldn't remember all their names and was inclined to cling to those with whom she had made acquaintance in the first few days: the Ainslies, Madge Rheinhart, whom everyone knew because she organised things, Stella Englefield who had buried two husbands and was somewhat deaf. Who was going to sit with whom at meals? Friendships had been forged; territories staked out. It reminded Evelyn of boarding-school, a period in her life which she remembered with painful clarity. Madge's efforts to move people around at dinner had been firmly resisted by those who had found congenial companions and were determined to stick with them.

This morning Evelyn had taken pity on Muriel Donnelly, the latest arrival, and had joined her at a table for two next to the toilets.

'They try to do an English breakfast,' said Evelyn. 'But it's not the same, of course.'

'Milk's funny,' said Muriel Donnelly.

'It's boiled. I think it's from buffaloes. The Ainslies are very adventurous – look, they're eating little puffy things filled with curry. When in Rome and all that.'

'I go to Spain for my holidays,' said Muriel. 'My son's got a villa.'

'How nice,' replied Evelyn.

'It's not hot like this.'

'It's the humidity, you see.' Evelyn enjoyed being the expert. 'Before the monsoon, apparently, it's insufferable. Now it's getting better and it should be very pleasant all winter.'

The ceiling fan creaked. At the next table, Madge anchored an airmail letter with the teapot.

'There are plans, apparently, to open another retirement hotel in Ooty,' said Evelyn. 'That's up in the hills where it's cooler. The British used to move there in the summer months. Apparently it's just like East Grinstead.'

The Marigold was, too. Sealed into their compound the residents lived in a world which was, in many ways, more familiar than the England they had left behind. It was an England of Catherine Cookson paperbacks and clicking knitting needles, of Kraft Dairylea portions and a certain Proustian recall. Now the summer was over the *mali* was planting out English annuals – marigolds and cosmea – widely spaced in damp depressions of earth. Evelyn itched to get her hands on the flower-beds; gardeners here knew nothing about colour and mass.

Outside the walls, India clamoured. So many people, such need and desperation. Evelyn had only ventured out a few times; she found the experience disorientating. The moment she stepped through the gate beggars stirred and clambered to their feet.

97

Skeletal dogs nosed through heaps of rubbish. Even the holy cows, wandering between the cars, were cruelly thin. And then there was the legless young man, sitting on his trolley in the midst of the exhaust smoke.

'We can go for a walk later, if you'd like that,' said Evelyn. 'It's all very different, I must say. I mean, in England people have got so much, yet they're becoming rather rude, don't you find? Here they've got nothing at all yet they're very polite. *How are you?* they ask. *Where do you come from?* Oh they pester you but in the nicest way.'

Muriel didn't appear to be listening. She was probably suffering from jet-lag; after all, for her it must still be the middle of the night. Somebody had mentioned that she had been left on a hospital trolley for two days. Oh well, thought Evelyn, at least she's got her legs. India, she was discovering, made one thankful for small mercies.

'I met some charming schoolchildren,' Evelyn said. 'White socks, so neat and clean, and they called me *aunty.*'

Muriel pushed away her plate. Her face was the colour of putty.

'Are you all right, dear?' asked Evelyn.

'Got a pain in my guts.'

'You poor thing.' Jean Ainslie leaned over from her table. 'Probably Delhi Belly. We've all had it.'

Evelyn scraped back her chair and stood up. 'Come along. I'll take you to the nurse.' She reached for Muriel's arm.

'I can manage.'

Muriel was a stubborn old thing. A Cockney, of course. They were an independent bunch.

'When *I* went to the nurse with tummy trouble,' said Jean Ainslie, 'she insisted on looking at my feet.'

Evelyn left Muriel with the nurse – a.k.a. Mrs Cowasjee, the manager's wife – and walked into the garden. It was already hot. The *mali*, holding a dribbling hosepipe, squatted in the flower-bed. Round his waist was tucked a chequered *dhoti*. She had once owned a summer frock made out of the same material – D. H. Evans, if she remembered correctly. Up in the tree, rooks cawed.

A man stood at the gate. 'Memsahib!' he called out, hoarse with his secret. His bicycle was laden with bundles. 'Memsahib! You want T-shirts? Slacks? Good price, madam!'

Evelyn feebly raised her hand in a gesture of both greeting and dismissal. Maybe she should buy a T-shirt and look like Madge; she already felt sapped of energy, however, and it was only ten o'clock in the morning. The heat exhausted her. The need out there, the vastness of it, drained her. In a moment of rebellion, staggering in its boldness, she had decided to embark on a new life. Was it a sign of despair, a recognition of how little she was needed? Brick by brick she had created a family. Like the walls of this garden they should have shielded her from the terrors of the world outside. One by one, however, the bricks had been removed and she was left alone in a foreign country.

Up in the nameless tree the rooks bounced from branch to branch. If only she could believe what Beverley had said: that those birds had once been people, that this was not the end. Deep in her heart she had never believed the Christian thing, she had realised this in recent years. Nobody calling himself God could let what happened happen. Maybe Indians, to whom tragedies happened on an incomprehensible scale, had the sense to hold nobody responsible. For lives so desperate, so pitifully short, there must be a comfort in knowing that theirs was just a journey through the animal kingdom. No wonder they looked so resigned – serene, even. Maybe the limbless beggar, to whom she had timidly given a rupee the day before, believed that next time round he would return as a rook, hopping across the lawn on strong, springy legs.

Evelyn stood on the path, trying to work this out. She should have listened to her daughter, who had gone on about her holy man. The trouble was, Theresa was inclined to lecture and Evelyn had drifted off. She also had an uncomfortable feeling that Theresa was seeking some emotional nourishment she had been denied at home. Evelyn herself had never really spoken to an Indian. Until recently the only ones she had met had been behind the counter at the post office or punching her ticket on the train to London. They were in a position of servitude. Once, the British had ruled this place. The Raj, however, like her certainties, had long since crumbled. Now it was she herself who was the ethnic minority. In this sprawling city there were millions of Indians and she hadn't the faintest idea what went on in their heads. Maybe they possessed a spiritual belief that made sense of the senseless; that was the only way they managed to survive. It was all most confusing.

Hugh's laugh boomed in her head. *Brace up, old girl!* How she envied the Ainslies, striding off hand in hand to explore the unknown! Evelyn had to make her own journey, with no companions except these near-strangers who sat on the veranda reading paperback novels with magnifying glasses. Some of them were already dozing. Creepers snaked up the wooden pillars of the hotel and smothered the roof tiles. It was like a scene from *The Sleeping Beauty*. The old building was crumbling; soon nature would engulf it and in years to come there would just be a pile of rubble. No, even this would have been scavenged; nothing lay around for long. It would be as if she and her fellow residents had never existed at all.

Norman, too, was asleep. He had returned from his mission; the newspaper lay on his lap. Evelyn crossed the lawn. Outside in the street, cars hooted. From the servants' quarters came the sound of a radio – warbling Indian singing, eerily high.

Evelyn approached Norman. A fly, attracted by a ketchup stain on his jacket, buzzed around his chest. His tie, scattered with ash, was askew.

Evelyn stepped nearer. Norman's purple hands lay on the *Daily Telegraph*. It was open at the Deaths page. He seemed to have underlined some of the words. Evelyn put on her spectacles. '*Peacefully*', she read, '*after a long illness.*'

Evelyn looked around; nobody was watching. With great care, she eased the paper out, from under the weight of his hands. He stirred; a phlegmy sound came from his throat. She waited.

He flung his head back and started snoring – loud snores that made his body shudder. She knew the sound only too well from her nights next door. His mouth hung open, revealing the plastic gums of his dentures.

Evelyn's heart beat faster; this was the most lawless thing she had done for years. Grabbing the newspaper, she hurried away. It was not until she reached the lobby that she burst into giggles.

It wasn't what she had expected, the nurse's room. Muriel had imagined a clinical place smelling of Dettol. Hospitals, for obvious reasons, filled her with dread.

This wasn't like that at all. Mrs Cowasjee lived with her husband in the annexe, a brick extension built on to the side of the hotel. She ushered Muriel into a room that smelt like church. A joss-stick smoked in a brass holder. The shelving unit was filled with ornaments – china animals, plastic flowers – and a booklet lay on the table: *Foresight Horoscopes: Only God Knows Better*. A fountain tinkled into a shell-shaped bowl, complete with cherub. In a funny way it reminded Muriel of her own front room. There was even a shrine, like her husband's to the Virgin Mary. This one, illuminated by fairy lights, held a figurine of a fat little man with an elephant's head. A candle flickered in front of it.

'What's that?' she asked.

'He is Ganesh, the god of prosperity and success,' said Mrs Cowasjee.

'Why's he got an elephant's head?'

She shrugged. 'He's the son of Shiva and Parvati.'

That seemed to explain it. 'Do you say prayers to him?'

Mrs Cowasjee nodded. Muriel stifled a giggle. Fancy worshipping an elephant!

'We have many gods,' said Mrs Cowasjee. 'Millions. In my country anything can be holy. You see, God is everywhere.'

Mrs Cowasjee was a handsome, middle-aged woman wrapped in a mauve sari. No nurse's uniform, nothing like that. Muriel had thought that all Indians were the same colour but Mrs Cowasjee's skin was paler than her husband's, like milkier coffee. There was a smudge of crimson in the parting of her hair. It reminded Muriel of her own wounds and the chain of events that had brought her across the world to this exotic boudoir.

'I got a pain in my stomach,' she said. 'And diarrhoea.'

'Sit down, dear, and take off your shoes.'

Muriel, mildly surprised, sat down in an armchair. She removed her shoes and peeled off her stockings.

Mrs Cowasjee seated herself opposite. She stared at Muriel's feet. There was a silence. '*Hai Raba!*' she said. 'Your feet are in a terrible state.'

Muriel nodded. 'It's the bunions.'

Mrs Cowasjee drew her chair nearer. She lifted up Muriel's right foot and rested it on her lap.

'See the bones here, and here? They are quite deformed. And the corns here, where your shoes have rubbed. Really, Mrs Donnelly, you should have looked after yourself better. Have you never visited a chiropodist?'

Muriel shook her head.

'If you take care of your feet,' said Mrs Cowasjee, 'they will take care of you.'

'Used to be a cleaner,' said Muriel. 'On my feet all day. That's when I got my varicose veins. My husband had beautiful feet. So did his brother Lenny. That's because they were so poor, see, they didn't have any shoes when they were little.'

'Indians have beautiful feet for the same reason,' said Mrs Cowasjee.

Her own peeped out from her hem – slim and brown, in bejew-elled flip-flops. Next to them Muriel's feet looked swollen and blotchy – deformed, even. Muriel had never compared herself to an Indian before.

'I too come from a poor family,' said Mrs Cowasjee. 'When I met my husband, it was love at first sight.' She sighed. In the corner, the fountain tinkled. 'My family are Hindus, and not high caste. The law forbids the caste system but of course it still continues as strongly as ever.'

'Same where I come from,' said Muriel, with feeling. 'Same in this place. I'm a fish out of bloody water.'

'His family, it is very prosperous. They're Parsees. They are like your Jews, they do very well for themselves.' Mrs Cowasjee sighed again. In the corner was a lava lamp; its orange blob rose to the top. 'I was looking forward to a peaceful old age but it hasn't happened like that.'

'Not with me either,' said Muriel. She had had to organise this all by herself, with the help of her neighbour Winnie. Tickets, packing, the renting of her flat to Winnie's niece, who had promised to move out if Muriel decided to return to Peckham. Not a word from her son, her light-of-her-life, her Keith. But she had done it. After all, she had her own pressing need for coming here.

Muriel's foot, like a lump of uncooked meat, still lay in Mrs Cowasjee's lap. It looked as if it belonged to somebody else. They both gazed at it.

'Oh yes, it was a love match,' said Mrs Cowasjee. 'Then.'

In the lamp, the blob slowly descended. Watching it made Muriel's stomach sink.

'You see, my husband is a weak man,' said Mrs Cowasjee.

'So was mine. People took advantage of him. Then he lost his job and sat about all day watching telly.' Muriel stopped. She shouldn't be saying all this to a foreigner. 'About my tummy –'

'The main problem, in this country, is burning soles.'

Souls? 'What? In the bonfires?' Muriel knew that widows flung themselves on their husbands' funeral pyres. She had seen it on the TV. It seemed a daft idea to her.

'No, dear, I'm talking about feet,' said Mrs Cowasjee. 'In the temples you have to take off your shoes, as a mark of respect, and the floor can be very hot. It damages the skin.'

Muriel gazed at the shelf of knick-knacks. Amongst them she spotted a Charles-and-Diana mug. It was the same one that she had, with the wedding photograph printed on it. *In my country anything can be holy*. Prince Charles . . . an elephant . . . She thought of her cat, buried in her son's garden in Chigwell. Maybe she could put a candle in front of Lenny's photograph, like Mrs Cowasjee had done. For a moment, Muriel felt at home. Just now it was that woman at breakfast, Evelyn with her posh voice, who seemed the foreigner.

'Shall I scrape those corns now?' asked Mrs Cowasjee.

'What about my tummy?'

Mrs Cowasjee lowered Muriel's foot to the floor. 'Drink plenty of plain tea,' she said abruptly. 'With cardamom and ginger. I'll tell the cook.'

'That all?'

'If it continues I'll call for Dr Rama.'

Mrs Cowasjee had lost interest. She seemed to be a moody woman; during breakfast Muriel had heard her shouting at her husband.

Muriel pulled on her hold-ups, easing them over the barely healed wound on her shin. Mrs Cowasjee seemed not to have noticed it. A funny sort of nurse, Muriel thought. And how could she do her job properly when she was swaddled in chiffon?

Muriel eased her feet into her shoes. They were beige courts, made of imitation leather that made her feet sweat. They were also too tight; her bunions throbbed.

From his niche, the elephant god watched her labours. He had a pot belly and a startled expression, as if somebody had goosed him. Maybe I should ask *him* to make my tummy better, thought Muriel. She felt a giggle rising, like a burp.

Mrs Cowasjee followed her gaze. 'We pray to Ganesh before an important undertaking. We are needing his blessing, you see, to remove any obstacles in our path.'

'You really believe all that?'

'If it happens, it happens.' She shrugged. 'It's our karma.'

Well, if it makes you feel calmer good luck to you, thought Muriel. She got to her feet, steadying herself on the arm of the chair. Taking a last look at the elephant, she thought: I know what I would pray for.

I would pray to find my son.

Evelyn stood in the lobby, clutching the *Daily Telegraph*. She waited for her heartbeat to return to normal. There was nobody around; no sound except the sweeper's broom and the tick-tock of the grandfather clock. It was an hour slow but nobody seemed to have noticed. It didn't really matter, she supposed. At Delhi Airport the Ainslies had pointed out a man squatting behind the clock, moving its hands. People scraped a living for themselves in whatever way they could. Somebody at dinner – Madge, the most *risqué* – said that eunuchs got paid to not lift up their saris and display their private parts. Even this, disgusting though it undoubtedly was, seemed touching in its desperation. At least they weren't layabouts living off benefits as their British counterparts would be doing, according to the *Daily Mail* which Evelyn used to borrow from her cleaner.

Half past ten. England would still be slumbering. Only postmen would be stirring, and those who had woken up early to catch a flight. People moved around the world as if they were popping down to the corner shop. Evelyn's own grandchildren, who lived in New York, were more familiar with Bali than the byways of Sussex. How different it was from her own youth, with its once-a-year trip to Marshall & Snelgrove! The technicolor present had outshone these timid treats, dimming them into monochrome. Evelyn thought of Gatwick Airport. Somewhere beneath its tarmac lay her own lost childhood.

'Madam would like some coffee?'

Evelyn jumped. Jimmy stood there, grave in his turban.

'No thank you, Jimmy.' Nobody could pronounce his real name. 'I'm looking for a photocopier. Does Mr Cowasjee have one in his office?'

Jimmy waggled his head. *If you want him to have one, he does.* He was trying to be helpful. Evelyn was fond of the old head bearer. He seemed to be permanently on duty, existing solely for the guests in a way that would be inconceivable in England. He anticipated their needs, fetching balls of wool or a cushion almost before they had thought of such a thing themselves. His advanced age made Evelyn feel like a spring chicken. In England, no doubt, he would long since have been put out to grass. In India, however, people seemed to carry on until they dropped.

Jimmy crossed the lobby to the lounge. With an effort, he wedged the door open. In this climate, woodwork warped. It was the humidity. In their bedroom drawer, Evelyn's own smalls had become mildewed.

She went behind the counter, knocked on the office door and went in. Mr Cowasjee was on the phone, jabbering away in his own language. Hindi? Something else? Just for a moment the hotel proprietor, in his khaki bush suit, looked impenetrably foreign. He was a plump, middle-aged man; a natty dresser. His hair was slicked back with pomade, she could smell it from where she stood.

He replaced the receiver and sprang to his feet. 'How may I help you, madam?' he asked.

'I'm so sorry to disturb you. I wondered if I could photocopy the crossword.' Evelyn wanted to add: It's my only way of feeling useful. This country makes me feel so helpless. Mr Cowasjee wouldn't understand this. Despite his affability he was still an Indian.

He clapped his hands. 'A splendid idea!'

Evelyn relaxed. 'Norman – Mr Purse – he does rather monopolise the paper.'

'How many copies would you require?'

She made a swift calculation. 'Fifteen, say. I'll pay you, of course.'

'Out of the question, madam.'

Mr Cowasjee lifted the lid of the machine and positioned the *Daily Telegraph*, which she had folded on the appropriate page. As he did so she remembered Muriel.

'Mrs Donnelly was taken poorly. I do hope she's all right. I took her to your wife.'

'You are a kind and thoughtful lady, Mrs Greenslade. You shall earn your place in heaven.'

'You don't believe in that, do you?' Evelyn stopped. This sounded impudent. 'I thought that – well – you believe you never die, you just come back as something else.' She didn't add: a woodpecker or something.

'That is the Hindu belief, madam. The soul migrates through a series of bodies.'

'Even animals?'

He nodded. 'Only by good deeds can they break the cycle of death and rebirth, and attain nirvana.'

'Goodness,' said Evelyn.

'However, I am a Parsee. We follow the teachings of Zarathustra. Like yourself we believe in a day of judgement. Either we will find solace in heaven or suffer the torments of hell.'

'To be perfectly honest,' said Evelyn, 'I'm not sure *what* I believe any more.'

Mr Cowasjee didn't reply. The machine hummed and a piece of paper slid out.

'Too faint.' He picked it up and passed it to her.

'My eyesight's rather poor.' Evelyn fumbled for her glasses, which had become caught in her blouse. 'Even distances are getting blurry now.'

He adjusted a dial on the machine and pressed the button again. 'The problem is, we are dying out.'

'Don't say that. *I* am, but you're still in the prime of life.'

'I mean us Parsees, Mrs Evelyn. There is too much inter-marriage.'

'I thought people listened to their parents here,' she said.

'Not always, madam.'

There was a silence. Evelyn thought of her son, at the age of forty, announcing his engagement to an American woman Evelyn had never met. It hadn't crossed his mind to ask his mother's opinion.

'I think parents know best,' she said. 'Their minds aren't muddled up by –' She was going to say *sex*. 'By an impulse that might soon burn itself out. My son became ensnared by a most unsuitable woman. When we finally met her, my husband and I, she terrified the life out of us.'

Mr Cowasjee didn't reply. Evelyn wondered if she had gone too far. One by one the pages slid out of the machine and fell sound-lessly into a plastic tray.

Suddenly Mr Cowasjee swung away, squatted on his haunches and pulled something out from under the cupboard.

'Madam, I'm going to show you something I have shown to very few people in my life. You, however, are a woman of under-standing . . .' Pushing aside some papers, he laid the bundle on the desk. It was an object wrapped in embroidered fabric. Mr Cowasjee broke the string – feeble Indian string that snapped like cotton – and opened the cloth. A pair of shoes was revealed. 'These are the shoes I was wearing when I met my wife.'

Evelyn touched the leather with her forefinger. 'They're very nice.'

'Exactly. Bata, 550 rupees.'

'Very smart.' She didn't know what to say. 'Did you meet her at a party?'

He shook his head. Good Lord, he was blushing! She didn't think Indians could blush. 'Tell me, Mrs Evelyn, what are your seven deadly sins?'

'Heavens, I can't remember them all. Murder, of course, and worshipping graven images.'

'You have committed none of them, I'm sure. That is why your memory fails you.' Mr Cowasjee wrapped up the shoes again in the cloth. Tiny mirrors were sewn into the fabric; they winked in the light. 'Vanity and lust, I'm sure they are two of them.'

'Oh yes, there's covetousness. Thy neighbour's ox and his wife. And . . . well, adultery, of course –' She stopped.

'Vanity and lust,' Mr Cowasjee muttered to himself. He squatted down and put the bundle back in the cupboard. Despite the slicked-back hair she noticed, now, that he was thinning on top.

'Good God, what are you doing? Your A levels?'

Norman stood on the veranda, staring at the ladies. They sat at the tables, pens poised, each with a sheet of paper in front of her.

'Bit old for exams, aren't you?' he asked.

Jean Ainslie pretended to slap him. 'Don't be so rude, you naughty boy.'

Norman peered closer. They were doing the crossword.

Madge Rheinhart removed the biro from her mouth. 'Anyone got *Primates taking the wrong place by cathedral choir*, four letters?'

Eithne Pomeroy, a gentle soul who had befriended the local cats, smiled at him. 'It's so kind of you, Raymond.'

'Norman.'

'I think you're a very nice man, whatever they say.' Eithne turned to the others. 'I've only got one.'

Madge looked at her sheet. 'And it's wrong, sweetie. Try *viaduct*.'

'What did you say, dear?' asked Stella, fiddling with her hearing aid.

'Keeps us out of mischief,' said Jean Ainslie, with a wink.

'It's *apse*, Madge!'

Norman felt confused. Was he finally losing his marbles? He still had the *Daily Telegraph*, firmly gripped in his hand.

'Aha, I've got Six Down,' said Madge. 'Give me a rupee, girls, and I'll tell you.'

Norman turned to her. With her chestnut hair and clanking jewellery Madge was one of the few almost-fanciable women here. He pointed to her sheet of paper. 'Er, who gave it to you?'

'Evelyn, of course. She said you wanted to share it.'

'Oh. Yes, of course.' Norman looked around. Evelyn was nowhere to be seen. Typical! Those quiet, genteel women were always the worst. Passive-aggressive, of course – a phrase his daughter used about her starched-shirt of a husband. He attempted a smile. 'Always glad to be of service, ladies.'

'What did he say?' Stella's hearing aid whistled.

'Nothing,' said Madge.

Muriel Donnelly was drinking a cup of tea. 'Ugh.' Lips puckered, she replaced the cup in the saucer. 'Tastes of cat's wee-wee.'

'Are you feeling better, dear?' asked Stella.

'I was, till I drank this muck.' Muriel glared at Norman, as if he had made the bloody stuff himself. It was clear that, alone among the women, Muriel was immune to his charms. But then she possessed few of them herself. She sat there, a cockney battleaxe, legs planted apart, stockings wrinkled around her ankles.

Norman gazed at them, heads bent over their crosswords like elderly schoolchildren. A few of them had bravely dyed their hair but the grey roots were showing. Some, like Muriel, were distinctly bald on top. The heat was oppressive. A couple of them were preparing to move inside, into the sepulchral lounge. Norman, too, felt oppressed by the female atmosphere. Where had all the men gone? What made women cling so doggedly to life?

Two ancient sisters, whose names he had forgotten, were approaching the veranda. One of them clutched a video.

'Look!' she said. 'That kind Mr Khan found us *Upstairs Downstairs*.'

There was a general twittering.

'The pavement's in a terrible state,' said the other sister. 'It looks like somebody had been mugged.'

'What's that?' asked Muriel sharply.

'Blood everywhere, great splashes of it.'

'That's *paan* juice,' said Norman. You silly cow. 'Stuff they chew, then they spit it out. The Indian does a lot of hawking and spitting.'

There was a pause. They all gazed at him, God knew why.

'It's a purification thing,' he said.

'So that's what it is,' said Madge. Somebody giggled.

What were the old bitches getting at? Norman felt outnumbered. *Women.* It reminded him of his wife and daughter, giggling behind closed doors.

Norman decided to beat a retreat. He walked down the rickety steps and made his way round to the back of the building in search of male companionship. This crosswords business had thrown him off balance. How could that Evelyn woman have snatched his paper? He had stayed alert, he was sure of it. Here he was, on the other side of the world, and landed in the same foetid nest of female manipulation he thought he had left behind in the various Homes in which he had been incarcerated. Indian women wouldn't have behaved like this. Indian women knew how to please a chap.

And he hadn't even done the blithering crossword himself yet. He made his way across the threadbare lawn, past the wheelchair ramp and round the corner towards the kitchen. This was a breeze-block extension at the back of the hotel. Behind it was the servants' quarters: a couple of huts, with corrugated iron roofs, sagging against the garden wall. It still startled him, these few steps into primitive village life.

A naked child stared at Norman as he relieved himself beside the crate of empties. It wasn't worth trekking to the khazi. Besides, it had been almost continually occupied by Muriel since her arrival. Thanks to the op, the piss flowed more freely now. In the waste land beyond the wall – soon to be a building site, he suspected – the natives relieved themselves every morning. Norman had seen them through a gap in the brickwork: rows of them squatting in the pearly light of dawn. Though Indians were a modest race they defeated quite openly, turning their backs to the road in the pathetic hope that this posture made them invisible. A good country for elderly incontinents, thought Norman. If they were off on a jaunt somewhere and caught short, the old girls could just pull down their knickers and have a piss in the street.

Norman chuckled as he zipped up his fly. A mangy puppy lay slumped on the earth. Like the rest of India, it seemed to have succumbed to lethargy. Weren't puppies supposed to gambol, without a care in the world?

Cooking smells drifted out from the kitchen. Norman went in and blinked in the gloom. Fernandez, the cook, was slicing a tomato. The kitchen boy had taken off his flip-flop and was slapping at a cockroach. It was a miracle that meals were produced from this place at all, meals for fifteen people and vaguely on time. Two gas burners supported pans filled with something-or-other bubbling away. Some onion rings were heaped in a bowl. Otherwise there was no indication that lunch would be served in an hour's time.

Fernandez nodded a greeting. Norman offered him his flask. The cook lifted it to his lips. Norman dropped in most days; there was something undemanding about this grease-spattered little hovel. Despite his rudimentary English Fernandez was usually game for a chat. Minoo was often distracted and Sonny only popped in now and then. The bowed old cook, however, was always on the premises; in fact the chap never seemed to have a day off.

This morning, however, Fernandez seemed to be upset. 'Memsahib,' he said, rolling his eyes. How well Norman knew that shrug, the eyes raised heavenwards. It was the same gesture the world over. The cook took another gulp of the whisky. No doubt Mrs Cowasjee had been shouting at him again. Norman found the sari-clad firebrand faintly arousing but she seemed to make the servants' lives a misery, bossing them about and setting them against each other. 'She says always she is working,' said Fernandez. 'The feets, the food . . . lunch and then dinner, too much working.'

'The feets?' asked Norman.

'Old memsahibs, very bad feets.'

Maybe I could get her to cut my toenails, thought Norman. Need a bloody hacksaw nowadays.

Fernandez seemed disinclined to talk. Swaying slightly, he crossed the floor and heaved the pot off the gas. It was a shame. Fernandez came from Goa and Norman enjoyed hearing tales of the topless beaches where the cook's son owned a café and seemingly enjoyed the favours of a string of Dutch and German nymphomaniacs. According to Fernandez, Goa was one long orgy. Pauline had promised to take Norman there the next time she came to India.

Norman left the kitchen. Outside the *dhobi* arrived on his bicycle. It was laden with laundry. Norman's hankies were returned starched and pressed so beautifully it seemed a shame to use them. Since his op, of course, there had been less need. *'Won't know if I'm coming or going.'* Norman still chuckled at the joke. He could always retire to his room, switch on Star TV and watch scantily clad Mumbai models cavorting to film tunes. Even for him, however, there was something dispiriting about this in broad daylight.

Norman crossed the garden and emerged into the street. The heat was blinding – a glare that made him stagger. The crossroads teemed with people – office workers, hawkers, beggars. The sheer movement of humanity made him feel seasick. A policeman stood on his plinth, blowing his whistle and vainly trying to direct the traffic.

Norman walked up the road. He would go to one of the big hotels – the Taj Balmoral, the Oberoi – and sink a pre-lunch beer. Today might be an auspicious day – they believed all that nonsense – today he might be lucky and meet an accommodating female with a taste for mature men. He walked past the United Ice Cream Parlour and Khan's Video Rental, past the Hideaway Pub – *The Hot Spot That's Really Cool* – a throbbing den into which he had once unwisely ventured, to find its customers of kindergarten age. The road was being dug up in the torpid Indian manner; one man squatted with a bucket whilst another man, clutching a spade, listlessly tipped in teaspoons of

112

rubble. A sign had been erected showing an arrow pointing right, while another sign was propped up saying KEEP LEFT. This didn't seem to matter as the traffic took not a blind bit of notice anyway. As usual, various young men took it upon themselves to accompany him.

'How are you, sir?'

'You are from which country, sir?'

'Please step inside, sir, you want fine tarts?'

Norman stopped. 'Fine tarts?'

'Fine brass, sir. Come inside my shop.'

'You are from which country, sir?'

'London, and bugger off.' Suddenly Norman felt homesick for London – the rain, the incurious inhabitants, his daughter who despite everything loved her old Dad. It had been nice when Pauline was here, bustling around, putting his Wisdens on the bookshelf and settling him in. India had powerfully affected her. Every day she had doled out sweets to children who had flocked around her, pulling at her legs. It probably came from having no kids of her own. Now she was long gone, and not due back for months.

Across the road was a park. It was just a small place: dried-up fountain; a few trees, bristling with starlings. Families sat on the grass drinking soda-pop. In each group sat a grandad. Norman stopped. Supporting himself with his stick, he gazed across the traffic. How right it was, that they brought their old grandads along; how happy they looked, the patriarchs, surrounded by their loved ones! Lucky bastards.

Beside him a taxi stopped and a woman climbed out. She was a gorgeous creature, maybe thirty years old, wearing a silky tunic and slacks. She stopped and looked at him.

Norman rallied. Nothing ventured, nothing gained. With an effort he cranked into gear, changing from neglected paterfamilias into a grizzled Casanova. What a seductive smile she had! What glistening, crimson lips! The invitation was unmistakable.

He would ask her to accompany him to the Taj Balmoral to partake of some liquid refreshment. Norman opened his mouth to speak, but then she spoilt it.

'Do you need help?' She stepped closer, her face concerned. 'Are you lost, uncle?'

It took a moment for this to sink in. 'Certainly not!' said Norman, and marched away up the street.

3

Caring for the daily needs of a Hindu god is similar to coping with a bedridden invalid. At midday the god is given a hot bath and anointed with saffron powder. Sandal paste is applied to the statue's breast and feet. It is clothed in clean garments and decked with jewels and garlands of flowers. When the god is ready, the curtain is reopened so that the god can be seen by the devotees. Next comes lunch, specially prepared by Brahmin cooks in the temple kitchens. Baskets of food are placed before the god. Finally the statue is offered quids of betel-nut and its mouth is washed with water.

(Peter Holt: *In Clive's Footsteps*)

The hotel was sunk in somnolence. It was the middle of the afternoon and most of the residents were having a nap. Some of them slept for hours, as if preparing for the sleep from which they would never awaken. Even the servants slumbered. Evelyn's room looked out over the back. Through the iron grille of her window she could see the *mali* snoozing on his rope bed. The puppies lay strewn around like dead things. In the shadow of the wall the sweeper, apparently an Untouchable, lay on the earth where he was indistinguishable from a pile of rags. Evelyn felt an intruder, gazing at these exposed lives, but in fact she liked this room better than her original one overlooking the garden. She had more privacy, a luxury denied to the staff.

Evelyn sat on the bed and wriggled her toes. Mrs Cowasjee had given her a pedicure. She had painted her nails a pearly pink. Evelyn knew that it was trivial to find pleasure in such a minor thing but there was no denying that it was a morale-booster. She had missed Beverley's sagas, of course – she had written her manicurist a letter but had received no reply – and Mrs Cowasjee had seemed even grumpier than usual. Evelyn's tentative enquiries about the shoes, and her first meeting with her husband, had been met with a contemptuous sniff.

Evelyn walked to the lounge. Jimmy, who was dozing in a chair, struggled to his feet. Despite her protestations that she could do it herself he went to the fridge and fetched her a Thums-Up (*Absolutely No Natural Ingredients*), a drink to which she had become mildly addicted.

Evelyn went out to the veranda, stepping over a line of ants that were making their way into the hotel, presumably to carry on eating it. Only yesterday she had opened a biography of Dr Crippen, one of the books that had been left behind by former visitors, and found its pages crumbling to sawdust.

She sat down with her drink. Jimmy hovered in the doorway.

'It's all right, Jimmy.'

'Madam would like something else?'

'No, thank you.'

Still he stood there, a shadowy waxwork. Always, everywhere, eyes were upon her – people wanting to serve her, to sell her something, people simply wanting to accompany her in the street in a desire to be helpful. Indians were so very hospitable and polite, so eager to welcome a visitor to their country. It certainly made a change from England but it could become somewhat wearing. Though Jimmy was a servant he was still more or less a man and she didn't want him to see her bare legs, so pitifully white and bruised from the slightest knock. Of course there were worse sights in India than her thread veins but she still had her pride. In fact, when she was young her legs had been her best feature. She could remember the exact moment when, puzzled by the phrase *a nicely turned ankle*, she discovered that it was a compliment and applied to herself. Even now she could recall the blush of pleasure. It was at a tea party in Horsham, when she was sixteen years old.

'Watch out for snakes.'

Evelyn jumped. Madge Rheinhart stepped out on to the veranda.

'Eithne swears she saw a cobra,' said Madge, 'but you know what a nervous little ninny she is.'

Madge looked beautifully groomed, as always – burnished helmet of hair, silk blouse and slacks. Sleep never rumpled her. Even with her glasses on Evelyn couldn't detect a wrinkle on that face. It was hard to believe she was as old as Evelyn; she seemed a different species altogether. Evelyn suspected a few nips and tucks. She wondered if it made one feel any younger, to stall time in this way. It was not a question she could put, even to Madge.

'I wish I could jettison my tights,' said Evelyn. 'In this climate . . . well . . .'

'Things can get a little clammy,' laughed Madge. 'Be a devil and go native. You've got gorgeous feet. Mine are hideous, Mrs C nearly had a fit.'

'You've been to her too?'

Madge nodded. 'We're all going, she does a mean pedicure. What you need are some glamorous sandals.'

'I don't have any,' said Evelyn.

'Come along. We'll go to the Oberoi, it's got the best shops.'

'But –'

'Come along, sweetie. The nice thing about India is you never have to think about money because everything's so cheap.'

For those on a fixed income this wasn't entirely true, but Evelyn surrendered. A thing she missed, since Hugh's death, was another person making the decisions.

The Oberoi Hotel was only a mile up the road but Madge ordered a taxi. It was too hot to walk and besides, they would get pestered. Evelyn liked the taxis; they were called Ambassadors but they were really old Morris Oxfords and reminded her of trips to the seaside when she was little.

'Such a happy time.'

'What did you say?' asked Madge.

'Nothing, dear.' Evelyn liked Madge; Norman called her the Merry Widow. Madge already knew her way around the city – Prada shops, Gucci shops. She said that all the best boutiques were to be found in the big hotels.

They were just getting into the taxi when Muriel Donnelly hurried up. 'Got room for one more?'

Later it all made sense. At the time, however, Evelyn was mildly surprised. She presumed that after three days of being confined to the Marigold, feeling poorly, Muriel wanted a jaunt. Her behaviour, however, was odd. On the way she didn't speak. The driver swerved around cows and scooters; Muriel gripped the torn hole where the doorknob had once been and stared fixedly out of the window. When they passed a group of Europeans she swung round and gazed at them until they were out of sight.

'How can anyone sightsee in this weather?' asked Madge.

'The Ainslies do,' replied Evelyn. 'They've gone to the Bull Temple.'

'Doesn't that woman drive you round the bend?' said Madge. 'So bloody smug. Dragging her husband around like a prize exhibit, crowing because she's got one and we haven't.'

'Madge!' said Evelyn.

'Boasting about her bloody son. Sometimes I wish something would happen to her, just to wipe that self-satisfied expression off her face.'

Muriel didn't join in. She stared out of the window. They drove through the Oberoi gates, past emerald lawns, their sprinklers rainbows in the sunlight, past palm trees. Muriel muttered something under her breath.

Madge paid. Even her rupee notes were crisp, unlike the oily rags most people had scrumpled up in their purses. A handsome doorman in a braided uniform bowed as they entered.

'How different from our own dear Jimmy,' whispered Madge.

Muriel, however, seemed distracted. She wandered across the lobby, looking around as if she had made arrangements to meet someone. The lobby was a vast, marble place and pleasantly cool. Evelyn could feel the powder drying on her face. Behind them a group of package tourists arrived – big men in shorts, maybe Germans. A hostess greeted them: a graceful girl in a sky-blue sari. She bowed and placed her hands together. Another young beauty put garlands around their necks and painted a blob of crimson on their foreheads. Muriel stood there, scanning their faces.

'This way to the shoe shop,' said Madge, leading Evelyn towards the arcade. A function board displayed names: *Welcome to Glaxo International, Krishna Room 4th Floor . . . Jayanti Wedding Party, Skyline Room . . .* Evelyn marvelled at the sophistication of the place – why, they could be in Houston or somewhere. It seemed a world away from their ramshackle hotel and its scruffy little bazaar. She felt a wave of loyalty towards the Marigold.

Just then a man she recognised appeared. He was hurrying across the lobby, talking on a mobile phone.

'Hallo, Sonny!' called Madge.

He finished his conversation, came over and vigorously shook their hands. 'Mrs Rheinhart, Mrs Greenslade! Ah, and Mrs Donnelly!'

Now Evelyn remembered: Sonny ran the retirement company. He was restless; his eyes flickered around as he talked like the maître d' of a restaurant, checking that the customers were being served.

'Everything is OK, ladies?'

'Well, nobody's died yet,' drawled Madge. 'But I wish you'd get us some more men. I mean we might be sad old bags but – honestly, Norman and Graham! We're not that desperate.'

'What can I do, madam?' Sonny raised his hands in a gesture of hopelessness. 'You are the powerful sex, you shall outlive us all. We are just the poor males of the species.'

'Don't talk such tosh,' said Madge. 'This is bloody India.'

'Yes, but behind every Indian man there is his mother.' Sonny's voice throbbed with emotion. 'He is the mere puppet, she is pulling the strings.'

'Rubbish,' said Madge. 'Oh well, I'll just have to find myself a nice rich maharaja.' She looked at Evelyn's startled face. 'Oh I loved my husband to bits, sweetie, but he's gone now. I don't want to die alone.'

'You've got us,' said Evelyn.

There was a silence. Madge gave her a small smile.

'You are not happy in your retirement home?' asked Sonny.

'I prefer to think of it as a hotel,' said Madge. 'The word "hotel" still has possibilities.'

Evelyn was aware of music playing. It emanated from a lady harpist, stationed beside a potted palm. The tannoy asked a Mr Willoughby to come to Reception.

Sonny took his leave. After he had gone Evelyn said: 'You seem to know him quite well.'

'He and Arnold, they did business together in London,' replied Madge. 'That's how I heard about this place. Sonny owns a lot of property here – that hideous place opposite our hotel, call centres, high-tech stuff. He knows everybody.'

'That true?' Muriel asked, her voice sharp.

'Most of them are his relations. But that's India for you.'

Muriel turned away and hurried after Sonny. Evelyn watched her waylay him and ask him something. He shook his head, or maybe it was one of those waggles. She still hadn't got the hang of them yet.

'Come on,' said Madge. 'Let's hit those shops.'

Sonny hurried outside to where a driver waited beside a white Mercedes. Muriel went up to the Reception desk. She stood there, a stocky figure in her floral dress, talking to the clerk. Her behaviour was really rather odd.

'What's Muriel doing?' asked Evelyn.

Madge followed her gaze. 'Maybe she wants an upgrade,' she laughed.

By the time they returned the afternoon shadows had lengthened. After the chaos of the streets the Marigold felt like home; for the first time Evelyn felt it might be possible to make a life for herself here, with her new friends.

Maybe it was something to do with the light. In India this time of day was very beautiful; for some reason they called it cow hour. It reminded her of the long, golden afternoon of her childhood, an afternoon that never seemed to end, when birdsong echoed and her mother was calling her to come in to bed, a call she pretended not to hear. Maybe it was to do with the freedom she felt, bare-legged, wearing her new sandals.

In the hotel somebody was playing the piano. Whoever it was played hesitantly, sometimes missing the note.

'Who is Sylvia? What is she –'
Evelyn herself used to sing it.
'That all our swains commend her . . .'
On the veranda stooped Eithne Pomeroy, in her yellow dress.
She was putting out a saucer of milk for the cat she had befriended.
Graham Turner, the ageing bachelor, had come to a standstill in
front of the aviary. Evelyn looked at his back view – the thinning
hair, the sloping shoulders. He often stood for long periods, lost
in thought.
'Is she kind, as she is fair?
For beauty lives with kindness . . .'
Evelyn hummed the tune. Actually she had never believed this
bit. Cecilia Shaw, at school, had the looks of an angel but she had
made Evelyn's life a misery with her bullying. Suddenly Evelyn
was seized with fury. No feelings since then – not for her husband
or her children – were as fierce as that tumult of half a century
ago, caused by someone who might now be dead.
'Come on,' said Madge, 'drinkipoos.'
She led Evelyn to the veranda and ordered gin and tonics, like
a husband. This was the best moment of the day. Evelyn had never
been a drinker but hotel life had liberated her. This wasn't home;
nor was it the stuffy prison of Leaside. *The word 'hotel' still has*
possibilities.
'Then to Sylvia, let us sing . . .'
The piano was out of tune, of course. Whoever was playing,
they must have learnt it as a child. Evelyn had learnt it too. She
had squirmed on the piano stool, longing to escape into the green
light of the garden.
Under the table Evelyn pushed the sandal off her foot; it was
already rubbing. Once she had stayed out all day, running wild,
crashing through the undergrowth. Now she was exhausted by a
taxi ride. Once she ran through the grass, her shadow following
her as the sun sank. Now she was in a country where the shadow
cast by the sweeper was so polluting that a higher-caste Hindu
had to disinfect it. Mr Cowasjee had told her that. How could
such kind people be so terribly cruel? It was as bad as Cecilia,
holding her nose when Evelyn walked past. Yet the sweeper, the

lowest of the low, seemed unperturbed. To him, perhaps, this life was as insubstantial as his own shadow.

Evelyn watched the *mali*. He walked slowly across the lawn, stooping to pick up Norman's cigarette butts. Cecilia, the bully, was the only girl at school who smoked. It seemed thrillingly wicked. She developed, too, before anyone else. Evelyn and her friends, inspecting their flat chests, used to chant: '*I must, I must, improve my bust.*' Would they ever become women? Would anyone, ever, want to hold them in their arms?

With an effort, the *mali* straightened up. His back was as stiff as her own. What had happened to Cecilia? She had probably had scores of lovers, Catholic girls were known to be fast. Evelyn had only had one: her husband.

The drinks arrived. Madge signed the chit and sat down. Evelyn was flattered that the glamorous Madge had singled her out. It was just like school, all over again, but freed from the pain.

'Why did you come here?' asked Evelyn.

'Because I was bored out of my mind,' replied Madge. 'Ever been to Stanmore?'

Evelyn shook her head.

'Well, then.' Madge lit a cigarette. 'I wanted to have one last go at it.'

'Indians seem to have a lot of goes,' said Evelyn.

'I don't think one should give up. Someone told Clark Gable that he was bad in bed. He said: *That's why I have to keep practising.*'

Startled, Evelyn laughed. She smelt dinner cooking. 'I liked what you said about hotels,' she said. 'I don't fancy the word *retirement* either.'

Madge fished out a slice of lime with her fingernail. Sucking it, she gazed at the residents sitting at their tables. 'Actually, sweetie, it's more like a waiting-room. Just don't look at the departure board.'

There was a silence. Deep in the hotel, the piano-playing stopped. Evelyn wished Madge hadn't said that.

She thought: We've only got each other now. We mustn't say upsetting things, doesn't Madge realise that? She tried to think of something else. She pointed to the *mali*, on the far side of the lawn. He was dropping the cigarette butts into the hem of his *dhoti* and tucking it around his waist.

'They do the most menial jobs, don't they? I mean, look at the gardener. Yet they're not like the British, they don't seem to mind. It must be their religion.'

'What do you mean?' asked Madge.

'Picking up Norman's butts.'

Madge laughed. 'He smokes them, silly. I've seen him round the back.'

Evelyn paused. 'Oh.' She thought: How can I work everything out, all on my own? She remembered how Hugh used to explain things in the newspaper. How he lent her his glasses. How he whipped the parking ticket out of her hand.

Just then the *mali* turned. They followed his gaze. A rickshaw was driving through the gates. It puttered up to the front door, emitting clouds of exhaust smoke. Douglas and Jean Ainslie extricated themselves from its back seat.

Something was wrong. They hurried up to Mr Cowasjee, who was handing out dinner menus.

'There's been a little accident,' said Douglas. He supported his wife up the steps. 'Jean's been bitten by a monkey.'

There was a general stir. 'We were at the Bull Temple,' said Jean.

'She was feeding it a banana,' said Douglas.

'It's here.' Jean looked pale. She showed the manager her hand. 'I think I should see the nurse.'

'Tetanus shot,' said Douglas.

'Come with me, madam. I will telephone for the doctor.' Mr Cowasjee snapped his fingers. 'Jimmy, ring doctor-sahib. *Jaldi, jaldi!*'

'But surely your wife –' began Douglas.

'My wife cannot administer an injection.'

'But –'

'Dr Rama is a tip-top doctor, sir,' said Mr Cowasjee. 'He'll be here in a trice.'

They went indoors.

Muriel got to her feet and hurried over. 'See?' she said. 'See what happened?'

'What?' asked Evelyn.

Muriel's eyes glittered. 'See?' She pointed to Madge. 'She wanted something to happen to her, to Mrs Ainslie, and it did.'

How strangely Muriel was behaving! Evelyn wondered if she was quite right in the head. But then she herself sometimes felt the sense of things slipping from her grasp.

And at dinner she forgot all about it. They were tucking into their soup (cream of tomato) when suddenly the conversation, never that lively, faded away.

A man was crossing the dining-room. He was tall, with an abundant head of black hair that shone in the strip light. He wore a blue shirt and carried a leather case. Evelyn recognised him from the photograph. Dr Rama was even more dazzling, however, in real life; more dazzling, even, than Omar Sharif in his prime. Accompanied by the manager he strode past the tables, smiling at the diners, and disappeared down the corridor in the direction of the Ainslies' room.

There was a hush, then a fluttering sound, like hens settling down.

'Blimey,' said Madge. 'He can give me an internal examination any day.'

Somebody clapped their hands together. Evelyn thought it was applause. But it was just Norman, squashing a mosquito. 'Got the bugger!' he said, wiping his hand on his trousers.

It had been a day packed with incident – a pedicure, new red sandals, a monkey-bite, a handsome doctor. There had been many more images, however, that crowded Evelyn's head – a man washing his ox beside the petrol pump; a boy, balancing a tray of tea glasses, weaving through the traffic . . . more than this, much more. The street outside teemed with life; she didn't really have to go anywhere at all. What a change it made from her village back home, with its shuttered weekenders' cottages. Nowadays English streets were empty; people stayed at home, gazing at their computer screens she supposed, blowing up the Houses of Parliament on video games.

It was late but Evelyn couldn't sleep. The sight of Dr Rama had stirred feelings she had long ago thought extinguished. She had only known one man's body. She remembered Hugh's smell, the peppery scent of his sweat; she remembered the fleshiness of him, his naked body in bed – well, to be accurate, he usually kept his pyjama tops on. She had never really speculated about other men; there hadn't been time, what with children and the sailing each weekend, let alone that enormous garden. She remembered Douglas's words on the plane: *you only have the one life.*

Evelyn sat up. She pushed back the mosquito net and switched on the light. Unlike herself, this room had known many lives. How many people had passed through it? There was little sign of their brief occupation – a cigarette burn on the dressing-table, that was all. *A waiting-room.* For Indians it must be different; from what she understood, life for them must be a series of waiting-rooms. And then what?

She slid her feet into her slippers. Outside, a dog barked. It was answered by more dogs in the waste land beyond the wall where people lived in conditions of staggering squalor. A kerosene lamp shone in the servants' quarters where the staff shed their uniforms and, just for a few hours, lived their unfathomable lives.

Evelyn padded along the corridor to the lounge. It was dimly illuminated by the light from the lobby. She sat down at the piano and lifted the lid. She hadn't played for years; her joints were stiff. Tentatively she moved her fingers over the keys, trying to remember the Moonlight Sonata. She wasn't going to play it, of course, it would wake people up. But surely, hidden deep within her fingers, there remained some memory?

It had gone. Evelyn closed the lid. She got up, unbolted the veranda door and stepped out into the night. The evening warmth welcomed her, it was as warm as her blood. How cold England had been, for old bones! Scent drifted from the tiny, unknown blossoms that made a hedge around the lawn. Somewhere a cat miaowed. Several of the ladies in the hotel – Eithne, Stella, Hermione Somebody – or was it Harriet? Evelyn couldn't ask now – some of the ladies fed the strays with food they saved from dinner. There was an undercurrent of rivalry about this. They each had a different name for a bald old tom that they considered theirs alone. No fool, he responded to all of them.

It was then that Evelyn became aware of a light. It was flickering in her old room, now inhabited by Muriel. She walked up the path and peered through Muriel's window.

The room was transformed. For a moment Evelyn couldn't recognise it. Candles were stuck along the dressing-table; smoke wreathed up from incense sticks. Dimly, Evelyn could discern a sort of shrine.

Muriel, in her nightie, was sitting on the bed. The window was open.

She swung round. 'Who's that?'

'I've been mugged, see,' said Muriel. 'And burgled.'

'I heard,' said Evelyn. 'It must have been terrible.'

'It's my nerves. I keep thinking they're coming back. They stole my home from me and my peace of mind, they took it all away. My whole life I'd lived in that place and they stole it for a telly. I keep having these nightmares. I wake up, me heart going like the clappers. I keep seeing their faces, like they're here.'

'It's all right, dear,' said Evelyn. 'They're not.'

'Keep seeing 'em everywhere. See, they found out where I lived.'

'You're safe here, really. You're on the other side of the world.'

'Two black boys,' said Muriel. 'They killed my Leonard.'

'Who?'

Muriel pointed to a framed photograph on the dressing-table. It was draped with a garland of marigolds. Evelyn got up and peered at it, in the candlelight. It was a photograph of a cat.

'The Huns killed my Leonard and those niggers killed my cat. It was the same person, see, he was in his body. I always knew it but Mrs Cowasjee, she told me it was true. I could've saved him if I'd seen the signs.' Muriel's voice rose; she was highly agitated. 'They evacuated me, see.'

'What, the police?'

Muriel gripped Evelyn's arm. 'They made me go and live in the country and that's why he was killed.'

'I thought you lived in London?'

'It's all my fault. That's why I had to marry Paddy.'

'Paddy?' Evelyn couldn't grasp this conversation but it was probably her own fault. 'Is that why you came here?' she asked. 'Because they evacuated you?'

'What's that?'

'After the burglary?'

Muriel stared at her. 'What are you talking about?'

Evelyn took a breath. She spoke clearly. 'Is that why you've come to India?'

Muriel stared at her as if she were retarded. Evelyn realised that there were several shrines. There was a Hindu god, the one with all the arms, a photograph of Princess Diana and even a small plaster Virgin Mary. Muriel certainly believed in hedging her bets.

'Don't tell anybody, promise!' hissed Muriel.

'I promise,' said Evelyn.

Muriel lowered her voice. 'It's all fate, see. It's karma. The mugging, the brochure that the doctor sent me, and then what I heard about my son. What the neighbours told me, where he lived.'

'Your son?'

Her grip tightened. More bruises tomorrow, Evelyn thought.

'Don't tell the police!' whispered Muriel.

'What have the police got to do with it?'

'He's here, see.'

'Who is?' asked Evelyn.

'My Keith,' said Muriel. 'That's why I've come here. He's here, in India.'

'Your son's here?'

'That's what the neighbours told me, that he's come to India. It's a business matter. I been looking at everyone to see if it's him, looking at the faces. I asked at that hotel, it's his sort of place, the sort of place he'd stay. But he'll find me. Keith's like that. He'll know his old Mum's here and he'll find me in the end.'

It was late. Within their rooms the residents slumbered, dreaming of Dr Rama who lifted their nighties with his caring

127

brown hands. Jean Ainslie typed a round robin email to her friends while her husband tried to sleep. Madge, who had been taught computing skills by her grandson, sat at her screen; the blue light illuminated her face as she logged on to her diminishing stocks and shares. Stella was swallowing her pills – heart pills, joint pills, Prozac – with a glass of soda water. In his room at the back of the hotel Graham Turner played Dinah Washington, 'Mad about the boy', at the lowest volume. Somewhere in the garden a bird screeched. The servants slept, wherever it was that they slept.

Outside, at the crossroads, lorries drove through the night. Brigade Road ran past the Marigold, out beyond the big hotels to the new city of office blocks where nobody had been because it was another world. The second road led to the Old Town and its maze of streets that only the most adventurous had dared to penetrate. The third road led into the city centre with its Victorian buildings that reminded them of home. The fourth road led to the airport. In England an airport was just a place which one made use of from time to time. Here its presence could be palpably felt. It was their place of arrival, which had delivered them into this foreign land. They had stepped out of the plane with a return ticket that in all probability would never be used. And it was a place that might deliver up to them, from a country that now seemed shrunk and unreal, those they loved.

'Namaste!' wrote Jean:

> Sorry I haven't written to you folks sooner but Doug and I have been busy busy busy settling into our new home and exploring this bustling Indian metropolis. Though lacking the obvious charms of some of the places we've visited on our former trips (see missives number 9 and 24), Bangalore is not lacking in interest and, as Douggy jokes, there are plenty of ancient monuments right here in our hotel!! Seriously though, the Marigold is a pleasant place, delightfully 'Old Raj' and boasting the usual erratic plumbing! Our fellow residents are well past retirement age but as you know

128

we believe that age is all in the mind and if one is open to new experiences one will always remain young at heart (enough lecture: ed!). Most of them are female, so Doug is enjoying himself and I have to keep him on a tight leash (just joking). One or two of them grew up in India so for them it's like coming home. We too feel very 'at home' here but then you know what vagabonds we are! We've always enjoyed 'going native' and have introduced the delights of 'dhosas' and 'idlis' to our more conventional fellow diners whose idea of local cuisine starts and ends with chicken tikka, a dish unknown to most Indians!

We are also learning the language of Karnataka (Kennada) and can already carry on a simple conversation with the staff. We can see that they appreciate us taking the trouble to master a few words. As you know, we've always believed in respect for other cultures and though McDonalds has popped up its ugly head (sorry, its golden arches!) India is still an ancient and many-layered civilisation. Of course there is a great gulf between rich and poor (you should see the bargains!) but we make a practice of giving alms to the beggars – a few rupees can make all the difference to a poor family.

All in all we have no regrets. Devon seems a distant memory and our only sadness is missing our many friends (do come out!) and of course our children. Amanda has been promoted to Deputy Head and finds time in her busy schedule for her beloved salsa dancing (Stage 4, well done Amanda!) and the annual 'Baroque Around the Clock' festival which she seems to organise single-handedly! Adam goes from strength to strength at the BBC (do catch his latest documentary, details enclosed, we think it's his best yet: thought-provoking and hilarious). Emails are of course a blessing and Douggy has finally overcome his Luddite tendencies and can hardly be parted from his new digital camera. The accompanying photo shows muggins here with the local snake charmer!!

That's enough for now. As they say here, 'phir milenge'

(we'll meet again), or, for those of a Muslim persuasion, 'khoder hafiz, insh'allah'!
   Love, Jean and Doug

PS: Idli is a steamed rice cake. Dhosa is a type of rice pancake. Lesson over!

4

Remember, you are everything or you are nothing. If you are every-
thing, then your heart is so big it can hold all of humanity within
itself, you have no jealousy or narrowness. You are in the heart of
every creature and every creature is in your heart. There is only
bliss.

(Swami Purna)

It was his wife who organised it. Of course Christopher had
planned to visit his mother at some point but it was Marcia who
suggested a date and sorted it out.

'Christmas in India!' Marcia said. 'Evelyn'll be thrilled. And
it'll be great for the kids, an awesome experience.'

So Marcia took it in hand. She downloaded holiday packages
that included Bangalore on their itineraries and settled on an
upmarket company that specialised in cultural tours. *South India
Highlights* included Mysore, the temples at Halebib and Belur,
'with their intricate carvings of dancing figures, animals and
friezes', and a two-night stay at the five-star Taj Balmoral Hotel,
Bangalore. 'A spacious city with many parks and gardens', she
read, '. . . now a thriving business centre, known as the Silicon
Valley of India.' Within a few days it was all set up, including an
optional extra: a week at the Colva Beach complex, Goa, where
they could unwind before returning to the States.

Christopher felt his usual mixture of powerlessness and gratitude. The woman was so damned efficient. Not only did she
hold down a demanding job in a top-flight brokerage firm, keep
herself fit with a punishing regime at the gym and organise the

131

children's own packed schedules, she had also masterminded yet another makeover of the apartment and was negotiating to buy some real estate up in Wellfleet, Cape Cod as a retirement home for her father and stepmother. Marcia was an exemplary daughter in this respect. Christopher attributed it to her Jewish and Italian blood. She came from a large achieving family where it was taken for granted that children cared for their parents.

This made Christopher feel guilty, of course. So did the fact that she was paying for this holiday; Marcia was a generous woman in this respect. Of course, she earned more than he did; when they met, in fact, she had been his superior though upon moving to New York she had transferred to another firm. His sister Theresa, who had never liked Marcia, assumed that she was bleeding him dry with her high-maintenance life-style. Christopher had only half-heartedly disabused her of this; after all, a man had his pride.

It was a Saturday in November and he was taking Clementine to Central Park. His daughter was eleven, going on sixteen. She had wanted to go to the beauty place to have her eyebrows done but he had insisted she try out her new rollerblades. Marcia had stayed behind to help Joseph with his math.

'*Kirsty's* had her eyebrows shaped,' said Clementine.

'That doesn't mean you have to,' he said. 'Stay a child for a bit longer.'

'Duh?' Her face said *Don't be a dork, Dad*. It was a new expression – curled lip, pitying smile.

They walked down Madison, past the fashion shops. Christopher wished she would slip her hand in his but she had recently ceased doing this.

'Are you looking forward to India?' he asked.

'Yuk. India's gross.' They were passing Ralph Lauren. Clementine caught her reflection in the glass and held in her tummy.

'You'll see some marvellous sights,' he said.

'India's full of poor people. They'll smell like Constancia.'

'That's not nice. Anyway, Constancia's from Haiti.' Constancia was their maid. 'And you'll see Granny Greenslade.'

'You said she was doolally,' said Clementine.

'I didn't! I don't even use that word.'

'I heard you talking to Mom.'

'I just said she was a little vague. She is seventy-three.'

'Gross.'

'Stop saying that, sweetie.' He thought of the fortune they spent on her education.

'She can't even *email*.'

'Just because you spend half your time glued to the screen.' He was sure Clementine was spending it in some unsuitable chat room, probably run by a paedophile. He remembered his mother's face as she gazed at the laptop he had given her. '*Christopher dear, it's too late for me to learn.*'

Clementine stopped outside a Starbucks. 'I want a frapuccino.'

'Not now. Afterwards.'

She groaned. They trudged on. Wasn't this supposed to be fun? Clementine's state-of-the-art rollerblades weighed a ton. Nowadays Christopher felt like a pack-mule, carting his children's consumer durables from one activity to another. Maybe his daughter should be carrying the rollerblades herself – earned pleasure, all that English stuff. The trouble was, he wouldn't dare suggest it. She wouldn't have a clue what he was talking about and would gaze at him with that Elvis sneer that was becoming so familiar.

Christopher's daughter unnerved him. Nowadays she seemed to regard him with contempt. In fact he felt this about the rest of his household too. It was a struggle to retain any dignity at all in a place where even the maid seemed to treat him with conde-scension. In Haiti, no doubt, men were still men. Over the years the suspicion had been growing that he was surplus to require-ments. Having inseminated his wife – it had been a late marriage for both of them and time was running short – he felt he had little to offer a woman who was so very capable of doing every-thing else herself.

Once he had found this stimulating. When they met he had been thirty-nine, working in the City and living in bachelor squalor in Clapham. He had his routine – squash on Tuesdays, the pub on Fridays. In fact with his Golf GTI convertible he considered himself quite a man about town. One by one, however, his friends had deserted him; the pub crowd had dwindled, picked off by the sniper fire of the opposite sex.

That he himself hadn't found the right girl was due to inertia. He realised this when Marcia blazed into his life with her power suits and organisational skills. She had been seconded to the London office for six months and for some reason made a bee-line for him. Maybe the old biological clock was ticking, for – not to put too fine a point on it – she was no spring chicken. She had been too busy working her way up the corporate ladder to think about starting a family. Nor, he had to admit, had he found Marcia that attractive on first meeting – sallow skin, heavy features and the thick eyebrows her daughter was to inherit. He, however, was powerless, drawn by the force-field of her personality. What a bracing contrast she was to his conventional English upbringing!

Within a week he surrendered himself up to her flashing eyes and vigorous lovemaking. Within a month she had moved in and sorted things out. 'You take your WASHING home to your MOTHER?' He remembered so well that slack-jawed, pitying look. He had become familiar with it over the years, particularly when the various investments he had made, on his family's and his mother's behalf, had gone so very wrong. Of course the market had been depressed since 9/11 but he had to admit that he had made some unwise decisions. Still, they were all right, weren't they? A comfortable life-style on the Upper East Side and his mother settled in a home that didn't drain her finances and that had many advantages compared to its equivalent in England. And her letters sounded cheerful enough, all the little comings and goings. She had been twittering on about some new sandals. For the old, the world shrank to their immediate surroundings; it scarcely mattered where they were. It was as if they were babies again; apparently her hotel even served jelly and custard.

They walked past the Met. An elderly woman sat on its steps. She was surrounded by plastic bags and held an empty styrofoam cup. A well-dressed woman, she bore a faint resemblance to his Ma.

134

Christopher felt a lurch of guilt. How easy it was to persuade himself that everything was all right! He had always been good at self-justification. In fact – to be really, truly honest, he had reduced his mother to penury. She deserved a contented old age in the bosom of her family and what had he done? Fuck all. Off he'd buggered to New York and weeks went by when, absorbed by his own distracting life, he didn't think about her at all.

The woman's gaze met his. *What have you done?* Christopher fumbled for his wallet. *I gave you life itself, and you dumped me like a bag of rubbish.* A police car sped past, its siren wailing.

It was then that he realised his mistake. The cup contained dregs of coffee. The bag-lady was simply an exhausted shopper.

Christopher had barely paused, thank God. Nobody had noticed.

In Central Park, Christopher strapped his daughter's skinny legs into the boots. She tottered along the tarmac. She managed to do even this as if humouring her old Dad, as if this hour with him was just an interval before she got back to her real life.

'That's the girl, Clem! Great!' He heard his own voice, over-boisterous. She wobbled. He held out his hand but she was determined to do it alone.

Three black dudes sped past. One carried a ghetto-blaster; music thumped out. People were biking, jogging, practising obscure Eastern postures. Marcia was a New Yorker. He loved this energy in the city, the utter lack of self-consciousness. The trouble was, he couldn't let himself go. He felt as if he were an onlooker at his own life, watching his actions from a distance. At this moment he was a father having quality time with his daughter – over-reacting, over-enthusiastic, his voice booming with false bonhomie. He could see that it was a beautiful autumn day – foliage on fire, the twin spires of the San Remo building rearing into the sky – but all he was thinking was how to describe it later to show Marcia he had noticed.

One of the black guys swerved and turned with consummate grace. He was simply himself; he wasn't split in this awful English way. Christopher thought: If only I could fuse myself together. His sister Theresa, who was into all that Indian stuff, went on about wholeness, about shedding the something to reach a higher state of awareness. She had even sent him a book, printed on what looked like lavatory paper, written by a Bhagwan thingy and with the passages on *stress* underlined. Theresa meditated; she did yoga. How come, then, that she was the unhappiest person he knew?

'Can we go now?' asked Clementine.

'What, already?'

'We've been here for *ages*.'

She steadied herself on a bench and bent to undo her boots. At that moment one of the black guys drew up, with a hiss, and came to a standstill beside her.

'Hey, you stopping so soon?'

He held out his hand. Clementine blushed pink. She hesitated, glancing at her father. Then she slipped her hand into the large black one and they were off.

Christopher watched them rollerblading side by side – Clementine tiny, the man huge. She was laughing – really laughing, childish shrieks of excitement. The man slowed down for her. His red T-shirt matched her jacket.

Sitting on a bench, Christopher watched them. Or, to be accurate, he watched himself – a middle-aged man, paunchy now, wearing grey tracksuit bottoms with a vinaigrette stain on the knee – he watched himself watching his daughter spirited away by a black god and laughing for joy.

5

What we are today comes from our thoughts of yesterday, and our present thoughts build our life of tomorrow: our life is the creation of the mind.

(Dhammapada)

Dr Rama had a powerful effect on the female residents of the Marigold. During November several of them became ill. Their complaints were not life-threatening but were apparently beyond the scope of Mrs Cowasjee, whose area of expertise, indeed, was somewhat limited. Dr Rama would be summoned to attend to the patients in the privacy of their rooms. Later, when they compared notes, they discovered that he had put them all on antibiotics but that didn't lessen him in their esteem. After all, antibiotics were meant to cure practically everything, weren't they?

'Dr Rama, what a charmer,' crooned Stella, gulping down the pills with a glass of boiled water. She was quite alone in the world. 'To be frank, it's him who's the best tonic.'

'Is anything more handsome than a handsome Indian?' said Madge, who had been frequenting the hotel bars in search of her rich maharaja. So far she had only found one: he was eighty-six, however, and looked like Yassar Arafat. '*One does have some standards,*' she had sighed.

'Norman's nose is out of joint,' said Evelyn.

'Serves him right,' said Madge. 'The old coot.'

For Norman was no longer cock of the roost. Some of the women had been immune to his charms but a surprising number had responded blushingly to his gallantries and laughed, sometimes uncomprehendingly, at his blue jokes. Madge had been right; in some sense, when one reached a certain age, any man would do. They had all witnessed this back in England where any recently widowed male, however unappetising and dilapidated, found himself inundated with females eager to take care of him. The reverse, of course, was not the case. Such was the brutal fact of life.

Muriel was not a member of the Dr Rama Fan Club. She said there was something funny about him.

'He's not like a real doctor,' she said. 'When I had my palpitations he put the stethoscope the wrong way round.'

Evelyn put this down to racism. She knew, from what Muriel had said, that the woman didn't trust foreigners. Early on she had heard Muriel muttering about darkies and wondered why on earth she had come to India if she had that sort of attitude. Now, of course, she knew the reason: Muriel's son was in the country. It all made sense – well, a sort of sense. What blind faith could lead Muriel to believe that just because she was in the same subcontinent as her son she would find him? Muriel hadn't told her much: just that Keith was wanted by the police for some fraud he hadn't committed – according to Muriel, he hadn't – and had fled to India to track down the business associate who had betrayed him. It all seemed highly improbable. Muriel had sworn her to secrecy and not spoken of it since. In fact, she seemed to be avoiding her. Evelyn tried not to take this personally; she knew, from experience, that those who receive confidences can be subsequently resented.

The irony was that despite her prejudices Muriel had sopped up more Indian ways than any of them. The Ainslies presumed themselves superior in this respect but Muriel seemed to have absorbed subcontinental beliefs straight into her bloodstream; it seemed to answer something in her nature. She regularly read her horoscope with Mrs Cowasjee, with whom she had become pally; she had had her fortune told by the man with the parrot in the bazaar opposite. The scent of joss-sticks drifted from her room and Stella swore that she had heard her chanting some incantation, though Stella's hearing was not to be trusted.

One day in late November an outing was planned to the Nrityagram Dance Village, twenty miles away. A minibus was booked but Muriel refused to go.

'It's an inauspicious day,' she said. 'Mrs Gee-Gee told me.'

She meant Mrs Cowasjee, of course. 'Why do you call her Mrs Gee-Gee?' asked Evelyn.

'Well I can't call her Mrs Cow can I?'

Stella lowered her voice. 'She can be a bit of a cow sometimes.'

'It doesn't mean the same thing here, Stella,' said Jean Ainslie. 'Cows are holy in India, it would probably be taken as a compliment.' She turned to Muriel. 'Why is it inauspicious?'

'Search me. She just said it was.' Muriel chuckled. 'Watch out or you'll get bitten by another monkey.'

As it turned out, the minibus broke down on the journey home. It had taken a while to repair, apparently with a length of twine donated by a roadside coconut-seller, and they were late for dinner. Plus Madge had lost her sun-glasses.

'See what I meant?' said Muriel triumphantly. 'What did I tell you?'

Evelyn alone knew the reason for Muriel's belief in supernatural forces. Prayers, spells, who cared? She was prepared to enlist any help in her quest to be reunited with her son. A bit of a long shot, but then this was India, land of miracles.

Dinner was cream of something soup, nobody could quite work it out, followed by a choice of fried fish or mutton pillau. People talked about the day's expedition: the charming dancers, the pot-holed roads, the lack of air-conditioning on the bus, for that too seemed to have given up the struggle for life. Evelyn had stayed behind; her hip was playing up and besides she relished a day when she had the hotel practically to herself. She had written letters and ventured out to the bazaar, where she had given a rupee to the legless beggar and bought some oranges. She even knew the word for oranges now: *santara*.

She was sitting with the Ainslies and Olive Cooke, a chatty woman whose husband had worked for BP and who had lived all over the world. They were discussing Hong Kong.

'Our son Adam made a documentary there,' said Jean. 'About Norman Foster's buildings. It was nominated for a BAFTA.'

As always, the Ainslies made Evelyn feel inadequate – their happy marriage, their achieving son at the BBC, their worldwide travel experiences. Evelyn thought of her own village, its high spot the yearly Cross-stitch Extravaganza in the community hall.

'His old boss is arriving here next week,' Jean said. 'A woman called Dorothy Miller, quite a legend apparently. We're dying to meet her, aren't we, Douggy?'

'Sounds a bit formidable,' said Douglas. 'What *is* this soup? Any ideas?'

Evelyn was thinking about her own son. She was looking forward to his visit with mixed feelings. Of course she wanted to see him, and the grandchildren whom she had not seen for so long, but she simply couldn't imagine Christopher in India. How would he react to this place? And what about that daunting American wife of his? What would she think of the stained table-cloths and fly-bespattered strip light? Americans were so hygienic. Seeing the hotel through Marcia's eyes made Evelyn realise how shabby it was.

Jimmy, with trembling hands, lifted up her soup plate and took it away.

'To be honest,' whispered Douglas, 'it should be *us* looking after *him*.'

What would Christopher think of the palsied servants, of the taps that coughed out brown water? Maybe he would sweep up Evelyn and take her back to New York. If he were Indian he would do that, but then if he were Indian he would never have let his mother come here in the first place.

Actually, thought Evelyn, I wouldn't want to go. Sitting there at dinner, she realised she had grown fond of her fellow residents. They were all in the same boat, all deserted in one way or another by those they had loved, and now they had to stick together. After two months they had become a sort of family; even those she didn't particularly like had grown so familiar that concepts of liking or disliking had become irrelevant. England was distant now, it was another life; it was these people now who concerned her. Some might get ill and go into hospital. Some might succumb to homesickness and return to Britain. The slightly odd ones would no doubt become odder, herself included. Some might – they would – die. They would all die.

'You on for *Inspector Morse*?' asked Douglas.

Evelyn nodded. Graham's great-nephew had sent a video of *Inspector Morse* from England. Graham didn't look like the sort of man who had relatives, but he obviously had. Maybe nobody had asked him. Those not exhausted by the trip were planning to watch that nice John Thaw after dinner.

Evelyn ate a mouthful of trifle. It was startlingly coloured, with hundreds and thousands on top. It reminded her of her children's birthday parties and there was a comfort in that. Whatever happened, there was always comfort to be found in the small things of life.

Pauline passed the fax to Ravi. 'Dad says this new woman is completely bonkers.'

'What?'

'This Dorothy Miller. He says she wanders around singing nursery rhymes.'

'Your father thinks everybody's bonkers except himself,' said Ravi. 'He's so bloody competitive.'

'Surely she can't be senile? I thought everyone had to have a doctor's report before they went there.'

This sounded like an accusation. Pauline hadn't meant this but whatever she said nowadays came out like a complaint. It was Ravi's fault. He was so prickly.

'Don't you want to read it?' she asked. 'It's quite funny.'

Ravi glanced at the fax but she could see he was only skimming. She tried to change the tone.

'One of my clients, her mother has Alzheimer's,' she said. 'The old dear turned up at the airport carrying three handbags. It took them ages to get through the security checks.'

Ravi paused, lost in thought, and went on loading the dishwasher. He rinsed the plates so thoroughly that it seemed a pointless exercise to put them into the dishwasher at all.

'*And* she was wearing a body belt,' said Pauline.

Still no response.

Pauline indicated the fax. 'Did you read that bit about the birthday cake? The cook spelling birthday with a U?'

Ravi closed the door of the machine and turned the dial. Suddenly Pauline broke out in a sweat – menopause, anger, one or the other. 'You don't seem to care what happens there, as long as you're making a profit.'

'That's not true –'

'You used to be such an idealist.'

'But what's wrong with the place?' said Ravi. 'You tell me. You said it was charming, you said it was as if time had stood still. You said you'd live there yourself if you were old enough.'

'The whole thing was extraordinary. I wish you'd been there.' Actually, Pauline thought, I don't.

'You've been quite different since you've come home,' Ravi said.

'The country had a strong effect on me.'

'Everyone says that about India.'

'I'm not everyone –'

'You British go there – oh the poverty, oh the sunsets!'

'Stop lumping us together –'

'You romanticise the place, you always have, but you're all the same, you take what you want from it, the British always have, then you get the hell out and it carries on just like before –'

'*You* got the hell out.'

'That's because I couldn't stand it,' he said.

'Why?'

Ravi folded a tea towel. 'You haven't the remotest idea what it's really like. You all come back with your bazaar bargains, mouthing a lot of mystic tosh –'

'Why couldn't you stand it?' she asked.

'Because I was suffocating.'

Ravi left the kitchen. From the lounge, she heard the sound of the ten o'clock TV news. She knew from experience that there was no point in continuing this conversation.

Pauline went upstairs. Nowadays she and Ravi no longer built up to quarrels; their life was one long rumbling argument interrupted

142

by work or sleep. It was a chronic argument with a life of its own; it was an intestinal parasite sucking their nourishment, sucking them dry.

She had thought it was the Ravison business that had changed her husband but India had made her realise something: Ravi hadn't changed at all, he had just become more himself – chilly, focused elsewhere, not really a husband at all. He was a single man who happened to have a wife. Maybe this was how most married Indians behaved and she hadn't realised until she had gone to a country full of Ravi look-alikes. Marriage was something you got settled before you carried on with your life. He simply didn't connect with her at all. Oh she knew he had to put up a self-protective shield, simply to do his job at the hospital. No doubt caring for strangers was easier than caring for those one loved. The trouble was, the more neglected she felt the less lovable she became. She watched herself becoming whiny and resentful; she was becoming hateful to herself.

Pauline sat down on the bed. The springs creaked. How she had desired him once! It was Ravi's foreignness that had aroused her; the jolt of the unknown. She remembered their first date, a meal in a French restaurant long since gone, his brown hand laid on the white table-cloth, the glimpse of his throat in the open-necked shirt, the thick black hairs there. She had pictured his brown cock, as yet safely zipped in his trousers. Maybe tonight we shall kiss. Will his saliva taste different? Will he smell different? Tonight, maybe, I will wrap my legs around the naked body of an Indian man. Weak with desire, she could hardly eat.

Love is perverse, she thought. The very element that inflames can carry, within itself, its own destruction. What had seemed mysterious now seemed simply opaque. Impenetrable. *Dull*.

India had explained her husband. Like a kaleidoscope, India had shaken Ravi and settled his pieces into a different arrangement. She saw him more clearly now; she could even understand why he had left. *I was suffocating*. Being in India was like being in the tube in rush hour – all those people, the press of them, the clamour of them, you had to shut down. If not, the sheer volume of that teeming, inert desperation would destroy you. And then

143

there was his family, some of whom she had met over the years when they visited London. *You romanticise the place.* At the beginning she had envied him his parents and siblings and cousins. Coming from a small family herself she had indeed romanticised them. She could see now, however, that there was something oppressive about their demands. No wonder he had simply bailed out.

The awful thing was that now she finally understood her husband she was no longer interested.

Outside, a gale was blowing. It had been a wild autumn. Pauline opened the wardrobe and took out a plastic bag. It was filled with photos. She took them out and spread them on the bed.

Some of the photos were of the Marigold: the peeling bungalow smothered with creepers. They called it a bungalow but in fact it was two storeys high. In one photo she saw a face in an upstairs window. Who was gazing out? She hadn't noticed at the time. Another photo showed her father sitting on the veranda outside his room; she could tell, by the tilt of his head, that he was listening to the cricket on the radio. During her stay she had grown fonder of him; it was easier without Ravi being around to wince at her Dad's daily bulletins on his bowel movements. Her father seemed to be tolerated at the Marigold more easily than at his other Homes, perhaps because there were no pretty females on the staff. Or maybe Indians were just more accepting of odd behaviour, especially by the British. They had had to put up with it long enough.

Pauline shuffled through the photos. One showed a lady, whose name she had forgotten, painting at an easel. Another showed four of the residents, all women, sitting in the garden. The photo was over-exposed and somewhat blurred. She couldn't work out what they were doing, if in fact they were doing anything at all. Nor could she recognise them; the women were as insubstantial as ghosts in their pale summer dresses. There were only a few of them then, the first arrivals, but already they had faded from her memory, outdazzled by the life outside the garden walls.

For during the afternoons, when her father was dozing, Pauline had explored the neighbourhood. Most of the photos were of the children she had met in the streets. They had clamoured around, jostling to get in the picture. In the photos their smiles were stilled, their hands outstretched for boiled sweets. They melted her heart. It was a feeling that made her legs weak, a feeling more profound than the desire she had felt for Ravi all those years ago in the Antoinette restaurant. Most of the children were boys; in one photo they danced in the water from a burst pipe. They were desperately poor, but how different from the shaven-headed thugs from the estate behind Plender Street, kids with men's faces who smashed wing-mirrors as they swaggered down the street. Theirs was a different kind of poverty. *You take what you want from us. The British always have.* If only she could give them back their photos; these were probably the only photos that would ever be taken of them, proof of their existence. But how could she send them? She didn't know these children's names and addresses. She could hardly write to: *Two boys, c/o the Rubbish Heap behind the Paradise Cinema, Bangalore.*

She knew that she was going back. It wasn't just her father's presence that was pulling her there. Pauline replaced the photos in their bag and went downstairs.

Ravi was watching some cop drama. This mildly surprised her; he never watched that sort of thing. She could tell, by the back of his head, that he knew she had come into the room. She thought: He's as miserable as I am.

She said: 'Let's go there for Christmas. Please, Ravi.'

Please say yes or I might go there and never come back.

'Have you heard from your charming daughter?'

'She's fine,' said Norman. 'Absolutely fine.' He was having a drink with Sonny in the Gymkhana Club. 'Got a phone call yesterday. She's coming out for Christmas.'

'Excuse me!' Sonny jumped up and ran after a man who was crossing the bar. Norman watched him gesticulating. The fellow couldn't sit still. Their conversation had been interrupted twice already by Sonny's mobile phone.

Sonny returned to the table. 'Please – carry on.'

'You should calm down, old chap,' said Norman. *'We're* the ones who're supposed to be having the heart attacks.'

'What can I do? There's nobody I can trust, everything I'm having to do myself. These people I do business with, they cheat me, they do another deal behind my back . . .'

Sonny rattled on. Norman wondered when he could bring up the subject he had come to discuss. It was a matter of some delicacy. A tiger's-head was mounted on the wall nearby; it stared glassily ahead, avoiding Norman's eye.

'Any problems at the hotel? You must tell me, Norman old boy.' Sonny twinkled. 'You are my spy.'

'They're all obsessed by that bloody doctor. Got them in a twitter. You'd think the sun shines out of his arse.'

'Women!' Sonny shrugged.

Norman took a breath. 'That's what I wanted to talk to you about –'

'Please! A moment.'

Sonny jumped up and waylaid a group of men who were just leaving the bar. Norman subsided into his chair. The Gymkhana Club was a vast old building filled with potted palms and slaughtered animals. It was built for the British of course but now it was full of brown faces. Norman had been there a couple of times before, as Sonny's guest – the only way a chap like him could get in nowadays. Relics of the Raj remained – photos of past presidents hanging in the lobby and a list of team members, inscribed in gold, fixed to the wall of the cavernous billiards room. Cockaded bearers, carrying trays of drinks, glided from table to table. From his sojourns in the tropics Norman was familiar with clubs like this one. In the past he had found them reassuring. Now he was older, however, a place like this made him feel as if he were already extinct.

Sonny returned to his seat. Norman lit a cigarette. 'You're a man of the world, old fruit,' he said. Almost family, in fact. The realisation always gave him a jolt. 'Must have knocked around a bit.' He knew Sonny had a wife but the man never seemed to mention her. 'Thing is, a chap can get lonely for a bit of female company. I've heard that the women in Bangalore can be very, well, accommodating. If you get my drift.'

Sonny was fidgeting. His eyes flickered around the room. Norman soldiered on.

'I was wondering if you could point me in the right direction. You know, make some sort of an introduction. Something of that kind. In the most discreet sense.'

'What?' asked Sonny.

'I'm looking for a friendly, experienced woman –'

'But you're surrounded by women.' Sonny chuckled. 'You could go bedroom-hopping, a different lady every night.'

Norman put down his drink. 'You must be joking. Bit long in the tooth, aren't they?'

'So are you, old chap.'

Norman shifted in his seat. Really, the fellow needn't have put it like that. Had the man no tact at all?

Sonny, who seemed anxious to leave, called for the chit. Norman took an auto-rickshaw back to the hotel. It bounced over the potholes; the driver's gee-gaws – little bells and mascots – swung on their strings. Norman crouched under the plastic canopy. The conversation had, of course, humiliated him. Didn't Sonny understand that, when he reached a certain age, a chap might start experiencing problems of an intimate nature? The prostate op hadn't helped, but to be frank he had been experiencing difficulties in the hydraulics department for some time now. Only a professional woman could help him – indeed, had been able to help him in the past. They had to be foreign of course – Nigerian, Thai, Malay. Only a different colour skin could get his mojo working. Women like these knew how to satisfy a man, it was in their culture.

The rickshaw bounced along the road, past Cubbon Park. Norman gripped the rail as it swerved around a roundabout. In the middle sat a statue of Queen Victoria, spattered in bird-droppings.

With women like that, a chap didn't have to engage in embarrassing conversation; no demands of that nature.

And they didn't laugh at him.

Sonny was fuming. He tried the number on his mobile again. No bloody answer, of course.

147

He leaned forward in his seat. 'Guess who I met at the club,' he told his driver. 'That rascal Freddie. He knows where that son-of-a-bitch PK has gone. The fellow looked shifty to me.'

They were speeding along MG Road, weaving in and out of the traffic. Jatan Singh was an adept driver; like many Sikhs he had a profound love of motors. For twenty years he had been working for Sonny and knew more of his secrets than anybody in Bangalore.

'He thinks he can give me the slip, the *haraami*,' said Sonny. 'I'll track him down, Jatanji, I'll track him down and roast him alive.'

PK, his erstwhile associate, had been eluding him for three weeks now. There had been a couple of sightings. Sonny's brother-in-law had seen him at a ministerial cocktail party; somebody else had glimpsed him at one of his building sites, an office complex out beyond Defence Colony, but for all Sonny knew he could have flown to the States or to London where he had business interests. PK was a crook, of course. By judicious backhanders his company had landed the contracts for several major developments, including a residential building on a plot of land Sonny had bought on the Airport Road. All that was acceptable enough. The trouble was, the man had sub-contracted the building work to his own brother's construction outfit which, by faking invoices, had used sub-standard materials.

'I'll have his guts for garters,' muttered Sonny as the car sped along MG Road. Three weeks ago, when only half-completed, the bloody building had collapsed. Investigations had revealed that there had been too much sand in the cement and now the *chootiya* had disappeared.

'Step on it, Jatanji!'

His mobile rang. It was a familiar voice. 'Where are you, *mera chota beta*? Is your life so busy that you've forgotten your poor old mother who has been sitting here waiting for you since an hour?'

Hai Raba! He had forgotten that he was supposed to take her to the optician.

'No, I can tell you have better things to do,' his mother sighed. 'I'll tell Anand to call for a taxi –'

148

'No, Mummyji –'

'I can go alone, my legs will have to carry me –'

'Wait –!'

'They're not giving me too much pain today, and I will tell Mr Desai that you have more important things on your mind –'

'I'm coming! Give me ten minutes!' Sonny switched off the phone. 'Turn the car round! *Jaldi!*'

Sonny sank back in his seat. And he had forgotten to pick up a box of *gulab jamuns* from her favourite shop, Darpan's Electric Bakery. He had promised, when he left the house that morning.

Sonny's temples throbbed. He pictured his mother, vast, steaming with impatience, waiting by the door. If only his wife could calm her down but for the past week they had not been on speaking terms. Sonny could no longer remember the cause of this particular row nor, to be truthful, did he care. Something to do with the kitchen arrangements, no doubt.

After a prolonged and active bachelorhood Sonny had married, late in life, a woman he had thought would be no trouble – plain, self-effacing, grateful to find a husband at all. Her apparent pliancy, however, disguised a steely determination to get her own way. This was usually attempted by pleading illness, a technique with which, in his mother, she had met her match. *Females.* How could anyone understand them? Norman Purse, he could tell, was a fellow sufferer. Still, thought Sonny, bugger me if I'm going to be the chap's pimp. What would happen if word got out, to Norman's daughter or to Ravi-sahib? It would put Sonny in an embarrassing position. Besides, the fellow was too old for that sort of caper. He should be enjoying a peaceful retirement in his hen coop.

The Merc inched down Brigade Road. The street was clogged with traffic. At the intersection two buses blocked the thoroughfare, each refusing to budge. Men, clinging to the sides, dropped down on to the road to join in the argument. Sonny leaned out of the window and yelled at them to get out of the bloody way.

Slumped back in his seat, Sonny gazed at Karishma Plaza. It had been his first property speculation; in a moment of filial piety he had named it after his mother. Twenty years had passed, however; the windows were rusting.

Across the street rose the wall of the Marigold. Bougainvillaea frothed over the top; behind it rose the flame trees. Sonny thought of the shady garden and its occupants, passing their twilit years in the safety of its compound. In England people dumped their parents in places like this, it was perfectly acceptable. Then they got on with their own lives. Sonny imagined this. It gave him an airy feeling, as if somebody had cut his strings and up he floated, into the sky. Horn blaring, the car shunted forward. He pictured his mother's outrage if he suggested such a thing. Not just outrage – total incomprehension. Just for a moment, however, it seemed an excellent idea. He could visit her once a week and give her a box of *jalebis* instead of dreading the return to his own home.

For he did dread it. As the car drew nearer he was gripped by the familiar feeling of guilt and suffocation. It grew stronger by the minute. He felt like a small boy – he, a man of fifty-two.

Suddenly Sonny realised that he always felt like this. However busy he was, flying hither and thither across the globe, underneath it all he remained a son. Oh, he might look like a man but appearances are deceptive. After all, this was India.

6

*The person who is searching for his own happiness should pull out
the dart that he has stuck in himself – the arrow-head of grieving,
of desiring, of despair.*

(The Sutta-nipata)

'Hi Mum, I'm here.'
    'Where?'
    'Here, in India.'
    'What?'
    'I'm here, in India!'
    'Where?'
    'Uttar Pradesh.'
    'Utter what?'
    'I'm in Uttar Pradesh!'
    'You're *here*?'
    'In an ashram.'
    'What?'
    'I'm in an ashram! I'll be with you for Christmas.'
    'What?'
    'I'll see you at Christmas!'
    'But I'm just wrapping your present.'
    'What?'
    'I was going to send it to you.'
    'You can give it to me instead. Honestly, is that your only
reaction?'
    'What?'
    'I said –'

'I can't hear!'

'I thought you'd like a surprise.'

'What?'

'Oh never mind. I'll ring you when I'm coming.'

The line went dead. Evelyn put down the phone and slumped back on her bed. Of course she was thrilled that her daughter was coming but she also felt drained. She had forgotten this particular brand of exhaustion that only Theresa could produce. Why hadn't she told her earlier? Evelyn had known her daughter was going to visit at some point but why hadn't she given her any warning? Of course, Evelyn knew the answer. Theresa didn't function like that. Evelyn's heart thumped. Where was her daughter going to stay? As far as she knew, the hotel was full. Theresa wouldn't – oh please God – sleep in her room, would she? There was a twin bed. Maybe Evelyn could get it removed. She could pretend it had never been there.

Had Theresa come to see her, a daughter–mother thing, or to find spiritual solace? Evelyn guessed the answer to this. Over the past years it had become clear that India had given Theresa something that she herself could not supply.

Oh Lord, Christopher would be here too. Did Theresa know this? Christopher and his family were coming just before Christmas, though thankfully staying at the Taj Balmoral Hotel. Oh Lord. Christopher. Theresa. *Marcia.*

She must phone Christopher and warn him. No – not warn him, of course. Tell him the good news that his sister was coming.

Oh heavens. If only she could pray but Evelyn knew, definitively, that prayers no longer worked. If only she were Muriel she could offer up something to a god. Krishna, the one with the blue face, was Muriel's current favourite; she had installed a plaster figurine in her room. She had even been spotted removing a shortbread finger from the sideboard to give him after tea. But then Indians believed that God is everywhere. They prayed to film posters, to anything. They simply draped them in flowers and believed.

Evelyn looked at the possessions she had brought from England – framed photos, her silver hairbrush, the water-colour of West

Wittering. She could hardly ply them with biscuits, she wasn't completely ga-ga. Anyway it hadn't worked, had it? Muriel's son still hadn't appeared. Only the day before, she had asked Muriel if there was any news from the neighbours in Chigwell, Muriel's only contact. '*Not a sausage*,' Muriel had replied. If her son didn't know his mother was in India how on earth could he find her, with or without divine intervention?

Poor Muriel, thought Evelyn. At least I have my children.

This thought was less of a reassurance than she had hoped. She gazed at the soapstone buddha she had bought Theresa for Christmas. On Tuesday there had been an outing to the First Choice Craft Emporium on Mahatma Gandhi Road. This was an establishment owned by a charming gentleman who said he would give them all a special price as they were friends of his good friend Sonny-sahib. As Christmas was coming they had all gone a bit mad, buying more or less useless objects made of sandalwood and brass. It had taken ages, as these transactions always did, a clerk laboriously filling out forms in triplicate and getting them stamped by the man behind the desk. Now Evelyn could give the buddha to her daughter in person!

Evelyn lifted up the phone. It was early morning in New York, she could catch Christopher before he went to work.

The line was dead.

Evelyn got up and went downstairs. It was early evening: cow hour. On the landing the young sweeper squatted beside his plastic bucket. He dipped his rag in the water, squeezed it and flicked it round the floor, rolling on his haunches, moving crablike across the landing. His torso was bare. His shoulderblades were so delicate, his neck so slender. Suddenly Evelyn was overwhelmed with tenderness – a pure, maternal rush, long lost on her own children. He smiled at her, a smile so dazzling her heart melted. Funny that he was an Untouchable when she longed so strongly to touch him – to hold his thin body in her arms and to stroke his beautiful skin. He was very dark. Indians, she had realised, were as variously coloured as the British. Dun skin, greeny-olive skin, glistening mahogany – as many variations as Norman's purple nose, Madge's leathery tan or her own papery pallor.

The sweeper edged into the corner to let her pass. He smiled, his teeth startlingly white. How simple, to radiate such goodwill! How very easy it would be to love him – no guilt, no recriminations.

Evelyn went downstairs. The lobby was empty.

'Memsahib would like a sherry?'

Evelyn jumped. It was Ayub Khan, the other elderly bearer. He was an unfortunate-looking man whose face was cratered with scars, either from acne or smallpox. For him, too, Evelyn was overwhelmed with emotion. Pity, in his case. She wanted to touch him and make him better. She wanted to touch them all.

'No thank you, Ayub.'

Goodness, thought Evelyn, this country is having a funny effect on me. Pull yourself together. Of course it was easier to feel warmth towards foreign people whose lives were wretched. Certainly easier than the large complicated human beings to whom she had given birth and whose imminent arrival filled her with such turbulence.

There was nobody behind the desk. 'Is Mr Cowasjee here?' she asked. 'The phone seems to be broken.'

Ayub Khan waggled his head. The calendar, hanging on the wall, showed a photograph of kittens. It said *November*. Evelyn had a feeling that December had already begun; in this place one lost track of time. In a few weeks her son would arrive. She must tell him the news; Christopher had always needed to prepare himself, well in advance, for the unexpected.

Evelyn gazed at the glass table, next to the settee. On it lay *Reader's Digest*, *Newsweek* and an Air France inflight magazine. They had lain there undisturbed since her arrival. Next to them, in the ashtray, lay the stub of one of Madge's cigarettes, stained scarlet. It had been there for days. Just then she couldn't imagine anyone, ever, having the energy to remove it.

Her reverie was broken by the sound of footsteps. It was the Ainslies, back from some jaunt or other. They walked briskly across the lobby.

'It's hard to believe it'll soon be Christmas,' said Evelyn brightly. 'This wonderful sunshine.'

'We've got a cassette of the King's College Carols,' said Jean.

'Doug and I play it at Christmas, wherever we are in the world.'

Evelyn stepped behind the desk, lifted the calendar off its hook and turned the page. As time went by they had all grown more proprietorial about the hotel, treating it like home. Indeed, this had become more necessary as the proprietor himself seemed less and less in evidence. December's photograph was cocker spaniel puppies.

'Both my children are coming for Christmas,' said Evelyn. She felt a timid flush of triumph about this; amongst the residents there was an undercurrent of rivalry on this subject.

'How lovely for you!' said Jean. 'Of course Adam's longing to come but we told him not to, we're quite happy. Anyway he's terribly busy, he's doing some huge series for the BBC.'

Evelyn felt deflated. The implication, of course, was that her own children had such failed lives that they had nothing better to do. Oh Lord, was this true?

Douglas looked at his watch. 'Sun's over the yard-arm,' he said. 'Time for a snort, girls?'

Evelyn declined, saying she needed to make a phone call but the line seemed to be dead. Yesterday there had been a power cut. It seemed a miracle that this country functioned at all, let alone supported a high-tech industry whose glittering office blocks rose into the sky only a mile down the road.

'Where *is* Minoo?' asked Douglas.

Evelyn lowered her voice. 'I think they're having another Domestic.' Raised voices had been heard earlier, in the annexe. 'It's such a curse. I must phone my son.'

And then she remembered what somebody had told her. There was a call centre across the road.

The Ainslies sat in their room, drinking whisky with Olive Cooke. It was cheaper than running up a tab at the hotel bar and Jean, who believed in economies, had found a liquor store at Richmond Circus and brought back a bottle of Scotch. Safe in the bedroom they felt freer to gossip.

'Guess who we saw in town,' said Jean. 'Dorothy.'

'Off on one of her walks?' asked Olive.

155

'We were just coming out of the bank – you know, Grindlays Bank in Lalbagh Street – and there she was, just wandering around looking odd.'

'The poor dear,' said Olive.

It was generally accepted that Dorothy Miller, the BBC lady, behaved strangely. For one thing she wandered off alone for long periods of time, sometimes even missing meals, and never told anyone where she had been. '*Just walking*,' she said. And with her arthritis too.

'We followed her down the street,' said Jean. 'She stood for ages outside the Mevali Tiffin Rooms, leaning on her stick.'

'Perhaps she just fancied a cup of tea,' said Douglas.

'No, there's something odd about her.' Jean refilled Olive's glass. 'Yesterday we saw her in the Old Town. We were having lunch, a simple *thali*, quite delicious. We often eat pavement food, don't we, Doug? It's perfectly safe.' She lowered her voice. 'I'm sure it's Alzheimer's, early stages.'

The residents of the Marigold, suffering the usual afflictions of age – memory loss, general vagueness – were alert for symptoms of more advanced senility in others. There was a shamefully triumphant feeling when this was spotted. Stella's report of the nursery rhyme singing had surely, in Dorothy's case, been proof of this. Apparently it had been 'Baa-Baa Black Sheep'.

'They do wander,' said Jean. 'Our friend Amy got dementia, didn't she, Doug? She went walking down to the main road in the middle of the night, in her nightie. They had to lock her up. She kept watching a video of *ET. I want to go home.* That was the bit she liked.'

'That's where they try to go,' said Olive.

'What, home?'

Olive nodded. 'To the home they've lost. Perhaps back to their childhood, who knows?'

'Funny they call a place like this a Home,' said Jean.

'It's not a Home,' said Douglas sharply. 'It's a residential hotel.' He drained his glass. 'And I don't think we should talk about her like that.'

Douglas was fond of Dorothy Miller. In general, however, she wasn't popular. This was partly because Dorothy was a late arrival, an outsider when friendships had already been formed and patterns established. This would not have been a problem if she had joined in but she was generally considered stand-offish. She ate alone, a book propped in front of her, and refused to play bridge. Of course there were other loners – Graham Turner, for instance – but he was a sad old bachelor whom everybody pitied. Nobody could pity Dorothy.

Douglas, however, felt a certain admiration for her. This was partly because she had been a support to his son, Adam, in his career. But it was more than that. Surrounded by chattering women it was a relief to find somebody with no small talk, somebody so entirely unfluffy. He liked Dorothy's plain face and square hands. She occupied the next room and when he woke at night he heard, faintly, the sound of her radio. Surely nobody entirely ga-ga would listen to the World Service?

Douglas looked at his wife. Her nose was peeling. Two weeks ago an arrangement had been set up with the Meridian Hotel, a concrete edifice that loomed up beyond the waste ground at the back. For a nominal fee its pool had been made available to the residents of the Marigold. Several of them had been going there to swim and to sunbathe, an unwise decision in Jean's case. Not only did she burn, she also broke out in a mildly disfiguring heat rash. Douglas couldn't dissuade her, however; she enjoyed sipping cocktails and showing off her German to the airline crews.

Douglas turned away. He was suddenly overcome with such a powerful feeling he could scarcely breathe. Don't think it, he told himself. Don't even *think* of thinking it.

Darkness had fallen. Evelyn paused beside the *paan*-seller's stall. A stack of leaves glistened in the light from his spirit lamp. He had a chopping board and little pots of paste, like the glue pots at school. Madge, always game, had tried chewing some *paan* but she said the little bits of nut got caught underneath her bridge.

Beyond the stalls stood the shabby concrete office building. 'Karishma Plaza' was inscribed over the entrance. Lights blazed from the windows. The call centre seemed to be open all night;

Evelyn had seen the lights on her nocturnal rambles in the garden.

'Madam would like a *santara*?' The fruit-seller held out two oranges, one in each hand like a juggler.

Evelyn shook her head and, stepping round a shrouded body, hurried into the building. In the lobby a man sat behind a desk. She asked for the call centre and he pointed upstairs.

Evelyn walked up a flight of stairs, pushed open a swing door and found herself in an open-plan office. It was divided by partitions into little booths. In each booth sat an operative, wearing a head-set. There must have been fifty of them. They all seemed to be talking at once.

Evelyn clutched the piece of paper. It had Christopher's New York phone number written on it. Nowadays she had to write everything down. The only phone number she could remember, curiously enough, was the Hotpoint repair man in Chichester.

A minute passed. Nobody seemed to notice her, they were all too busy. Evelyn was mildly surprised. She had vaguely expected a reception desk and customers waiting to use the phones, something of that kind.

Then she noticed another curious thing. Affixed to each booth was the name of its occupant. She could only read the ones nearest her: *Sally Spears, Michael Parker, Mary Johnson*. But the people sitting in the booths were Indian – young men and women, dressed in jeans but definitely Indian.

Evelyn listened to the girl in the nearest booth. 'Good afternoon,' she said, 'this is Sally Spears calling, may I take a moment of your time?'

Good afternoon? It was seven o'clock at night. Evelyn's head span. Really, she must be getting confused. She was always getting things wrong. It was Hugh's death that had done it. She had been perfectly all right until then; afterwards, however, she had felt like Alice stepping through the looking-glass into a world where nothing quite made sense any more.

'Hi, are you looking for anybody?' The young woman removed her head-set.

'I want to make a call to New York,' said Evelyn.

The young woman frowned. On the wall hung a sign: *You Don't*

Have To Be Mad To Work Here But It Helps.

'I think I've come to the wrong place,' said Evelyn.

'This is a call centre,' said the girl. 'You can't make calls here.'

'But isn't – I mean –'

'*I* can make calls, aunty, but you can't.'

Sally explained. She and her colleagues were calling businesses in England and selling them things over the phone – life insurance; cheque recovery schemes, whatever they were. 'It's telesales,' she said. 'That's why we work at night, because of the time difference.'

'Goodness.'

'Quick!' Sally pulled Evelyn into her booth. 'The super's watching, the old dragon.' She sat Evelyn down on the swivel chair and squatted beside her. 'They tell us things about England but I've never been there. I want to go so much.'

'I'm sure you will one day.'

'You can help me, please!' She grabbed Evelyn's wrist. 'Tell me about England.'

'Well, it's not like here. It's a lot colder –'

'You see, some of the people we call, they smell a rat.'

'Why?'

'Because we're supposed to be calling from England! We mustn't let on that we're in Bangalore. That's why we've got English names. I'm really Surinda.'

'That's a pretty name –'

'We have to pretend we're English, we've been learning how to sound English, *do re mi*, all that junk, a teacher comes and gives us lessons.' She lowered her voice. 'Tell me about Enfield, aunty.'

'Enfield?'

'That's where we're supposed to come from, all of us.'

Evelyn tried to gather her wits. 'Enfield. Now let me see . . .' She tried to remember if she had ever been there. Surinda, lips parted, was gazing at her. She was a little plump, but very pretty. Her T-shirt said FCUK. 'I remember,' said Evelyn. 'I went to a tea dance in Enfield once . . .' Suddenly it was there, crystal-clear. A June day, it was always June. She wore her dress with the white

159

collar and the tiny red roses. 'It was in the Windsor Hotel, and I
went with my friend Annabel because she lived near there, a big
house with lots of dogs, and I was jealous of her because she was
coming out and I wasn't –'

'Coming out?'

'And I danced with Teddy Ramsbottom who had been terribly
brave in the war, he still had a piece of shrapnel in his leg but he
danced so beautifully . . .' Evelyn's voice trailed away. She sat
there, lost in her memories. 'We sat out a dance in the garden,
and I only saw he had a limp later, when he was walking to his
car, it was his father's car, an Austin Seven, and that was the last
I saw of him.'

There was a silence. Through the partition she could hear a
voice. '. . . it's at a very affordable price, Mr Bishop, and we can
offer a discount if you pay within fourteen days.'

'Is Enfield near Liverpool?' asked Surinda.

'No, dear. It's near London.'

'Oh. I thought it was where the Beatles came from.'

'No, only Annabel.' Evelyn paused. 'And she went to live in
Australia in 1953.'

Evelyn hurried up the drive. Dinner must have already begun.
Outside was the hooting traffic, the cacophany of the street, but
once through the gates a hush fell, as if the hotel created its own
silence.

In the lobby she met Madge and Sonny. They were both dressed
up, Sonny in a cream silk tunic, a little too tight.

'See you later alligator,' said Madge. She wore a sequinned top
that revealed her tanned, wrinkled cleavage. 'We're off to a
wedding. Sonny's going to introduce me to a maharaja who's got
his own plane.'

'So your children are coming for Christmas!' said Sonny. 'A
little birdie told me. I knew I was right.' He chuckled. 'Quicker
than Connex South-East and almost as cheap!'

'I've just had an extraordinary encounter across the road,' said
Evelyn. She told them about the call centre.

'Ah, the manager is a good chum of mine,' said Sonny. 'It's a very popular place to work, they're all graduates you know, a lot of get-up-and-go. You see, Mrs Greenslade, it's the only place where boys and girls can meet together, in the workplace, without their families breathing down their necks.'

'They want to know about England,' said Evelyn.

There was a silence. Sonny stared at her. From the dining-room came the faint clatter of plates.

'Come on, Sonny,' said Madge. 'I've already been waiting two hours. Does nobody do *anything* on time here?'

Sonny was gazing at Evelyn. 'Mrs Greenslade, you are a genius.' He lowered himself to the ground. 'Please permit me to kiss your feet.'

After dinner Evelyn stepped into the garden. The *mali* had watered it thoroughly for once; she smelt the drenched lawn, the earth exhaling in relief. Now it was winter the weather was perfect; cool nights, cool enough for a cardi, and days as perfect as that June afternoon when she had sat under the clematis with Teddy. She heard, faintly, the sound of Peggy Lee. The music drifted from Graham Turner's open window. He had one of the smaller, cheaper rooms at the back of the building. '*It was just one of those things . . .*'

She wondered about Teddy, the other life she had dreamed for herself that day in Enfield. It made her feel dizzy, the possibilities. She gazed into the darkness. Through the tangled branches she saw the lights in Karishma Plaza. All those boys and girls . . . they were spinning their lies in there, dreaming their own Enfields, but they were young and anything was possible. Their youth made her want to weep.

'Psst!'

Evelyn turned. Muriel was beckoning from her window. Evelyn hurried up to her.

'I saw a holy man today,' whispered Muriel. 'Mrs Gee-Gee took me.'

'A holy man?'

'He was in this little room in the temple! Don't tell nobody, they'll laugh at me.'

161

'What was he like?'

'He had mud on his hair, it was all long and matted like the Rastas, you know? There's lots of them in Peckham.' Muriel pointed to her forehead. 'He put this spot here, with his thumb. Can you see it? I haven't washed. I gave him some money and he blessed me and said my Keith was coming soon. He had staring eyes, they stared right into me. He said my Keith's coming to find his Mum.'

They arrived a couple of days later, twenty girls and boys from the call centre, and filed into the lounge. The residents were already ensconced; the young visitors sat at the feet of their elderly hosts. Sonny, who had arranged it, ordered Pepsis all round.

Surinda sat next to Evelyn, her head resting against the side of the armchair. 'I could sleep for a week, Evelyn aunty,' she said.

'You poor thing, working all night.' Evelyn longed to stroke Surinda's shiny black hair. It reminded her of her brother's old labrador, Toby.

'It's really stressful,' said Surinda. 'When I get my bonus I'm going to take a course in hotel management.'

'When will you get your bonus, dear?'

'When I've made a thousand sales,' said Surinda.

'How many sales have you made so far?'

'Twenty-seven.'

They laughed. Evelyn felt a maternal rush. She longed to take care of this lovely plump girl. In fact she felt a proprietorial fondness for all these young people; after all, it was she who had found them in the first place. We're all desperate for somebody to love here, she thought; that's why we put out milk for the cats.

'There's some handsome boys here,' she whispered. 'Have any of them taken your fancy? What about that one?' She pointed to a young fellow who was lounging on the floor, propped up on one elbow.

'Oh, that's Rahul. Just because he's US-returned he thinks he's the bee's knees.'

'What's his English name?'

'Ramy Gold.'

Evelyn paused. 'That's not very English, dear.'

'He got it by looking out of the window,' said Surinda. 'He saw the sign for your hotel.'

'What do you mean?'

'Marigold. It's an anagram. Well, sort of.'

Evelyn burst out laughing. She hadn't enjoyed herself so much for ages. She leaned across to Madge, who sat in the next armchair.

'They get their surnames from products – Johnson's Baby Powder, Parker pens.' She felt proud, knowing something nobody else did. 'My friend here got hers from that Britney Spears.'

'She's not a product, sweetie,' said Madge. 'She's a singer.'

'That one's a Beckham.' Evelyn pointed. 'And one of them's our very own hotel.'

Sonny clapped his hands. 'Silence, please! Now, my good friends, the aim of this gathering is for you to ask our distinguished Britishers here about their home country, Enfield in particular. They are kindly giving up their time to help you to perform your jobs to a higher standard. Let's roll!'

Conversations broke out around the room. Norman's voice boomed out. 'I remember Enfield. Used to stop at the Spider's Web, out on the arterial road –'

'I went to school near there,' said Olive. 'Wood Green. Well, *quite* near there.'

'Where *is* Enfield?' asked Hermione.

Norman said: 'Used to drink pink gins with a floozie called Fay –'

'I went to the cinema there,' said Olive. 'The Gaumont.'

'Is it near Acton?' asked somebody.

'That's Ealing, dear.'

Everybody seemed to be talking at once. It was a novel sensation, having people interested in what they said. The young telephonists sat there, drinking in every word.

'I remember when the newsreel came on saying Gandhi had been shot,' said Olive.

'I was drinking my milk.' Stella's eyes were bright. 'I heard it on the wireless.'

'I was in rep in Enfield,' said Dorothy. 'I was playing the maid in *Dear Brutus*.'

'You were an actress?' asked Madge.

Dorothy nodded. 'For a few years. There was a Lyon's Corner House in the high street. One day I saw Nye Bevan driving past. It was like seeing God.'

'Who was he please?' asked a young man.

'He created our National Health Service,' said Dorothy. 'So people no longer died in the streets, as they do here. The next day I decided to give up acting and started making programmes for the Labour Party.'

'Bully for you!' said Norman, who was drinking whisky.

'I know Enfield quite well,' said Graham Turner.

The residents turned.

'I grew up there,' he said.

'I never knew,' said Madge.

'In Maybury Road,' said Graham. 'We had an Anderson shelter at the end of the street. When the air raid sounded I tried to smuggle in my pet hen.'

'A hen?'

Graham nodded. 'I was rather fond of her.' He sat there, his cheeks flushed, in his shirt and tie. He had never been seen without his tie.

Evelyn looked round. Some of the young workers had fallen asleep. No wonder, poor dears, slaving away all night. They slept beautifully. Sleep was so simple, when one was young.

'My fiancée, Amy, worked at the Army & Navy Stores,' Graham said.

'Fiancée?' Norman drained his glass. 'Well, I'll be buggered.'

Graham's bald head glistened in the lamplight. 'Thursdays were her half-days. I used to travel down to London, on the bus, and take her to tea at Gunter's.'

He stopped.

'What happened to her, darling?' asked Madge.

Graham didn't reply. They gazed at him. For the first time

Evelyn noticed his hands. They were thin and liver-spotted, knotted together in his lap.

'She passed away.'

There was another silence. Stella blew her nose.

'Why didn't we know that?' Evelyn whispered to Madge.

'We didn't ask.'

It was half an hour later. The curtains had been drawn in the TV room. Squashed together, they were all watching a video of *EastEnders*. Packages of these would arrive, at irregular intervals, from Olive Cooke's grandchildren. They never labelled them properly so people would watch the episodes in the wrong order, which even for the most clear-headed could be somewhat confusing.

Surinda whispered to Evelyn: 'Why did you all leave England?'

'Various reasons, dear. Some of us found we couldn't manage to live there any more.'

'What do you mean?'

'Various – well, provisions we had made – didn't turn out to be quite what we had been led to expect. Pensions and so forth.'

'Why didn't your children look after you?'

Evelyn paused. 'It's different in England.'

On the TV, a woman battered at a man's head and burst into tears.

'Do you miss it, aunty?'

'Sometimes,' said Evelyn. 'I miss the rain.'

'Wait for the monsoon!'

I miss the Sussex Downs, thought Evelyn. I miss the wind blowing over the pelt of the barley field, brushing it silver. A family called Harbottle lived in her house now. 'I miss my garden. I know it sounds silly, but I long to get my hands dirty. I'd love to get cracking on the garden here, plants just plonked down in a row.'

'I want to go to England,' sighed Surinda.

Evelyn smiled. 'You probably want to go for the same reason we wanted to leave.'

'Ssh!' Madge turned up the sound. On *EastEnders* two young men with shaven heads hurled abuse at each other.

Evelyn whispered: 'It doesn't belong to us any more. We don't understand it. Britain belongs to other people now.' She hoped this didn't sound racist. She hadn't meant it like that.

Just then there was a small commotion. A girl got up and pushed her way through the bodies. She sat down beside Surinda, shifting her aside.

'Norman uncle just groped me!' she said.

Surinda giggled. 'Put Kamila next to him.' She turned to Evelyn. 'Ever since she called herself Karen she's become a real slapper. She's anybody's now.'

'What, even Norman's?' asked Evelyn.

They spilled into the garden. The sun was sinking; it was time for the young people to go to work. Sonny paced up and down the lawn, talking on his mobile phone.

Norman stumbled over to Surinda and took her arm. 'You're a fine-looking girl,' he said. 'Let me escort you to the Hideaway Pub tomorrow for a glass of their finest rum.'

Surinda removed his hand. 'No thank you,' she replied.

Norman pointed to the young men making their way down the drive. 'They're no bloody use. Shirt-lifters, the lot of them.'

'Pardon?' asked Surinda.

'I've seen them in the street, holding hands.' He leaned towards her, breathing heavily. 'My dear girl, they bat for the other team.'

'Piss off!' Surinda said.

'Come on, don't be coy –'

'*Jao, karaab aadmi!*' said Surinda.

Sonny hurried over. 'That's enough, old chap –'

'Bugger off, you twerp!'

'Don't make a complete fool of yourself –'

'Leave me alone!' roared Norman. 'You Paki nit-wit!'

Sonny grabbed Norman's arm and yanked him away. Norman stumbled against him. Sonny set him upright and pushed him towards the veranda steps.

There was a silence. Eithne Pomeroy, the cat lover, suddenly laughed. It was an eerie, high-pitched sound, like the bird nobody had seen, the bird that called from the flame tree at night.

When Evelyn turned, the young telephonists had melted into the gloaming.

It wasn't just Norman who drank too much that evening. Some of the others became decidedly squiffy too. Eithne started singing 'Rose in the Bud' in her high, cracked voice.

> *'Rose in the bud, the June air's warm and tender,*
> *Wait not too long and dally not too late –'*

'No, pet,' said Madge. 'It's *trifle not with fate.*'

Dinner was late, that was why. In fact it was eight-thirty and there was no sign of dinner at all. Minoo was glimpsed hurrying through the lounge; raised voices could be heard but no delicious curry smells drifted from the kitchen (it was chicken bhuna that night). The residents sat on the veranda, drinking. They had long ago cleaned out the bowls of small, dry crackers, always in short supply at the best of times.

Norman was nowhere to be seen. The incident with the Indian girl had bonded the others together; even Dorothy, the BBC lady, had joined in.

'He really is a menace,' she said.

'Poor girl!' said Evelyn. 'What can she think of us?'

'Not much of an ambassador, is he?'

The Ainslies had missed the excitement, having been to a lecture on Tagore. By now they had heard all the details.

'So embarrassing.'

'So terribly un-British, just lunging like that –'

'Pretty typical, I would say.' Dorothy put down her whisky glass. 'English men are useless at foreplay.'

A *frisson* went around the table. Eithne tittered.

'Hang on,' said Douglas.

'It's our ghastly public schools,' drawled Madge. 'Why do you think I married a Jew?'

'I had a Hungarian friend once,' said Dorothy. Her voice was slurred. 'He blamed home ownership. On the continent people rent their places but in England men are dying to get back to their DIY.'

'What did she say?' Stella fiddled with her hearing aid.

'No, it's public schools,' said Madge. 'They all bugger each other at fifteen –'

'Madge!' squeaked Eithne.

'– they enjoy it so much they spend the rest of their lives terrified they're gay.'

'That's not true about public schools,' said Jean. 'Take our son Adam –'

'Exactly,' said Dorothy.

'What?' asked Jean.

Dorothy drained her glass. 'At least he's honest about it.'

There was a silence. A roar of laughter came from one of the other tables.

Jean whispered, 'What did you say?'

'What did she say?' A whistling sound came from Stella's ear.

Douglas pushed back his chair and got up. 'Darling.' He touched his wife's shoulder. 'Let's pop along to our room. I've forgotten my specs.'

Jean didn't move. She sat there, her face frozen. Douglas took her hand.

'Come along, old girl,' he said. 'You might know where to find them.'

Gently, he helped his wife to her feet. He steered her across the veranda to the door. Jean moved stiffly, as if sleep-walking.

When they had gone Madge turned to Dorothy. 'What was *that* all about?'

Dorothy didn't reply. She sat there, her mouth open. Madge thought: The poor thing. Maybe it was true, what they said about her – the wanderings, the mutterings. She did, indeed, look quite dotty.

There was a strange atmosphere during dinner. It wasn't served until after nine, by which time people were dizzy from hunger and the effects of alcohol. Nor was it chicken bhuna, a general

168

favourite. It seemed to be a hastily assembled dish of fried chicken with tinned tomatoes ladled on top.

Both Norman and the Ainslies were absent. So was Graham Turner, always such a nebulous presence that it took them a while to realise he wasn't actually there. Perhaps he had been overcome by his own revelations.

'Fancy having a fiancée who died,' said Olive Cooke, scraping the sauce off her chicken-leg.

'No wonder he looks so, well, unused,' said Madge.

They had nearly finished working their way through the chicken before the rice appeared. Jimmy put down the bowl on the table. Evelyn whispered to the old bearer: 'Is anything the matter out there?'

'Trouble in the kitchen, memsahib,' he said and glided away.

Madge looked around. 'Dorothy's not here either. It's just like the Ten Little Niggers.'

'Indians, dear,' said Evelyn.

'Who's going to be next?'

Dorothy and Douglas sat in the garden, hidden from the hotel by a clump of bushes. They could hear the far clatter of dinner. Beside them the aviary was silent, its budgies long since gone to sleep.

'I'm so terribly sorry,' said Dorothy. 'I presumed she knew.'

'It nearly happened once before,' said Douglas. 'He'd broken up with a Spaniard called Marco. This was years ago. Marco phoned up but we weren't at home. When I got back I heard this message on the answering machine.' Donald paused. Something rustled in the dead leaves. Maybe it was the snake that nobody had actually seen but which had distinctly been heard. 'It told us that our son was gay. Not just that, it itemised in some detail all the things he'd been up to. You can imagine, I dare say. It went on for ten minutes.'

'Good Lord,' said Dorothy.

'Jean was away for the night. I knew she mustn't hear it, I knew it would destroy her, but I didn't know how to erase messages. Our daughter had given us the machine and I hadn't got the hang of it yet. So I pressed Rewind and phoned up everybody we knew,

169

saying how Jean would love to hear from them. She's been feeling a bit low, I said, and could they give her a tinkle.' Douglas paused. Various cats were miaowing in the darkness. By now Eithne and the others were too inebriated to feed them.

'She came back the next day to find eight calls on the machine. *How are you, Jean, haven't seen you for ages.* Things like that. *We've been thinking about you, do pop over.* She was so chuffed. And the calls lasted more than ten minutes, so the original message was swallowed up. All that love taped over all that hatred. And she never knew, till now.'

'I'm so sorry,' said Dorothy again. Beyond the wall, somewhere in the waste ground, a dog howled.

'She would have found out sooner or later.' Douglas got to his feet. 'Better see how she is.'

Douglas patted Dorothy's shoulder and left, his footsteps crunching on the gravel. Dorothy sat there in the darkness. What an evening. It reminded her of her youth in rep – the drunken confessions, the elderly roué making a fool of himself, the thrum of homosexuality. The little group marooned in the middle of nowhere.

Except it wasn't nowhere. She knew every inch of this garden. It had altered, of course, as places alter in dreams, but it was still the same earth under her feet. It was terrifying. All those years – school, the BBC studios, the flats in Lancaster Gate and the Marylebone Road, all the people she had met and the places she had been, all the meals she had eaten, all the seventy-four years of her life – it had drained away, as if she had hardly lived it, and here she was, back where she began.

Dorothy thought: What must it feel like, for somebody to love you enough to rewind that tape?

Douglas stopped outside the bedroom door. He pictured his wife's face, puffy from weeping. He stood there in the corridor, gazing at the bamboo-printed wallpaper. To be honest, he was glad that Jean knew about their son. It disburdened him of the secret he had kept for so many years. He himself hadn't minded at all. At the time, his own equanimity had surprised him. Other people

170

would probably have been shocked. Disappointed. He had thought: Oh well, that explains things then. I just hope Adam's happy.

It was at that moment, standing in the corridor, that Douglas realised he didn't care that Jean was upset. He didn't mind how she felt, the woman with whom he had shared his life for forty-eight years. *I don't mind. I don't care. In fact, I don't even like her.*

Strangely enough, this didn't disturb him. It was as if the words had been waiting, patiently, for him to notice them. The mist had cleared, revealing them like standing stones. And they didn't even surprise him.

How strange, and yet not strange at all. Perhaps nothing could reach him. Perhaps there was nothing to reach. Something in this country answered a certain lassitude in his soul. It was the enervating weight of the place, the mass of its humanity who couldn't do anything about anything either.

Douglas gazed at the picture hanging on the wall. It was a photograph of a waterfall. The glass was cracked. Somewhere in Kashmir or wherever, that water was still falling. So his wife was upset. That too would pass. He was too old to leave her, he hadn't the energy to go, nor the energy to cope with her distress. Life would continue, the water would pour over the rocks and he was as resigned as the beggars who sat outside the hotel, their hands outstretched.

Douglas moved towards the door. Maybe none of this was important, this thing they called life, maybe he had realised a great truth. Or maybe he was just incapable of feeling anything at all and had long ago given up.

All this should have been shocking, but what the hell. Douglas turned the doorknob and went into the bedroom.

It was eleven o'clock, way beyond her bedtime, but Evelyn was awake. Carrying the plastic bags of newspapers she crossed the road.

'Memsahib!'

She heard the rattle of trolley-wheels. The legless beggar propelled himself towards her but Evelyn shook her head. Her

171

hands were full. She squeezed her way between the stalls. The little bazaar was still busy. Did nobody in this country ever sleep? She couldn't get 'Rose in the Bud' out of her head.

> *Life is too short and love is all, I'm thinking,*
> *Love comes but once, and then, perhaps, too late.*

When she was young she had thought this song the height of romance but now she realised the words were footling. In fact she could have fallen in love with any number of people. There were men, perhaps dead now, who could have made her as happy as Hugh had done. Maybe happier, who knew? If she hadn't been so well behaved she could have fallen in love during her marriage. Hugh's sailing partner, Tim, had made a pass at her, and her widowed friend Angus had once murmured 'Barkiss is willing' during a flute recital at Arundel Castle. If she had allowed herself, she could have found both men desirable. Exciting, even. And, as this seemed a night for confessions, she could even admit to a mildly unsettling fantasy about the man at the post office.

Evelyn entered Karishma Plaza and walked up the stairs. One of the carrier bags was splitting – Indian plastic was so flimsy, it was no use at all. She hoisted the bag under her arm. Up in the office, she looked at the rows of dark heads clamped with head-sets. Michael Parker, Mary Johnson. They sat there selling things nobody needed. Pity flooded through her. What must it feel like, to pretend to be somebody else because you were Indian and therefore not to be trusted? And yet they hadn't complained; in fact they seemed to think it was quite natural to pretend to be British. They certainly had better accents than some of the young people she knew, even friends of the family.

Evelyn paused outside Rahul's booth. It was papered with Bollywood posters.

'. . . if you commit now,' he said, 'we can offer you a substantial discount . . .' Today his hair was oiled into spikes. 'No, sir, I'm calling from England . . . Yes, Enfield, do you know it? A very pleasant town. I live there with my floozie.'

172

Oh Lord. Evelyn moved away and eavesdropped on the next booth. She could swear she heard the words *'Army & Navy Stores'*.

The supervisor was nowhere to be seen. Evelyn stepped into Surinda's booth.

'. . . never mind, madam, thank you for giving me your time.' Surinda, heaving a sigh, pulled off her head-set. 'Stupid old bag,' she said.

'I came to apologise,' said Evelyn.

'What for, aunty?'

For everything, really, thought Evelyn. For you, having to pretend. For not thinking that's terrible. She said: 'For the behaviour of Mr Purse.'

'That's OK. He's just a dirty old man.'

'And I've brought you some English newspapers. I feel we gave you rather a misleading impression of Britain.' Evelyn put the bags on the floor. 'They'll help you to keep up to date. Except, of course, some of them are rather old. Oh well, never mind. It's always the same news, somehow, isn't it? You'll find the crossword's been done already.'

Surinda unwrapped a stick of gum and offered it to her. Evelyn declined. 'Not with my teeth, dear.'

Surinda chewed for a moment. 'Your hotel's pretty crummy, isn't it?' she said cheerfully.

'Is it? I rather like it.'

'Why?'

'I suppose it feels like England.'

'I want to work at the Oberoi,' said Surinda. 'They have a great disco.'

'I think I'm a bit beyond discos.'

'You're as old as you feel.'

'Then I feel old,' said Evelyn.

Surinda got up and indicated her chair. 'Sit down, aunty.'

How polite they all were! Evelyn thought of the lager louts in England stampeding through the train, how she clutched her handbag to her chest.

'I have a friend like you in England,' Evelyn said. 'A young woman who painted my nails. I was very fond of her. To most people one is quite invisible.'

A voice floated over the partition. '. . . you'll find we're a more competitive supplier than British Gas, Mr Potter, and can reduce your quarterly bills by thirty per cent.'

Evelyn said: 'The thing is, I was married for a very long time. It's quite a shock to come out into the real world. Until then you don't think you're old. You've been together for so many years you're somehow the same people as when you first met. You don't notice the grey hairs.' She paused. 'And having someone with you is so – well, distracting. In a comforting way. Them being with you, going on. It stops you thinking about dying.'

'Never mind, Mr Potter,' said the voice in the next booth. 'Have a good day and toodle-pip.'

Evelyn said: 'You have so many choices when you're young. Or at least you think you do.' She gazed down at Surinda, who was sitting on the floor. 'Will you have a choice, dear? Will you be able to marry the person you love or will somebody arrange it for you?'

'You think that's really bad, don't you?' said Surinda. 'Like, weird.'

Evelyn shook her head. 'It's probably as good a way as any.' If only Christopher had listened to her he would have married that nice Penny Armstrong-James who had adored him but finally, disheartened by his inertia, had gone off and married somebody else.

Oh heavens! She still hadn't rung her son. That was the reason she had come to this office in the first place. A great deal seemed to have happened since then.

'Good night,' she said to the *chowkidar* who sat, wrapped in his blanket, beside the gate. He waggled his head. Somebody had told Evelyn how to say 'good night' in the local dialect but it had slipped out of her mind.

It was nearly midnight. Nights were beautifully clear here; the stars were so bright you could touch them.

Raise thine eyes to heaven
When thy spirits quail,
When, by tempests driven,
Heart and courage fail.

Evelyn thought: One day I shall die. I must learn the Indian words so I can say good night to my new friends.

She listened to the crickets trilling. Ahead loomed the black bulk of the hotel, most of its lights extinguished. She thought of the dramas that had taken place within it during the past few days, the dramas it must have seen since it was built in the middle of the last century – no, the century before the last one. Good Lord! It wasn't just the days that were whizzing by. It was the years. The *centuries*.

A shape was approaching down the drive. She saw the glimmer of a white shirt.

'Mrs Evelyn! You are out so late?'

It was Minoo. The gravel crunched as he walked up to her. They stood peering at each other in the darkness.

'Have you come to look for me?' she asked.

He was highly agitated. 'Mrs Evelyn, please accompany me.' He took her arm and turned her around, back towards the gates. 'You, of all people – you will understand.'

'What's happened?'

He held up something in front of her. It was a pair of shoes. 'You recognise these items?'

She peered closer. They were the shoes he kept in his office.

'These shoes, madam, have brought me nothing but heartbreak.'

'Call me Evelyn, please.'

'In this country we express our devotion by bending down at a personage's feet.' Minoo had stopped dead in the driveway. 'The *Rig Veda*, it tells a good Hindu to prostrate himself, to say *I am like the dust on your feet.*' He paused, breathing heavily. 'Yet the foot is the most impure part of the body! The head of primordial man gave rise to the high caste and his feet to the low caste. What confusion is that!'

From where they stood, in the garden, the lights in the bazaar were merely a flicker. Above them, in the offices, the windows blazed.

'I kept these shoes for sentimental reasons,' said Minoo. 'My little shrine to love. But now I am at breaking point. My wife has brought me nothing but misery. Tonight she has sacked the cook.'

'What happened?'

'Norman-sahib was very upset. He took a bottle of whisky into the kitchen and they drank it together. Fernandez became drunk of course, he is a drunkard, you understand. He is a Christian. Then he fell asleep and there was no dinner cooking and my wife threw him out. Always she makes the servants unhappy, shouting at them and putting them against each other. That is all she does, that and sitting on her big bottom reading her magazines and never lifting a finger. You see, madam, I love this hotel, it is my family home, but Razia has no respect for it and no respect for me and how can a marriage be happy when there is no respect?'

Heavens, he was crying! They were at the gates now. Evelyn saw his streaming face in the light of the passing cars.

'There there,' she said. 'Surely it's not that bad?'

'If only I had listened to my mother!' Minoo blurted out. 'I should have married the woman of my parents' dreams!'

Evelyn was suddenly overcome with such weariness that she longed to lie down in the dust. A few yards away a little family slumbered together, the children laid out like dolls beside their parents.

'What are you going to do with the shoes?' she asked.

'I shall give them away.'

Minoo strode across the road. A man on a bicycle wobbled and swerved. Evelyn hurried after the distraught manager.

'Who will you give them to?' she asked, catching him up. 'Your beautiful expensive shoes?'

'I shall give them to the first person I see who deserves them.' Minoo stood at the crossroads. Shaking with sobs, he looked around wildly.

Then he spied the man on the trolley. He rushed up to him, arm outstretched, holding out the shoes.

Evelyn hastened over to Minoo and touched him on the shoulder. 'I wouldn't give them to him, dear. He hasn't got any legs.'

Part Three

1

*Who everywhere is free from all ties, who neither rejoices nor sorrows
if fortune is good or is ill, his is a serene wisdom.*

(*The Bhagavad Gita*)

Theresa sat in her hotel room, trying to read. '*He who is in the
sun and the fire and in the heart of man is One. He who knows
this is one with the One.*' The room cost 150 rupees a night, cheap
even by Indian standards, and there was only a dim bulb hanging
from the ceiling. '*In the centre of the castle of Brahman, our own
body, there is a small shrine in the form of a lotus flower, within
can be found a small space. The little space within the heart is
as great as this vast universe.*' Theresa squinted through her spectacles. These were a recent acquisition, bought from Boots in
Durham before she left. She was aware of the significance of this
purchase – another shunt into middle age, along with the flabbi-
ness of her upper arms and of course the tummy. She always wore
loose clothes in India, in this case *shalwar kameeze* pyjamas that
modestly covered her body. Even in England she had favoured
Indian dress and now she could see the point of it.

She was soon to be fifty. This was an alarming thought. During
this trip she had noticed a change in people's reactions. Men no
longer tried to chat her up. Everywhere she went, of course, there
were questions – 'Where do you come from? What is your name
please?' – but this was just the friendly curiosity one encountered
in India. It was no longer sexually pressing. As she travelled from
place to place, squashed on buses, sweltering on trains, people gave
up their seats to her as if she were already her mother. Even the

Babu at that ashram in Benares who was notorious for the twinkle in his eye – notorious, in fact, for going further than a twinkle in his union with his disciples – even he, during their private *satsang*, had treated her with impeccable gravity. This was, of course, liberating. True freedom only came through the transcendence of the flesh.

Theresa's bowels ached; she had had diarrhoea for the past week. Outside in the street was a placard: WE HAVE SOUGHT PERFECTION IN CONCRETE. One needed a strong stomach to face the lavatory down the corridor. She knew she should eat something but the thought of food made her nauseous. The only thing she could imagine possibly eating, ever, at some far distant point in the future, was a boiled egg with Marmite soldiers.

Exhausted, Theresa took off her flip-flop and inspected her foot. She had stood on something sharp in the temple of Hanuman, the monkey god who freed people from their troubles. The skin had been punctured. What happened if she got an infection and died, alone in a hotel room in a country where nobody cared for her? Where nobody, except her mother, knew her name? Even her mother didn't count because the idea of Evelyn living in India was so bizarre that Theresa simply couldn't picture it, not until she had seen it with her own eyes.

Theresa closed her eyes. She shifted into a cross-legged position on the bed.

'*Om* . . .' she said. '*Om* . . .'

She tried to pull the energy up, up from her toes through her diaphragm, through the *chakras. At the base of the spine lies Kundalini, the coiled serpent power* . . . She tried to concentrate.

A vision, however, kept swimming into view: crisp white sheets on her bed at home in the Old Vicarage. The rattle of a tray approached and her mother was coming in, carrying the egg, the soldiers and the latest issue of *Bunty* magazine.

'*Om* . . . *om* . . .'

The room was sweltering. She couldn't open the window because the hotel was opposite the bus station and the noise was deafening. The exhaust fumes made her sick.

'*Om* . . . *om* . . .'

Crisp white sheets . . . a clean lavatory in a large, carpeted bathroom; a new roll of Andrex hanging within reach; more rolls of Andrex in a cupboard filled with large, soft bath-towels . . . A bath . . .

Attachment was illusion. Attachment was fear. Theresa gave up and turned back to her book. *'Two birds sit on a tree. One gorges on the ripe fruit while the other sits serenely. The seasons change and the fruit disappears –'*

Thumps and giggles came from the next room.

'The first bird flies round frantically searching for the fruit. The second sits patiently waiting for his friend to realise the delusion of attachment, of pain, sorrow and reliance.'

It was a Dutch couple; Theresa had seen them arriving with their backpacks. Their energy seemed inexhaustible; they had kept her awake most of the previous night. She needed to get some sleep because tomorrow morning she was catching the early bus to Kerala. Since her watch had been stolen, in Mumbai, she had lost track of time. Of course this was liberating, too, but there were certain disadvantages.

'The unchanging self is all that exists.'

The woman cried out. Last night Theresa had counted her orgasms – muffled screams, yelps, smaller squeaky noises, waves of these that went on for ages. It had been like counting sheep but without the desired result. How did the woman have so many orgasms in her?

A cockroach scuttled across the floor. Theresa gave up on her meditation and opened her exercise book.

'Dec. 16' she wrote:

The ashram in Pattipurnam was a little disappointing, as after a two-day journey I arrived to find Swamiji was not in residence, having gone to Germany. However his presence could be felt in the holy atmosphere and of course a spiritual journey need have no goals. I shared a room with a pleasant woman from Des Moines who calls herself Prem. She has been in India for many months and described a visit to the Bench Swami in Tamil Nadu. He has been sitting on

181

his bench for twenty-five years, in silence, his eyes closed.
She sat with him for many hours. Finally he opened his eyes
and she was filled with a powerful feeling of joy. Apparently
he used to be a postman until he achieved enlightenment.

There is something childlike about the Babajis I have met.
They emanate a sense of wonder and sweetness. They also
have a delightful sense of humour. How we laughed when,
during darshan, one of our number put up three fingers and
asked: 'Guruji, how many?' Swamiji, his eyes twinkling, said:
'Four.' Most of my time however has been spent in medita-
tion or just sitting quietly listening to the discourse. I have
travelled for many miles, from one ashram to another, but
as Sri Baba says, a journey has no beginning and no end –

The biro ran dry. She had only bought it that afternoon in the
bazaar but Indian pens, like so much else, had a short life
expectancy. Theresa put away the book. There was no need to
write. For whom was she writing her journal anyway? One by
one, by choice or circumstance, her possessions had disappeared.
She should feel lightened, of course.

She had to admit it: this visit was turning out to be something
of a disappointment. Last time she had returned from India on a
high but this time the drug didn't seem to be working. There had
been some moments of heart-stopping beauty. She remembered
a dawn outside Allahabad, piles of refuse, smoking fires and the
beggars rising from the ashes . . . an ineffable grace in the midst
of squalor. Such epiphanies could be found everywhere, for those
with eyes to see them. But somehow the connection she sought
so keenly hadn't been made. This time, somehow, she hadn't
managed to rise above the delays and frustrations, the general
hopelessness of everything. On several occasions she had lost her
temper, a humiliating experience in a country whose people,
however cruelly they were treated, seemed to possess no rancour.
One didn't take things personally here; there was simply no point.

Maybe she was becoming too old for this sort of thing. But age
shouldn't be relevant; after all, many of the Swamis were no longer
in their bodies but their presence was as powerfully felt as if they

sat there twinkling at their devotees; death was an irrelevance. Why then did she feel so mortal, with her thickening waist and churning bowels? Shivabalayogi sat in a cave for eight years, meditating twenty-three hours a day and only returning to ordinary circumstances to bathe and drink a glass of milk. His body was gnawed by rodents yet he emanated a spiritual bliss so intense that thousands of people came to sit in his presence.

The longer you stay in India, the less you know.

Actually Theresa did know the reason. It was the fault of her upbringing. She had come to India to be made whole but this wasn't possible when she herself was a cracked vessel. No amount of spiritual glue could mend her until she had learnt to love herself, and feel loved. She saw this all the time with her clients; that was why she had gone into counselling in the first place. So many of them, like herself, had been given no sense of validation, of self-worth. In every case she had enabled them to trace it back to their parents. This had made it possible, with a great deal of work, to move on.

Darkness had fallen. Theresa got up and hobbled to the window; her foot had started to throb. Outside, in the bus station, was a mass of humanity – people carrying bundles and suitcases, people carrying children, people disgorging from the buses or queuing to embark. Traffic was at a standstill. Horns hooted in that passionless Indian way – nothing personal, just a reflex action. Tomorrow Theresa herself would be moving on. There was one more place she had to go, before she travelled to Bangalore. All her hopes now resided in a remote Keralana village. Here, surely, she would find the love that had so far eluded her.

For in that village, Vallickava, lived the Hugging Mother.

2

Real faith does not live merely in words. It lives in actions, the actions of everyday life. So that everything is done with great devotion and contemplation.

(Dr Svami R. Anand Giri Purna: *Discourses*)

Madge and Evelyn stood looking at the *lingam*.

'Nobody we know, darling,' said Madge.

Evelyn laughed. Stella fiddled with her hearing aid. 'What did she say, dear?'

The *lingam* certainly was an impressive sight – four feet high, at least, and made of stone polished smooth by the hands of devotees. Evelyn felt a curious melting sensation.

'Is that what I think it is?' asked Stella.

'I used to see them when I was little,' said Eithne. 'My parents used to hurry me past. Of course I had no idea why.'

Eithne Pomeroy, the cat lover, had spent her early years in Calcutta but had left when her father was posted back to Britain. She had volunteered the occasional memory of that time but was in general somewhat vague. '*Away with the fairies*,' said Norman with a snort.

The four women were visiting a temple, whose name Evelyn hadn't caught, somewhere on the outskirts of Bangalore. Madge had organised the outing. '*You must come, Evelyn, or else your daughter will think you're a fuddy-duddy.*' News of Theresa's imminent arrival and her interest in things Indian had gone round the hotel.

Evelyn, however, was none the wiser. The temple was a dark little room where Indian families chattered away as if it wasn't sacred at all. For them, of course, God was everywhere so maybe this place wasn't holier than anywhere else. The elephant one, spattered with paste and strewn with flowers, sat in a niche. He looked like the sort of thing you won at a fairground and then wished you didn't have to take home. It was all rather charming but their guide, as guides so often did, had reeled off a list of dates and measurements that had simply gone in one ear and out the other. Why did guides always tell you the things you didn't want to know?

The four women went outside. The temple was on top of a hill; it had nearly killed them, climbing the steps. The light was blinding; in the distance they could see the modern skyscrapers of the city shimmering in the heat, a mirage of commerce. Evelyn sat down, creakingly, and pulled on her sandals.

'At least you can tell your daughter you've been,' said Madge. 'And that's the main thing.'

A monkey, suckling its baby, watched them. The baby removed its mouth from a long dry nipple and glared at Evelyn with malevolence. She thought how once she had suckled the two grown-ups who were slowly but surely converging on her from the other sides of the world. This gave her as odd a sensation as the *lingam*.

Eithne leaned towards Evelyn. She indicated Madge, who had unclicked her compact and was re-applying her lipstick. 'Do you know,' she whispered, 'I've forgotten her name.'

'It's Madge,' whispered Evelyn.

'Silly me!'

'Don't worry,' said Evelyn. 'I forget names all the time.'

'I'll be forgetting the name of my daughter next,' said Eithne with a small laugh. Eithne's daughter, Lucy, was married to a test pilot and lived in Australia. Lucy had promised she would come and visit soon. They all said that, of course; it was a question of finding the time.

They walked down the steps, between the rows of stalls. 'Whose daughter are you talking about?' asked Stella.

'Get a grip, Stella!' said Madge. 'Eithne's. She's called Lucy and lives in Sydney.'

'Sidney who?' asked Stella.

'My Lucy's going to come,' said Eithne. 'She says it'll be a surprise.'

'Don't let her surprise you, pet,' said Madge. 'It'll give you a heart attack.'

They reached their hire car. The guide, a bespectacled man, very thin, gave each of them his card. It said *Dr Gulvinder Gaya, BA (Failed)*. Evelyn put it into her bag to join her growing collection of business cards. Everywhere one went, people thrust them into one's hand. They tipped him – Rs 30, they had planned this in advance – and drove off. Madge had boldly volunteered to sit next to the driver.

Evelyn sat squashed in the back, discreetly scratching her mosquito bites. They were discussing dinner. Thursdays were usually a choice of biriani or cutlets. 'I'd kill for a decent piece of cheddar,' said Madge.

Fernandez, the cook, had returned to work the day after he had been sacked. Apparently this was a regular occurrence. Evelyn had told nobody, however, about Minoo's confession. Two weeks had passed and the poor man looked even more miserable. His wife was glimpsed occasionally barking at the servants but she hardly spoke to the residents any more and was unavailable for pedicures. Jean Ainslie, too, seemed somewhat muted. The reason for this was not generally known but it contributed to the odd atmosphere. It was as if they were all waiting for something to happen. Maybe it felt like this when the heat built up in the summer, before the monsoon broke.

'Look!' Stella pointed out of the window.

They were crossing a river. On its banks stood a forest of washing, strung on poles. Rows of sheets hung shimmering in the heat. Tiny figures slapped clothes in the water.

'That's a *dhobi-ghat*, dear,' said Eithne. 'Our laundry is probably there.'

'Maybe I can spot my pink slacks,' said Madge.

'No!' said Stella. 'I mean – look. It's Dorothy.'

They told the driver to stop. A lorry blared its horn. It passed, belching fumes. Putting on their specs, they stared out of the window.

Next to the washing was a group of huts, roofed with plastic.

A black-and-yellow taxi was parked there. Even at this distance they could make out that the woman beside it was Dorothy: blue trousers, white blouse. She was talking to one of the washermen.

They sat there, gazing at her. 'What on earth is she doing there?' asked Evelyn.

'Maybe she's lost her smalls,' said Madge.

Dorothy was there at dinner. None of the four asked her what she had been doing at the *dhobi-ghat*; one simply didn't, with Dorothy. She sat at a table with Graham and the Scottish sisters, a pleasant but dull pair of widows from Fife. Due to Madge's efforts seating arrangements had become more sociable: tables had been shoved together to make places for four, a number which Madge said made for better conversation. Two was too pressured; more than four and the deafer ones couldn't hear. Madge was a veteran of many cruises and knew about such things. There was a musical chairs aspect to this, however: those last to arrive found their choices dwindled to Norman Purse or Hermione Fox-Harding, another of the cat-lovers, who suffered from flatulence. The trick, of course, was to enter as a group and stick ruthlessly together.

Evelyn sat next to her companions of the afternoon. She eyed Dorothy with curiosity. This changed to astonishment when Dorothy ordered a bottle of wine. Nobody drank wine, it was exorbitantly expensive, as rare a treat as when they were young. People drank local beer, Indian spirits or, if feeling extravagant, imported liquor. Jimmy carried in the bottle, holding it like a firework, and had to be helped with the corkscrew.

'Not your birthday, old girl?' boomed Norman from the next table. He eyed the bottle greedily.

Dorothy shook her head. After a long interval Jimmy re-appeared with four dusty wine glasses, trembling on a tray.

Evelyn, some yards away, inspected Dorothy's face. There was an air of suppressed excitement about her, as if she had heard some news on the radio of which the rest of them were unaware. Dorothy speared a slice of egg mayonnaise, lifted it to her mouth and then, lost in thought, put it down again.

Until recently Evelyn had defended Dorothy against the

rumour of barminess that had been circulating. Eccentricity, like good cheddar, was one of a dwindling list of things of which the British could be proud. Until they had arrived at the hotel many of the residents had been living alone for some years, a situation that fostered odd behaviour. Evelyn herself frequently spoke aloud to Hugh.

Only the day before, however, she had found Dorothy in the garden, talking to the *mali*. When she drew nearer and could make out the words she had discovered that Dorothy wasn't speaking English at all; it was some sort of gobbledegook. No wonder the *mali* had looked bemused and shaken his head. Or done that sort of waggle. *Of course, if that's what you want to say, you dotty old Brit.* We all have our strange little ways, thought Evelyn. It was just that some were stranger than others.

Take Muriel Donnelly. In recent days Muriel had grown more agitated. The visit to the holy man hadn't produced the desired result: there was still no sign of her son. She had phoned his home in Essex many times: no answer. His neighbours hadn't heard a dicky-bird. Muriel's efforts to track down his wife and her two children, Jordan and Shannon, had failed too. Maybe the wife had run away as well. Muriel had no idea. The two of them had never got on.

Yet Muriel still persisted. Miracles could happen. After all, without hope she would probably lose the will to live.

After dinner Evelyn sat in the lounge, reading an old *Good Housekeeping*. From the TV room came the sound of *Porridge*; somebody had discovered a pirated copy at Khan's. In the armchair opposite dozed Hermione, her exercise book on her lap. She was writing her memoirs for her grandchildren.

Muriel came up to Evelyn and whispered: 'Guess what. I'm having me leaves read tomorrow.'

'Leaves?'

'It's going to tell me the future.'

'Do you think that's a good idea?' asked Evelyn.

'It's got the answers written on it,' said Muriel.

'How? I thought they just made a sort of shape.'

'What does?'

'Tea-leaves.'

'Not tea-leaves, ducks,' said Muriel. '*I* can do them. This is palm leaves. They even tell you when you're going to die.'

Opposite, Hermione had fallen asleep. Her memoirs slipped from her fingers and fell on to the floor.

Ammachi, they say, is the embodiment of Devi, the Divine Mother of the Universe. At her ashram in this small fishing village by the Arabian Sea – built on the site of her birth-place and childhood home – thousands of people from around the world come to experience her unique darshan, in which she holds each devotee in her arms like a mother embracing a child.

Theresa sat on the rocks reading *From Here to Nirvana*. The waves pounded the beach and withdrew, hissingly. Their rhythm lulled her. Each wave was her consciousness, washing over her and then retreating and leaving her cleansed. Now she had arrived she was filled with peace.

Earthy, vital and archetypically maternal, the Hugging Mother personally receives every person who comes to her – laughing, scolding, consoling and finally wrapping the devotee in a mammoth hug (usually accompanied by a chocolate kiss or some other sweet as prasad). She's been known to embrace over 15,000 devotees in one night, greeting each one with the same radiant, unforced smile. Her disciples estimate that to date she has hugged about twenty million people.

How rare were the hugs of Theresa's own mother! Evelyn hadn't been a physical person at all – too frigid, too English. The thought of her having sex with Theresa's father was too grotesque to contemplate. Once, when she was little, Theresa had crept into their room and tried to climb into bed with them. Her mother had wordlessly picked her up and carried her back: Theresa's first experience of rejection, the first of many.

Theresa became aware of a smell. She looked down. In the cleft between the rocks was a pile of shit. She got up and, crossing the rocks, limped down to the beach. Her wound was now a dull ache. Indian Elastoplast was useless; it fell off after a few steps.

In fact, her mother's hugs weren't really hugs at all; just a brief clasp against her rigid body, a kiss on the cheek. These clasps were treacherous, for they spelt farewell. A brief embrace and then her parents were gone, driving away in their Rover, back to their happy marriage, and leaving Theresa to face the horrors of boarding-school. How could they have sent their child away? What sort of love was that? They had always loved Christopher more, of course, their darling boy. Oh Christopher could do no wrong.

Theresa limped back to the village. If only she could find a foot-guru, to heal her wounds. If only she could find a bowel-guru to heal her diarrhoea. Judging by the evidence dotted around in the sand she was not the only one to suffer from the runs.

She made her way past a row of coaches. The village was crammed with pilgrims, many of them westerners.

'Hey, mate, how're you doing?' Two English youths hugged. 'We met in Varanasi, remember? Pandit's Chai Shop.'

It was with some difficulty that Theresa had found a room: a concrete cell in a house on the main road, next to the cyber-café. Theresa sat down on the bed. Outside traffic inched past. She could hear people's voices as they walked past her window.

'I'm living in Wembley at the moment,' said a girl. 'But I'm looking for a place in Kensal Rise.'

As a rule Theresa avoided the British but she suddenly longed for a conversation, even the limited kind she would have with a stoned Londoner half her age. She took out her packet of Moist-Wipes. There was only one left. She tried to clean her wound but the Moist-Wipe had dried up.

Never mind, she thought. Tomorrow I shall be hugged.

3

He who feels neither excitement nor repulsion, who complains not and lusts not for things; who is beyond good and evil, and who has love – he is dear to me.

(*The Bhagavad Gita*)

'Look, Jo-Jo, elephants!' Christopher pointed out of the jeep.

'I *seen* an elephant.'

'That was only one. Look, there's a whole herd of them here, a Mummy elephant and a Daddy elephant and a little baby elephant –'

'Dad,' said Clementine.

'Mom, I'm *tired*.' Joseph, his thumb in his mouth, snuggled against his mother in the back seat.

'You can't be tired,' said Christopher.

'They got up at six,' said his wife.

'Do look, kids! It's a whole family of them!'

'You're shouting, honey,' said Marcia.

'But they've never seen elephants before, in the wild!'

'Yes they have.'

'When?'

'In Kenya, remember? The Masai Mara.'

Marcia sat there, draped with their children. Clementine, who seemed to have regressed on this trip, was sucking her thumb too. The driver, a helpful chap called Hari, had stopped the jeep.

'Elephants, sahib,' said Hari.

Christopher took a photo. Somebody had to show willing, just for the sake of the driver. The elephants were simply grey

191

boulders amongst the scrub. Christopher urged them to do something interesting.

'Got some photos anyway,' he said brightly. 'We can look at them when we get home.'

Nobody replied. Hari started up the jeep and drove on. Christopher wanted to say to him: Don't blame me. I know they're spoilt kids but honestly their friends are just as bad. You have no idea.

In the back seat, the children lolled against their mother. Marcia hugged them in a proprietorial, excluding way. She really did spoil them dreadfully. Guilt, of course. Career women over-indulged their children, it came from hardly ever seeing them. How different it was from his own upbringing.

They bounced along the track. He wished she wasn't so, well, physical. All that hugging, especially with their son. Christopher suspected it wasn't entirely healthy. Surely it was storing up trouble for later?

The Mudumalai Game Reserve was only Day Four of their holiday and already the children were bored. They had seen temples and beaches; they had travelled on a boat through the backwaters of Kerala and helped themselves to vast buffets in staggeringly luxurious hotels; they had swum in pools the size of Piccadilly Circus whose palm trees rustled with parrots; flunkeys had served them, bringing them elaborate non-alcoholic cocktails and picking up the sodden towels they left strewn around their rooms. So far the only sign of animation from Clementine was when she met somebody who had met Johnny Depp. As for Joseph, most of the time he had stayed plugged into his discman, only coming to life when the batteries died.

'Me and your Grandad, we went camping once on Dartmoor,' said Christopher. 'Tramped for miles, just an apple and a piece of cheese in our pockets. In the evenings we made our own amusements – playing Battleships, things like that.'

Clementine looked at him, her lip curled. 'Dad, that *so* is sad.'

'It wasn't. It was grand.' *Grand?* He had never used that word before in his life.

Nowadays Christopher felt himself becoming unrecognisable. He was playing at families. He gazed at his angel-faced son, seven years old and already unnerving; at his mulish daughter. Oh, he worried what life had in store for them but in truth he felt that they hardly belonged to him at all. Now he was away from home, in their company twenty-four hours a day, he saw them all with horrible clarity. Why couldn't they just be happy, like families were supposed to be?

The jeep bounced along the track, past miles of scrub. It was an overcast morning, the light flat. A few birds flew around but Hari had given up pointing things out. Christopher turned in his seat, to smile encouragingly at his little family. Bare of make-up, Marcia's skin looked sallow in the early morning light. She didn't show her age, he had to admit that, but she really was a remarkably plain woman.

He suddenly had a vision of the villages they had passed, in Kerala – glimpses of a life so simple, so achingly beautiful that he couldn't shake it off: a laughing child waving at the boat, a sari-clad woman gracefully throwing grain to her hens. *Keep that breathless charm.* Each little house they passed, nestling amongst its banana palms, drenched in sunlight, was a vision of Eden. It was a vision of such unattainable happiness that he wanted to weep.

'When are we going back to the hotel, Mom?' whined Clementine.

'Soon.'

'Then we're off to Ooty!' said Christopher. 'Then we come down from the hills on a steam railway, then we go to some amazing temples at a place called Halebib –'

'Look Mom, some bug's bit me!'

'And a beautiful city called Mysore –'

'Look! It's all swollen!' wailed Clementine.

'There's a wonderful palace there –'

'Am I going to die?' asked Clementine.

'Darling,' said Christopher, 'don't be such a drama queen.'

'She's worried!' snapped Marcia. She turned to her daughter. 'Sweetie, we'll put some stuff on it when we get back to the hotel.'

'And then on to your Granny!' said Christopher. 'Granny Evelyn. She can't wait to see you guys.'

'Will she be wearing a diaper?' Joseph snorted with giggles.

193

'That's silly,' said Christopher. 'Of course not.'

'Old people wear diapers, like babies.'

'*You* wore diapers once,' said Christopher.

'Gross!'

'Will she give me a Christmas present?' asked Clementine.

'I'm sure she will.' In fact his mother was famously stingey but surely she would buy them *something*. By Christmas Day, in fact, they would be gone; they only had two nights in Bangalore and then it was on to Goa. Christopher knew they should be spending the day with his mother but the dates hadn't worked out. Still, it was near enough. And Theresa would be there for the actual festivities. Surely that was all right, wasn't it?

Christopher felt the usual guilt, rising like nausea. He was useless, both as a father and a son. He closed his eyes.

There she was: one woman, glimpsed from the boat. She wore a pale blue sari. Squatting at the water's edge, she squeezed out her washing. The sun caught her hair. As the boat passed she raised her head and smiled at him, a dazzling smile. Just for a moment the mist cleared. Her smile, like the sunshine, dissolved it away.

'Mom, it's gotten all red!' wailed Clementine.

'Yuk,' said Joseph.

Christopher glanced at the driver. The brochure had promised them a qualified wildlife expert but never mind; in India, he had noticed, such promises seemed to evaporate. In this case they had been given an elderly man who could hardly speak English. Christopher looked at Hari's thin ankles, his dusty grey toes. How much did the man earn? Per week, probably less than a gin and tonic.

Ah, a gin and tonic . . .

Hari drove out through the game reserve gates. Boys emerged from some huts, and ran up to the jeep.

'What is your name?' they asked.

'Topher,' said Christopher.

When he was a schoolboy Christopher had tentatively made up this nickname for himself. However, it had never caught on; none of his class-mates had used it and the whole thing had disintegrated in a vaguely humiliating way.

'Topher, Topher!' shouted the boys. 'You are from which country please?'

'England. But I live in New York.'

Christopher looked at them. Suddenly he had a powerful urge to tip out his own children and gather up these laughing boys instead.

To them I'm Topher! he thought. I could start all over again with a woman in a blue sari who simply smiled at me, glad that I existed.

'Hi! My name is Madhu Sengupta and I'm twenty-six years old. I'm cheerful, well educated and from a good family. I have a BA Com in Systems Management but despite my modern exterior I'm very traditional at heart. My interests include bridge, music and conversation –'

'She's nice, Rahul,' whispered Evelyn.

'I'm looking for a man I can depend on and who can depend on me –'

'Forget it, sweetheart,' Surinda said to the face on the TV screen.

'Shut up,' said Rahul.

A group of the residents sat in the TV room. They were watching a video of prospective brides for Rahul, the young man who worked at the call centre.

'– and who is reasonably good-looking –'

'That counts *you* out,' chortled Surinda.

'Please supply a horoscope.'

Rahul lounged between Evelyn and Madge's feet, his hair shining in the glow from the screen. He said he wanted some input from people whose opinions he valued. They had been charmed by his confidence.

Another face appeared on the screen. *'My name is Kiran Shrivastav and I am a Christian,'* she said, *'five feet six inches tall. I am looking for a partner with marriage in mind, he should be well settled and with a good sense of humour. I work as a dental assistant and my age is twenty-two –'*

'Twenty-two?' crowed Surinda. 'In your dreams, darling.'

'I am fluent in Kannada, Hindi and English and would prefer a non-smoker. Please email me at the above address.'

'They all look so pretty,' said Evelyn. She wished one of *them* had married her son.

Another face appeared. '*I am a divorcee, no encumbrance, and I'm looking for a respectable professional man, any age, caste no bar –*'

'Poor thing, *she's* desperate,' said Surinda.

'The next one is the one I like,' said Rahul. 'I've replayed her four times –'

'Oh pu-leese,' said Surinda.

'What do you think, aunties?' he asked.

A pretty girl appeared on the screen, eyes downcast. '*I like dance, drama, and eat-outs,*' she said. '*I'm an affectionate and caring graduate –*'

'Hey, I know her!' said Surinda. 'We were at college together. She's a slag, Rahiji.'

'What did she say?' asked Stella.

'*And* she's got a fat ass!'

Just then Evelyn noticed a man standing in the doorway. It was Minoo. He was gazing at the TV screen. Even in the gloom she could see that he was upset.

Eithne pointed to the TV. 'That one's just like my Lucy. Hardly darker at all –'

'Sssh!'

'She says she's sending me a surprise for Christmas,' said Eithne. 'It's her, I know it is! She's coming to see me, all the way from Australia –'

'Do shut up!' somebody called out. 'We're trying to find this nice young man a wife.'

When Evelyn turned, Minoo had gone.

The video ended. The elderly audience got to their feet, their knees cracking like pistol shots.

Evelyn went outside. In the darkness Minoo sat slumped on the veranda steps. She lowered herself carefully and sat down beside him.

'Were you thinking of your lost bride?' she asked.

He nodded.

'What was her name?'

'Bapsi.' He turned to her. 'Mrs Evelyn, I can't go on like this. The hotel is falling to pieces around my head.'

'Is it?' She looked up, alarmed.

'I can't work, I can't sleep. Did God put us on this earth to suffer such unhappiness?'

She lowered her voice. 'Have you thought about divorce? In England nowadays people do it all the time. They have a very short fuse.'

'I've been divorced,' said Madge. They swung round. 'Am I butting in?'

'Sit down, madam, please,' said Minoo.

'Best thing I ever did.' Madge sat down beside them. 'Because then I met Arnold. Honestly, it was as if I was born again. Another crack at it.' She turned to Evelyn. 'You wouldn't have recognised me with Howard – that's my first. I was such a mouse.' She lit a cigarette. 'With Arnold I became a different person. He made me laugh, you see. Oh we did have fun, right up to the end. I remember once, when he was bending down to get something from the floor – he had a terrible back – he said *Now I'm down here, is there anything else you want?*'

They sat, gazing into the darkness. At the far end of the veranda Eithne called: 'Tommy . . . Tommy . . . ?' She was looking for the cat.

'I only had the one husband,' said Evelyn. 'He seemed enough for me at the time.'

Another voice in the garden called out: 'Tinker? Tinker? . . .' Hermione too was searching for the cat.

'From what I understand, you lot can have another life but only after you've died,' said Madge. 'Some of us can have another life when we're still alive.' She drew on her cigarette. 'It makes you feel you've lived longer, like a two-centre holiday.'

'I thought I believed in God, ladies,' said Minoo. 'But I've been having doubts.'

'To be perfectly honest,' said Evelyn, 'so have I.'

'May I have one of those please, madam?'

Madge gave Minoo a cigarette and lit it. Evelyn liked cigarette smoke, it reminded her of Hugh. Besides, it kept the mosquitoes away. The three of them sat there, absorbed in their thoughts. The voices called faintly in the garden. A third one had joined them: 'Felix . . . Felix!' Far away, beyond the wall, the traffic hooted.

Just then a figure appeared, walking up the drive. It was difficult to make out who it was – just a glimmer of pale clothes, like a ghost.

A hush fell. For a moment, all they could hear was the scrunch of footsteps on the gravel. The figure drew nearer. It was a woman.

'Lucy!' A voice cried out from the other end of the veranda. The plate clattered as Eithne dropped the cat's food. 'Lucy darling!' Eithne rushed up to where they sat on the steps. They moved aside to let her pass. 'It's my daughter!' she said breathlessly. Gripping the rail, she descended the steps.

Maybe she tripped. Nobody knew. Suddenly there was the sound of tearing wood. The rail broke and Eithne fell, heavily.

The three of them jumped to their feet.

'Eithne, are you all right?'

Evelyn, however, wasn't looking at the prone body lying on the ground. She was looking at the woman who was near them now, approaching through the darkness: a middle-aged woman dressed in Indian clothes.

'Theresa!'

'Hallo, Mum.'

Evelyn hurried across the gravel and hugged her daughter – an awkward thing to do, with the rucksack getting in the way.

Eithne's accident had a powerful effect on the residents. She had been taken to the Victoria Hospital with a broken hip. In their hearts they all knew what this meant. One thing led to another; those who went in with a broken hip seldom came out again. 'It's the beginning of the end,' said Hermione, not known for her tact.

The Ainslies visited Eithne the next day. Like an advance guard, they reported back their impressions of the hospital. Families around every bedside, they said, full-scale meals being set up, but otherwise the place wasn't that different from a British hospital, including the brown faces of the staff. Eithne's daughter had been notified and, despite her mother's feeble protestations that there was no need, was flying out from Australia and would arrive the next day.

'One down, nineteen to go,' said Madge to Norman. 'We're like those lobsters in a tank, you know, when you go into a restaurant. Soon someone's going to point a finger and say *I'll have that one.*'

Norman liked Madge. She was a good-looking woman; must have been quite a trouser-stirrer in her youth. She smoked too, unlike most of the niminy-piminy old biddies with whom he was surrounded. At one mad moment he had considered confiding in her. Most of his fellow residents looked the way old people were supposed to look; something beige about them, and they all had the same hair-dos. Impossible to imagine they had ever had sexual intercourse. A few of them, however, like Madge, looked like ordinary women who happened to have got on a bit. Of these, Madge was the best specimen. She'd obviously had a lot of experience in the bedroom department and maybe could give him some reassurance about his little problem. *Your hubby Arnold, did he find, as time went by, that he had less snap in the old celery?* Norman, however, didn't entirely trust Madge to keep it to herself. If his secret got out he could never hold up his head again.

He had made up his mind to get some professional advice and had found the address of a clinic in the pages of the *Bangalore Times.* 'Impotence,' said the small ad. '*Premature Ejaculation, Sexually-transmitted Diseases, HIV Testing, Confidence Guaranteed.*'

Norman sat crouched in the auto-rickshaw as it puttered along Elphinstone Street. The road was clogged with traffic. It was 18 December, a momentous day. To admit he had a problem was one step; actively to do something about it, to lift the phone and make an appointment, was loin-girdingly bold. He needed to get it over with before Pauline arrived. It would be difficult to slip away when she was on the premises, being the dutiful daughter.

The rickshaw swerved around a bus. Its exhaust fumes made his eyes water. Why wasn't Pauline bringing that husband of hers? Surely the chap would want to visit his own country and check up on his investment? Still, they couldn't complain about Norman's behaviour this time. Nobody had chucked him out of the Marigold yet. Of course, the temptations hadn't been numerous.

He thought about Eithne, the poor old bird, languishing in hospital. He wished he hadn't told her that her glasses made her look like Rosemary West.

'Is she a friend of yours?' Eithne had asked.

'No. Serial killer. Gloucester.'

'Pardon?' asked Eithne, never that bright at the best of times.

'Fred West, all that,' replied Norman. 'Remember?'

Eithne had made a small, startled noise in her throat.

Really Eithne should sue the bloody hotel but their generation didn't do things like that. It wouldn't cross her mind. Besides, if Sonny had anything to do with it, which he did, the place had probably never been inspected or had any sort of official certification in the first place.

The rickshaw veered across the traffic and came to a halt on a pile of rubble. Norman eased himself out and straightened up, with a groan. Up above him loomed a peeling building: Elphinstone Chambers. Signs attached to the various floors proclaimed the businesses within. *Ishmail Tailoring, Suitings and Shirtings. Rahman Travel Agency.* He looked further up. *Third Floor: Meerhar Clinic.*

'These Indian post-its are hopeless,' said Evelyn, picking one off the floor. 'They don't stick at all.'

'You don't need attachments, Mum,' said her daughter. 'Just let go.'

'Don't be silly, dear. I won't remember anything if I don't remind myself.'

'It's a *joke*, Mum. We did a lot of laughing in the ashrams.'

They left the bedroom and walked down the corridor. Theresa was still limping but Mrs Cowasjee, in a rare moment of goodwill, had bandaged her foot. Theresa wore her mother's bedroom slippers: powder-blue, trimmed with fluff.

'Lucky it was just your foot,' said Evelyn. 'I was so worried about you. One hears such stories.'

'I was fine,' said Theresa.

'Muslim terrorists –'

'Not in India –'

'Muslims are such trouble, bombing things, praying all the time –'

'Mum! Not all Muslims are terrorists.'

'Anyone who has ground elder can understand terrorism,' said Evelyn. 'Pull up one bit and there's still a whole lot more, breeding away under the soil –'

'Mum –'

'Pulling it up only encourages it, you see. Another bit pops up where you least expect it.'

'Mum!' Theresa stopped. 'Don't be so *silly*.'

'You shouldn't talk to me like that,' said Evelyn sharply. 'You sound about twelve years old.'

Evelyn couldn't help it; her temper was short that day. Eithne's fall had upset her and her own daughter, after only two days, was starting to irritate her. She looked at Theresa. Grey wires had appeared in her hair; Evelyn hadn't noticed them before. Her daughter's skin, bare of make-up, looked pasty. Really, six weeks in India and she hadn't even got a tan. And those miserable, colourless pyjamas! They looked nice on Indian women but Theresa looked as if she'd been in bed with the flu.

'You must snap out of this cycle,' Evelyn said. 'It just goes round and round. If you snapped out of it and grew up, then you'd be happy.'

'Good grief, Mum. You sound like a Hindu.'

'I do live here, you know.'

Theresa grunted. They walked into the lounge. Evelyn realised that things had shifted between them. She wasn't the same person who had arrived so apprehensively three months earlier. Now she felt freer, with her bare legs and her new young friends. She had grown fond of Surinda and Rahul, who was less blasé than he looked. And then there were her fellow residents who were by now so familiar that they were almost family. Above all it was this baffling and beguiling country which was altering her. And her daughter, whom she loved but whom she found so infuriating, had remained exactly the same.

Norman sat in the waiting-room, looking sideways at the other men. There were eight of them, all Indian of course. Some of them smoked. They looked as if they had been sitting there since last year. Indians had that air about them, when they were waiting for something. What were they thinking about? All the shags that had finally come home to roost? Wondering if it had been worth it? You could bet they weren't suffering from impotence. Indians were at it all the time, you only had to look at those swarms of children to realise that the average Bangalorian had no problem getting it up. And they were well versed, too, in the arts of love. The *Karma Sutra*, which Norman had eagerly read in his youth, listed eight kinds of nail marks – *eight* – to be used during coitus. Norman had only scratched a woman once, and that was involuntarily, in pain, when her watch-strap caught his pubic hair.

What would the doctor do? Get him some Viagra for starters, see if that worked. Maybe he could prescribe some exotic elixir made out of powdered rhino horn or something. After all, this was India. At the last resort there was apparently a pump thing but surely it wouldn't come to that.

'Fancy a gasper?' he said to the man next to him.

The chap waggled his head, *no*, and took one.

'Speak English?' asked Norman.

The man waggled his head again and said nothing.

They all looked like bank clerks – thin; poorly paid. You could sense the desperation. They probably went home to a couple of chapattis. Funny, really, that they had nothing except the one thing that Norman would give his eye-teeth for, if he still had any eye-teeth.

The door of the surgery opened and the nurse called out: 'Mr Smith!'

Nobody moved.

'Mr Smith?'

She was looking at Norman. He jumped. He had forgotten he had given a false name.

202

Norman made his way across the room. He felt horribly conspicuous. For the first time in his life he wished he were brown. *Invisible*, in fact.

The nurse opened the door and Norman stepped into the surgery. The doctor, dressed in a white jacket, sat behind a desk. He got to his feet.

Norman stood, frozen to the spot.

'Good God,' he said. 'Dr Rama!'

Theresa felt suffocated. Initially she had been relieved to have found her mother in fine form – even flourishing. For a conventional Englishwoman, Evelyn seemed to have adapted remarkably well. In fact her mother looked years younger. She had stopped wearing face powder – '*It just slides off*,' she said, '*so I gave up*' – and her skin was lightly tanned. The warm climate had eased her arthritis and she seemed altogether rejuvenated. '*Just looking at the people in the street*,' she said, '*well, it makes you count your blessings, doesn't it?*' This, of course, was a great relief. Theresa didn't feel quite so guilty about her now.

She had also been surprised by how pleased she had been to see her mother. Maybe it was a reaction to the loneliness and disappointment of her trip (yes, she could admit it now). She had just wanted to hug her.

Two days had passed, however, and the goodwill was evaporating. The trouble with visiting people so far away was that once you arrived you had to stay for such a long time – two weeks, in her case. How maddening her mother was! It was odd, feeling the old irritations rise to the surface in these foreign surroundings, like hearing a nursery rhyme in the middle of a raga. Of course Theresa knew that wherever people went, they carried their baggage with them, but it was still an unwelcome sensation. And the hotel was getting on her nerves. At first glance it looked charming but really what a ludicrous place it was, a time-warp for grannies, *is there honey still for tea?* A place that reinforced every stereotype and confirmed every prejudice. They called the head bearer Jimmy, for God's sake; didn't they see how degrading that was? None of them seemed to have learnt a single word of Hindi or the local language, Kannada, and Theresa's efforts to interest them in the simplest tenets of Hinduism had been met with blank incomprehension. That awful old Norman Purse, the one with the purple nose, had even sniggered at the word *lingam*. It was extraordinary how the British could live in their own bubble. Of course they had had centuries of practice.

It all stemmed from denial. Denial was the British default setting – denial of sexuality, denial of one's feelings. Theresa herself had had to work on that; it had taken her years of therapy to realise that she hated her brother. Denial, of course, produced fear. Theresa could see it in the faces of the old people, so damaged by the western culture in which they had been brought up. No wonder they knocked back the gin-and-tonics.

Funnily enough, the only person who seemed to be on Theresa's wavelength was a working-class woman, Muriel Donnelly. They had sat in Muriel's delightfully kitsch room and discussed reincarnation. Muriel was not an intellectual, by any stretch of the imagination, but Theresa had discovered that this could be an advantage for those who followed a spiritual path.

'They think I'm barmy,' said Muriel, 'but you should see that Stella Englefield, she's a sandwich short of a picnic. And that Dorothy Miller thinks she's so hoity-toity but I've heard her singing "Here we go round the mulberry bush" when she thinks nobody's listening.'

She had told Theresa about a holy man she had visited in the Old City. Theresa had decided to go there and had obtained directions from the manager's wife. After two days in the Marigold she felt the need of a spiritual hit.

For Bangalore was far from exotic: a sprawling, featureless city filled with office blocks. On her first day Theresa had hired a car and taken her mother around; the driver had insisted on giving them a tour of the various IT buildings, including a glass edifice soon to be occupied by Newscorp.

'This is our Silicon Valley,' he said proudly. 'Mr Rupert Murdoch, you have heard of him? He is setting up a digital software facility for his global networks.'

204

'It's just like Milton Keynes,' said Theresa.

'Sssh, dear,' said her mother.

'I've come half-way round the world to get *away* from this.'

Theresa could hardly visit a holy man wearing bedroom slippers. Her wound had nearly healed; she took off the bandage and slipped on her flip-flops. The manager had found her a box room, crammed with two beds, at the top of the hotel; there were no other spare rooms, apparently.

Theresa wrapped a *dupatta* around her shoulders and went downstairs. The old dears were just shuffling in to lunch.

'Do stay and eat,' said her mother.

'No, I'll see you later. Bye, Mum.' 'Mum' sounded babyish – after all, Theresa was a middle-aged woman – but what did one call one's mother? Could she change it to 'Mother' at this late stage?

Theresa was pondering this when the door burst open and Norman Purse arrived. His face was brick-red.

'Guess who I've just seen!' he barked at the queue. 'Your precious Dr Rama!'

'What do you mean, dear?' asked Evelyn.

'The fellow's a bloody clap doctor!' Norman gave a snort. 'Always knew there was something fishy about him. Smarming around with that hair.'

There was a silence.

'The man's a charlatan!' said Norman. 'He runs a clap clinic in Elphinstone Street!'

'What were you doing in a clap clinic, sweetie?' said Madge.

'I was walking past on my way to the bank.' Norman's small, fierce eyes challenged her. 'Saw the fellow coming out.'

There was another silence. One by one they turned to Minoo.

'Is this true?' somebody asked.

'That's got their knickers in a twist,' chuckled Muriel. 'No wonder he gave 'em all antibiotics.'

Lunch was over. The news of Dr Rama's treachery had had a powerful effect on many of the residents who had now retired to their rooms for a brood and a nap. Muriel sat on the veranda with Douglas Ainslie, who as a man had been less susceptible to the

205

doctor's charms and who therefore felt less keenly a sense of betrayal.

Douglas, however, seemed miles away. Over the past weeks the man had changed. The breezy, suntanned extrovert, with his thick white hair and gold-rimmed glasses, seemed somehow diminished. He sat for long periods gazing into space, and the expeditions with his wife had all but ceased. Nobody knew the reason. Maybe he was sickening for something. Better call the doctor, thought Muriel, stifling a giggle.

The news hadn't shocked her, of course. Muriel had never had much faith in foreign doctors anyway. What was disappointing, however, was the collapse of her new-found enthusiasm for the more spiritual side of Indian life. She had to admit it: this partic-ular medicine hadn't worked either. Her recent visit to the palm-leaf reader had told her nothing about her son, only the date of her own death.

Not surprisingly, this had knocked her for six. The leaf thing was called *Nadi*. An old man, sitting in an incense-filled room, had asked her when she was born and had taken a print from her left thumb. He had then flicked through a bunch of palm leaves, tied with string. Finally he had pulled one out. It was covered in tiny writing, as if an insect had been let loose on it. He started reading out the contents.

Some of it was familiar enough: ups and downs, loss of a loved one. She had heard that before, often enough. Then he told her the other thing.

Muriel had to admit it; after hearing the date of her death she had hurried from the room. *'Peacefully,'* he had said, *'after a short illness.'* And then the time and the place.

It gave Muriel the collywobbles just to think about it. She had told nobody, not even her confidante Mrs Cowasjee.

Douglas had finished his coffee and left. Muriel was alone on the veranda. Gazing at the empty chairs, she thought of the people who had occupied them. For each of them there was a palm leaf. Far off at the gate, a bell tinkled; a man stood there with some-thing to sell, trying to attract her attention.

Some of the chairs were pushed back from the table, where a

206

person had got up. Soon Jimmy would emerge from the dining-room and straighten them. A gecko was stuck like a brooch to the wall; it sat there for hours, without moving.

Plenty of time left, Ma. Keith's arm was around her shoulders. *Hey, don't cry.* He kissed her cheek. *I'll miss you something rotten but just think, at least you know you're not going to be knocked over by a bus tomorrow.*

Muriel heard footsteps. She wiped her nose with the back of her hand. It was Dorothy. She emerged from the front door and walked down the drive. Despite the stick there was a purposeful air about her, as if there was no time to waste.

Muriel got up and grabbed her handbag. The woman was off again on one of her expeditions. This time, thought Muriel, I'll find out where the old lunatic's going.

Muriel hurried down the drive. The city held no fears for her now; no accidents could happen, she had been told they wouldn't. Just for a moment she was glad she knew her fate.

Out in the street Dorothy crossed the road and approached the rickshaw-stand.

'Memsahib!' The drivers stirred themselves. 'This side, memsahib!' She climbed into a rickshaw and it drove off down Brigade Road.

Muriel climbed into another rickshaw. She pointed to Dorothy's vehicle, disappearing amongst the traffic.

'Follow!' She flapped her hand as if shooing away a fly. 'Follow it! Quick!'

'I'm at my wits' end, Sonny *baba*!' Minoo was on the phone. 'The residents are very upset and who can blame them? Now they're thinking we're diddling them, oh why did we start on this foolish venture –'

'Calm down, man!' said Sonny.

'The situation is driving me out of my mind, you have no idea –'

'Listen –' began Sonny.

'– they'll tell the authorities and I'll lose my licence, what am I going to do?'

Sonny switched off his mobile. Shit! This was all he needed, on top of his other troubles. That bastard PK, the snake-eyed *maderchod*, having swindled him out of lakhs of rupees, was still nowhere to be found. He must have paid off the police for even Sonny's closest confidant in the force, a fellow Rotary Club member too, had stopped answering his calls. No doubt PK's thugs were also responsible for the beating-up of the foreman at the depot, who was now in hospital and refusing to identify his attackers. Sonny's troubles had taken on a life of their own. He had had to borrow heavily to cover his losses and now the bank was threatening to call in his loan. Another of his projects was in trouble, planning permission having mysteriously been withdrawn. Back at his residence things were at breaking point, his wife having sacked the old servant who had been in the family for twenty years. And on top of all this, his cousin Ravi was pestering him with emails demanding to know about plans for the worldwide expansion of Ravison Retirement Homes. Didn't the fellow understand that Sonny was at breaking point?

Sonny sat at his desk, turning the biro round and round in his fingers. Outside, the traffic was gridlocked in Brigade Road. His office was two blocks from the Marigold, a place which only a few months earlier had seemed the answer to his dreams. The business world was based on shaky foundations – only too shaky, in the case of his Defence Colony project. The stock market was plummeting, the economy tottering, one by one the great corporations – Enron, World.Com – imploding. The only thing a chap could be sure of, in this life, was that he would grow old and need someone to look after him. In his own small way Sonny was enabling that to happen. How well he remembered his eureka moment at the Royal Thistle Hotel, Bayswater! Now the whole project was threatened by that interfering old bugger Norman Purse.

How could he have snitched on them, he whose own daughter had a stake in the business? How dare he stir up trouble in the one operation that was going smoothly?

Sonny sat there, seething. He would get even with the old *chootiya*. He just had to think of a way to do it.

* * *

'Imagine that you have an appointment with a stranger.' Later, Theresa remembered the page from her book of meditations. *'When you meet, the radiant presence of this person astounds you.'* She was standing in an alley filled with rusting car parts. On either side, stalls were heaped with exhaust pipes. Men sat drinking tea. They gazed at her. She was somewhere deep in the Old City, clutching the piece of paper with Mrs Cowasjee's directions written on it. *'How can you describe this person? What makes him or her so special? You ask the stranger's name and are told that you are looking at a part of yourself. Thank the stranger and say goodbye. Acknowledge your own inner beauty.'*

Theresa stepped over an open drain. Something was going to happen. It hadn't happened with the Hugging Mother, an experience in which she had invested so much hope. Hundreds of devotees had waited but Theresa, being a European to whom time was more precious, had been ushered to the head of the queue. Ammachi was a smiling, middle-aged woman who had hugged her and given her a boiled sweet. Maybe Theresa had been distracted by her throbbing foot. For then it was over and she had felt no different at all. Nothing.

There was nobody to whom she could confess it, least of all her own mother. *Why would you want to be hugged by somebody else, dear? The woman doesn't even know you.*

TURN RIGHT THROUGH CLOTH MARKET. Theresa looked at the alley. It was narrow, just a slit between the buildings, and crammed with people. No sunlight penetrated here. The smell of sewage filled her nostrils. This is the real India, she told herself, this is where I feel at home.

Theresa was lost. Now she was squeezing her way through a spice bazaar which wasn't mentioned in the directions at all. Mounds of coloured powder – russet, ochre, crimson – were heaped in sacks. People jostled past. 'Baksheesh, memsahib!' Somebody waved his stump in front of her.

TURN LEFT AT GANDHI MARKET. Was this Gandhi Market? A banging drum drew nearer; somebody was playing a trumpet. A group of *hijras* pushed their way through the crowd, ogling the people as they passed. The eunuchs in India unnerved Theresa, with their plastered make-up and men's faces. One of them waggled his tongue at her. They wriggled past in their saris, off to some wedding or other, off to bless or curse, or lift up their skirts.

Theresa didn't panic. *If I find him, I find him.* She had been lost in these crumbling mazes often enough before. There was no sense in battling against it.

Suddenly she was gripped by loneliness. She longed for the Marmite soldiers. If only she could be tucked up again in bed, everything would be all right. She knew, of course, that she could never again slip between the sheets. The room had long since been dismantled, along with her childhood. That bliss was as lost as nirvana – a state she knew, now, she would never attain.

Theresa stumbled on, past stalls hung with cooking pots. At the end, alleys led off in several directions.

'Janpath Lane, *kahaan hai?*' she asked three old men who sat chewing *paan*. They waggled their heads and pointed in three different directions. What was the name of the sadhu?

It was then that she saw him: a European man pushing his way through the crowd. Dark-haired, drenched in sweat.

'Hey sweetheart, you English?' he asked.

Theresa nodded. He was close to her now, breathing heavily as if he had been running. There was something dodgy about him – stubble, dark glasses. Something feline. She felt a melting sensation in her guts.

'Fuck, am I glad to see you.' He took her arm. 'Know the way out of here?'

A figure squatted in the central strip of grass, spraying it with a hose. Muriel's rickshaw puttered along, overtaken by cars that rocked it as they passed. Office buildings – Motorola, Meyer Systems – were set back amidst landscaped lawns. More buildings were under construction; workmen clambered up flimsy wooden scaffolding, passing each other buckets. It was another world out here, in Silicon Valley.

Ahead, Dorothy's rickshaw shimmered in the heat. Muriel imagined it disappearing, a mirage. What on earth was the woman doing?

Muriel gripped the rail. In front of her, the driver's head was wrapped in a dirty cloth. He was an old man, older than she was. He sat hunched in his seat as if he were driving a dodgem. That was how they drove, here. She thought of the fairground on Clapham Common, Keith's small hand in hers. Gypsy Rose Lee – not the real one, she was dead – had told her she would travel. Now Muriel knew what she meant. Maybe this journey would never end. This tattered white ghost would drive her on and on, far into the unimaginable land that lay beyond this city – deserts? Mountains? He would drive through the years until he reached the day of her death and she would dissolve like a mirage. *Peacefully.* And then Leonard would be waiting for her, still young, the handsome young man she had once loved. He had stopped while she had grown older because he existed outside time. They were all waiting – her parents, her brothers and sisters, her husband Paddy – and now she knew she would meet them. Maybe they were like that flock of parrots – emerald-green, exploding from the palm tree as if someone had fired a pistol. Muriel watched the birds. Who knew? Her beliefs were as shaken up as her insides, jolted by the ride. Only one thing was certain and she didn't want to think about that.

Just then she realised that they had passed Dorothy's rickshaw. It was parked at the side of the road.

'Stop!' Muriel grabbed the driver's shoulder. 'STOP!' He was skin and bone.

The driver swerved on to the verge and stopped.

'Wait here,' she said. 'Don't move, see?'

He waggled his head. She got herself out.

The other rickshaw was parked outside some gates fifty yards down the road. Next to the gate was a guard's hut. Dorothy was talking to the gateman who sat inside.

Muriel felt awkward. The BBC lady hadn't seen her yet but she was bound to turn round. Muriel would have to say she was worried about her, they were all worried, the way she buggered off without a word to anybody. She might have got lost. In fact she was probably lost now, and asking the way back to the hotel.

211

Muriel walked along the verge. Cars hurtled past, blowing dust in her face. She and Dorothy were marooned here beside the motorway; they had left the teeming streets behind.

The sign at the gates said TEXAS INSTRUMENTS HEADQUARTERS BUILDING. Through the gates Muriel saw a drive, which led past flower-beds to a handsome bungalow. Like their hotel, it was an old building; this place, however, was smartly painted: white with green shutters. Expensive-looking cars, and jeeps like Keith's, were parked outside. Next to it was a patch of waste ground where piglets snuffled plastic bags.

Dorothy still hadn't noticed her. She was leaning on her stick and gesturing with her free hand. The *chowkidar* was an old man wearing a grey uniform.

Muriel walked nearer. Dorothy sounded exasperated. She jabbered away in a strange language. The traffic drowned the words. The old guard frowned at her. Talk to him in English, ducks, urged Muriel.

'*Mai is ghar mey rehti thi!*' Dorothy raised her voice. 'I'm dotty!' she cried.

Muriel, standing behind her, caught the man's eye. She tapped her temple conspiratorially. Screw loose.

'I'm little dotty!' cried Dorothy.

Not a little, darling. A lot.

Dorothy shouted: 'I'm little Dotty! Dorothy! Don't you remember me?'

Muriel stepped up to her and touched her arm. 'Come on, love. Time to go home.'

Dorothy swung round. Her eyes glittered. 'He doesn't recognise me! This is my house, I used to live here. His father was our driver, he and I used to play together when we were little!' She didn't seem to register Muriel at all, she was too upset. 'He doesn't recognise me!' She turned to the gateman. '*Mai Mr. Miller ki beti hoo!*'

It was then that the *chowkidar* realised. A smile broke out on his face.

'Dotty?' he asked in a strangled voice.

He stumbled out of his hut. For a moment it seemed that Dorothy was going to hug him. She recovered, however, and put out her hand. The old man shook it. Then they both burst into tears.

Theresa flung herself back and lay beside Keith. Their bodies were slippery with sweat; the sheet was bunched up under their feet. They lay there panting like dogs. Above them the fan creaked round.

After a while their breathing returned to normal. They both burst out laughing.

'Go on,' he said. 'You were saying?'

'What was I saying?' Outside the sun was sinking; his hotel room was bathed in golden light.

'What you were doing in the bazaar.'

'Oh, I was looking for a sadhu,' Theresa said.

'A saddo?'

'No! A sadhu. A holy man.'

'You don't need a holy man,' he said. 'Look, you can worship me.'

Theresa propped herself on her elbow. She ran her finger down Keith's chest – tanned above the waist, paler below. 'Fancy yourself, don't you?' she said.

He grinned. She touched the damp hairs around his cock. He had the most beautiful cock she had ever seen. So many men's were red and angry, bursting at the veins with aggression. They seemed disconnected to their sometimes inoffensive owners. Keith's was smooth and beige, a natural part of his body.

It seemed perfectly natural, too, to have gone to bed with him. She had just done it, just like that. *Making love* seemed an inappropriate phrase for two people who had only met a couple of hours ago; *having sex*, however, didn't seem the right words either for such an incandescent experience. Such rapture.

'An old woman sent me to see him,' she said. 'A funny old baggage at the hotel I'm staying at. The last sort of person to seek a sadhu, one would have thought.' She hooked her foot around Keith's. He held it between his own feet.

'Why were *you* there?' she asked. 'In the bazaar?'

'It's a bit of a long story. Let's just say somebody sent me there to meet somebody but I smelt a rat.'

'Only one? I saw about six.'

'It was a set-up,' Keith said. 'I realised that just before I saw you. Can't tell you how glad I was. See, I've been in a spot of trouble.'

'Tell me about it,' she said. 'I'm a counsellor.'

'Don't need a counsellor, darling. I need a hit man.'

A thrill shot through her. 'Are you a criminal then?'

'I'm a businessman.'

You're not, Theresa thought. You're an animal, in the purest, most ravishing sense. 'You've been doing something dodgy, though,' she said. *Dodgy*. The word made her shiver. 'Hindus believe that if you do something bad you pay for it in the next life.'

'No you don't, love. You go to prison.' Keith rolled on top of her. 'Anyone told you you've got the sexiest mouth?' He kissed her deeply. *Seriously*. It sucked the breath out of her body. He moved his head down and ran his tongue between her breasts, down to her belly.

'Don't,' she said. 'I'm so fat.'

'You're not, you're gorgeous.' He licked her navel. 'A gorgeous woman.'

'I feel so flabby.'

'Don't be stupid.' He shifted round between her legs, lay upside down on her and rummaged on the floor for his cigarettes. Theresa thought: I don't even know his surname. I don't want to know. I just want to lie here, with the weight of him between my thighs, until it gets dark. She stroked his buttocks as he lit up. Smoke curled up from the end of the bed.

She hadn't done this for a long time. Six years, in fact; a drunken cellist, after a party. How strange and lovely it was, that bodies could be so companionable.

'I've always wanted to do Tantric sex,' she said. 'You can go on and on, apparently, without an orgasm.'

'Sounds a daft idea to me,' he said. He moved back and flung himself beside her.

'You just apply pressure to the *chakras*,' she said. 'You release vital energy without penetration. Hours and hours you can do it.'

'Sounds like the plumber,' he said. 'You stay in all day and nobody comes.'

Theresa burst out laughing. It was an unfamiliar sensation.

'Into all that stuff, are you?' he asked.

She nodded.

'Don't tell me. You're a vegetarian.'

'No I'm not,' she replied.

'Thank God for that.'

She lifted his cigarette from his fingers and took a drag. 'I'm a vegan.'

Keith snorted with laughter. 'I'd kill for sausage and chips.'

'How long have you been here?'

'Too bloody long.' He paused dreamily: 'And a bottle of Rioja.'

'You don't look like – well, the sort of English person one finds here.'

'I told you. It's business.'

They lay there. She watched the smoke-rings rise towards the ceiling. She hardly dared look at him, he stopped her heart.

His fingers laced through hers.

'I'm so happy,' she said. 'It's simple, isn't it?'

Outside, the muezzin called through the loudspeaker for evening prayers. The sound echoed in the street. She had no idea where the hotel was. Out near the airport somewhere, in a scruffy little commercial area.

'How old are you?' She wanted to call him *darling* but she couldn't make it sound natural.

'Fifty-two.'

They were near enough the same age, but what different lives had led them to this disordered bed. She had never been intimate with a man like Keith before, he wasn't her type.

Yes he was. Did he have a wife? Her professional life was spent listening but just now she didn't want to hear.

'I've been traipsing round ashrams,' she said.

'Now why would you want to do a thing like that?'

'Good question,' she said.

Keith laid her hand on his chest and stroked each of her fingers, one by one.

'Families and stuff, I suppose,' she said. 'Families are so compli-cated, aren't they.'

He shifted on top of her and reached out to stub his cigarette in the saucer on the bedside table. *Don't move.*

'Look at my free gift.' He gave her a small square envelope: BUSINESSMAN KIT. 'Open it.'

Inside she found a paper clip, a rubber band and a small biro.

'That'll come in useful,' she said. 'For your business.'

'Very handy.'

They laughed. Maybe it really was this simple. Do business with the aid of a paper clip. Lie in bed with a stranger who has a boxer's broken nose and a tattoo on his shoulder.

'I've been travelling light too,' she said. 'Well, most of my things got stolen.' The molten light shone on his possessions, heaped in the corner: an open suitcase, a laptop, some papers. She said: 'I had this dream of shedding everything and just – being. You know?'

'What I miss is the swimming-pool,' Keith said.

'You've got a swimming-pool?'

'Back in Chigwell. Kept it heated all year round, cost an arm and a leg. The kids used to drop stuff in it, crisps and stuff, drove me round the bend.'

Kids. Theresa paused. 'Do you miss them?'

'They're not mine. Tell the truth, it's my Mum I miss the most. Keep phoning her but there's no reply. I told Sandra to look after her but Sandra's fucked off. God knows where.' He sat up abruptly, swung his legs over the side of the bed and stood up. 'I'm ravenous, darling. Want something to eat?'

'I can't. My mother will be worried.' Oh dear, that sounded dowdy. 'I'm staying with her at this hotel full of old people, a sort of retirement place.'

'I want my Mum to go to one of them but she's too blooming proud.'

'So I suppose I ought to go back.'

'Suit yourself.' He pulled on his boxer shorts. They were printed with little locomotives. Only a woman would buy boxer shorts like that. Now she looked at Keith properly she was gratified to see that he was thickening around the waist.

'I'd rather have dinner with you,' she said.

'Know something, babe?' He zipped up his trousers. 'You saved my life out there.'

'Really?'

He lunged towards her, cupped her chin in his hands and kissed her eyes, one and then the other. Then he sat down and put on his shoes. His Rolex caught the setting sun. She reached for her clothes.

'I'm going to take you shopping,' he said.

'What?'

'Those pyjama-things do nothing for you. I'll take you out tomorrow, OK?'

She smiled. 'OK, Keith Whatever-your-name-is.'

Sonny got the idea on the way home. They were driving along Sixth Street, a residential area. In one of the houses a wedding was taking place. Fairy-lights were slung through a neem tree; a row of cars was parked outside.

It was then, sitting there seething about Norman Purse, that Sonny had one of his eureka moments. It was an idea so staggeringly bold, so bloody appropriate, that he chuckled out loud.

Jatan Singh, at the wheel, half-turned. No doubt he was surprised that, things being what they were, Sonny-sahib was laughing on the way to the battlefield that had once been his home.

Sonny said nothing. He took out his mobile and punched in a number.

It was eight o'clock, quite dark now, and Theresa still hadn't returned. Dinner was being served but Evelyn was too worried to eat. She stood at the gates looking up and down the street.

'Baksheesh, memsahib?' It was the elderly beggar to whom Minoo had finally given his shoes, that night of tears and confession.

Evelyn shook her head. 'Not tonight, darling.' *Darling?* What was the matter with her? She looked down at the old man's feet. The shoes were dusty now. They were really too big for him; his ankles were as thin as sticks. What an effort it took, simply to remain alive!

217

Where was Theresa? She had been away for hours. Evelyn wished she hadn't let her daughter go alone to the Old City; by all accounts it was a dangerous place, especially at night. She might have been robbed. Raped!

I'll be all right, Mum, don't fuss! My goodness, her daughter was irritable nowadays. Theresa was pushing fifty, she really shouldn't be behaving like a teenager.

Just then a rickshaw drew up. Evelyn's heart leaped.

However, it wasn't Theresa inside. In the light of the street lamp Evelyn could see two women, squashed in the back. They extricated themselves. Muriel and Dorothy.

Evelyn was mildly surprised. She didn't think they were particular friends, they had little in common. In fact it was Muriel who claimed, more triumphantly than any of them, that Dorothy was barmy.

Muriel linked her arm through Dorothy's as they walked up to the gates. She stopped when she saw Evelyn. Her face was tense with excitement.

'This is her home!' she said, indicating Dorothy.

'We prefer not to call it a Home, dear,' said Evelyn. 'It's really a hotel.'

'No,' said Muriel. 'Bangalore's her home. This was where she lived when she was a little girl.'

Dorothy pointed to the Marigold, its lights glimmering through the trees. 'This building was my school,' she said. 'My first school. St Mary's, it was called.'

Norman had raced through dinner. Showered and shaved, dressed in a fresh shirt, he made his way down the drive towards the flickering lights of the rickshaw-stand. Three women – Dorothy, Muriel and Evelyn – stood in the darkness.

'Night night, ladies!' he said cheerfully as he passed. They didn't respond; they were too busy talking. Norman walked through the gates. 'Night!' he said to the *chowkidar*.

Out in the street he paused, checking that his tie was straight. Swaying slightly, he adjusted the handkerchief in his breast pocket. He was about to cross the road when a rickshaw puttered up and came to a halt beside him. Somebody climbed out. It was that Theresa woman, sour-looking creature, Evelyn's daughter.

'Hello, Norman!' Good God, the woman was smiling. 'Where are you off to at this time of night?'

'Aha,' he said. 'That would be telling.'

Theresa coquettishly raised her eyebrows. Surprised, Norman gave her a conspiratorial wink.

Then he climbed into the rickshaw. 'Take me to the Gandhi Market, my good fellow!' he said. 'The Old Town! Chop chop.'

Dinner was over. Four of them were sitting in Dorothy's room drinking whisky. It was the first time Evelyn had seen the BBC woman's bedroom. Shelves were crammed with books and on the wall hung a painting that was apparently by Howard Hodgkin, whoever he was. Its brush-strokes glowed in the lamplight.

Word had got around, of course, that Dorothy had been born in Bangalore and lived there until she was eight. She had only discovered the location of her family home that very afternoon for the city was largely unrecognisable to her now, it had changed so greatly, so many of its old buildings destroyed. Her childhood home lay outside the centre and was now the offices of some multi-national corporation or other. She had finally tracked it down through an old *dhobi-wallah*.

'We saw you there,' said Evelyn. 'At the washing place.'

And this hotel had been her school. Seventy years ago she had played in the garden and sat on the floor in the dining-room singing 'Baa-Baa Black Sheep'. This explained the nursery rhymes, of course. It was a relief that Dorothy could no longer be classified as senile; that sense of communal slippage had gone. Still, it was annoying that she had excluded them from her secret.

'Why didn't you tell us?' asked Evelyn.

'I didn't know you well enough,' replied Dorothy.

'We're all you've got, dear.'

Beside her, Theresa shifted. *Don't be so tactless, Mum*. But she didn't speak.

'What I mean is,' said Evelyn, 'we would have understood.'

219

'I wanted to be sure of it first,' said Dorothy. 'When I got the brochure I thought my memory was playing tricks with me.'

'Can't you see she's tired?' said Muriel, who had been behaving somewhat proprietorially. Maybe she felt guilty for her earlier remarks. 'It's been a big day, hasn't it, love?'

Dorothy nodded. There was something about the way she sat there, on the bed, that made Evelyn feel like an intruder. She thought: There's so little privacy here, just the small sanctuary of our bedrooms. In this communal life we struggle to keep ourselves intact. Turning away, she gazed at the painting. She had never caught up with the abstract movement and now she never would. Somehow the colours seemed so sure of themselves – bold brushes of brick-red and indigo-blue. Perhaps you didn't have to understand; you just had to look.

Dorothy was crying. Theresa jumped up and put her arm around her. Evelyn resented this. Still, it was her daughter's job, she supposed. Counsellors knew when a hug was in order.

'I'm so sorry,' said Dorothy. 'I'll be better tomorrow.'

'Do you want to talk about it?' asked Theresa.

Dorothy shook her head. 'Not just now.' She sat there, a big plain woman, shuddering with sobs. Evelyn gave her a tissue.

It was clear that she wanted to be alone. They left. Outside the room Theresa turned to her mother. 'What a day!'

'What a day.'

'I'm exhausted,' Theresa said. 'I'm going to bed.'

'I never asked,' said Evelyn. 'Did you meet your holy man?'

'Not exactly.' Suddenly Theresa put her arms around Evelyn and hugged her. 'Night night, Mum.' Half-way up the stairs she turned and said: 'Actually, I came to India because I missed you.'

The rickshaw chap seemed unwilling to take Norman any further. Probably the alley was too narrow. Norman paid him; the rickshaw swung round and juddered off in a cloud of exhaust smoke.

Norman's heart pounded. What an adventure! How they would be twittering, back at the hotel, if they knew! Here he stood, in the middle of the Old City, in a street that smelt of drains and sandalwood, on his way to visit a lady of the night. *This woman*

Sikra is a sorceress, old boy, said Sonny. *What breasts, what a pussy! I tell you, Norman-sahib, a honeypot like hers will bring the dead back to life!* Norman paused, swaying. He had shipped a few brandies before embarking on this enterprise. Crumbling buildings loomed up on either side. Lights shone in a tea-house where various villainous-looking men sat about smoking. Somewhere a radio was playing. *She's waiting for you, my friend. She is my Christmas present to your esteemed self.*

Shop-keepers were pulling down the shutters; Gandhi Market was packing up for the night. Norman made his way down the alley. It was so narrow that those unsteady on their feet could bump against one wall and then the other. He arrived at the Hindu temple, as per instructions. On the step sat a dog, licking its private parts. *Walk past the temple until you come to a blue door. Knock loudly and ask for Sikra. Mention my name and they will lead you up the stairway to heaven.*

'You are from which country, sir?' Little boys clamoured around him.

'Bugger off!' Norman waved his stick.

They reassembled like flies. 'Please sir, you are from which country?' They pulled at his trousers.

'Piss off and go home! It's past your bedtime!'

Norman tried to concentrate. Breasts. Great voluptuous breasts the size of melons. He felt a faint stirring in his groin. See! There was life in the old todger yet. Stupid of him to have been worried. Those months – years – of doubt, and all he needed was this: darkness, a foreign land, exotic flesh . . . the only combination that was guaranteed, more or less, to get the old equipment up and running.

Still, his heart hammered against his rib-cage. He arrived at the blue door. Touching his tie – all shipshape – he knocked smartly with his walking-stick.

The children seemed to have melted away, thank God. Norman heard a movement behind the door. Somebody hawked and spat. The door opened, just a little. He glimpsed a painted face.

'Good evening,' he said. 'Mr Sonny Rahim sent me. Do you speak English?'

221

'OK.' The head waggled.

'I'm looking for Sikra.'

'OK.'

Nothing happened. He suddenly had a vision of his daughter. *Dad, what on earth are you doing?*

The door opened and he stepped into a passage. It was illuminated by a fly-bespattered strip light. He smelt perfume and incense. The sari-clad figure pointed upstairs and disappeared into a room. Norman heard the sound of voices, then the door closed.

He paused. Suddenly he pictured the Marigold, so blithely abandoned. He pictured his room – Wisdens on the shelf; radio, tuned to the World Service, waiting on the bedside table. His heart pumped. He had to admit he had expected something a little more salubrious. A chap didn't expect a welcoming committee but there was usually a hostess of some kind, and a frilly lamp.

Norman rallied. He had better go through with it. If Sonny found out he'd flunked it he would never live it down. A fellow had his pride.

He made his way up the creaking wooden stairs. Staggering slightly – they seemed to be rocking – he arrived on the landing. A door stood ajar.

Norman stepped into the room. Breathing heavily, he tried to regain his balance. This looked more like it. The room glowed with rosy light. On the wall hung photographs of Doris Day and Bruce Willis. There were plastic flowers in a vase, and a collection of Dinky cars on the shelf. And there was a bed, covered with an apricot satin eiderdown and a heap of soft toys.

Nobody was there. It was an odd business, he had to admit it: carnal union with a complete stranger. Somehow it never quite lived up to expectations. One always felt a bit let-down afterwards, post-coital *tristesse* and all that. But how could a chap tell, otherwise, that he still had blood in his veins? That he wasn't, to all extents and purposes, already dead?

The door opened and a figure appeared. She was startlingly tall, and smoking a cigarette. Her face was heavily made-up and she wore a pink sari trimmed with gold.

Norman put out his hand. 'Sikra, I presume?'

222

She grinned and patted the bed. There was no doubt she was a handsome woman; something commanding about her but that was all right, in a situation like this he welcomed a female who knew what she was doing.

'I'm Norman Purse,' he said. 'Pleased to meet you. Mr Sonny Rahim sent me.'

'*Acha*.' The woman stubbed out her cigarette in an ashtray shaped like a corgi. Her bangles tinkled. 'You want soft drink?' She smiled invitingly. 'Thums-Up? Limco?'

'I'm fine, my dear. Drunk quite enough tonight.' Norman cleared his throat. 'I've heard a lot about you.'

She patted the bed again. He sat down beside her, the sateen sighing. Sikra leaned over and unknotted his tie. What big, capable hands she had! She took off his jacket.

Norman looked down at his own purple hands, resting on his knees. Should he start undressing her? Is that how they did it, here? He wasn't sure about the Hindu way of going about it and didn't want to offend. The girls in Bangkok didn't have any sort of culture thing.

'I live on Brigade Road,' he said. 'Do you know it?'

Sikra moved her head a little and pulled off his tie.

'Never been to India before,' he said. 'Born at the wrong time, I suppose. I would've enjoyed it in the old days. Feel in a way I'm at the fag-end of history. For my lot, of course,' he added hastily, 'not yours.'

She moved closer.

'Haven't done this for a while,' he said. 'Years, in fact. Might be a bit rusty.'

He had never seen so much slap. The woman's face was plastered with the stuff – pale powder, pink rouge. He couldn't imagine kissing her but that probably wasn't called for. His faint stirrings subsided. He tried to superimpose his fantasies – the nipples as dark as chocolate buttons, the sari unravelling as she span like a top.

'You want sex now?' asked Sikra. She had an attractive husky voice.

'May need a little encouragement.' Norman tried to laugh. Unlike his penis, his heart seemed to have a life of its own. It jolted so hard he rocked on the bed. Sikra unzipped his fly and slid her hand in. Her fingers sought his balls and started kneading them. Norman stroked her chiffon-clad thigh. Where did one start with these damn saris? There seemed to be no visible opening.

Sikra's face loomed closer. She stuck out her tongue and waggled it, startling him. Her hand remained in his trousers, stroking his flaccid member. Her bangles tinkled faster. Nothing doing.

She wrenched off his trousers, down to his ankles, pulled down his underpants and pushed him back on the bed. She pulled up her sari in a workmanlike manner, as if rolling up her sleeves, took his hand and put it between her legs.

Suddenly Norman realised. That strong jaw, that blue shadow beneath the powder! He froze with shock. Pain shot across his chest.

Dorothy couldn't sleep. She stood in the garden listening to the trilling of the crickets. Where the aviary now stood there had been a Wendy house. They had sat in it for hours – herself, Nancy Mayhew and Monica Cable – crooning over their dolls. Her schoolfriends no doubt had grown up to have babies of their own, now middle-aged. They had dared to love, and been loved in return.

Dorothy knew she had been ungracious earlier but it was all so overwhelming. Years, it had been, since she had cried in public. She knew, of course, why she hadn't told them earlier. The pity, the sympathy, the fluttering around her – it would have been suffocating. Now the lid had been lifted. She could stir in her box and feel people's breath on her face. Back home, in her former life, the waxworks stood on their plinths. When she was young she believed that at night they woke up. They stepped down and mingled, chattering across the centuries.

In a former life she too had stood on a stage. Her career as an actress had been a failure. Even at the time she had known the reason. To surrender yourself, the freefall of it, you had to trust others to catch you. Tonight she had come nowhere near explaining but she had felt the kindness of strangers.

Dorothy walked down to the gates. Wrapped in a military blanket, the *chowkidar* slept. As she stood there, something unclosed within her. Across the road the little bazaar was dark. In the street light she could see bodies slumbering; they lay like waxworks that nobody would pay to see. Nearby, the elderly beggar lay in his usual spot. He was swaddled in a cloth. Only his feet protruded, wearing surprisingly smart shoes.

It was three in the morning. In Karishma Plaza, however, the lights blazed. When she was little this office block didn't exist. St Mary's Convent had stood across the road, shaded by tamarind trees. Her teacher, Sister Ruth, had owned a pet monkey. Once Dorothy had seen two nuns sitting on the swing, laughing like young girls. They *were* young girls.

She remembered the office building across the Marylebone Road, the security guard swivelling round on his chair. He was Indian too. Maybe he was dreaming of his lost homeland, just as she did, the traffic sliding between them.

Dorothy walked back towards the hotel. In the bushes a cat miaowed for Eithne, who had deserted him. It was cool; Dorothy wrapped her dressing-gown around her. From their pots, the lilies exhaled their perfume.

> *The moon shines bright; in such a night as this,*
> *When the sweet wind did gently kiss the trees*
> *And they did make no noise; in such a night*
> *Troilus methinks mounted the Trojan walls*
> *And sighed his soul towards the Grecian tents*
> *Where Cressid lay that night.*

Dorothy paused on the driveway, looking up.

> *Look how the floor of heaven*
> *Is thick inlaid with patines of bright gold.*

At the side of the hotel a light shone, illuminating the veranda. It was Muriel's room.

'Norman's not back,' Muriel hissed from her open window. 'He was sozzled tonight.'

Dorothy went indoors to Muriel's room, and sat down. Muriel

climbed back into bed. She wore a winceyette nightie printed with flowers.

'It's just like school here, isn't it,' said Dorothy. It *was* school.

'He's dead, I know he is,' said Muriel.

'Norman?'

'No. My Keith. Somebody's died tonight.'

'Don't be silly,' said Dorothy. 'A lot of people have died tonight but your son's not one of them.'

'I can feel it.'

'I'm sure he's fine.'

She felt close to Muriel tonight. Muriel had seen her childhood home. Afterwards they had travelled around the city and Dorothy had pointed out the few places she dimly remembered, the few that remained – Nancy Mayhew's house, now the Inspectorate of Highways; the bungalow in Cunningham Street where Dorothy had gone for dancing lessons, now a restaurant serving Steak'n'Seafood Sizzlers. The fog dissolved, revealing the landscape of her past. She thought: How could my parents have sent me away, across the world?

'Children are what keep you alive, see,' said Muriel.

'Do they?' asked Dorothy. 'I wouldn't know.'

'They're how you carry on after you've passed,' said Muriel. 'I've given up this Indian rubbish. It doesn't work.'

'I think the only thing that lasts is art,' said Dorothy.

'I wanted to tell Keith what happened, see,' said Muriel. 'I never did, I kept putting it off and now it's too late.' Her fingers kneaded the coverlet. Without her teeth her face had fallen in. 'They sent me away because of what happened with Leonard.'

'Leonard?'

'They had me evacuated to Melton Mowbray,' said Muriel. 'It was like the end of the world, like further than here. They took away my baby, I was only sixteen, see, they took away my baby and sent me away.' She started crying. 'And when I got back Lenny was dead. He was the love of my life, Dotty, he had such lovely hair. And then I married his brother and Keith was born and Paddy was his father but somewhere there's this other little boy but Keith doesn't know and this other little boy, Charlie was his name,

226

he was made with love.' Muriel raised her face. It was terrible to see. Dorothy looked around for a Kleenex but there weren't any.

'I'm so sorry,' Dorothy said. 'So very sorry.' Just for a moment she thought: This would make a good documentary.

Muriel wiped her cheeks with the coverlet.

'I was sent away too,' said Dorothy. 'When I was eight, not sixteen. My parents sent me away from here, to boarding-school in England. It was the end of my world.' There, she had said it. 'I'm sure it was for my own good but I felt utterly unwanted. India was stolen from me. India stole my parents from me. Nobody could love me after that because how could they, when my parents didn't? Oh I don't know. My whole life has been a mess.'

She stopped to catch her breath. She thought of her friends, the bright young men with whom she had worked, so many of them dead from AIDS; she thought of her Hungarian lover and others before him and she realised: I've never told anybody this. Here I am telling it to a toothless old lady from Peckham who's probably not that interested anyway.

Far away in the lobby the phone rang. There was nobody around to answer it.

It rang and rang, while the two women sat there, lost in their thoughts, and then it stopped.

4

If thy soul finds rest in me, thou shalt overcome all dangers by my grace; but if thy thoughts are on thyself, and thou wilt not listen, thou shalt perish.

(*The Bhagavad Gita*)

Norman's death stunned the residents. A heart attack, apparently. They sat in the lounge, under a solitary paper-chain; the stringing-up of the Christmas decorations had come to a standstill.

'I can't believe it,' said Hermione. 'Such a character. Such a life-force.' She was a churchgoer and nice about everybody.

'I still don't understand how it happened,' said somebody.

'He lost his way in the bazaar,' said someone else.

'But what was he doing there?'

'Buying something, I suppose. A Christmas present.'

'But wouldn't the shops be closed?'

'Perhaps they stay open late at Christmas, like Dickins & Jones.'

'In the *bazaar*?'

'But surely they don't believe in Christmas, here.'

'Yes they do, dear. We taught it to them.'

'For God's sake!' interrupted Madge. 'The man was on the razzle, the randy old tomcat.'

'Madge!'

'He had a heart attack on the job.'

There was a silence. Hermione shifted in her armchair.

'What job?' asked Stella.

'Peter Sellers went that way.'

'Did he really?'

228

'Who are you talking about?'
'– with his wife. That film star.'
'His poor daughter.'
'Whose, dear?'
'What are we going to tell her when she arrives?'
'If one has to go it's got to be the best way. Quick.'

Outside it had clouded over. A breeze blew through the door, chilling their cheeks. After all, it was December. The paper-chain shivered.

'I know! Britt Ekland.'

Minoo had told them the news at breakfast. Norman's body had been taken to the hospital to await instructions. His daughter had been informed and would be arriving the next morning, a day early. What's the hurry? thought Douglas. Norman's son-in-law, apparently, had changed his plans and would be accompanying her. It seemed you had to die before people travelled across the world to visit you. Neither of Douglas's children was coming for Christmas; that must be because he and Jean were still alive.

Douglas had had mixed feelings about Norman but his death had affected him deeply. Already he had been feeling rocky. That night, weeks ago, he had put something into words and nothing could erase it. The word 'ghastly', which he never normally used, had lodged itself in his head. *I am married to a ghastly woman. She's boastful. She's boring. She's fathomlessly smug. The thought of spending the rest of my life with her is too ghastly to contemplate.* How strange that he had never realised it before. They had always been so busy rushing around, off to Portugal, off on some NADFAS tour. Maybe it had been lurking but he hadn't dared to admit it because then, like the nuclear bomb, it could never be uninvented.

Norman's death had demonstrated, if such proof was needed, that life is short. If only good manners worked, when it came to death. *After you. No, after you.* They had been precious little use in the past. In fact it was good manners that had made him marry Jean. Oh, she was lively and attractive, he had enjoyed going to bed with her, but to be honest he had married her because she had presumed they would and he didn't want to be considered a

229

cad. Forty-eight years had passed, seemingly in his sleep. And now, sooner rather than later, he would die. *YOU first!* Like jumping into the sea on a freezing day. *You go first and tell me what it's like.*

No doubt the women in the Marigold envied his marriage. How little they knew. He had a strong desire to confide in Evelyn. She and Dorothy were the only people who might understand. This was impossible, of course. He must take his secret to the grave.

Lunch had been served – coronation chicken or fried pomfret. Life had to go on, meals had to be cooked and cleared away. The servants, no doubt used to the presence of death, carried on with their duties. The residents, of course, had suffered their losses but India seemed to display the flimsiness of life on a larger scale than the one to which they were accustomed. Olive Cooke swore that a bundled-up body lying beside Gulshan Crafts, opposite, had been there for two days.

The sun had come out. Evelyn sat on the veranda, a sparrow in her lap. It had been walloped by the ceiling fan and lay there, stunned. This had happened on several previous occasions. Various women had nursed the birds on their laps but so far none had revived.

'Just off, Mum, see you later.' Theresa crossed the veranda.

'Where are you going?'

Theresa smiled. 'Shopping.'

Good Lord, her daughter was wearing lipstick! The effect was transforming. The last time she had worn it was for Evelyn and Hugh's silver wedding.

Evelyn watched Theresa walking briskly towards the gates. She suspected that her daughter was going to buy her a Christmas present. She hoped she wouldn't have to be polite about it; usually Theresa got her some item from the Greenpeace catalogue that Evelyn discreetly passed on to her cleaning lady.

'Any sign of life?' asked Douglas from the next table.

Evelyn looked in her lap. The sparrow hadn't stirred. 'Not yet.'

'Oh well, hope springs eternal.'

Douglas sat with his wife, who was writing a letter. His Wilbur

Smith was propped in front of him but Evelyn knew that he hadn't been reading it. They were all somewhat distracted by the news. It was already disorientating, to realise they were living in Dorothy's old school. Today, however, there was a jumpiness in the air. One-and-a-half down (Eithne being the half); whose turn was next?

So Norman was, as Madge somewhat crudely called it, *on the job*. It was called *le petit mort*, Evelyn knew that. From her own admittedly limited experience, lovemaking was a companionable rather than near-death thing. She wondered if Graham Turner was a virgin. He sat under the peepul tree writing in a notebook. One only had to look at him to guess that this was probably the case. What had he got to show for a lifetime in the civil service?

Then there was her own daughter. Theresa, too, hadn't had much luck in that department. The few love-affairs that Evelyn knew about had ended in a welter of recrimination. Theresa made things so complicated. She wanted to turn everything into a relationship, a word that to Evelyn always spelled trouble. Once people called it that, everything seemed to go wrong. Why couldn't Theresa just be happy? Time was short – terrifyingly short. *Gather ye rosebuds while ye may*. Evelyn had learnt that at school where of course it hadn't meant a thing. Here, despite the little fusses and annoyances, she sensed she was in the company of people who, somehow or other, had this at the back of their minds.

And tomorrow Christopher would arrive, with family in tow. She knew he had booked this holiday especially to see her but the prospect filled her with dread. It would all start up again as if there had been no interruption . . . The blame, the resentment. *You always sided with Christopher, you and Dad, I was never the sort of daughter you wanted me to be.* Boarding-school, no doubt, would rear its ugly head. Good Lord, Dorothy had been banished across the world at eight years old and she was all right. Well, maybe not all right, but she had survived.

And Theresa was so indiscreet. Had she no sense of decorum at all? *In our family nobody believed in talking*, she said. She had certainly made up for it since. At their first breakfast she had tried to explain Munchausen Syndrome to Jimmy, the bearer, who was serving them Sugar Puffs. She believed that servants were people and should be included in the proceedings.

'I used to pretend I was ill,' Theresa told the old man. 'Just to get people's attention.'

'I don't think he understands, dear,' said Evelyn.

'I used to limp on walks.'

'Theresa, they don't have to *pretend* to limp here.'

She had to admit that Theresa seemed to have perked up since yesterday. That hug on the stairs had been something of a breakthrough. But Theresa was a turbulent woman and at a tricky time of life. It must be terrible to realise that the possibility of children had finally been extinguished. After all, without children who would look after a person in their old age?

Who? Evelyn ignored this thought. She gazed into the garden. Graham Turner put away his notebook and went indoors for his nap.

Evelyn touched the sparrow. It was rigid, either from fear or from death. Whichever reason, she would let it lie there a little longer.

'I keep thinking he's going to burst out of the hotel booming *fooled you all!*' said Douglas.

Evelyn presumed he was talking to his wife but Jean had dozed off; he was talking to her.

232

5

'*With a rising population of eight million, Bangalore is one of
the fastest-growing cities in Asia,*' read Christopher. '*Listen, kids.
At the cutting edge of the technological revolution, Bangalore is
a thriving modern metropolis with pubs, clubs and great shopping opportunities.*'

They were travelling on the coach from Mysore. Across the
aisle the children sprawled in their seats.

'Sounds promising, eh?' said Christopher. 'If you're all templed
out.'

'Temples suck,' said Clementine.

'Buildings can't suck, sweetheart,' he replied.

Beside him Marcia flung back her head and glugged from the
water bottle. He thought of her lips clamped around his cock. *That
woman sucks me like chrome off a trailer-hitch.* Where had he
heard that? Some film. His wife thrummed with energy. To be
truthful, her demands on this holiday had been somewhat overwhelming – sucking, straddling, pressing his buttocks into her as
she experienced her spectacular multiple orgasms. After each one
he thought she had finished but no, another was on its way.
However soft and shrunken he had become she still availed herself
of his body; in fact it hardly seemed to matter whether he was
inside her or not. Whether he was there at all. To be perfectly
honest she could be rubbing herself against a traffic bollard. The

233

night before she had summoned him into the shower. Whilst attempting to pinion her against the tiles he had slipped on a bar of soap and nearly ricked his back. Of course the noise she made was gratifying but he worried that the children would wake up in the next room. India seemed to be having an unsettling effect upon her.

The coach had come to a standstill. The driver hooted. Outside the window was a truck stop, a scruffy place puddled with oil. HORN PLEASE was painted on the parked lorries. GOOD LUCK. Christopher's fellow holiday-makers leaned into the aisle to see what was holding them up.

Beside him truck drivers lounged on rope beds. How contented they looked! They lay there, smoking cigarettes. Sealed into his air-conditioned coach Christopher felt thrust into intimacy with these strangers. The place reminded him of his flat in Clapham – undoubtedly squalid but somehow simple in its demands. Nobody asked anything of these men: they drove, they slept, they smoked without Marcia reacting as if she had caught them masturbating. Christopher had a sudden desire to wrench open the coach door and step into another life. GOOD LUCK! He could climb into a gaudily painted lorry and drive away. In America his wife did the driving because she said he drank too much. In America he had screwed up his career and financially ruined his mother. In America his children treated him like a servant.

Christopher closed his eyes. He could step into another world and start all over again; the coach would drive on and nobody would notice he had gone. He would be like Jack Nicholson in that film, when he crossed the forecourt at the petrol station. In his new life Christopher would have children who laughed at his jokes and a beautiful wife who called him Topher in her lilting Indian voice filled with love. Who would squeeze out his shirts in the river and straighten up, when she heard his footfall, shading her face from the sun. He would be cherished.

The coach moved on. Christopher gazed at the passing countryside. His old life could evaporate, just like that. The lumber of it – the skis and pasta machines, the *things*, the *stuff* – they could disappear with a click of the fingers. Nothing had weight here, it was all insubstantial. He thought of the moths that fluttered in the wardrobe back in Sussex. One clap and they were smears of powder between his palms.

The coach shunted forward. Marcia closed her eyes. She was back in the temple at Halebib. A group of young men were wandering around looking at the friezes. Young Indian men, office workers maybe – short-sleeved shirts, oiled hair. They moved into the inner sanctum, and stopped.

Marcia lay on the plinth, her skirt bunched up around her waist. The stone was warm under her skin. Look at me, a goddess of sex! Her blouse was unbuttoned; with one hand she stroked her breast. She stroked with a gentle, circular movement; her forefinger brushed her hardening nipple.

Her legs were spread open. Luxuriously she pleasured herself. As she did so, she turned her head to look at the young men.

They stood there, gazing at her. Their hands moved to their crotches. Closing her eyes, she heard their collective breath . . . rasping, quickening . . .

'Mom, are we nearly there?'

Marcia opened her eyes. They were travelling through the outskirts of a city – open drains, apartment buildings topped with a scribble of TV aerials.

'Soon, honey,' she said.

'I'm thirsty.'

She passed the bottle of water.

'I want a *Coke*.'

Marcia closed her eyes again. Each night, in bed with her husband, she concentrated on different faces. As she lay there, gripping Christopher's soft, middle-aged flesh between her thighs, it was a brown face that loomed above her; it was a big brown dick pumping inside her, making her cry out. And while she was doing it there were more men watching her, she brought them into the bedroom too. Those Kerala fishermen, naked except for loincloths, sat against the wall; they gazed at her open legs, her hips rising and falling. A row of sweepers, ravishing young men grey with dust, fondled themselves under their *lunghis*.

Everywhere in India men were watching her. Christopher never looked at her, not really. Too damn English. These men hungered for her; they brought her to life. They delivered up a new Marcia to herself – desirable, thrillingly pale, and beautiful at last.

For the rest of his life Christopher replayed that moment. A number of years remained to him; the date of his death was written on a palm leaf but he was ignorant of its existence. For the rest of his life, which was a long one, he remembered that moment when the doors of the Taj Balmoral sighed open and he stepped into the lobby. Musak played. A turbanned doorman bowed and a woman stepped up to him. He supposed his family was with him but they evaporated as if they had never been.

She wore a midnight-blue sari shot with silver. Of course she was beautiful but then most Indian women were exquisite. There was something else about her – a yielding, ineffable sweetness, a grace. She lifted up a garland of flowers. Christopher bowed his head and she laid it around his neck.

'*Namaste*,' she said, placing her hands together. Her bangles, tinkling, shifted down her wrists. She bowed. *You are my lord and master.*

'*Namaste*,' he said, sounding like a berk.

She was blessing him; she was making it all better. She dipped her finger into a pot and pressed it to his forehead. As she concentrated, the tip of her tongue protruded between her teeth. Her eyes met his and she smiled.

'Welcome to the Taj Balmoral,' she said. 'We hope you enjoy your stay.'

Christopher had never believed in love at first sight; not until that moment. He simply felt accepted, in all his pallid clumsiness. Later she told him she was just finishing her shift. Five minutes later and she would have gone for lunch. Christopher, newly sensitised by love, had pictured the many obstructions he had encountered on eight days of Indian roads. Another herd of goats, another crashed lorry, another holy cow just standing there. Another blithering comfort stop, and Aisha would not have stepped into his life with her marigolds and musky, dizzying promise of happi-

236

ness. Such was the fragility of it all. Out of its chaos India had delivered him up a miracle. It would bring suffering in its wake, but then India knew all about suffering, too.

Ravi had insisted on accompanying Pauline to Bangalore. 'Of course you can't go alone, not now.' Pauline suspected that now her father was no longer in residence the Marigold was a more attractive proposition. She couldn't say this, of course, not when Ravi was being so supportive. He thought she needed him in her hour of grief.

In fact her father's death had affected Pauline less painfully than she had expected. It was the strangest sensation, the world without him in it, but Norman had led an enjoyable life entirely devoted to satisfying his own needs and had died at a ripe old age, waited on hand and foot by kindly staff and surrounded by pleasant companions. There seemed worse ways to go. Pauline was surprised at her own equanimity. Maybe she had absorbed some Indian fatalism without realising it. In fact it was Ravi who seemed more upset. She suspected this stemmed from guilt.

Sonny, too, seemed powerfully affected. Pauline couldn't understand this. Was the busy little wheeler-dealer really that fond of her father? She knew that they sometimes had a drink together but Sonny's reaction to his death seemed out of all proportion; the man seemed genuinely upset.

Norman was cremated the day after they arrived and a small service was held at St Patrick's Church. Sonny snuffled throughout. Afterwards they went outside. Pauline pointed at the gravestones: the young subalterns cut down in their prime – *Lawrence Lennox, Standish Wilson* – their wives and children too. 'Look, typhoid fever and only twenty-two years old,' she said. 'Only *six*.' She put her arm around Sonny's plump shoulder. 'Compared to them, my Dad had a good innings.' Really, she thought, it should be *Sonny* comforting *me*.

She suspected that the true causes of his distress were the various crises that had gripped the hotel in the past few days. Dr Rama had been sacked. The manager's marriage had broken up and his wife had moved out to her sister's. The cook, upset by

Norman's death, had gone on a drinking binge and hadn't been seen for the past two days. The residents seemed unaware of these backstage dramas; meals had been cobbled together by Minoo and the kitchen boy and Mrs Cowasjee had all but retired from public life anyway.

'No doctor, no nurse,' whispered Ravi. 'What happens if anybody gets ill?'

'They've always got you,' said Pauline.

Ravi didn't reply. Along Lady Curzon Street the sun was sinking. They were returning from the church in a minibus Sonny had organised for the residents to pay their last respects. Tongas clopped home from Bangalore's modest tourist attractions. Pauline looked at the skinny horses, at the concrete buildings molten in the evening light. The sunsets were so beautiful here they brought tears to her eyes. It seemed to be India, rather than her father, that had the power to make her cry.

Ahead lay the melancholy task of sorting out her father's things. It would be an odd Christmas, celebrating with near-strangers. But no odder, she thought, than it must be for them.

Evelyn was having dinner at the Taj Balmoral with her son, his wife and Theresa. Her grandchildren, thank goodness, had been sent to bed. She had to admit that their behaviour had disappointed her. Those two little darlings, Joseph and Clementine, had grown into American brats. She could hardly believe they were relations of hers at all, and, by the look in their eyes, she suspected they felt the same. Not a word of thanks for the gifts she had given them nor the slightest interest in their surroundings; all they did was whine that the TV didn't work. How could children who had everything be so ungrateful? Indian children, who had so little, were by comparison enchantingly polite, even when asking for money.

Apart from this the visit had been an unexpected success. Christopher and his sister hadn't quarrelled once. It was strange how the thing you most dreaded could just evaporate. The two of them, in fact, looked somewhat distracted – dreamy, even. Nor did Theresa show any of her normal hostility to Marcia. And how attractive Theresa looked – almost vampish – in a red strappy dress trimmed with spangles. It must have raised a few eyebrows in the ashrams.

Evelyn had told them about the cremation that afternoon, about Dorothy's revelations and the manager's marital troubles. 'He sent his wife packing on Tuesday. The poor man was so unhappy. Nobody knew except me; we're friends, you see. He even showed me the shoes he wore, when they met.'

'Has he fallen in love with someone else?' asked Christopher, putting down his fork.

Evelyn shook her head. 'He just felt beaten down by her. His wife was very bossy.'

'Really?' asked Christopher.

'Don't be fooled by those saris,' said Evelyn. 'Indian women can be very domineering. The man was a wreck, she made him feel so inadequate, you see.'

There was a silence. Christopher toyed with a prawn.

Marcia gazed at the sitar player, a young man in full Indian dress who sat on a plinth in the corner. 'Isn't he beautiful?' she murmured.

Marcia wore a turquoise top embroidered with mirrors. They seemed to be flashing messages of whose significance only their owner was aware. Perhaps India was having a beneficial effect on their marriage, Evelyn thought. The last time she had seen the two of them relations seemed strained. Marcia was such a nervy woman but now it seemed that her inner wires had been cut. She looked relaxed; almost pretty.

Evelyn would never discover the reason. Tomorrow, Christmas Eve, they would be gone.

'Just think, Christmas on a beach!' said Evelyn. Her son and his family were travelling to Goa.

'I'm sorry we can't be here,' said Marcia. 'It's the itinerary.'

'Don't worry, it's been lovely seeing you,' said Evelyn. They had been to the Bull Temple and the Botanical Gardens, they had crammed a lot into the two days. The visit could be counted a success despite the strangely bland atmosphere as if everybody were sleep-walking.

'I feel very spoilt having you with me at all,' said Evelyn. 'Some people have relatives flying out in January, after they've spent the actual day with their nearest and dearest.' She stopped. Weren't *grandparents* supposed to be one's nearest and dearest? 'Muriel Donnelly thinks her son's going to appear, poor soul. It's the only thing that keeps her going. Hermione's been praying for her each Sunday.'

'Where is her son?' asked Theresa.

'God only knows.' Evelyn smiled. 'Perhaps that's why Hermione's been asking him. No answer so far. He sounds rather a rum character.'

'Who, God?' asked Theresa.

'No dear, her son. Into all sorts of shady dealings, apparently.'

'What sorts?' asked Theresa.

'Haven't a clue. Nor has Muriel.'

A horrible suspicion was dawning on Evelyn. Perhaps Theresa was taking drugs. That would explain the long absences, sometimes for a whole afternoon. She returned bright-eyed, her cheeks flushed. Bangalore was apparently awash with drugs, Evelyn had read it in *The Times of Karnataka*, their reliable supply of English newspapers having died with Norman.

'Organised crime is rife in the city, with corruption at the highest levels. Crores of rupees are at stake in the escalating drugs traffic.'

Evelyn watched her daughter. Theresa swabbed a piece of *naan* bread around her plate and tore at it with her teeth. As she did so, she gazed dreamily into space. In the candle-light, Evelyn squinted at Theresa's arms. Were those needle-marks or mosquito-bites?

Evelyn felt a sinking sensation in her bowels. Oh Lord. Perhaps this explained her daughter's frequent trips to India. *I'm an India junkie*, she had said once. *I need my fix*. Evelyn wasn't entirely ignorant on these matters. Oh Lord.

'How're your young call-centre friends?' asked Christopher.

Evelyn rallied. 'Surinda got the sack last week, I'm afraid. Her heart wasn't in it. She kept asking people about England and never got around to making any sales. Such a shame.'

Maybe she should ask the doctor's advice – the real doctor from England, Dr Ravi Kapoor, not the VD one with the hair. *The fellow's a charlatan!* Suddenly, ridiculously, she missed Norman. Surinda too had disappeared from her life. It had been nice to have young faces around, faces that didn't mirror back her own mortality. Living with old people was so ageing. That was the point of families – well, one of the points. Different generations thrown together. Now she had lost her surrogate granddaughter, Surinda, and her own daughter, the drug addict, would soon be gone.

The Lotus Restaurant was on the top floor; below them spread the lights of the city. Tonight India felt alien to Evelyn, alarmingly so. Her efforts to tune herself into the place during the past weeks felt phoney and misguided. Having no option, she had willed herself into feeling at home. In fact this country had transformed her children into strangers – adults with secrets she could no longer penetrate. Look at them, toying with their napkins and smiling to themselves!

No doubt this is natural, she thought. It doesn't take India to turn one's children into middle-aged adults with lives of their own. Oh Hugh, she thought. Oh Hugh.

'Happy Christmas, Ma.' Christopher leaned across the table and gave her a package.

Evelyn opened it. Inside lay some beautiful cloth, folded up: deep red silk with a gold border.

'It's a sari,' he said. 'I know, I know, but maybe just once, for a special occasion.'

'Where did you get that?' asked Marcia sharply. Evelyn suspected that it was Marcia who usually bought the presents.

'Just a shop,' he said. 'It's a *banarasi* sari.'

'A what?' asked Marcia.

'A *banarasi* sari, for special occasions.'

'How do you know that?' Marcia stared at him.

Christopher cleared his throat. 'I read it in the guide book. Now who's for pudding?'

Evelyn thanked him, though she couldn't imagine ever wearing a sari, nor an occasion special enough to warrant such a thing.

Widows in India wore white ones, as if they were already ghosts. She was glad Christopher hadn't got her one of those.

'He's great, isn't he?' said Marcia.

Evelyn nodded. 'So generous of him.'

Marcia didn't mean Christopher, however. She was gazing at the sitar player.

'Look at those hands,' Marcia said softly. 'The way they hold the instrument.'

Evelyn folded up the wrapping paper. Her generation, like Indians, never threw anything away. It might come in handy later.

'The way they move over the strings,' said Marcia, and relapsed into silence.

Pauline took her husband's hand and led him through the garden.

'I want to show you something,' she said.

It was late. She led him past the servants' quarters. A light glowed through the window; someone hawked and spat. Here, in their own homes, the familiar old bearers were strangers.

'Where are you taking me?' Ravi whispered.

'Through the wall.'

The moon was full. It was a clear night, the stars mirroring the lights of the city below. They were making their way through the furthest corner of the garden, where none of the guests ventured. In a pile of rubbish, something stirred.

Ahead was the door, half-obscured by creepers. 'The servants use this route,' Pauline whispered. 'When they go out. Errands and things. Back to their villages, perhaps, on their day off. I don't know.'

She turned the knob. The door creaked open. They stepped through and emerged into the waste ground behind the hotel. There was a smell of shit. Ravi lifted his foot and inspected his shoe. Thorn bushes stood frozen in the moonlight; plastic bags were caught in their branches. Beyond them were the huts where the rag-pickers lived.

'Isn't it like *Alice Through the Looking Glass*?' Pauline whispered. 'Stepping into another world?'

'What do you want to show me?' Ravi was trying to be kind.

242

After all, today her father had been dispatched to wherever it was that people went.

'Dorothy's parents knew people who lived here,' she whispered. 'She told me today. Years ago there was a garden here, and a bungalow. They were called Colonel and Mrs Hislop and she drank lemonade while they played bridge.'

She wanted her husband to feel the magic of this place. Surely it was still hidden in him somewhere, a connection?

'Sweetheart, I promised Minoo I'd look at the accounts,' he said. 'The poor chap'll be longing to go to bed.'

'I want to look after people,' Pauline said. 'You've done it all your life but I want to do it now. Those children I met, I've got their photos but I'll never find them. Imagine building them a home here, the ones who're alone in the world. I could be some use, Ravi.' She looked at his beautiful, grave profile. 'Old and young people could be together. Don't you see, it makes sense?' She pointed to the hotel behind them. 'They miss young faces around them, they pine for them. They could teach them things, they both like the same sort of food, they think the same way. Old and young people have an awful lot in common, second childhood and all that. And they have all the time in the world.'

She stopped. It had come out more tepidly than she meant. Ravi's presence had somehow sapped her.

He leaned towards her and pushed a strand of hair behind her ear. 'It's a lovely idea, darling. But I think they're going to build a shopping mall here.'

Ravi felt terrible. He knew he should be sympathetic but this place was dragging him under. It always happened, this slow suffocation. Back in the room the phone would be winking: his mother calling from Delhi, *When are you coming, my little Raviji? . . . Your father's chest pains . . . your sister and that no-good husband of hers . . . your brother has been calling from Toronto, a divorce is on the cards and who's going to pay his debts and what's going to happen, that boy is wrecking his career . . .* Sonny, too, changed here. He shrank, a beleaguered man.

Life was so simple when you lived abroad, the weight fell off you. London was heedless and unjudgemental. The friends you made had earned, through kindness and compatibility, a place in your heart. And Mozart was there, to take your hand and lead you to heaven.

Ravi had tried to explain this to Pauline but she was fresh to his country, she couldn't understand the remorselessness of it, the impossibility of change. India would steal Pauline from him and then abandon her. He wanted to grip his wife's shoulders and yell: *Don't you see? You'll never get anything done!* But he didn't yell, and now they were walking back to their room in the hotel. It was her father's room, hardly conducive to marital high-jinks. The linen had been changed, of course, and the twin beds pushed together but Norman was still there. People didn't die; their presence was as powerful as ever. Even more powerful, because charged with one's own guilt and the impossibility of reconciliation.

They walked along the veranda. The wood was rotten, it creaked beneath their feet. The missing hand-rail, where Eithne had fallen, had been replaced by a length of rope. How flimsy the world seemed, tonight. Maybe those who had children felt anchored. How was he to know?

Ravi's heart ached. For himself, for Pauline. Still fresh, still horribly alive after all those years, grief waited in the darkness, ready to pounce.

The front door was locked; it was later than he thought. As Ravi rang the bell, Evelyn and her daughter walked up the drive. They had been out to dinner.

'Everyone seems to have gone to bed,' said Ravi.

The old bearer, Jimmy, hobbled up to the door, muttering like the porter in *Macbeth*. Ravi watched him through the glass, fiddling with the key.

'We adjourned to the Balmoral bar,' said Evelyn. 'It's a lovely hotel.' Good God, the woman was squiffy. She frowned at Ravi. 'I was going to ask you something but it's gone right out of my head.'

The door opened. 'Come on, Mum,' said Theresa, taking her arm.

Evelyn turned to Pauline. 'I'm so sorry about your father,' she said. 'Such a cheerful man. I miss him sitting on the veranda with his whisky and soda.'

'I still don't understand how he died,' said Pauline. 'What was he doing in the bazaar all by himself?'

There was a pause. Then Evelyn said: 'Don't you know?'

'Know what?'

'He was buying you a Christmas present, of course.'

Pauline stared at her. 'Was he?'

Evelyn moved away. 'I'll just get it from my room.'

'Goodness,' said Pauline. 'He never bought me presents. My mother always did it for him.'

They waited in the lounge. A Christmas tree had been installed; it was hung with dusty paper lanterns. Somehow, the decorations made the room look even shabbier. Ravi gazed at the mismatched armchairs and threadbare rugs. He had to admit that the hotel had been something of a letdown. It was hard to believe that this was supposed to be the beginning of a new British empire, a global trade in the elderly.

You don't understand, Pauline had said. *To these people it's charming. All the things you hate about India are the things we like. I'm in the travel business, I should know. Anyway it reminds them of home.*

Theresa sat on the arm of the settee. She removed a sandal and inspected the sole of her foot.

'Anything the matter?' asked Ravi.

'It's OK, it's healed now.' Theresa's toenails were painted crimson. They didn't match her red, somewhat tarty dress, but the effect was invigorating. Though sharp-featured, Theresa was a handsome woman and looked in good health – lustrous hair, bright eyes. Ravi wondered if she was on HRT. Pauline had just started taking it but she seemed as moody as ever. Hardly surprising, of course, at the moment.

'Do you know a man called PK?' asked Theresa.

'PK?' asked Ravi.

245

'He's a big businessman here, apparently. He knows everybody.'

Ravi shook his head. 'I live in Dulwich.'

The grandfather clock chimed midnight. As it did, Evelyn returned. She carried a package wrapped in festive paper.

'I looked after it for you,' she said, giving it to Pauline.

Pauline unwrapped it and withdrew a long length of cloth.

'It's a sari,' said Evelyn. 'A *baranasi* sari, for special occasions.' Theresa made a small movement but Evelyn took no notice. 'Your father was very fond of you,' she said.

'Was he really?' Pauline fingered the silk.

Evelyn nodded. 'He talked about you a great deal. How glad he was you gave him a home, back in London.' She paused. 'It meant a great deal to him.'

Pauline stroked the gold border. 'I'm glad he was thinking of me.' She smiled at Evelyn. 'I never thought he did, much.'

Ravi looked at the sari. It seemed a surprising present for the old man to buy. Maybe he had misjudged his father-in-law. He thought: How little we know of what lies in another's heart.

'So you've had five wives,' said Theresa.

'I wasn't married to two of them,' said Keith.

'Ludmilla and Maureen, right?'

Keith nodded. 'Ludmilla didn't last long. She was from Vladivostok.'

'And Shannon and Jordan are Sandra's kids.'

He nodded.

The whole thing was complicated, painfully so. Theresa kept probing, however, like a tongue returning to an abscess. She thought of the thousands of times Keith had made love to other women. *Live in the present*, she told herself. His gold Rolex lay discarded on the bedside table. *Shed the past*. These afternoons in his hotel room, they stepped outside time. She wondered if he thought the same.

Keith took a swig of beer, leaned over and laid his lips against hers. She swallowed from his mouth.

The desire for possession stems from fear, Swamiji said. *Attachment is illusion.*

'What went wrong?' she asked.

'Wrong?'

'You seem to have had a lot of failed relationships.' Oh dear, she sounded shrewish.

Keith shrugged. 'Easy come, easy go.'

'That's such an avoidance tactic.'

'It's not a tactic, sweetheart.'

Oh God, maybe he wanted to watch the football or something. Theresa soldiered on, however, she couldn't help it. 'You seem to have a bit of a problem with commitment.'

'They were shagging other blokes too. Sandra was banging her fitness instructor.'

A soul opened to God is opened to change within, Swamiji said. Keith seemed in tune with that. And yet one's dharma was to accept one's condition, to live with it in complete acceptance. Theresa's head swam. Honestly, the more she studied Hinduism the less she knew. Which was the point of it, of course.

She said: 'My problem is that my parents were too happy.'

'For God's sake, woman.' He laid the icy bottle on her belly. She yelped.

'Life's simple for you, isn't it?' she said.

'Simple?' Keith drained the bottle. 'It's not simple, darling. It's bleeding diabolical.'

By now she had learnt a little of what had happened. Not a lot. *You don't want to know,* Keith said, thrillingly. Big money was involved; property dealing, something like that. Theresa suspected that drugs came into it. Bangalore was riddled with corruption, right up to ministerial level, and Keith had tracked down the man who had swindled him out of a great deal of money and who had shopped him to the police. He had crossed the world to find him, flying first to Delhi and then tracing him to Bangalore. The man was called PK and he had connections in high places. However, he was proving elusive.

'To be perfectly honest, darling, I'm at the end of the road.'

'Can't you go back to England?' she asked.

'You must be joking. I'd get arrested.'

'What about your Mum? Aren't you worried about her?'

'Tell me about it.' Keith lit a cigarette.

'Can I have a puff?'

He passed it to her. 'I've left messages for her,' he said. 'See, I could get to Spain, I got friends there, they'd look after us. I want to get her there and then we could lay low for a while.'

How different it was from her childhood in Sussex! Theresa tried to imagine her own mother dodging the police and going to ground in the Costa del Sol with a bunch of crooks swigging malt whisky. She tried to picture herself there. Would such people find her counselling skills of use?

It was disorientating to be with a man whose life was in danger. It must have been like this in the war. Keith could step out of this hotel room and never return. PK's thugs could be waiting around the corner. It cast an elegiac air over the most banal utterances. Just now she was all he had.

She said: 'Most people I work with, their biggest problem is an eating disorder.' She thought of the people outside, picking through the rubbish.

Keith rolled on top of her. 'You're a great listener, babe.'

'It's my job.'

'And a terrific fuck.'

They put their arms around each other. As he entered her she cried out. He made love so tenderly, his body said all the words they had never uttered. They both knew they were two strangers and this would never last. *Easy come, easy go.* Swamiji would have said it like this, if he had known the words.

The sun had slid down the wall. Outside the muezzin called like a landlord. *Time gentlemen please.* They stood in the shower, gravely soaping each other.

'What are you going to do tomorrow?' she asked.

Keith shrugged. His hair was plastered to his face. *I adore you,* she thought.

'Come for Christmas dinner,' she said. 'You mustn't be alone.'

He lathered her arm. 'I don't want to get you into any trouble, sweetheart.'

'I hardly think a group of British pensioners has a hot line to the Indian mafia,' she said. 'Do come, please. They'd love it, you could flirt with them. None of their relatives are coming, do say yes.'

He washed her with a focused thoroughness, like a boy washing his first bike. 'Who'll you say I am?'

'Just my boyfriend.' Theresa blushed. 'If that's what you are.'

6

Would The Last Person To Leave Please Turn Out The Lights.
(Notice in the TV room, the Marigold)

Ravi was cooking the Christmas dinner. Circumstances had forced this emergency measure; a new cook had been engaged but was not due to start work until the following week. With the help of the boy, Ravi had been busy all morning, chopping, peeling and basting the turkey which Minoo had bought in the Gandhi Market and transported home, as large as a guest, in the back of a taxi.

Ravi found a profound satisfaction in cooking. After the demands of his patients it had always restored him, to make dinner. Vegetables were silent. The bald body of the turkey demanded nothing of him except to be transformed into a meal. He was a creative man; in another life he would have been an old-fashioned wife for his homemaking skills were superior to Pauline's. He knew the secret of roast potatoes: parboil them, toss them in seasoned flour and then fling them into hot fat. As they spluttered he felt an unfamiliar sensation: joy.

'*Garam pani lao,*' he told his young helper Pramod, a listless youth whom Ravi suspected was suffering from anaemia. The boy was a vegetarian and could do with some red meat in his bloodstream.

Brussels sprouts being unavailable, they were cooking cabbage. The secret of cabbage was to blanch it in a little water then toss it in butter, garlic and caraway seeds. Boiled cabbage, as Sonny had pointed out, smelt like an Old People's Home.

'*Ocha pani,*' Ravi told the boy. Pramod was a Tamil speaker but

250

they stumbled along in Hindi. Speaking it, Ravi felt himself reverting to a looser-limbed, more expressive version of himself, a young man he had long ago left behind. His shirt-sleeves were rolled up, his armpits sodden. Growing up in India, he had never romanticised physical toil; with no stretch of the imagination could the lives of the labouring millions be considered enviable. In his family, in fact, they weren't considered at all. But today, as he heaved up a saucepan and dumped it on the burner he felt a muscular pleasure in these simple tasks. He remembered passing a building site in Lewisham and hearing the workmen whistling.

Pauline hobbled in. She wore the sari her father had bought her for Christmas – that he had died whilst buying in an act of startling, and uncharacteristic, generosity. Ravi felt a wave of pity for Norman; for Pauline too, who looked so awkward in the sari – English women never knew how to move in them – and whose complexion was drained by the vibrancy of the colour.

'How's it going out there?' Ravi asked.

'Fine. They're drinking Sonny's special cocktails.' Pauline opened her hand to reveal a heap of coins. 'I thought I'd put these in the puddings.'

'They might get stuck in their throats,' he said. 'What happens if someone dies choking on a rupee?'

'What a way to go through life,' she replied sharply.

Ravi paused. Norman had called him a fuddy-duddy. Once he had crowed with triumph when Ravi picked up the safety leaflet on a train. But Ravi had only done it for something to read, to stop the old bastard talking. And now Norman had gone.

What the hell. If they died, they died. Ravi's professional instincts had evaporated in the steam of cooking. This was India, after all.

'Sorry, darling,' he said. 'Go ahead.'

Pauline shot him a look. She was a big-boned woman. In the sari she looked too wrapped-up, somehow, like an unsuitable Christmas present. She had tied back her thick auburn hair with a butterfly clip; it made her jaw squarer. Ravi was overcome with another wave of pity. Amidst the fluster there was a stillness about her; a terrible sadness.

251

'Are you all right?' he asked. Silly question.

'It's strange,' Pauline said. 'I'm an orphan now. I've been shunted to the head of the queue.'

Ravi looked at his wife. He should put his arms around her but he was holding a chopping knife. There always seemed to be something in his hands. Despite her need, the simplicity of it, Pauline seemed as unknowable as a woman he had just met. Now they were in India, would they finally lose each other? Or would they learn how to love each other, all over again?

Dinner was to be served at four. It was strange, of course, to spend Christmas Day with the temperature in the eighties but by general consent this was preferable to the drizzle one experienced nowadays in England – white Christmases, like so much else, being a thing of the past. Besides, many of them had spent previous festive seasons abroad – Florida, Portugal. According to Jean Ainslie, she and Douggy had listened to their King's College carols in seven different countries. It was still somewhat disconcerting, however, to hear 'Good King Wenceslas' while a mynah bird screeched in the bougainvillaea.

Some of the residents had gone to church. Some had received phone calls from their families back home; there was an undercurrent of rivalry about who was summoned most frequently to the lobby. The awkward question of gifts had been solved by a lucky dip organised by Madge: each person contributing a small present to be rummaged for, at random, in the brass spittoon.

Now they sat on the veranda drinking cocktails made of rum and mango juice.

'Nice, but slightly viscous,' whispered Evelyn.

'Vicious?' asked Douglas.

'No. Viscous. I suspect they used a tin.'

The smell of roasting turkey drifted from the kitchen – turkey cooked by the real Indian doctor, not the sex one. In the dining-room the tables had been pushed together to create the banquet effect. There were crackers. There were table decorations created by Stella and Hermione out of exotic foliage strewn with tinsel. Two extra places had been laid for the mystery guests, a source

252

of speculation amongst the residents. One was Madge's new gentleman friend. Her socialising with Sonny had borne fruit for, although not a maharaja, Mr Somethingunpronounceable was rumoured to be a man of considerable wealth, a widower in the pharmaceutical trade whom she had met at a buffet for Nestlés.

'Never too late to have another crack at it,' whispered Douglas.

'I'm not sure about that,' replied Evelyn. 'One does get a lot more reading done.'

Startled, he asked: 'Think that's a good swap?'

'No.'

There was a silence. They looked at each other.

The other guest, apparently, was Theresa's new friend. He sounded like one of the waifs and strays to whom she devoted her professional life. 'He's here on business,' Evelyn told Muriel. 'His family's in England and he's all alone, poor thing.'

'Should have your family round you at Christmas,' said Muriel bitterly.

'I'm so sorry about your son,' said Evelyn.

'Thought I'd hear from him *today*.'

'Maybe the police should be alerted. Interpol or something.'

'Don't want no police.' Muriel sat, a squat figure in the wicker chair. There was a hooded look in her eyes. Evelyn suspected that Muriel knew that her son was up to no good. She offered her a cheese straw.

To tell the truth, Evelyn's mind was on other things. Why had she spoken like that to Douglas? The words had just come out of her mouth. Then there was Theresa's mystery friend. Was he the man responsible for her daughter's newly discovered skittishness and plunging necklines? Maybe the culprit wasn't drugs at all. The two of them were due to arrive any minute. One look and Evelyn would be able to tell.

Almost as thrilling was the news about Surinda. In the New Year Minoo was recruiting her as a trainee manager to replace his wife who, according to rumour, hadn't been a nurse at all but simply a chiropodist's assistant, a fact that explained her interest in feet. They were all fond of Surinda in whom they took a protective interest, suspecting that for all her brash talk she was a romantic at heart and secretly in love with Rahul, who was treating her fast and loose.

Surinda had been invited to the meal. At that moment she was in the garden, dressed in slacks and a sun-top that left nothing to the imagination. She stood there, frowning at her mobile. 'Can't get a bloody signal,' she muttered, walking up to Evelyn's table.

'Sonny could.'

'This place is a time-warp, aunty.' Surinda wrinkled her nose. 'Even mobiles don't work.'

Evelyn drained her glass. 'That's why we like it, dear.'

Without Norman's presence there was an emptiness in the air, as if a burglar alarm had stopped ringing. Other absences were more palpably felt, for Christmas is the cruellest season. It had to be remembered that even in England this could be the case. Eithne, however, had returned for the day. Though nobody's nearest and dearest she had been greeted like a soldier returned from the Front. Sitting in a wheelchair, she had visibly suffered a *coup d'âge*. She had been transferred to a private nursing home out in Phase Six Colony but still had hopes of returning to the Marigold in the New Year.

Graham Turner sat with Dorothy. He had been drawn to her, as one unclubbable spirit to another, and over the weeks a diffident friendship had developed. Clearing his throat, he placed a parcel in her hands. 'A small seasonal gift,' he said.

Dorothy unwrapped an exercise book: *A History of the Marigold*.

'I've been doing some research at the British Council Library,' said Graham. 'I've always been keen on local history. It keeps me out of mischief.'

Startled, she looked at him.

'Go on,' he said.

Dorothy opened the book and gazed at the hand-written pages. 'Good God,' she said. 'Sister Eileen O'Malley.'

'Remember her?' he asked. 'She was the Principal when you were attending the school, am I right?'

'Old Mally,' said Dorothy. 'Well, she seemed old to us but she was probably about thirty.' Her eyes travelled down the page. 'Oh my goodness, here are my class-mates. Dora Hethrington . . . Monica Cable, my best friend. Bobby Miles, I remember him. He got a lentil stuck up his nose.' She paused. 'I haven't thought about him for sixty years. Seventy.'

Evelyn joined them.

'Nancy Pringle,' said Dorothy. 'She was such a bully, she made me cry.'

'There was a girl like that at my school,' said Evelyn.

Eithne wheeled herself over.

'Look, there's your name!' said Eithne. '*Dorothy Miller*.'

Dorothy raised her head. 'I can't thank you enough,' she said to Graham. Her face was tense with emotion. 'I can't thank you . . .' She stopped.

Thanks for the memory. Ella singing it, with the Duke Ellington band. Graham had it on CD. He had Dinah Washington singing it, on a long-playing record. He sat there in the afternoon sunlight, sipping his cocktail and gazing at Dorothy's grey head as she pored over the book.

> *Oh we said goodbye with a highball*
> *And I got as high as a steeple,*
> *For we were intelligent people,*
> *No tears, no fuss, hooray for us . . .*

He thought of his bedsitter in Swiss Cottage, his solitary dinners at the Cosmo Restaurant – *wiener schnitzel* and boiled potatoes, that was his customary fare. The restaurant was run by Austrian *émigrés* and long since gone. Graham thought of his past Christmases with his sister's family in Pinner, the loneliness and longing, the painful solace of jazz. With surprise he realised: I'm happy. For the first time in my life I'm a part of something, I'm amongst companions and we're all, at last, in the same boat. They've caught me up.

He gazed at his fellow residents sitting around the tables – beaded cardigans, floral dresses. Eithne, in her wheelchair, wore a smart magenta shirtwaister. Jimmy walked from table to table, refilling glasses. Hermione demurely covered her glass with her

255

hand. The sun shone through the leaves of the creeper that hung like a veil over the roof of the veranda. Suddenly Graham's heart swelled with love. For Dorothy, for all of them.

The gong boomed. They got to their feet with difficulty. Dinner was late and they had drunk several of Sonny's excellent cocktails.

'I miss Mrs Gee-Gee,' said Muriel. 'They're not all the same, the Indians, not when you get to know them.'

Surinda walked towards the dining-room with Pauline. 'My English is pretty good but your father used some phrases I didn't understand.'

'What phrases?' asked Pauline.

'Like, Indian men play the pink oboe.'

Pauline stopped. 'He said that?'

'Is it the same as a shirt-lifter?'

Pauline's eyes filled with tears. 'The silly old fool,' she said, her voice thick. 'Oh I do miss him.'

'Was he talking about sex?'

Pauline nodded. 'I think he was terrified of it. He was certainly terrified of women.'

They moved back to let Eithne pass. Stella, dressed in a yellow frilly blouse, was pushing the wheelchair. 'Sail before steam!' she said. Oh Lord, she was pissed.

Madge's guest had arrived. He was a bald, diminutive gentleman in a black silk tunic. As Madge bent down to whisper in his ear, the sunlight flashed on her jewellery. He laughed. Her husband, apparently, had also been short but she had cited Tom Cruise as an example of a desirable midget. They paused at the dining-room door, ready to make their entrance; beside them, the barometer was set to FAIR.

'Where's my daughter?' asked Evelyn fretfully. 'And her friend?'

She hurried down the garden to the gates, though why this should bring Theresa home faster she had no idea. The elderly beggar stood there, wearing Minoo's shoes. To him, she supposed, this particular day was no different from any other. He was still

256

as hungry as he was yesterday, and as hungry as he would be tomorrow.

She rummaged in her purse and found a five-rupee note. What was that in old money – one and ninepence? Quite a lot, in fact, when she was a girl. More than a month's pocket money, in fact.

She put it into his tin. 'Happy Christmas,' she said.

Theresa sat squashed next to Keith in the rickshaw. It puttered along past walls spattered red with *paan* juice, past a building which bore a sign saying GOVERNMENT WORK IS GOD'S WORK. Whenever it stopped, the engine died. The driver had to yank the handle until, in a cloud of exhaust smoke, it coughed into life.

'My mother will be consumed with curiosity,' she said. 'But in a well-bred way.'

Keith lit a cigarette, his hand jolting as he flicked the lighter. During all these days together he had seldom asked her a personal question. In the long run, no doubt, this lack of curiosity would annoy her. She suspected, however, that there would be no long run. *Thank the stranger and say goodbye.*

'At least you won't have to meet my brother,' she said. 'He's gone to Goa. He's married to an awful ball-breaking wife who's destroyed his self-esteem but he's too weak to leave her. He's always been a coward. Or just lazy, which can come to the same thing. Who said that evil comes from inaction?'

'I hate this bloody country,' said Keith.

Theresa knew he was depressed. Christmas was always a bad time for her clients; in fact she felt guilty, leaving them. At Christmas you needed to be surrounded by those you loved. Despite the passion between them, she guessed that for Keith she wasn't included in this category. Though his thigh was pressed against hers, she felt suddenly alone.

I want my Mummy! she thought. Men might come and go but a mother was always there. For a little longer, anyway.

Ravi, flanked by the two elderly bearers, stood at the head of the table. He was carving the turkey. Its appearance had been greeted by a flutter of applause. *Those cocktails do grow on you*, Stella had said. More drink waited on the table: beer, sherry (the Ainslies' contribution) and several bottles of imported French Bordeaux, bought at some expense by Sonny.

Sonny's solicitude in the past few days was a cause of puzzlement. Since Norman's death he had seldom been off the premises and he was strangely subdued. It was Christmas Day, did the man have no home to go to? Several people remarked that he had lost weight.

Evelyn sat next to two empty places. Maybe her daughter was in some drugs den, shooting up or whatever they did, in the company of her unknown corrupter.

'Children, even when middle-aged, are such a worry,' she said to Pauline, who sat on her other side. 'Nobody tells you, it's one of those secrets.'

'I always wanted children.' Pauline took a gulp of wine. 'I had a miscarriage once and that was that.'

'Oh, my dear, I'm so sorry.'

'After it happened Ravi and I went through a rocky patch.' Pauline's cheeks were flushed. 'These damn saris!' She flung the material back over her shoulder.

Sonny tapped his glass and stood up. A hush fell.

'My dear ladies and gentlemen,' he said, 'please allow me to welcome you to your first Christmas at the Marigold –'

'I want to set up a children's home here,' whispered Pauline, 'but where's the money? Besides, Ravi's not keen.'

Sonny said: 'I am sure, my friends, that you are aware of some teething troubles but what grand venture does not bring problems? I must thank you for your kindness and patience and want to inform you all that we are fortunate to have engaged the services of a new cook and assistant lady manager who will take up their positions in the next week.' Sonny cleared his throat. 'And now, to be serious for a moment, I would like us to raise our glasses to the gentleman who can no longer be with us.'

There was a general murmur as they hurriedly filled their glasses from whatever was nearest to hand.

'Mr Norman Purse,' said Sonny. 'A great man, and my very good friend.'

The bearers passed round the plates of turkey. The diners paused, uncertain whether to begin. Was he going to continue?

Yes. 'I admire your esteemed selves for your courage, for you have shown that it's never too late to embark on a new experience. By opening your hearts to the hospitality of my country you have shown that in the twenty-first century the world has no borders. As the wise man said, geography is now history!' Sonny wiped his brow. 'As your co-director it's gratifying to see you flourishing in our sunshine, for as many of you have been so kind as to say, our country has given you a new lease of life.'

'Try telling that to Norman,' muttered Madge.

'Throughout the centuries my country has enjoyed a unique bond with yours,' Sonny continued. 'As you have made my people welcome, so too we have made yours. I hope our modest venture will be the start of a whole new export market – no longer cotton, but people!'

'What, by the kilo?' whispered Douglas.

'For India has bypassed the industrial revolution, my dear friends. She has leapt from agriculture straight to the service industries –'

'What *is* he going on about?' whispered Evelyn.

'Maybe he's drunk,' whispered Pauline. 'He's been rather odd since my father died.'

Sonny continued: 'This has been a difficult year for myself too, in ways I won't elaborate now –'

'Thank God,' whispered Madge.

'Can we start eating now?' hissed Olive.

'And I would like to inform you that I propose to wind down my other commitments and devote my energies to this enterprise, for here in my country we have a tradition of reverence for older people, we respect their wisdom and their place at the head of our families –'

'Hear hear!' said Douglas.

'We don't abandon them in nursing homes or on hospital trolleys,' said Sonny, 'this is not the Indian way –'

'No, but you press baby girls' faces into sacks until they suffocate,' whispered Theresa, sitting down beside her mother.

259

'Darling!' exclaimed Evelyn. 'Thank God you've arrived.'

'– you burn brides to get their dowries, some lousy VCR. You force children into labour.' Theresa leaned close to her mother. 'I'm going off India. This is Keith.'

Evelyn shook hands with a man, rather charming in a rough-diamond kind of way. Keith had pale blue eyes and a pugilist's nose.

'You can't be her Mum,' he whispered.

'Can't I?' Evelyn felt the warmth rising up her neck.

'Sorry we're late,' said Theresa. 'Rickshaw broke down.'

Keith gazed at Evelyn, his eyebrows raised. 'I can see where she got her looks,' he said.

'Don't be silly,' Evelyn simpered. That was how it felt – *simpering*. 'Welcome to Bournemouth-in-Bangalore,' she said.

Sonny was still droning on. Nobody seemed to be able to stop him.

Suddenly someone screamed.

Muriel was staring across the room. 'Keith!' she cried, her voice strangled. 'KEITH!'

Stella, who was sitting next to her, touched her arm. 'Don't distress yourself, dear, it's just Theresa's young man –'

Keith stared across the table.

'Fuck me!' he said.

Scraping back his chair, he jumped to his feet and stumbled past the diners. Heads turned as he charged round the table. Jimmy, holding a tureen of cabbage, was blocking the way. Keith moved him to the side as if he were a hat-stand.

'Mum!' He opened his arms and scooped Muriel up. Holding her tightly he lifted her off her feet and whirled her round. They bumped against the bamboo bookcase. It wobbled; several volumes of the *Encyclopaedia Britannica* fell to the floor.

'My son!' cried Muriel, and burst into tears.

Outside, darkness had fallen. The meal seemed to have gone on for hours. The residents, paper hats on their heads, sat amongst the debris – slimy coins spat out from the Christmas puddings; torn cheese wrappers. These were Theresa's contribution to the feast – individual portions of cheese which she had bought in the bazaar near the airport. She suspected they came from airline meals, pocketed by cleaning staff and sold on to the stallholders, but didn't let on. 'Camembert!' cried the diners. 'Cheddar!' They slipped the spare ones into their handbags, for later.

Muriel sat next to her son. People had shifted around so that the two could be together. Her shock had given way to a dazed gratification. 'It's like all my Christmases have come at once,' she said.

'In India,' said Theresa, leaning across the table, 'sooner or later you bump into the person you want to meet.'

'That true?'

'No,' said Theresa. 'But it's not entirely untrue either.'

Muriel had told her son about the mugging, the burglary, how she had buried her cat in his garden before going back to Peckham, packing up her life and coming to India to find him. 'It's all fate,' she said. 'That first tumble, and me meeting that nice Dr Kapoor.' She beamed at Ravi down the table. 'I've even got those black boys to thank, who took my bag, because here I am and I'm never going home, never. And you *can't* go home so that makes two of us.'

The miracle of this reunion had affected them all. The prodigal sons . . . the daughters, disappeared into the demands of their adult lives . . . at any moment, they felt, the door would open and in would step their lost families, drawn to India by its transforming magic. The effects of alcohol gave this a Spielbergian radiance, as if they were sitting at their own movie, awaiting the scenes of reconciliation and final credits.

'It's been go-go-go these past few weeks,' Madge whispered to her new boyfriend, whose name was Mr Desikachar. 'Dorothy told the Ainslies their son was gay, the manager kicked out his wife, the cook's gone, the doctor's gone, an old soak called Norman died in a brothel but his daughter doesn't know, she thinks he was buying her a Christmas present. And that's just for starters.'

'I thought this was a *Retirement* Home,' said Mr Desikachar.

'Life begins at seventy.' Madge smiled, dazzling him with her expensive dentistry. 'Seventy's the new forty, didn't you know?'

'Looking at you, Mrs Rheinhart, I find that easy to believe.'

261

She touched his knee. 'Do call me Madge.'

Down the table, Douglas tapped his glass. 'I think we should toast the cooks.'

They raised their glasses to Ravi. He rose to his feet. After thanking his helper, Pramod, he cleared his throat. 'As Sonny said, you have indeed shown great courage in moving to my country. More courage than I have shown.'

Pauline made a small noise in her throat. She was sitting at the far end of the table, a paper hat on her head.

'It's said that in Britain family life has broken up,' continued the doctor. 'That people no longer feel a duty to care for their parents any more. That's part of the reason we set up this company. I have to tell you, however, that this does not just apply to your countrymen.'

He sat down. Madge leaned to her neighbour, Douglas. 'What's that all about?' she whispered.

'Search me,' replied Douglas. 'Maybe he's tipsy.'

'He's been on the lime sodas, darling. The man doesn't drink.'

Oh well. He was Indian. However much you knew them, pockets of incomprehensibility still remained. Madge gazed at Mr Desikachar's hand as he lit her cigarette. He wore a heavy gold signet ring. Tufts of black hair sprouted from his finger-joints. She was so hungry for sex her throat was dry. I shall have one last adventure, she thought. Arnold would want me to be happy.

'You're lucky,' she said to Douglas.

'Why?' He stared at her.

'Not to be alone.'

Douglas looked at her cigarette packet. 'May I have one of those?' he asked.

Surprised, Madge lit him a cigarette. Douglas sat there, smoking. He wore a lemon V-necked sweater, like Perry Como. Beneath the bland, golfing-pro exterior, however, she sensed something thrumming. She knew men, she knew something was up.

Across the table, Graham Turner lit a small Panatella. His cheekbones were flushed. Leaning towards his neighbour, Olive Cooke, he said: 'People think we're waiting to die. Well, I'm starting to live.'

Startled, Olive toyed with the cardboard strip from their shared cracker. It had failed to explode. She had pulled out the strip in the same manner, she imagined, as the surgeon back in Hornchurch had pulled out her varicose veins.

Stella drained her glass of wine and rose unsteadily to her feet.

'Oh Lord,' muttered Madge.

'The tinkling piano in the next apartment,' sang Stella.

Graham joined in. *'Those stumbling words that told you what my heart meant . . .'*

They looked at him, in surprise.

'The fairground's painted swings,' they sang together,

'These foolish things, remind me of you.'

The sisters from Fife joined in, slightly off-key. So did Mr Desikachar, who had a pleasant baritone voice.

'The winds of March that make my heart a dancer,
The telephone that rings but who's to answer –'

Suddenly they were plunged into darkness.

'Oh oh, a power cut,' said Stella.

Minoo barked an order to Jimmy, presumably to find some candles. They heard the old bearer blundering against Eithne's wheelchair as he made his way from the room.

Eithne uttered a shrill laugh. 'What fun! We can play Murder in the Dark.'

'I know another game,' said Keith, making his way towards Theresa.

'Oh!' squeaked Stella.

'Sorry, wrong person,' said Keith.

'Do carry on,' Stella giggled. 'It was rather nice.'

'Let's play London Tube Stations,' said Madge. Her cigarette glowed in the dark. 'Guess the one that doesn't have any of the letters of *mackerel* in it.'

'That's just silly, Madge.'

'What did she say?'

'Dollis Hill.'

'No, it's got an *l.*'

Minoo said: 'I know. Think of the most comical Parsee name. Many of us are called by the name of a trade –'

'Euston!'

'No, it's got an *e* –'

'Cashmeresweaterwallah,' said Minoo.

'I give up, Madge.'

'Sodawaterbottleopenerwallah,' said Minoo.

'All right then,' said Madge. 'If you really give up. It's St John's Wood.'

They sat in the blackness, waiting for the lights to come on. Somebody cleared her throat. Faintly, they could hear the *tick-tick* of the grandfather clock.

After a moment a voice said: 'Do you think this is what it's like?'

'What?'

'*It*. Do you think it's like this?'

'For goodness' sake, Hermione, don't be so morbid!'

There was another pause.

'I know. Moorgate.'

'We've finished that game, Eithne.'

'Anyway it's got an *a* and an *r* –'

'And an *m* –'

Pauline felt a hand removing her paper hat. 'Are you all right?' asked Ravi.

She nodded. 'Are you?'

Maybe he nodded; it was too dark to tell. 'I've been thinking about what you said.'

'What?' she asked.

'The children's thing,' said Ravi. 'You really want to do it, don't you?'

She nodded. His hand stroked her hair.

Dorothy spoke in the darkness. 'There was a gully behind our house. Egrets, herons . . . I nearly drowned in it once. I used to dream about it.'

She fell silent. Outside, the veranda creaked.

'Someone's here,' said Douglas. 'Listen.'

Madge flicked on her lighter. Illuminated from beneath, she resembled a skull. She *was* a skull, of course; they all were. 'Can you see who it is?'

They heard the veranda door opening. 'Ma?' said a voice. 'Is anybody there?'

Jimmy entered with some candles. For a moment, a man was illuminated in the doorway. It was Christopher. Then the breeze blew the candles out and they were plunged back into darkness.

'Christopher, is that you?' asked Evelyn.

'What's happened?' he asked. 'Why are you sitting here in the dark?'

'Why are you back?' asked Evelyn, alarmed. 'Has there been an accident?'

Somebody scraped a match alight. Briefly they glimpsed Christopher's wild eyes.

'Why aren't you in Goa?' asked Evelyn. 'Where are the others?'

'Ouch!' yelped somebody as the match burnt her fingers. Darkness engulfed them.

'I can't talk now, Ma,' said Christopher, his voice shaky. 'I'll tell you some other time.'

'Tell her now, for God's sake,' said Madge. 'We'll find out, sooner or later.'

They sat in the darkness, waiting.

'I've left my wife,' Christopher said.

There was a gasp, like a wave pulling back over the pebbles.

'You've what?' asked Evelyn.

'And my children.' His voice was thick. 'Yesterday. The coach drove away and I just stayed there. On the pavement outside the hotel.'

'Crikey,' said Douglas.

'Like thingy in that film,' said Madge.

'Jack Nicholson,' said Graham. '*Five Easy Pieces.*'

'I fell in love with somebody else,' said Christopher. 'I'm going to live with her.'

'What about Marcia?' asked his sister. 'The children?'

'They don't need me.'

Suddenly the lights came on. Christopher stood there, dishevelled.

'You can't just do that,' said his mother.

'I know,' he said. 'But I have.' He stared at the room. They saw now that there was a suitcase on the floor. Jimmy instinctively moved towards it. Then he stopped, and glanced enquiringly at the manager.

'My God,' said Theresa. 'You, of all people.'

'Sit down, old chap,' said Douglas. 'You need a drink.'

Christopher didn't move. He wore a turquoise short-sleeved shirt. There were damp patches under the arms.

'Who is this woman?' asked Madge, with interest.

'She's the greeter at the Taj Balmoral,' he said.

'Ah!' exclaimed Sonny. 'Aisha or Jana?'

'Aisha,' said Christopher.

'Good choice.' Sonny nodded. 'She's the babe.'

Graham Turner loosened his tie. 'Well I never,' he said.

'Where is she?' asked Theresa.

'In the garden.'

'Why?'

'She's shy,' said Christopher.

'But I thought she greeted people.'

Christopher still seemed incapable of movement. He looked at Pauline. 'Isn't that the sari?' he asked, puzzled.

'No it's not!' said his mother.

'The sari I gave you?' asked Christopher.

Pauline frowned. 'What are you talking about?'

'Nothing, he's just confused.' Evelyn turned to her son. 'Do ask your lady friend in, darling. It's chilly out there.'

Christopher jumped. He swung round and walked into the garden. 'Aisha?' he called 'Aisha?' Deep in the darkness, a cat miaowed.

They sat there, waiting. Eithne gave a giggle. 'Goodness me. And such a nice man. He helped me wind my wool.'

Douglas drained his beer glass. 'What a day,' he said. 'Anyone else got something to tell us?'

'Douggy, this is serious!' said his wife. 'The man's left his family.'

Madge laughed her husky, smoker's laugh. 'At least nobody can accuse us of falling asleep.'

'Except for Dorothy,' said Pauline. '*She* has.'

They turned.

Dorothy sat in her chair, the paper hat crooked. There was something odd about the way she was slumped.

Ravi grunted. There was a scrape as he pushed back his chair and leaped to his feet.

7

When the Lord of the body arrives, and when he departs and wanders on, he takes them over with him, as the wind takes perfumes from their place of sleep.

(The Bhagavad Gita)

Dorothy's ashes were scattered in the garden of the Marigold, her lost Eden, where she had played as a child. Adam Ainslie, her protégé, had flown out; so had a distant niece, bearing out Douglas's observation that one had to be dead before anyone paid you a visit.

'Out, out, brief candle,' Adam read:

> 'Life's but a walking shadow, a poor player
> That struts and frets his hour upon the stage
> And then is heard no more . . .'

Douglas was deeply disturbed. *Is this what it's like?* somebody had said, during the power cut. He knew that it must have been an easeful death, simply to remain asleep when the lights came on, but he was gripped by panic.

'Are you all right, Dad?' asked Adam.

'Fine!' Douglas blew his nose.

'I feel so guilty.' Adam sat down on the veranda steps. 'I should have visited her. In London. I was always so busy, and now it's too late.'

Douglas looked at his wife. Jean was standing on the lawn talking to Evelyn. She shot a glance at their son. Sooner or later the three of them would have to sit down and discuss Adam's sexual orientation. The thought of this conversation – indeed, any conversation – filled Douglas's heart with lead.

I can't live the rest of my life with her.

So what did one do? Cross the garage forecourt, like Jack Nicholson, and climb into another vehicle? Evelyn's son had done it.

A chill wind blew. Evelyn hugged her cardigan to herself, wrapping it around her chest. It was an instinctive, girlish gesture. How frail she looked, as if a strong wind would topple her over!

'This has knocked us for six,' said Douglas. He remembered the plane, how he blew up the plump lozenge of the neck cushion and passed it to Evelyn. Already he had wanted to ease her passage through life. It was hard, travelling alone.

Evelyn, wrapped in the airline blanket. Recently the two of them had crossed the street to Khan's Video Rental. At the crossroads some women waited for a bus – village women, Muslims, enveloped from head to foot in burkas. *'Being old's like wearing one of those,'* Evelyn had said.

Had Evelyn's husband ever told her she was beautiful? Hugh sounded a breezy, no-nonsense fellow. Evelyn said he was devoted to their spaniel.

'Here, Dad.' Adam passed him a Kleenex. He was looking at him oddly. 'You loved her, didn't you?'

'Who?' asked Douglas.

'Dorothy.'

'Ah,' said Douglas. 'Yes.'

The sun was sinking. At this time of day the garden was transformed into a place of great beauty. Douglas looked at Evelyn, still miraculously alive, her shadow lengthening across the grass. Her hair was no longer grey. In this light it shone, the palest gold. He wondered if she had been blonde in her youth. Seventy-four years of her life were unknown to him, and yet here she was, utterly familiar.

And then Adam took the apple, and ate it. Douglas hadn't read the Bible since Sunday school. They were kicked out of the Garden of Eden, he knew that.

269

Douglas got up, went indoors and lay down on the bed, his face pressed into the pillow.

Later, when Adam and his mother had settled down for their little chat, Adam said: 'Poor Dad, he couldn't stop crying. It's not like him.'

'I never knew he was *that* fond of Dorothy,' said Jean.

'He's inconsolable.'

The next day Ravi and Pauline flew to Delhi to visit his family. She never discovered what had caused her husband to make that speech during the extraordinary Christmas dinner. Something had affected him powerfully but he had been unable to put it into words. Maybe it was the scent of loss in the air, for that day she had decided to leave him.

Now she wasn't so sure. They arrived at Delhi Airport where the hands of the clock had to be inched, laboriously, into the future; Pauline could see the knee of the man squatting behind the clock-face. Why can't we simply be mammals? she thought. We *are* mammals. Why can't we simply be warm bodies in bed, our arms around each other? The world is too terrifying to face alone.

Ravi touched her shoulder. 'There they are,' he whispered.

At the barrier stood his family – his parents, his sister, her two children, his Aunty Preethi. Ravi waved back.

'Here goes,' he muttered, like a boy of six.

'I wish you hadn't told me that, Ma,' said Keith.

'I had to tell somebody,' said Muriel. 'Now you know when I'm going to die, you know how long we've got each other for.'

'It gives me a weird feeling,' he said.

Three of them were walking through the Botanical Gardens – Muriel, Keith and Theresa – though none of them was interested in plants. Theresa said: 'Don't believe all that stuff, palm leaves and stuff. It creates such helplessness.'

'You've changed your tune,' said Keith.

'I want to go home,' said Theresa. 'I'm tired of it here, my clients need me, Mum's got Christopher now though God knows

270

what he's going to do here. I mean he's a sort of stockbroker or something.'

'Plenty of money in Bangalore, darling,' said Keith.

A monkey swung past, carrying a baby under its arm, but they were used to monkeys now. In two days' time Keith and his mother would be flying to Spain. He wore a red baseball cap pulled down over his forehead, and a shirt printed with pineapples. Already he seemed alien to Theresa. For two weeks they had been insepa-rable but now he was returning to unknowability. On 6 January he would, like Persephone, be swallowed into the Underworld, the sunlit Underworld of the Costa Del Sol, where in some incom-prehensibly dodgy way he would go to ground. I shall remember you all my life, Theresa wanted to say. I love you. Not in the way Swamiji wrote in his *Eightfold Path to Enlightenment*, however. There's nothing cosmic about my love; it's only too particular. I love your arms and your skin and the smell of you. I love you inside me. I love your eyelashes brushing my cheek when you blink and the way you make me laugh. These foolish things.

It was the next day. Sonny sat in the Gymkhana Club drinking whisky with Keith.

'I'm just a small fish, my friend,' said Sonny. 'That *maderchod* PK is too big for both of us.'

'What's a *maderchod*, mate?'

'Motherfucker.' Sonny drained his glass and snapped his fingers for more drinks.

'I'm cutting my losses and getting out of here,' said Keith.

'I must tell you something.' Sonny lowered his voice. 'I did a terrible deed and in my next life I shall pay for it. Revenge is not sweet, dear boy. It's a bitter pill to swallow.'

'What did you do, then?'

'It was I who killed Norman-sahib.'

'He died on the job, right?' said Keith, lighting a cigarette. 'That's the rumour, lucky old sod.'

'He died in the arms of a *hijra*.'

'A what?'

'A eunuch.'

271

Keith clapped his hand to his mouth.

'It's not funny!' barked Sonny. 'How can I forgive myself? I shall make amends to the old Britishers, I have decided to devote myself to their well-being, but how will I help his poor daughter, so sad and pale?'

The drinks arrived. Keith removed his ice cubes and put them in the ashtray.

Sonny spoke the words, not expecting an answer. He was merely thinking out loud in the company of his new confidant who might understand the pickle he was in, Keith-sahib being in a pickle himself. A worse one, Sonny suspected, for he himself had never been involved in the drugs side of PK's organisation. Keith Donnelly, he guessed, knew more about this than he was prepared to divulge. Sonny certainly didn't want to know, things being bad enough already. See no evil, hear no evil.

'How can I help this poor lady,' said Sonny, 'who in three days' time will fly home with only the ashes of her father for comfort?'

'You really want to help her?' Keith looked at him.

Sonny nodded. How simple it was in his boyhood, being passed from knee to knee! His mother's lips against his cheek, the smell of her perfume. If only he could rewind his video and dwindle into a child again, adored just for being a boy.

Keith smiled. 'I got an idea,' he said.

It was late. Douglas stood at the gates of the Marigold, gazing at the crossroads. There were four choices: the airport, the town, the office world, the Old City. He had come to a moment of decision. His skull felt tight. Nearby, the gateman's cigarette glowed. Douglas had given up smoking in 1986 but he needed one now.

In the light of the headlamps the legless beggar sat on his trolley. Evelyn said she only gave to two beggars, you had to make a decision on these matters. She gave to the legless man, for though young he was helpless. And she gave to the elderly beggar out of a feeling of solidarity. Their circumstances were worlds apart but she said it all boiled down to the same thing.

Douglas thought of the forty-eight years he had lain beside his wife. Dorothy had dreamed about the water buffalo in the stream behind her childhood home, now no doubt landscaped over to become a corporate lawn. Lying next to Jean's nightie-clad body, Douglas too had dreamed. The years he had spent with his wife had dissolved away as if they had never been. It was bloody terrifying. Exhilarating too. What was real, in this life? Had he ever grasped it, all those years of being a solicitor and a husband, of raising children and tramping across Dartmoor?

Behind him, in the darkness, the crickets chirruped. Maybe they were tree frogs, he had never discovered. He knew nothing except that they would go on chirruping through the night and the beggars would go on waiting.

How could he cause such pain when sooner or later they would all die? Was such monumental selfishness justified even in the young and heedless? Christopher, Evelyn's son, was bad enough, running away with an Indian lady and leaving his children fatherless. Here *he* was, apparently aged seventy-one.

'*Rose in the bud, the June air's warm and tender . . .*'

For a moment Douglas thought it was a record. But the voice was too tuneless.

'*Wait not too long and trifle not with fate . . .*'

Maybe it was Hermione. Her grandchildren were visiting. She had told them she was writing her memoirs, a statement that had been met with polite incomprehension. More relatives were arriving the next day, and several people were leaving – his own son, accompanied by the Howard Hodgkin painting Dorothy had bequeathed him in her will; Pauline and Ravi, accompanied by her father's ashes. Theresa, too, was flying back to England and Keith was taking his mother to start a new life in Spain.

'*Love comes but once, and then, perhaps, too late.*'

Douglas heard a smattering of applause. He thought: I wish I'd learned how to play the piano.

It's never too late. Madge was getting married in March. She was moving to New York with her cheery little millionaire. Anything was possible.

Douglas's heart thumped like a teenager's. He stepped into the hotel. The calendar still displayed last year's puppies although it was 5 January. On the desk sat an ashtray, containing a stub smudged with scarlet lipstick. It was Madge's. She no longer spent the nights at the hotel but went home with Mr Desikachar, *See you later, alligator*, reappearing at lunchtime the next day. There seemed something profoundly naughty about this.

In a while, crocodile . . . Standing in the empty lobby, Douglas made his decision.

Theresa tucked into her vegetarian lasagne. She was always hungry on planes. Beside it sat a portion of shrink-wrapped cheddar and two crackers. She looked at the cheese. How appreciated it had been, by the elderly people she had left behind!

She thought: I have eaten meat. I have drunk beer from the mouth of my lover. I can hardly recognise the person who flew out two months ago. I never had the showdown with my mother, the conversation I had been meaning to have all these years, but it has somehow become irrelevant. If there was anything to forgive, I have forgiven her. I didn't need Swamiji to tell me this, I have found it out all by myself. My mother is another generation, she has no vocabulary for my dissatisfactions. She and her friends at the Marigold, they are the last of a species. Their memories are of a world that is already history: a world where children were seen but not heard, where men looked after women. Where women cared for their men. The witnesses to this world are disappearing one by one. Madge's husband Arnold had survived Auschwitz. Their world was one of tragedies and certainties that have disappeared for ever.

The stewardess pushed the trolley past. 'Can I have one of those?' asked Theresa.

She took the small bottle, twisted off its cap and poured the wine into her glass. As she did so she thought: People like me, we won't be old like them. We'll have to make it up as we go along.

Then she thought: Maybe, despite the perms and the cardis, that's what they're doing too.

Theresa finished the lasagne and split open the wrapper. She gazed at the yellow rectangle of cheddar. To be frank, she was fed up with cheese, cheese and more cheese. No wonder she had put on weight.

You're not fat, you're gorgeous.

Theresa drained the glass of wine. Closing her eyes, she thought: What's it all about? What *is* it all about?

Within a month Christopher was back home. Marcia flew out to Bangalore, to his rented flat, and prised him out. It was easier than both had anticipated, as if he were an oyster already loosened within the shell.

To his surprise, Marcia was compassionate, almost tender. 'Honey, that's where fantasies should stay. In your head.' She sat on the bed while he packed. 'Else what should we do for dreams? Believe me, I know.' She had done something to her hair.

At the airport, by sheer force of will, she got them upgraded to business class. Christopher was helpless. The past weeks shimmered and dissolved. 'That story's not your story,' Marcia said. '*We* are.'

Oh, it was painful. But in retrospect he knew that the suffering he had inflicted, and experienced, was seen from his usual distance. Nothing had really changed. He had been a man watching himself embarking on a thrilling and impulsive venture, a man impersonating himself.

He sat on the balcony of their apartment. Way below, on 82nd Street, the traffic was stilled and released by the lights, over and over again. As winter progressed the sunlight inched down the building opposite. Marcia brought him out a glass of Chablis. 'What a silly boy you've been,' she crooned. 'A silly, silly boy.' She stroked his thinning hair.

8

*Eunuchs in New Delhi are helping out local telephone customers
by taking their complaints directly to telephone company offices,
where they stage sit-ins and even threaten to expose themselves
until the faults are fixed. Users have reported a marked improvement in services since the campaign began. 'Efficiency of the field
staff has improved and faults are often rectified without more ado,'
says one phone company official. 'It is the customer who ultimately
gains.'*

(*Guardian*, 13 February 2003)

Late in January Ravi and Pauline drove to High Wycombe, where
she had grown up. In her lap sat a Safeways carrier bag; within
it rested the casket containing what remained of her father. They
planned to see him off, not down the Ganges but scattered over
a smaller stream, deep in the beechwoods where long ago he had
liked to walk.

They parked the car and made their way through the wood.
Pauline remembered the path though it had altered, as if she had
dreamed it – the trees had grown taller, a new glade had opened
out where once there had been brambles. A rustic sign now
informed her that she was following the Chilterns Heritage Trail.
Her father had liked walking with a stick, slashing at nettles,
striding ahead so that she and her mother had to scamper along
to keep up.

The path dropped towards the water. Ravi took her hand, to
help her down. It was a blustery day; the wind whipped her hair
against her cheek. They both felt curiously exhilarated.

276

'What happens if he blows away in the wrong direction?' she asked. 'If he blows back in our faces?'

'I'd say *Your father always got up my nose.*'

Pauline laughed. There was a new easiness between them these days. Maybe it had been unlocked by her father's death. Pauline suspected it was more complicated than this, however – more to do with Ravi's family than hers – but was disinclined to ask the reason in case it broke the spell. They had even made love in his parents' house in Delhi – before dinner, in fact, with people chattering on the landing outside. Afterwards they had caught each other's eye during the meal and Ravi's father asked: 'What's the joke? Anything we can share?'

They inched down the path, gripping the trees on either side. Roots broke through the earth. Later Pauline remembered that descent, every step of it. She was thinking about the thorn trees in the waste ground behind the Marigold, the transformed landscape of Dorothy's past and how Dorothy had finally found peace there. She was thinking of her own dream for its transformation, a scheme that now had Ravi's support but which, in the chill of an English winter, seemed farcically unlikely.

Below, the water glinted. This was her father's moment, she should be concentrating on him, but she was thinking about how she could find a plot of land and whether Sonny would help, with his networking skills. Sonny had been curiously attentive towards her before she left, something odd in his manner. He had dealt with all the funeral arrangements and even fetched the casket from the undertakers.

They arrived at the stream. It was somewhere here – she couldn't be sure, not now – that the three of them had once had a picnic. 'Dad had brought back some biltong from Zimbabwe – maybe it was still Rhodesia then – and it was as tough as leather. It *was* leather.' Pauline remembered her mother sitting on the rug, inching the skirt up over her knees to let the sun warm her legs. They had been happy sometimes, hadn't they? Her mother's pleasures were modest ones. Her father had taken a snapshot but their photos had been destroyed when his bungalow burnt down.

Pauline squatted and lifted out the casket. It was surprisingly heavy but then you didn't know what to expect, did you? With her fingernail she picked at the adhesive tape.

'Are you OK?' asked Ravi.

She nodded. She ripped off the tape, scrunched it up and shoved it into her jacket pocket. This whole occasion felt somehow lacking. Should they sing a hymn or something?

There was a pause. They glanced at each other, then she unscrewed the lid.

Inside, packed tightly together, lay plastic bags of white powder.

Pauline gazed at them. For a moment she thought that this must be the Indian way of doing things. Then she looked at them again. 'These aren't ashes,' she said.

Ravi pulled out one of the bags. 'Good God,' he said. 'Is this what I think it is?'

A few days later another casket arrived from India. It contained her father's ashes. Accompanying it was a piece of paper with an address in Hackney where the white powder could be sold. It was signed *A Guilty Party*.

What guilty party? The image of Keith passed through Pauline's mind. She preferred to suspect him rather than Sonny, because she had known him so briefly. With a near-stranger, anything is possible. But why would anybody do this to them? And why did he feel guilty? Neither she nor Ravi discovered the answer to this.

They buried the bags in their garden in Dulwich. Months passed. Of course it was bizarre, to know they lay there, but no more bizarre, Pauline thought, than her existence on this earth, eating Pringles and brushing her hair. No more bizarre than two people endeavouring to spend their lives together.

Maybe she and Ravi would separate. They would fund new lives on the proceeds of a drugs deal. She would build a children's home in Bangalore, founded on heroin.

Oh yes?

There the bags remained. Call it moral rectitude, or a failure of nerve. But there, in the flower-bed, lay buried possibilities. Perhaps she and Ravi would forget all about them. Perhaps, some time in the future, a fox would dig them up and they would wake in the morning and think it had been snowing.

The monsoon had come and gone. At the Marigold the morning mist cleared. A hoopoe, like a clockwork toy, stabbed at the grass. The dew silvered the spiders' webs that draped the bougainvillaea. Soon the residents would be stirring. Over the past months there had been some changes. Several residents, for one reason or another, had returned to Britain. Jean Ainslie had gone to live in Surrey, with her daughter. More guests had arrived. Deep in the building, a radio bleeped a wake-up.

Outside, oblivious to the early morning rush hour, a beggar lay sleeping. He wore the Bata shoes, pukka leather, tip-top quality but somewhat battered now. It was no longer the elderly beggar, however, who lay there. His body had been removed some weeks earlier. The new shoe-owner was a good deal younger.

In India, nothing goes to waste.

Another year passed ... the heat, the monsoon, the radiant winter dawns. In his studio Vinod, the man who shot the promo-video for Sonny, was touching up a photo. He unsheathed his paint-brush and tested it against his finger. He dipped it into the brass water-cup. Outside, traffic thundered along the Airport Road. Each year the traffic was heavier. Soon this building was to be demol-ished to make way for a luxury apartment complex. Already the hoarding had been erected: *2 km from the Airport, 7 km from downtown Bangalore, Embassy Heights offers Discernment, Security and an Unrivalled Perfection of Design.*

The other businesses on his floor were vacating their premises. Soon Vinod would have to find a new photographic studio. Plus his tooth was throbbing. He was too much of a coward, however, to visit the Chinese dentist, Mr Liu, who would no doubt insist on pulling it out.

Vinod had bought a booklet called *Positive Thinking* from the stationery shop across the road. It supplied exercises in triumphing over physical affliction as well as the mental stresses of daily life. So far, despite repeated efforts, he had noticed no improvement.

Some occasions, however, had the power to lift his gloom. The recent wedding of Mr Douglas Ainslie and Mrs Evelyn Greenslade was one such case. That happiness could be found at such an advanced age had restored Vinod's spirits, simply for its promise that such a possibility existed.

Vinod's brush was sable, and so fine that he could barely see it without his spectacles. Head tilted, he inspected the photograph. It was matt finish, and thus capable of absorbing moisture. A trick he had learnt, however, was to stroke the brush across the glue strip of an envelope, before he began. This guaranteed that the paint would adhere to the surface,

He dipped his brush into carmine red. This he mixed with a little ochre pigment. Also some grey. Then he got to work on the cheeks – just a blush, scarcely a hint of pink. He did it tenderly, as if he himself were stroking the lady's skin.

Next, he darkened the pigment for their lips. He rinsed his brush and started work on the gentleman; first he traced the outline of the lips, then he filled it in. Mr Ainslie was laughing, showing teeth which Vinod had already whitened.

Outside a siren wailed. No doubt it was an important personage travelling to the airport – the minister, maybe, with full police escort. Each day thousands of people sped along this road, to be lifted into the sky and flung across the world. Vinod's own sons, who had once sat in front of the camera, fidgeting in their school uniforms, had long since gone. In the studio, however, nothing moved except Vinod's hand.

Half an hour passed. As he painted, Vinod thought of his own marriage. Here, in the photograph, lay proof that reincarnation of a sort was possible in this life rather than the next. To achieve this, however, a certain amount of ruthlessness was required. This was a quality he signally lacked. To judge from appearances, however – one of the requirements of his job – so did these newly-weds. They looked the gentlest of souls.

Another hour passed. Finally Vinod rinsed his brush, wiped it and laid it on the table.

There. *Shabash*. He had taken years off their age. A certain artistry was required, to restore the ravages of time. With modest pride Vinod gazed at the photograph of the bride and groom, sitting side by side against the faded wallpaper of the Marigold lounge.

In its small way, it was a miracle. With their blushing cheeks and pink lips, the elderly couple looked quite young again.

www.vintage-books.co.uk